Sac

[illegible]

CONTENT WARNING:
Most readers may find this content disturbing.
Trigger warning for graphic content, including but not limited to sexual content, sexual violence, death, torture, strong bloody violence and aggressive language. Non-Con, Dub-Con, torture (mental and physical), abduction, sadism, selling and purchasing of humans for vampire consumption, pretend/roleplaying Oedipal relations, breeding, bdsm Reverse Harem, MFM, MMF, MF, and MM, and a whole lot more naughty fun.

If you are related to me, don't read this book.

Our family barbeque in the summer is already awkward with Crimson Talon being a topic of conversation, and that story is dark with some smutty goodness, but this book isn't a little of murder with plots and some spanking.

Please don't make family events more uncomfortable by reading this!

ISBN: 978-1-7782336-2-3

DEDICATION

This book is for:
those who wanted something darker …
something far more twisted than what was here before.

CONTENTS

ACKNOWLEDGMENTS

Oh, my dear beloved Alpha, Beta and Arc readers!

Paulette
Shelby
Destiny
Carla
Jerry
Dorothy
Desiree
Marie
Marah

You are wonderful people, and I couldn't have asked for a more encouraging group!

Haya <keep being sassy, cause girl, you made me laugh so hard from your comment that I excitedly waited for your responses>

Deb: I will thank you later with the sappiest of all thank-you letter that will make you weep. Not because the sadist in me feeds on the tears of my friends and enemies alike… But only because it's becoming a competition between Cat and I on who can make you cry more from our appreciation notes for your editorial skills.
My dear friend, I adore you! I cannot thank you enough for all your help and publishing advice. You are a wonderful person and I appreciate your kindness beyond words. That I can surprise you (a woman who has read countless books) with my plots and twists makes me so thrilled!

HAH! See Catherine! You were wrong, I can write a book that is completely filled with smut and still has a plot. It's in there… somewhere. Now, you can claim all you want that what you said was 'if the book is filled with smut and has only some plot, then it's only considered erotica, not romance with erotica.'
And I literally wrote an entire book to prove you wrong based on misunderstanding a single sentence… pfffft.
HAHAHA, I love you! xoxo

PROLOGUE

A GLIMPSE INTO THE FUTURE

THE SERVANT

The servant watched as his master ripped the anal beads from the slave's puckering asshole, sending bits of feces and old sperm flinging through the air. Flecks of the secretions from the human toy's ass splattered the wall behind the ancient vampire, who had moved out of the way as he reefed on the rope. A small trickle of blood escaped the orifice, as he clearly had done some damage from the aggressive act.

Unnoticed, the ever-loyal servant stood at the entrance of the dungeon with his clammy hands clasped firmly behind his back, observing the pitiful toy's punishment. His eyes refused to stray from the young woman, who wailed in agony against the ball gag tied snuggly with a leather cord wrapped around the back of her neck. Her screams reverberated from the cobbled walls, echoing loudly. He noted beads of perspiration appearing and rolling down her tanned flesh.

The servant wasn't as sadistic as his master, but he couldn't help the increase in his heart rate as he watched the captive struggle against her restraints. Though, as always, he kept his expression vacant.

The girl coughed, retched, and wailed in protest, while attempting to free herself from the creature who tortured her during her every waking moment. The hollow ball gag did nothing to silence the young woman. It was far too large and had to be forced into her mouth, likely making her jaw ache more painfully the longer it was in there.

The Master could control every agony and each pleasure that the slave experienced. This was not the time for gratification, and there was nothing the toy could do to ease her suffering.

As the human cried, mucus oozed from her nose, dribbling down the ball gag, mixing with saliva as she drooled. At one point, the victim had even puked, though there had been nothing in her system, so phlegm and bile filled the gag before trickling in strings toward the ground. The secretions formed a small puddle on the floor beneath the prisoner.

The chains suspending her rattled loudly as the tortured toy trembled. The candlelight from the chandeliers overhead cast their shadows writhing in flickers across the room. They had a few candles on them, and only half of those were lit, but it was enough to light the girl's skin with a shimmering glow.

The servant's eyes flashed to the mess that accumulated on the cobblestone under the slave, knowing it was his responsibility to sterilize it. Always. He removed the filth, cleaning every physical sign of his master's depraved behavior, then guaranteeing the financials didn't leave a paper trail behind that could be followed.

The master had damaged her body from head to toe. He made bruises and cuts that marred her formerly flawless skin. Naturally, the human's marks could be readily covered to hide her deviant experience.

"Are you prepared to give up?" his drawling voice enquired of the young toy, as a nasty, toothy smile danced across his face.

Just from the set in his master's features, he could tell that the one he served hoped the slave wouldn't give in. However, he was far from finished tormenting the girl. Based on past experience, this torment could continue for hours if the victim was stubborn enough.

More tears spilled down from the human's eyes as she furiously shook her head, desperately straining to scream her displeasure from beyond the ball gag. The girl's body seemed to hover parallel to the ground. Ropes held her head back at an unnatural angle so that it forced her to stare straight ahead. The rubber cuffs that held her in place contracted tightly around her limbs as she trembled, cutting off more circulation to her extremities and causing her to sway in the air. The metal chains attached to the cuffs clanged loudly, sending vibrations along the bindings, increasing the intensity of all sensations.

The servant attempted to mentally soothe himself, knowing all too well how agonizing every movement and each breath was when hanging by those chains. The human was scarcely receiving a glimpse of what he'd spent his life enduring.

"What? I can't hear you…" the deadly vampire mockingly interrupted his victim's desperate pleas, giving a maniacal laugh for emphasis.

The creature's bare feet made no noise as he practically slithered his way around her suspended body to the girl's face. At the sight of his fangs, the human's eyes opened unnaturally wide with icy terror. She tried frantically to shake her head, but the movement caused vibrations to travel along the path of the chains holding her in this awkward position. The echoes of rattling chains nearly made the servant flinch as he became awash with memories of how the straps shot searing pain down his extremities.

The servant's eyes darted to the rubber cuffs around the human's limbs. They appeared to squeeze tightly, gouging into the skin, making the plaything cry out in agony, resulting in mucus trickling from the gag.

The master reached a hand forward, pressing on the ball gag. Sputum surged through the small holes against his palm. When the girl choked, more snot dribbled out of her nose.

"Oh- no…" whispered the maniacal vampire, putting on fake airs of concern like a horrible mask.

"You made a mess, my little toy," he cooed softly as he lightly caressed the side of the victim's face with gentle fingers.

Then he rubbed his palm under the slave's nose and across her chin.

He dropped the sincere mannerisms for a more homicidal tone as he aggressively washed the human's face with the collected mucus. "You can have it back!"

The chains rattled as the helpless creature struggled to avoid the vampire's icy hand, but in the end, all she could do was close her eyes tightly. Her jaw would have quivered if the ball gag hadn't locked it open as wide as her mouth could go. She retched loudly … followed by the smell of vomit becoming stronger. It mixed with the saliva and mucus that was being rubbed all over her face.

The desperate slave gave one last scream through the ball gag. Bits of spittle and puke flung out the holes in the gag, spraying in front of the vampire's precious little victim. When the girl was finally out of air and strength, she lost consciousness. The punishment was horrific…

The servant waited on the sidelines for his next order, prepared to do whatever his beloved master commanded.

1

THIS SHOULD NOT BE US

CHANCE

East Brooklyn apartment. The two-bedroom rental unit was mostly kept meticulously clean, so while she waited, there wasn't much to do to keep her occupied. Her TV was large, though she wasn't the one who used it. Her roommate's gaming console's red light gleamed, telling her he had forgotten to shut it off. There was a small stack of games piled haphazardly on the floor, but she refused to pick them up again. He wasn't really her roommate, but she hated calling him her boyfriend. She needed to put her education before the development of a personal relationship.

Chance stared at the clock that she was beginning to hate so much more than she logically should have.

2:30 AM.

She paced back and forth, rubbing her red, tired eyes

before staring at the luggage gathered in the living room's corner. She had her two midnight blue bags stuffed to the brim with everything she would need for her trip. She marched over to the bags and lifted her purse from the floor next to them, resting it on top of one bag as she riffled through it. A sigh of relief broke the silence in the empty apartment as she found her passport and plane ticket right where she left it.

2:45 AM.

He should have come home already! Chance quickly checked her phone for messages. Her stomach tightened into a knot of frustration as her hand squeezed the phone. Its edges dug into her fingers. Not even a text! She was so tired, and she was supposed to be leaving the following morning. It was only a few hours away. This was so unfair!

3:05 AM.

Chance finally settled onto the hard-cushioned beige sofa. She hugged one of the fuzzy green pillows to her chest as she swayed slightly. Maybe if she closed her eyes for just a minute…

Thump, bang…

3:45 AM.

Chance's eyes snapped open in surprise and immediately flashed to the clock. Why the hell was it so late?! A shuffling at the entryway told her that someone was there. Slowly, Chance crawled off the couch, coming to her feet as she brushed her bangs off her face. She cautiously moved toward the entrance.

The sight of her boyfriend sitting on the floor, struggling to pull off his black leather cowboy boots, put her mind at ease. Though, it wasn't for long.

Sighing softly, she folded her arms and leaned against the doorframe with narrowed eyes.

"You're late. Bar closes at two… It's almost four," she snapped through gritted teeth.

"Got paid for an after-party," Tyne snarled defensively at Chance without even giving her the decency of glancing in her direction.

When he got annoyed or even a little pissed, his English accent would immediately thicken.

The tall, muscular man came to his knees and teetered as he yanked open the closet door with far more force than necessary. He rose to his feet and kicked his boots in while throwing his leather coat on top of them in the closet's corner. He placed his hand on the wall for support as he turned to cock a dark eyebrow at Chance. His shoulders were broad, and he was so well muscled that their outline was distinctive beneath the cotton material of his shirt. His dark-blue eyes sparkled mischievously as he drew his bottom lip into his mouth while smirking at her.

"You could have called! Or messaged!" Chance replied, his smile pissing her off. She turned her back on her lover before adding, "but whatever, why would I matter? I'm just fucking leaving tomorrow!"

She could hear the ruffling of his clothing and the soft scuffle of his bare feet as he followed her from the entrance into the kitchenette area.

Chance stomped her way from the carpet onto the tiled floor while muttering, "I just stayed up to make sure you fucking eat…"

Reaching up into the cupboard, Chance pulled out a glass. She turned on the faucet and rinsed the cup, pouring out the liquid before letting it fill with cool water. Chance didn't even want to look at him as his voice sounded from directly behind her.

She felt his fingers slide up the forearm of her freehand as he spoke. "Don't be like that. You are the important one, you know that."

She recoiled from his touch, switching the hand that held the cup as she raised it to take a gulp. The cold liquid quenched her thirst but did nothing to cool the flames of her temper.

The manipulative bastard continued when she didn't respond. "You're everything to me. I need--"

"Am I?" Chance turned to face him with a glare. "So, are you going to say you didn't enjoy it?" She leaned back against the counter with her hands flailing in the air as she snarled. "That you like it only when you're eating and fucking me?!"

"You're the only one I need, baby." Tyne purred, sauntering closer, as if to corner her between the counter and his body.

Chance side-stepped, dodging his attempt to trap her.

She snapped, "You're practically a hooker!"

"Oh, fuck off!" Tyne snarled as he moved forward with lightning speed. He snatched Chance's wrist before she could take another step away and hissed, "You knew what I was when we met."

"Let go of me!" Chance yelled, trying to pull away from Tyne. "I'm so fucking pissed at you! You said you'd be home early tonight, that we'd actually get to spend some time together before I leave, and you were late!"

The big bastard smirked as he pressed Chance back into the fridge, knocking the wind out of her. He easily pinned her there using his body. Tyne snatched up both of Chance's wrists in one hand and effortlessly pushed them up over her head.

"Is that why you're so mad?" Tyne grinned playfully, before placing two fingers under Chance's chin to compel her head to tilt back.

There was no resisting his advances. He was far too strong. All she could do was cooperate while struggling. Her eyes narrowed as he forced her to look at him.

"Let go of me, Ty! I'm so pissed at you. What if the sun rose while you were still out partying, huh?!"

Tyne simply smiled before grazing his lips against Chance's, imposing the kiss upon her. She would never pursue a kiss, especially when angry like that. Tyne slowly trailed his fingers down Chance's jaw when the kiss broke off and she spoke.

"Stop it, Tyne! Just stop!" Chance hissed as she struggled against the muscular man's iron grip.

A demonic smile pranced its way onto Tyne's mouth before he pressed his lips against Chance's with a deep guttural growl. She felt his tongue slip from behind his teeth and glide along her lower lip. She wasn't about to give him access so easily, so she kept her jaw clenched tightly shut. She busied herself by struggling against the iron grip of only one of the vampire's hands, which pinned her in place. Tyne's fingers of his other hand released Chance's chin. As it slid down her throat, she felt goosebumps rise across her skin. From above the lace trim of her camisole, his touch followed her collarbone to her cleavage. Chance groaned as his hand cascaded south. Tyne's cold fingers paused at the buttons on Chance's jeans.

"This is what you wanted for your last night, wasn't it?" Tyne whispered, his lips tenderly brushing her earlobe. "There's still time, my love."

Chance whimpered softly. She longed to give in to Tyne. She yearned to give him everything. She was angry, not only at Tyne now, but at herself for her own uncontrollable desires.

Tyne's fingers undid the button and zipper on her pants in a single, swift motion. He moved to kiss Chance again, but the frustrated woman turned her face away with a disapproving groan. If she gave in so easily, what would that say about her?

"Don't be that way. You crave it too…" Tyne purred, pushing his body against hers.

His rock hard cock pressed against her stomach as he made his intentions clear. Her mouth watered with longing, but instead, she scowled up at him.

"No, I don't. I never want it… You're just too stupid to figure it out!" Chance growled, feeling tears of frustration threaten to roll down her cheeks.

"Is that so?" Tyne whispered, his expression darkening as his eyes narrowed in an annoyed glare. "Then I'll just take what I wish."

Tyne moved in for another kiss. Chance turned her face

away while scowling up at him from the corner of her eye. His teeth shone in the glare of the kitchen's light before he brought his mouth down to her neck. Tyne's lips tenderly brush against her throat.

"No, no… Don't." Chance whimpered, knowing what was coming.

Chance felt Tyne's fanged teeth sink into the flesh of her neck. The ever-familiar pain and pleasure sensations washed through her entire frame, resonating from the location of the bite. Chance's hips bucked into Tyne as desire overwhelmed her mind and body. The fiery, passionate need to have someone touch her assaulted Chance's with every thought as a wave of dizziness overtook her. She whimpered as the phenomenon swept across her flesh, starting from the wound and radiating between her thighs like a beacon of incomparable urgency.

After a few moments, Chance bowed her head forward until her forehead pressed into Tyne's collarbone as she closed her eyes. A soft moan escaped Chance's lips before she could stop it.

Tyne was drinking from her, and there was nothing she could do about it. Why did she always crave that bastard vampire like this? Chance was sure she wasn't interested. Before Tyne came into her life, she had never even looked at a man lustfully. However, in that moment, with Tyne's fangs embedded deep in her throat, Chance wanted nothing more than to wrap her arms and legs around her lover while forgiving every transgression.

Tyne finally released Chance's wrists, which fell loosely to her sides as she fought her desire to hold the devious creature. The vampire's hands gently slid along Chance's chest. One hand paused, pinching a nipple through her shirt and padded bra. The other continued to cascade lower. He withdrew his fangs, only to bite again, plunging them deeper than before. It sent a rush of sensations spreading across her body, making her moan and gasp while thrusting her hips forward.

Chance wheezed, tears filling her eyes. It was constantly like this. She always cried in the beginning, at least until she gave into the waves of passion and desire that threatened to crush her into oblivion. She slowly shook her head, feeling the weakness in her muscles increase from blood loss.

Tyne must have been hungry to drink so much. He had to have really worked up an appetite at the bar. The thought reminded Chance of why she was so angry. It was late, too late for Tyne to be coming home unscathed. Yes, Chance knew Tyne had been a stripper when they met, but that was all.

After she found out her new 'friend' was a vampire, everything had changed. It was as though Chance no longer had a say in anything. They moved in together; they did things that Chance could never tell her foster parents. This creature of the night completely trapped her, keeping her enthralled.

"Stop," Chance whispered softly, the same word she'd uttered so many times in the past.

Even though she said it, she did nothing to deter Tyne's caressing. In fact, she readily turned her face away to grant the beast easier access to his meal.

Tyne finally broke away from Chance's throat, blood oozing from his chin and the corners of his mouth. She watched him as she felt blood dribbling down her neck and into her cleavage beneath her shirt. The puncture marks healed instantly into two scarcely noticeable scars on the girl's throat. Chance could barely contain her disappointment. In fact, she didn't even bother to turn her face toward the vampire as she stared up at him from the corner of her eye. She wanted to be bitten again. Her breaths came in harsh panting as her hands reached out to the muscular man. Her fingers caught the edge of his shirt, gripping tightly as she lightly pulled on the material.

"I love you…" Chance whispered a desperate plea.

"Delicious as always. You should taste yourself…" Tyne responded, his fangs glimmering in the dim moonlight streaming in from the window.

His dark blue eyes suddenly glazed over with a solid black, turning demonic with bloodlust, though he still seemed amused. Within an instant, they became like two endless pools that could lead any mortal soul to hell.

The vampire pinched Chance's chin and forced her to look at him. He pressed his lips against hers, forcing his cold tongue into the warmth of her mouth.

Chance could taste her own blood on Tyne's tongue. The metallic richness made her head spin. But there was something sweet in the flavor too, something Chance had only ever experienced when kissing Tyne after he fed. She felt herself pressing against Tyne, with her tears drying on her cheeks. She wanted more.

She felt his lips curl into a smile while he maintained the kiss. His arm snaked around her waist as he turned Chance toward the hall that led to the bedroom.

As the pair made their way into the hallway, Chance's elbow knocked into a painting, which sent it clattering to the floor. The glass cover shattered, yanking her out of the trance-like state she'd found herself in.

"Stop it!" Chance suddenly shrieked, more pissed off than she'd been all evening.

She quickly shoved her hands against his chest to push herself out of the vampire's grasp.

"I'm not your god-damned toy!" she screamed, knowing that he had this freaky way of controlling her and that was exactly what he had done.

As Tyne tried to grab her wrist to stop her from moving away, Chance whipped around and smacked him across the face.

The slap was hard enough that any normal person would have stumbled backward. Any human, but not Tyne… Tyne wasn't human. He simply smiled at Chance, with his fangs glittering, making her skin crawl.

"All I am is a personal fucking vending machine to you!" Chance yelled, as her hands trembled while they floundered before her for emphasis.

"Don't throw a tantrum, Chance." Tyne muttered, his upper lip drawing back in annoyance.

"Get the fuck off of me, you- cheating sack of crap!" Chance responded.

Tyne grabbed Chance's wrists and slammed her backward into the wall, knocking the wind out of her. She banged the back of her head, but the discomfort went unnoticed compared to the searing agony she was experiencing elsewhere. Chance stepped on the glass from the picture, cutting the bottoms off her feet. She gasped in pain, but used it to keep focused.

"I can't be cheating if you won't even admit that we are together." Tyne growled softly, "But you *are* mine…"

"No, I'm not!" She lifted her hands and pressed them in fists against his chest, in an attempt to push him again, "Now, let go of me! You make me sick, I- fucking- hate- you!" Chance said everything she could to make Tyne move away from her, but nothing worked.

Chance was usually kind, spirited and soft-spoken, but everyone has their limits and Tyne had a mystical way of nudging Chance beyond her every boundary.

So, Chance stood there for a moment, her feet searing with agony from the glass in them, and let the blood sucker desperately kiss her.

Chance knew that things would not be back to normal till after her upcoming trip to Europe. She was the only applicant selected out of her entire state to study medicine abroad for several months with this all expenses paid opportunity. Not only was this the opportunity of a lifetime, but it was her avenue to escape the cycle she'd entered with the narcissistic vampire.

When he broke off the kiss, she whimpered, "I need to leave." Chance struggled to free herself from Tyne's grip.

Chance sobbed as Tyne pinned her against the wall with his body. She turned her face to the side, so her cheek pressed against his chest. Just having him this close made her pulse increase.

The vampire hissed between his teeth and slid a knee between her thighs.

"You're not going anywhere."

2

The Magic of Fangs

Tyne

"I need to leave." Tyne heard the delectable appetizer whimper against his chest as her struggles to break free increased.

Annoyed from the young human's constant escape attempts, Tyne shoved Chance against the wall, easily pinning the weak little creature using his body. The heat that radiated from her was like an oasis in a desert to a man dying of thirst. He slid a knee between her thighs, basking in the heat that radiated from every inch of her flesh. A timid moan from the girl made him smirk against the top of her head as he pressed his mouth to her. Her small hands balled into fists, grasping the material of his shirt.

"You're not going anywhere," the Englishman hissed as he easily pinned his curvaceous instant-dinner against the wall.

The vampire inhaled deeply through his mouth, tasting the aroma of the metallic essence that emanated from the cuts on the bottom of the girl's feet. He was a shark, and she was barely even a minnow.

Tyne forced another kiss upon her, desperate to taste the human one more time. He slid his tongue from its chamber behind his teeth to deepen the kiss, gliding the tip along Chance's lower lip. The young woman's jaw quivered, and her hands trembled against Tyne's chest as he basked in her flavor. Tyne drew Chance's bottom lip into his mouth and suckled on it lightly. His razor-sharp fangs easily sliced it, trickling blood into their mouths before the vampire's saliva caused the wounds to heal almost instantly. The only remaining evidence was two nearly invisible scars. Finally, Chance turned her face away, breaking off the kiss.

Tyne didn't let it slow him. He gradually kissed his way down the human's throat. The scent of blood had awoken him, making him desperate to devour the young creature in his arms. His fingers numbly extended into claws as they slid up the girl's ribs, dragging the shirt with it. When Chance didn't lift her arms giving him access, Tyne growled, before simply using those claws to shred the material off the object of his desire. The vampire passionately, but forcefully, licked and sucked his way across Chance's collarbone. He pulled off the remaining material of Chance's shirt, letting it flutter to the ground at their feet. Tyne's kisses moved down her abs to her delicate v-lines.

Chance's breath caught for an instant before a moan of desire escaped her throat as his lips dragged across the sensitive flesh just above the v-line. He knew it was her favorite spot because she always got squirmy when he touched there. It was possible that she was simply ticklish there, but her pulse elevated every time he gave the area any attention.

Tyne's fangs buried themselves into the juicy flesh just above the pelvic bone. His fangs pierced through skin and muscle alike. Chance gasped loudly, her hands circling the back of his head to hold him there. He had to suck hard to get a decent mouthful of blood. It wasn't his favorite place, but she seemed to enjoy it.

The girl's warm fingers twined in Tyne's sandy blond curls. He knew his venom would have an extraordinary effect on her. A numbing dizziness would spread across her entire body. Even the glass slicing her feet would become a muted whisper of sensation when compared to the extreme arousal that would overwhelm the young woman. The intense desire to be touched would crumble any physical barriers. Her hands moved to Tyne's shoulders to hold herself on her feet, as her legs were on the verge of giving way.

Tyne withdrew his fangs and sank them back into Chance's delectable flesh several times to ensure the human's complete compliance. Each time, he could feel her hips sway toward him as though she wanted him to bring his face lower.

Chance placed her hands on Tyne's cheeks. His head followed her lead by bowing down and turning so their eyes could meet. The young woman brought her mouth down to his. The blood on his lips smeared onto hers as she began desperately kissing him. She moved with a need that would only seem satiated by physical contact. She pulled his bottom lip between her teeth, biting down harder than she should have. He felt no pain from her aggressive advance. In fact, it only aroused him more.

Chance whispered into Tyne's ear, "I need you".

"If you want me, take me."

As if Chance didn't need more of an invitation than that, she grabbed Tyne's wrist and led him to the nearby doorway, every step leaving a bloody footprint behind on the tile floor. His venom had her so high that the pain shooting up her legs from the glass potentially felt good.

Once in the privacy of their bedroom, Tyne smirked down at Chance, who shoved him onto the bed. He laid back on the soft bedding with his arms folded behind his head as he watched Chance struggle to undo her bra. Tyne reached out toward the delicious morsel and allowed his clawed hand to glide across her luscious skin. As she straddled him, his hands seemed as if they were trying to touch every area of her body.

He heard her groan in frustration, before giving up on undoing her bra. The high human leaned forward to press her lips against his. The young woman moaned with absolute ecstasy as the vampire opened his mouth to invite her tongue to enter beyond his fangs. As Chance pushed her tongue into his mouth, those fangs slashed it.

Metallic flavored liquid splashed into their interlocked mouths from the unnoticed wounds that Tyne's fangs gave Chance's tongue. Tyne swallowed everything he could, though some trickled from the corners of his mouth before his saliva healed her wounds. The exotic flavors in her lifeblood overwhelmed Tyne with a rush of desire, putting his bloodlust in overdrive. Irritated by her bra, Tyne hooked the edge of the fabric with a single clawed finger. As the tearing began, Chance gasped loudly.

"Not my last bra!" she whimpered into his mouth, but it was already too late.

The strap snapped easily, but the bra remained trapped, compressed between their bodies. With an annoyed growl, Tyne grabbed a strap and yanked, rougher than necessary, freeing her luscious breasts from their prison and finally allowing her bare skin and hard nipples to be pressed against his icy flesh.

Chance's instinctive gasp resounded in Tyne's ears. The high was wearing off, so Chance sat up and covered her chest with her forearms. She still got uncomfortable with nudity. They'd been together for nearly a year, and it always took venom to encourage her into sexual obedience. Before he came along, she was completely inexperienced in the ways of men.

Tyne followed her lead and came upright, grabbed her hips as he pressed his mouth against hers once more. The girl was still blushing and trying to cover her breasts when he wrapped his arms tightly around her. He didn't care for her embarrassment and humiliation today; he needed to bury himself in her essence in every way possible.

Tyne easily rolled them over on the queen-sized bed so he could top the delectable woman. He broke off the kiss to press his lips against her cheek, then tenderly kissed repeatedly and with increasing fervor down her neck and throat. It took all his inner strength not to bite and drain her. He paused in his desperate kisses to glide his tongue along her collarbone, feeling Chance squirm beneath him.

Chance muffled her gasps and moans by placing a hand over her mouth.

"Wait… I can't-," Chance whimpered, but Tyne sank his fangs into the juicy flesh of her breast, using his venom to distract her from denying him.

Evidently, it worked like a charm, and the young woman felt so aroused by Tyne's mere presence that her hips bucked toward him with a desperate neediness. He pressed his throbbing weapon against the entrance of her ravenous sheath, feeling its heat through their clothes. He could feel its pulsating desire caress his member and it sent him spinning. The fire from her hearth was nearly unbearable, as he lingered on the verge of the most glorious abyss he'd ever explored. Soon, but it wasn't time yet…

His powerful hands grabbed her around the waist while he resumed passionately kissing Chance's flesh.

Tyne's cool lips brushed against her soft nipple, feeling it become taut. He pulled it into his mouth, feeling it harden more. His teeth scraped along her succulent skin. He drew his mouth away from the pink flesh to swirl his tongue around her nipple, feeling all the tiny bumps that appeared around its erect center.

Chance moaned and whimpered, arching her back to press her body against Tyne's. Her cupped hand over her mouth made the sound echo loudly in her ears.

"Please. Ty, I want you."

Tears filled the young woman's eyes as she desperately pleaded for Tyne to enter her. Chance moved her hips, rocking them to grind them against his groin. His lips became taut against her skin as he smiled into her flesh.

"Bite me," Chance blurted out, as if she couldn't stop herself. "Devour me."

It excited Tyne that the girl was so high with lust that she didn't even realize that his fangs were already plunged deep into her tender flesh. As he drank from his little victim, his tongue swirled around her excited nipple. There were some humans who were delicious, no matter what flowed from them, their blood, saliva, and even their cum. This was one of those rare humans. She belonged solely to him.

"Please!" she begged, her tears finally breaking free from her eyes and rolling down her temples. "Harder!"

Tyne basked in his prey's desperate pleading. Every word she uttered sent him into oblivion as it combined with his own narcissism. He had been careful not to take too much blood, as she already seemed to be more than a little lightheaded, but her pleas had him wanting to swallow every drop until she was an empty husk. Then, the delicious little treat would eternally be his.

He resumed slithering his way down her body. Tyne kissed the underside of her breast. On the left side of her ribs, he trailed tender kisses. He felt her abdomen tighten as she squirmed under his lips. He couldn't help the smirk that danced across his features as his fingers curled over the hem of her low rider jeans. He lightly pulled on the material, intending to remove them.

Chance wiggled beneath Tyne as he yanked on her pants. Her hips rolled against him, pressing her thigh against his hardening weapon. She moaned loudly, finally uncovering her mouth to put her fingers through his long dirty blond locks of wavy hair.

After he removed her pants, he drew his hand back to her breast. Its playful little nipple had been dancing there, just on the edge of his sight, fully erect and tormenting him with its need for attention. He pinched her nipple, twisting lightly.

Her skin felt feverish against his icy lips. As his fingertips slipped beneath the edge of her pants, she drew her knees apart to bend her legs.

For only an instant, Chance attempted to put her weight on her feet, digging her heels into the bed to lift her bottom up. Her plan instantly failed as she gasped out in pain. The scent of her blood filled Tyne's nostrils as her wounds reopened. She lifted her feet up in the air, leaving behind bloody footprints on the pale blue bedding.

"They hurt," Chance cried out, fresh tears rolling down her cheeks as she lifted her head in time to see her lover slipping her pants past her ankles. "No, Ty, my feet."

Tyne rested her leg over his shoulder and kissed his way up her inner thigh as he faintly heard the girl's begging. He had a little more self-control now. He could have stopped… had he wanted to. Instead, the vampire sank his fangs into the pulsating vein that beckoned deliciously to him. Sweet nectar spilled forth, filling Tyne's mouth and rolling from the corners, dribbling onto the bedding. The heat rushed into his mouth, warming him from the inside, and spreading across his body in a fiery blast.

This was his favorite place to drink from. It was the most sensual and Chance always reacted responsively to the location, when he could get beyond all her struggles.

"Ty!" Chance groaned and reached out toward him.

He withdrew his fangs, moving closer to her underwear, brushing her lips through the material with his cheek, but didn't turn his face toward the place of passion.

The sweet scent of her arousal intoxicating him once more, as her succulent core enticed him, beckoned to him invitingly. He sank his teeth once more into the meaty flesh of her inner thigh, feeling the heat of her womanhood radiating, as though caressing the side of his face.

3

WANTING YOU NOW

CHANCE

She used one hand to hold herself sitting up, while she had originally intended to employ the other to push the domineering vampire away. Chance's warm fingers encircled the back of Tyne's head as she moaned loudly. She couldn't help wanting more. It was as though dopamine had flooded her brain and cascaded across her entire body, engulfing her in a whirlwind of elated passion and undeniable desire.

Her entire frame felt heated. Her limbs were numb, with tingles running along them. The searing pain that seemed to reverberate up her legs pulled her from the head-spinning web she had been unaware she was in.

Just as her eyes became unfocused, and the world around her had devolved into a hazy void, her lover retracted his fangs from her flesh, not even leaving behind more than a kiss mark stained with blood. The feeling of weakness was so overwhelming that Chance could do nothing but allow her hand to drop to her side. Her shoulders retreated to rest on the pillow beneath her head. Her silky black hair tickled her ears and neck as she helplessly surrendered to her exhaustion and relaxed into the comfort of the bedding.

Chance felt Tyne smile against her skin as he tenderly pressed his lips to the flesh of her inner thigh. He shook his head, kissing as he rubbed his cheek against the dampening spot on her underwear. Her hips twitched in reaction to his caresses.

She was desperately trying to encourage him to touch her. She gasped loudly as he indulged her by pressing his lips against the material that offered very little protection for her womanly center. He opened his mouth, grazing his face against her. His nose nuzzled her clit as his fangs poked small holes in the fabric. She felt Tyne slowly inhale a large breath. He pushed his tongue out and greedily lapped at the material, moistening it with his saliva.

Chance closed her eyes tightly, her tears drying at the corners and upon her cheeks as she struggled to arch her back, rubbing her clit against his face. She was so tired and dizzy, but the idea that this was their last night together for the next month while she went overseas made her want him all that much more. The mere thought of surviving without the vampire's touch for a single night made her reconsider the career-altering opportunity of a lifetime.

Tyne slipped his arms under her legs so they could rest comfortably on the bed as he grabbed Chance by her hips. Chance's underwear felt moist against his lips as he kissed the fabric. His tongue pushed up against the material as his head buried between her thighs.

Her legs tightened as he violated her. Her thighs hugged around the sides of his neck as though they threatened to crush him. Chance moved one foot from the bed to circle that calf across the back of his neck, holding the vampire with his face pressed against the thin fabric that seemed to be the only thing protecting her pussy from him ravaging it. There was no doubt in Chance's mind that she could not force herself to leave until it was over.

"More," Chance cried out in response when his finger hooked the edge of her underwear, pulling it aside, exposing her in all of her glory.

As Tyne adjusted the material, Chance could feel his icy fingertip slowly glide across the tantalizing lips of her moistened entrance. She couldn't help the frantic shudder that rampaged about her body, triggering gooseflesh to rise and prickle her skin with sensitivity. Chance's arousal had reached a whole new level of intoxicating desire that left her utterly helpless in the man's cold, dead hands.

"Tell me what I want to hear," Tyne whispered, his icy breath caressing her, causing her hips to buck toward the source of frosty pleasure.

"I'm yours," Chance responded, desperately. "I'll belong to you until I perish. Take my life, my soul, devour me!"

She knew the words by heart like a chant that he demanded she speak before he would satisfy her. He encouraged her to learn one line at a time, gradually making the keywords more degrading.

"I'm nothing, your toy, your slave, your plaything. Please, my beloved master!" she continued, "I cannot live without your touch!"

Chance spoke the last of her creed, pressing the foot she had on the bed down to lift her hips toward his face.

The shards of glass burrowed themselves deeper into her flesh, causing her to yell out in pain. As her insides clenched from the agony, Tyne impatiently rammed two fingers deep into the core of Chance's pleasure.

"Good girl!" Tyne practically snarled before burying his face between the juicy lips of her ever-wanting piece of paradise.

Chance's ensuing scream rang out in a guttural sound of utter enjoyment, coming from deep within, as if her soul were being ripped from her body. His icy breath rolled across her skin, making her guts clench around his fingers as though they never wished to release him. Chance felt him forcefully push a third finger into her. She whimpered in pain, drawing her hands downward to slow his agonizing advance.

The cruel vampire did nothing to ease working the fingers in. There was no gliding or massaging as he punished her. He was using brute force, excruciatingly entering her. She was leaving him behind and needed to suffer for it, though he'd never admit out loud why he was being so brutal. She knew this, and would accept his torment, but only because a part of her wanted to suffer for her decision.

"It hurts!" Chance cried out as Tyne rammed a fourth finger into her, making her scream as he tore at her.

Her delicate hands found the top of his head in their attempt to make the pain stop. Tyne reached up with his free hand, catching random fingers, and held her in place.

"Please Ty. It hurts, I love you. Please, don't hurt me!" she begged, realizing how truly pathetic and weak she sounded, but not caring.

She loved and hated the beastly creature who had no respect for her. He did as he wished, when he wanted. Tears rolled down her cheeks as she lay there, powerless in his clutches. She would leave soon and could finally escape this relationship, even though a huge part of her heart didn't want her to go anywhere.

Through the pain, there was also pleasure as Tyne's fangs scraped and cut the hyper-sensitive area around her clit. The sensation was akin to razorblade lacerations that seeped with bliss instead of burning when the skin realizes it's been wounded. As the damage occurred, his saliva instantaneously healed her. Tyne briefly withdrew his fingers to lick where he had torn her, repairing the scratch before gliding his cool tongue from her hole along her labia to her clit. He began kissing and suckling on her, burying his face into the delicacy she had laid out before him.

Chance allowed herself to melt back into the mattress below her as the pain was relieved and waves of euphoria gradually mounted deep within her body. It radiated away from her most pleasurable area across her extremities, causing her to nearly swoon. She could barely force breath past her lungs as her head tipped back, arching her spine. Her perky little nipples became erect, beckoning their unfulfilled desire to be touched. The universe tilted with insurmountable agony as her delicate fingers clutched tightly at his chilly hand.

As Tyne looked into Chance's eyes, every ounce of resistance was slowly being washed away in waves of passion.

He ripped his hand from her grasp before grabbing a handful of breast to massage the flesh. He lightly squeezed, rolling the breast under his palm as he closed his forefinger to his middle, pinching the sensitive peak that wished for his affection. He wiggled his fingers back and forth, applying a moving pressure, making Chance gasp loudly. His motions sent ripples of reaction across her chest, making her wet with arousal.

With her hands suddenly free, Chance panicked for an instant, unsure of where she should put them as another orgasm rose from her depths. Finally, both of her hands flung down to the bedding, grasping the material tight, as if that would somehow cease the entire world from whirling around her. As Tyne messed with every sensitive area on Chance's body, she could do nothing but suffer through wave after wave of agonizing pleasure. He ravaged her breasts and toyed with her pussy while licking, kissing, and biting her.

As an orgasm threatened to rupture her insides, sending her into oblivion, she cried out through bated breath. Chance trembled so hard beneath her lover that the headboard rattled against the wall.

"Ty! I can't… Another. I can't handle another. Oh, my god!" she finished in a shriek as honeydew liquid erupted from deep within her, filling his mouth.

"No! Wait!" she pleaded as he continued to ravage her.

Chance's hips bucked wildly in resistance to the overwhelming sensitivity that engulfed her entire frame. Her toes curled and her hands clenched into fists so firmly she feared they'd never open again as her body seized from the oncoming of yet another climax.

"No more! No more! Stop!"

The muscles across her body wound so tight that a knot formed in the back of her thigh. She brought that leg higher, trying to ease the tension, but Tyne only took it as an invitation to increase the intensity of his movements.

She screamed out, holding that leg in the air while wiggling beneath the beast, who clearly had no intention of slowing.

"It's coming… wait!" she begged, dropping her leg onto his back as her entire figure clenched and contorted around another overwhelming climax.

Chance struggled to get herself under control, but as Ty growled loudly, rumbling that bestial sound from between her thighs, the vibrations sent her spiraling over that edge once again. As the victim of unadulterated pleasure, Chance breathed in her last puff of air while she ascended to oblivion. She writhed among tides of trembling rapture as her thighs pressed together, trapping the vampire's head. She couldn't even exhale the breath she'd drawn.

As her orgasm lingered, Tyne finally slowed in his motions. He grabbed her underwear in both hands and ripped the material. The tearing sound echoed through the small bedroom. He chuckled it to the floor beside the bed before resuming his tauntings. Chance normally would have been very vocal about her complaints, but at that moment, she was too busy gasping from the residual waves of her climax.

He trickled kisses up her pubis. When he found her tender spot just above her center, he dragged his cool, wet tongue along her v-line. He penetrated her with his fangs, creating a trail working his way across her abdomen. He would bite, then lick the wound, move up half an inch, bite and lick the wound to heal it.

Each time the vampire's fangs broke skin, Chance would gasp and twist beneath him as her head spun and her extremities turned numb. She whimpered helplessly, with her hips rotating forward and back on instinct. As he made his way up her body, Chance closed her eyes and tilted her head backwards, basking in every sensation that threatened to drown her.

When he finally reached her ribs, he licked his way up her breast to her nipple. His hand moved to her other breast and massaged that nipple, rolling it between his thumb and fingers.

He breathed out and his icy exhale cascaded across her flesh, making her nipples unbearably hard. The entire world felt as though it were moving sluggishly. Her skin tingled. She felt as though she couldn't get any more aroused. That was…until he slowly dragged his hand from her breast to her throat and squeezed. The pressure was perfect. It blocked some airway flow, but it was tender enough that it didn't hurt. The flesh on her face prickled in reaction to being choked. Her lips parted, and a moan forced its way past the stranglehold on her throat.

He released her nipple from his mouth and proceeded with his upward charge. His lips, tongue and teeth fought endlessly as they continued the onslaught up her breast, to her collarbone, then onto the side of her neck. He growled like thunder against the crevice at her throat, summoning goosebumps across her skin. The sound rumbling in her ear, giving her chills down her spine. Chance arched her back, pressing herself against Tyne, desperate for him to enter her.

When that didn't work, she became frustrated. With a shrill groan, Chance wrapped her legs securely around Tyne's waist and began attempting to pull him against her. His body was icy against her feverish skin, only making her want to touch him that much more. She pressed her lips against his collarbone.

Chance felt Tyne's hard throbbing cock penetrate her tightness as the lust and pain turned unbearable. The tip of his rod tickled her hole tauntingly. Without warning, Tyne thrust his entire length all the way into Chance, making her gasp loudly.

"Wait! It hurts," she cried out, but kept her arms wrapped firmly around him to encourage the vampire to continue.

"Accept the pain..." Tyne responded in a breathy whisper against her throat as he trailed his hands down her sides. His cool lips brushed her earlobe as he added, "I'm glad we could reconcile before you abandon me."

"I'm not leaving," Chance gasped out as Tyne rolled his hips harder, "forever... I'm going to be with you always..."

They became entangled in one another's arms as if perfection itself were being created between their interlocking bodies. She mewled as he thrust intensively into her, drawing out and pummeling his icy member back in. He growled loudly before sinking his fangs into her shoulder. His movements slowed as her blood filled his mouth. The blood loss and multiple orgasms were already making her head spin with delirium.

As he swallowed gulps of her elixir, his motions increased in pace again. Tyne frantically pounded his meaty flesh deep into Chance as though he had never intended to slow.

Chance wrapped her arms and legs tightly around her lover. Her fingers dug into his back. She didn't bother to be gentle as she scored his pale flesh with her nails.

Suddenly, and without warning, Tyne rolled away from Chance while sliding his arm under the back of her neck. He folded his free arm beneath his head and sighed in relief as he basked in the afterglow. Her blood was now drying on his lips.

Chance laid there panting as she struggled to get her breathing under control. He always stopped so abruptly. It was almost as if he became bored. Luckily, she'd already finished multiple times, so she didn't feel too dissatisfied with the anti-climactic ending.

Her sweat dampened skin glistened from the moonlight that streamed in through the nearby window, the sheer curtains doing nearly nothing to temper the flow of shimmering light as the breeze sent the material fluttering listlessly. A bat flew past the window, reminding Chance that she needed to shut the light canceling curtains for Tyne's protection.

Her mouth tightened in a knot as she turned her head to stare at the vampire who laid next to her with his eyes closed. Why did she feel the need to close the damn curtains for him? What was he going to do after she left?

Was she still leaving? Could she really abandon him here on his own? To fend for himself?

Yes. Yes. A thousand times, yes!

Chance took a deep breath and swung her legs off the edge of the bed. As she sat up, her hand raised to grab her head. A wave of dizziness nearly sent her slumping back down.

That she even considered giving up the opportunity of a lifetime to remain with him made her feel disgusted with herself. She had spent her life working and fighting to reach her goals. Chance leaned forward, resting her elbows on her knees. She pressed her palms against her eyes so hard that she could see white dots behind her eyelids.

Getting through the spins that came with blood loss was frequently the hardest part of being with a vampire. The other side effect was discovering how unexpectedly needy she was. That didn't start until after she had allowed him to feed on her.

Slowly, Chance twisted to stare down at the beautiful man who seemed sound asleep. He resembled a dead body when he slept. It always made her nauseous when she saw him like that. When he was up and moving around, his skin texture was smooth. His color would return to normal, though he felt a little cool to the touch. When he was resting, it was as though everything that animated him disappeared, leaving a husk of a body behind. When he was asleep, he was exactly like the cadavers she'd worked on at the hospital. The sight of him revolted her.

The moment Chance closed her eyes or looked away, she felt this strange desire to crawl across the bedding and curl up against him, never to leave his side again. Her jaw quivered as tears welled in her eyes. There were only a few hours remaining and if she allowed herself to watch him for the rest of the night, then she'd never be able to leave come morning.

Chance carefully stood and staggered toward the door. She'd go sit outside for a bit to clear her head. Then maybe, just maybe, it would make walking away from Tyne a possibility.

4

Too Late For Regrets

Chance

"It's still dark out," Tyne muttered, scaring the ever-loving hell out of Chance as she entered the doorway.

An obnoxiously loud gasp escaped her as her knees buckled. She barely caught her balance, grabbing the edge of the frame to keep herself from toppling over.

"It's almost sunrise," Chance snapped, before slipping out the door. "I'll be fine." She then slammed it shut behind her with an echoing thump.

She couldn't even figure out why she was so furious. *Why the hell was she mad earlier? Why was she angry now?*

Everything was still madly spinning. The world around her seemed to do that drunken 'slight turn one way, then swirl the other way' sensation, making her stomach want to revolt. She hadn't been intoxicated too often, and there were only once when she had experienced bed spins. This sensation was something akin to that.

Once she made it to the living room, a second of panic set in. She had felt so disoriented that she forgot to grab clothes. Chance stared at the bedroom door for a moment and shook her head. Tears welled in her eyes. Chance knew that if she entered that bedroom, she'd never find the strength to leave it again. Tyne would say or do something that made her think leaving the country would be the worst thing ever. He made her feel bad for even leaving the house to go to school or work on any regular day…

She felt awful for abandoning him. After being made to endure a guilty conscience concerning it, she was tempted to offer for him to accompany her. The bonus feature of travel was finally escaping this dark relationship. She'd be staying with her mother's friend there and would have no place for him. Her parents didn't even know about her affair with the vampire, they simply knew that something had changed about their daughter over the past year. Her confidence was lower, and her mannerisms had become demure. They could tell that something was wrong and had questioned her relentlessly about the change.

Every step she took gouged the glass further into the bottoms of her feet, sending shockwaves of searing pain through her as she made her way down the hall. Halfway to the exit, she stopped moving to give herself the opportunity to brace herself mentally against the pain. Her hand was placed on the wall to help her balance as she avoided the shattered pictures still on the floor outside the room. On her way toward the door, Chance picked up Tyne's t-shirt that he had left hanging over the back of the couch. Normally, she'd have already cleared it away, washed it and returned it to his drawer for him, but with the trip coming up, Chance hadn't had the opportunity to clean up his messes lately.

Chance made her way out of the apartment wearing nothing but that t-shirt. It was so large on her it hung midway down her thighs, exactly how a dress would. She approached the back stairs to the apartment building and went out of the emergency exit. She stood in the deserted alleyway behind the apartment building.

Chance's entire body trembled as she picked up the brick from behind the door and used it to stop the door from swinging shut and locking her out. That would be what she needed… to get locked out of her building, stuck in the alley behind it, in nothing but a t-shirt..

"Fuck," she cussed, fighting the urge to break down in full sobs of anguish. It was almost as though swearing helped ease some of that emotional pain. "Tabarnak…"

Chance stumbled down the three steps, gripping the railing as though her life depended on it. On the last step, she plopped on her bottom. She was careful to keep her knees pressed tightly together and the t-shirt tucked under her bare ass. She took a slow, deep breath of the pre-sunrise air. Her mind had fooled her into thinking it was going to be a clean, spring morning, fresh breath… but it certainly was not! She glanced at the enormous pile of rotting garbage on one side of the stairs, then at the dumpsters on the other side.

She sighed again, rubbing her eyes with the back of her hand. Chance winced as she lifted her foot from the cement. With every step she'd taken, she became more aware of the glass embedded in her skin. Twisting, Chance placed her ankle on the knee of her other leg and shoved the edge of the t-shirt down in the gap it made between her legs. She picked the glass out of the bottom of her foot, careful not to push any shards deeper. Chance ignored the blood that dribbled onto the pavement.

"Got in a fight with your boyfriend?" an unfamiliar voice asked.

Chance hadn't heard anyone approach, so her head whipped up as she dropped a fairly large shard of glass onto the pavement with a soft 'tink' sound.

"I-I don't have a boyfriend," Chance responded as she quickly wiped a drying tear from her cheek.

"Girlfriend then?" The stranger smiled.

"I- what? No. Please. I'm sorry, I would like to be alone." Chance's eyes looked down as she spoke.

She glared at the stranger accompanied by two large dogs. He wore only black. Jeans, shirt, and a leather jacket. His clothes seemed ragged, covered in stains, and worn down on his knees and at the hem across his ankles. He had shoulder length black hair that was unkempt and damp from the light rain in the night. The man had no shoes on…Could the man be a transient? He didn't look well maintained.

Chance self-consciously put her foot down and pushed her knees tightly together, mentally noting that she wasn't wearing pants or underclothes beneath Tyne's shirt. Then she also crossed her arms over her chest to hide the fact that she didn't have a bra on. The chilly morning air had caused her nipples to become erect, causing them to press sensitively out against the material, emphasizing just how naked she was.

While Chance adjusted herself, one of the man's dogs, a tri-colored collie, leisurely made its way up the stairs toward the door behind her. She couldn't help thinking that he really should have had a leash on the animal. What if the hound attacked her?

"There's a shelter close to here," Chance noted softly, trying to keep calm, while timidly pointing toward the opening at the end of the alley.

"How cute. She believes you're homeless, Choker." A female voice said from directly behind her.

Chance twisted her head and shoulders around to find a completely naked woman standing not even a foot away from her. The sound that erupted from the young medical student was something between a gasp and a gurgle as she choked in surprise. In a panic, Chance turned to face the woman who had appeared out of nowhere.

She staggered away from the stairs, limping as shooting pain vibrated up her legs from the shards of glass she'd missed. Before Chance could speak, she backed into someone. The homeless man grabbed her upper arms from behind her in an iron tight hold. She bowed her head, attempting not to stare at the nude lady who approached her. She could see her own bloody footprints on the rain-dampened pavement through the tears that welled in her eyes. Chance wiggled, trying to loosen the man's grip on her.

The woman placed her fingers on the center of Chance's chest as she spoke. "You smell like a vampire, little girl."

Chance's head whipped up so her gaze could meet the lady's.

The man behind her slid his hands down her arms to her wrists, making a sickly feeling bubble up in her stomach. She lightly struggled against the stranger's tight grip.

Her eyes flashed to the wall of the building, to the bedroom window of her apartment. The thought of screaming occurred to her, but would Tyne get to her before they hurt her? Would he care to try?

"The sun is rising," Chance warned the pair, assuming they were vampires. "If you don't get out of here, you'll die."

"Not to worry, sweet one… Not to worry…" the woman muttered as she reached past Chance's face and slipped her hand into the man's breast pocket.

They had trapped her snugly between them, making it difficult for her to even struggle against them. The naked lady's bare leg slid up between Chance's, spreading them slightly. Her hot thigh pressed right against Chance's femininity, rubbing it hard as they imprisoned the younger girl.

They both formed a warm cocoon around her. That was when Chance realized the pair weren't vampires. The woman pulled a small black case from the man's pocket and opened it as she stepped back. Chance used the opportunity to struggle against the guy's grip a little harder, while a horrified whimper escaped her lips.

At the sight of a needle loaded with some sort of clear liquid, Chance panicked. The realization that this was actually happening filled her with a numbing terror that spread up from her extremities. Chance flailed hard enough that the man stumbled backward, taking her with him. It created a gap between her and the woman.

"No! Get away from me!" she yelled and kicked her foot out at the woman.

Chance's strike smashed the naked woman's stomach, leaving a bloody footprint on the redhead's pale skin, while toppling her over. The needle fell to the ground with a glassy clatter. A deep, throaty growl erupted from the dog, which waited patiently next to the man. Chance prepared to scream for help, but the guy released one of her wrists to cover her mouth. This was her opportunity! She balled her free hand into a fist and flung her elbow backward, hitting her attacker in the ribs. The hound's barking fell silent.

Before she could react further, a wrestling match had begun, and Chance's tiny size didn't have a hope in the struggle. Someone threw her to the ground as three bodies landed on top of her. A hand covered her mouth, and she tried to scream out of her nose. Mucus shot out from the force of the air. The hand improved its hold on her by blocking her nose.

Where had the third person come from?! Why did it matter?

"Hurry, Pandora!" The new stranger snapped in a growl.

The woman had landed on Chance's left arm when they fell to the ground. Keeping that arm pinned, she struggled to reach for the needle that she'd dropped earlier. Chance tried to scream out, but there was absolutely no air flow. Little white flecks danced across her vision as a blinding headache erupted within her entire skull. Her limbs had become numb and tingly from the body weight of her attackers, cutting off blood flow. Chance would have whimpered when the needle was stuck into the side of her neck, if she could have made any sound at all.

The hand released her mouth, but Chance couldn't even focus on trying to scream for help. In a rush, she noticed herself losing the will to resist as she struggled to remain conscious. Her muscles and mind suddenly felt more relaxed than ever before. Many hands pulled her up to her knees and, though she concentrated hard on her desperate desire to fight against them, she also really wanted to comply. As she teetered on her scratched knees, she barely perceived her fresh wounds and scrapes, the remaining glass in her feet, or the dirt and stones from the wet ground that stuck to her shirt and thighs.

"Gotta love the vamp juice," the original stranger said and chuckled. "The venom already has her under its spell. Spot, run ahead home and tell the master that we caught a special treat for tomorrow night."

Chance's breathing had become slow, and everything tingled, even inside her mouth. She bit her bottom lip, trying to cause pain to help herself refocus her mind. Chance's eyes met the woman's and the naked lady awarded her with the creepiest grin before transforming into a dog. The hound seemed to smile at her. Either they gave her some really wild psychedelic… or…

"Werewolf?" She whispered faintly as the man wearing clothes picked her up, cradling her like a baby in his arms.

Yes, a werewolf that turned into a collie. Chance laughed softly as she stared around. The other man was gone too… maybe he was a poodle? She had to have been hallucinating. There were no such things as werewolves. Or transforming dogs…Mind, she would have said the same about vampires two years ago.

"Tyne," she muttered…dizzy as she closed her eyes, resting her head on the stranger's shoulder, "I'm still mad at you…"

It had to be Tyne holding her. No one else could carry her like she was a baby. She wrapped her arms around the man's shoulders and kissed a trail down his neck.

"I think I love you…" Chance groaned.

"I'm not your boyfriend, you're high," someone's voice snarled in her ear.

It wasn't Tyne's voice that echoed in her ears. It was the stranger's voice. Chance would have panicked if she could have felt anything besides lust and an odd floating sensation.

She was being abducted… But she was being taken where? And for what reason? What were they going to do to her?

"I don't care…" Chance breathed… "About… anything…"

5

Animals In Cages

Chance

Chance's eyes snapped open, and she sat up a little too fast.

"I'm late!" she blurted out from her lips before recent memories came cascading into her mind.

The very first thing she noticed was the horrific smell of the room. It gave her flashbacks to when her family lived on a farm and the septic system backed up into the house.

As she gagged, Chance realized that someone had stripped her of that t-shirt. She was naked! Chance's arms wrapped around herself as goosebumps rose on her flesh. There was an old holey blanket on her that was too small to cover all of her bare skin. The material was some aged itchy wool, and it smelled of urine, but it was better than nothing.

Her uniquely colored eyes stared around, trying to understand the situation. She was in a dog cage? What the hell happened?!

As Chance sat up, she made a mental note that the top of the crate was approximately an inch higher than her head. Lining the wall, like an abandoned kennel-style space, were at least 20 more cages identical to her own. Most of the crates had people locked in them. The room had two entrances. Chance's head turned from one direction to the other. On her left was a single cage, then the wall with one of those entrances. To the right were all the rest of them. She counted fifteen crates leading to the far exit.

A bubble of panic built in her chest. She lunged for the barred door, her hands fighting with the slider, only to find a small metal padlock holding it in place. She was trapped!

"Hello?! Let me out!" Chance yelled, leaning back and kicking at the cage door with her barefoot.

Her assault on the crate hurt a lot less than it should have. As Chance grabbed her foot to examine it, she found that the glass was gone, and the wounds had completely healed. Good! It would make booting the fucking gate easier. She rammed her foot into the door where the lock was.

"Stop!" the person in the cage next to her hissed in a panicked whisper.

Chance's face whipped to her left in surprise. "What?"

"You *don't* want them to come."

The stranger next to her pulled the ratty blanket off of her head to give Chance a wide-eyed stare. The girl's eyes were the most stunning lilac purple she had ever seen. She was slender and dark-skinned with curly black hair worn naturally, but was a matted mess on one side as though she spent a lot of time laying down. As she sat up, her blanket fell to her lap, exposing her unclothed breasts as though she'd lost her sense of propriety.

Chances' eyes snapped shut.

'*Why is everyone naked lately?*' she thought, struggling with her own discomfort.

Both women pulled their thin blankets protectively around themselves, though Chance didn't bother to hide the barely discernible bite marks on her neck and collarbone. They were nearly invisible unless one knew to look for them, and would completely disappear with time.

"Where the hell am I? What's going on?" Chance whispered at the stranger, as her eyes flashed up and down the hallway.

"Nice to meet you, too," she muttered sarcastically, followed by a sigh as Chance shot her a dark glare. "We all know basically the same things. They abducted us off the street, then are kept down here before they take us away."

"Taken away to where?" Chance questioned, her hand grabbing at the metal bars separating her from the other girl.

"Dunno. They just come and remove some of us. I think it's every few days…No one ever returns; they just leave permanently…" She pulled her knees to her chest as she spoke, wrapping her arms around them to give herself comfort.

Chance could barely fight the urge to hyperventilate. She was going to die! They were planning to kill her and the last thing she told Tyne was that she hated him… Unless that was a dream? It was hard for her to discern reality from her nightmares lately.

The last thing she said to her foster mum was that she'd call them for a video chat during Sunday breakfast because she wasn't going to be able to attend in person. She wouldn't be seeing her, though, because she stupidly got herself mixed up with a bloodsucker. This had to be Tyne's fault! A thought dawned on her.

"Are they all vampires?" Chance whispered, lifting her chin from its perch on her knees as she still attempted to remember what had happened the previous night.

Simply saying something like that made Chance feel as

though she sounded like some kind of nut and that she belonged in a whole different type of cage. Who would ask that so suddenly? But when her eyes met her new friend's, the other girl didn't look like she thought Chance was crazy.

"The monsters I've seen call themselves hellhounds," the woman responded, rubbing her forearms as if attempting to build up warmth from friction.

"Hellhounds?" Chance's face paled. "Like in mythology? The guards of hell?"

"That makes them sound scarier than they sometimes are, but I saw one turn into a Chihuahua." The girl gave her a half-hearted smile, as though trying to help the newest prisoner find some comfort.

Chance struggled to grant the woman a shaky grin of her own. Tears filled her eyes instead. Her hands trembled as they grasped at the blanket's edge near her ankles.

"Don't cry. They'll just laugh and make it worse… What's your name?"

"Chance Kimura… and you?"

"Lizzy," she responded… "That's an odd one."

"My dad was half Japanese." She told her softly.

"You don't look very Japanese or sound it." Lizzy tilted her head to the side. "You seem more French than anything."

"That's because my dad was only half-Japanese. He was also American and my mum was French-Canadian. So, I'm really barely Japanese." Chance's gaze dropped to her hands as tears welled in her eyes.

"It's okay, don't be sad…You might see them again someday." She tried to comfort Chance.

"Not likely. They're both dead. They passed away in an accident when I was twelve." She lifted her chin, meeting the gaze of the stranger.

"Your eyes." The girl gasped at Chance, noticing the mismatched colors.

"Yeah, I get that reaction a lot. My left eye was my mums; that's why it's green. I was in the car with them." She sighed softly. "What about you? Any deep darks you wanna get off your chest before we die?"

She laughed timidly. "Not really. I had a fairly normal childhood until a few weeks ago."

"What happened a few weeks ago?"

"I was kidnapped… and brought here. I'm sure it's been at least a few weeks." Lizzy sighed softly while her vibrant eyes, shimmering with unshed tears, stared nervously at the entrance to the far left.

"You've been here that long?! Do you ever think about escaping? Going back to your family?" Chance felt panicked as this all became far too real.

"All the time," Lizzy's voice trembled. "My mum and dad are probably so scared for me. Or they likely think I'm dead." Lizzy's gaze dropped in shame as her eyes filled with tears.

"My foster parents are expecting me to call on Sunday. We hold breakfast every week. They're going to show up at my house if I don't…" As the thought occurred, panic really exploded in her chest. "Oh, my god. They're going to wonder who the hell Tyne is and why he's in my apartment!"

They were going to look for her and find a *man* in her home. What if he told her parents that they were sleeping together?

"You were kidnapped by monsters, and you're worried your family will meet your boyfriend?!" The girl's jaw locked in far more anger than she should have felt. There was no way this girl was going to understand. Her parents clearly weren't Asian, and she could probably date as a teenager. Chance would still be a virgin if Tyne had never appeared in her life.

"He's not my boyfriend…" She sighed quietly, rubbing her eyes with her palms. "My foster parents are both Korean and are a little too strict."

"Sounds like they care," Lizzy said softly.

"Yeah… and I don't want them to think shameful things of me." Chance felt tears burning her eyes as a ball of stress built in her throat, making her voice hoarse. "I don't wish that to be the last thing they ever think of me."

"At least your family thinks nice shit about you," Lizzy whispered, resting her chin on her knees. "Mine probably aren't even searching for me…they likely believe I overdosed and am dead in a gutter somewhere."

Lizzy panted lightly as she spoke. Glistening tears dribbled down her cheeks as she struggled to maintain her calm.

"Are you having trouble breathing?" Chance added gently as she leaned toward the edge of her cage to get a better look at the other girl.

"I have asthma. This is a pretty dank basement." She rolled onto her side, pulling her blanket to her chin. "I'm amazed you noticed, though, not many would."

"I'm studying to be a doctor," Chance told her softly. "I've been going to school at-." She cut off as the door opened at the far end of the hall.

Chance leaned forward with her eyebrows furrowed as she strained to view who it was. A pang of disappointment struck her when she didn't recognize any of the newcomers. A tiny part of her had hoped to see Tyne, or the police, or even her parents, to arrive through the door.

Two rough-looking men in dirty jeans and black leather jackets entered, dragging an unconscious naked teenager between them. They marched down the aisle in a way that screamed they'd done this time and time again. They headed straight to the cage between Chance's and the wall at the end of the room. One man yanked open the door, and they shoved the comatose teen inside feet first while being careful not to damage his face.

After one man slammed the door, Chance announced, "Let me out. I have to pee!"

"I don't give a damn," another guy snarled.

"But I have to pee!" she insisted louder.

"Shut the fuck up!" the other man roared, pulling out a taser.

"No!" Chance yelled right back.

The stranger tapped the prongs to the crate while pressing the button. A shot of electricity sparked where the weapon made contact and sent a shock to zap Chance's ass, feet, and hand. Everything that touched the cage clenched with pain for a split second. She screamed in surprise and agony.

"Want it again, bitch?"

"No! No! please."

"Then shut the fuck up!"

Chance sniffled quietly as tears rolled down her cheeks. She pulled her knees to her chest and wrapped her arms around them as she nodded quickly to soothe the man's anger. Her eyes flashed at Lizzy, who was curled in a ball hiding under her blanket. The woman was trembling so badly that the material shook.

The two men marched down the hall toward the exit they had entered through. Chance growled softly in the back of her throat as she watched them leave, slamming the door behind them. Why hadn't they just gone out of the entrance that was closer to her, instead they walked the length of the hall to the other door? She couldn't let fear stop her from planning or making notes.

The clothes the hellhounds wore seemed dirty and unmaintained. The style of apparel was something like bikers gone hobo. Except, not all homeless people were unwashed like this and the few bikers she'd met through the hospital took good care of themselves. She'd only really gotten to know one homeless man. He would perch himself outside the hospital, panhandling for donations. On the days security didn't kindly ask him to leave, she'd often buy him lunch and give him some spare change. He would call her a vanilla-scented angel. Just seeing his face light up when she got to work would make her a little bit happier.

Chance surveyed the man they'd brought in, gasped, and looked elsewhere, blinking rapidly. OH MY! He was very naked, and they didn't even bother to cover him. As she turned her face away from him, her gaze fell on Lizzy.

"You okay?" she whispered as quietly as she could, glancing toward the door to make sure no one was coming in to hear.

"Yeah? Are you? I'm sorry. I should have warned you." Lizzy began trying to finger-brush her hair. "Don't talk to them unless spoken to, and… it smells so bad in here because…" Tears of humiliation rolled down her cheeks as her gaze dropped. "There's nowhere else to go but in your cage."

"I'm going to end up with a distended bladder…"

"That's the least of your worries." Lizzy picked at a hole in her blanket as she mumbled. "Sometimes they take one of us… the ones who don't behave… and all we hear are screams."

Chance blinked back her tears and moved to press her body against the back of her crate that lined up with the wall. The bars dug into her bare skin, and she could feel a chilly dampness through the stone wall. She pulled her thighs to her chest and tucked her blanket under her chin while resting it on her knees.

As she sat there, she considered her options. Eventually, she was going to make an escape attempt, but if she failed, she'd end up dead. The best time to run away would be during a transfer or change of location. It was often the weak point in a kidnapper's steps. Transition points. Ultimately, they'd take her and everyone else out of the cages, like Lizzy said. That would be her opportunity to try getting out. No, that wouldn't be the best time after all. If there were too many of them, she'd easily be overpowered. A few months of Tae Kwon-do classes at twelve does not make a battle-hardened warrior. She wished she hadn't begged her foster parents to put her in gymnastics instead. Being able to do the splits would not help her now.

After hours of quiet, Chance dozed in and out of wakefulness from pure boredom. Just as she was falling into a deep sleep, a blood-curdling scream erupted right next to her, jarring her from her rest. Chance yelped in surprise, dropping her sheet before snatching it back up to hug against herself while attempting to protect her dignity.

Tears rolled down her cheeks as she realized in her

freight… she peed. It all just came out and left her sitting in the warm liquid as it cooled in a puddle beneath her.

"Stop screaming!" she yelled at the young man in the cage next to her.

"Fuck you, bitch!" he snarled back before continuing to shriek and kick at his crate.

Chance leaned away from him, blocking her ears to help deafen the echoes of his screeching.

"You need to stop!" Lizzy made her own attempt at silencing him.

But before he could respond to her, the door at the end of the hall flung open so hard that it rammed into the crate behind it. Chance turned to stare at the angry hellhound who stood in the entranceway panting in rage. From the corner of her eye, she saw Lizzy curl into a ball beneath her blanket as if the girl believed it would offer a shield to protect her.

"Let me the fuck out!" the young teen in the cage next to Chance's roared as he stomped at the door.

She didn't know what she had expected, but she really didn't think the man in the doorway would simply smile at the captive. That smirk made her skin crawl. The hellhound pulled out the same handheld taser that someone used on her earlier.

The man next to her continued his shrieking, and she thought the hellhound would react the same as he had with her by shocking the teen's cage. Instead, still wearing that creepy smile, the asshole moved the taser to zap the cage nearest to him.

A feminine wail of surprise and pain echoed through the room. Then he moved to the next cage. The scream was more masculine, but had just as much agony behind it. As he approached Chance, she could see Lizzy shaking harder and harder beneath her blanket.

"Stop it, you fuckin freak!" the teenager next to her screeched as the hellhound reached the midway point.

It didn't slow him. Scream after scream, he drew closer. Chance glared, meeting the hellhound's eyes as he paused in front of her cage. She didn't want to shriek. She was going to try not to, but as the taser tapped her crate, the sound simply came out.

The hellhound took one last step to reach the yelling man's cage. He put his hands on his hips for a moment while grinning down at the fool. Chance quivered, but didn't let herself stop glaring at the bastard with the taser.

"Fuck you, asshole!" The guy barked at the hellhound moments before the creature shocked his cage.

The hellhound didn't lift the taser immediately like he'd done for each victim before. He waited, holding the weapon there, while the young man squealed, throwing himself around to escape the waves of agony. Chance eventually broke and closed her eyes tightly, unable to bear watching the boy in pain. The shrieking was endless. She turned her face away and raised her hands to block her ears as tears streamed down her cheeks.

When the screams were silenced, all she could hear was the brutal sobbing from the tortured teen. She opened her eyes to see that the hellhound had finally stopped shocking the cage. As he spoke, she closed her eyes again as more tears leaked from them.

"Oh, look at that..." the hellhound practically purred. "Battery ran out. Lucky you."

Chance could hear the sturdy thumping of boots marching away down the hall. The echo was drowned out by the young man's subdued sobs. Eventually, his sobs quieted into occasional sniffles. There was a certain point when crying just took too much energy and there never seemed to be enough tears to qualify for the amount of pain.

"Hey," Lizzy's voice broke the silence.

Chance opened her eyes to find Lizzy sitting up, nearly pressing her face against the side of her cage to see the young man.

"Wh-what?" he practically yelped.

"Shhhh!" both Chance and Lizzy hissed at him in panic.

Lizzy shook her head as she spoke. "If you whisper, they

won't come. So we need to be quiet."

When he looked on the verge of tears once more, Chance added, "What's your name?"

"Nathan." His voice was soft, as though he attempted to murmur, but it cracked loudly instead.

"I'm Lizzy, and this is Chance."

"How did this happen? I was on my way to yoga and…" Nathan trailed off, his black eyes moving from Chance to Lizzy as though one of them might have the answer.

Chance shook her head, shrugging her shoulders as she hugged her blanket to her chest, careful not to let it slip. Chance frowned at the young man. He looked just as terrified as she felt. She wished she could offer him words of comfort, but she barely maintained her own composure.

"I believe it helps if you just think about home," Lizzy whispered. "I visualize my family, my job, my hobbies… I picture it in my mind."

Nathan closed his eyes, taking a deep inhale, but a moment later, a tear rolled down his cheek. His face turned red as though he held his breath. He opened his eyes, shaking his head at her, looking like he was about to break into uncontrollable sobbing once more.

"I can't," he whimpered. "I just keep seeing them attack me."

Chance wanted to cry again. She wouldn't be sure if she was weeping for him or herself.

"It's okay. Close your eyes," Lizzy advised him. "I'll help you.

She also shut her eyes, willing to do anything to make this bubble of terror in her chest disappear. She took a slow, deep breath as she prepared to follow Lizzy's instructions.

"Picture where you work," Lizzy murmured. And after a few moments, she added, "Tell me about it."

"Downtown, at Olly's Coffee Stop," he answered, clearly struggling to prevent his voice from cracking again.

Chance pictured the hospital. She visualized she was wearing a white coat. She could almost feel her tablet in her fingers, like it was second nature.

"Imagine the smell of coffee. Let the scent bring you back there."

As another slow, deep breath filled Chance's lungs, she instantly regretted it. That was not the aroma of coffee, but urine. She made a face of disgust. This wasn't working for her. Maybe if she pictured the coffee shop near the entrance of the hospital. She grabbed her coffee every morning there.

"What would you be thinking about at work?"

"I umm… Midterms. I'm going back to get my grade twelve. I decided I want to be a lawyer."

"Why? Why is school so important to you now?"

"My brother was falsely accused of some stuff. The lawyer saved his life." He cleared his throat. "I wanna do that for someone, too."

"How are your grades? Did you study at work?"

Chance opened her eyes and looked at Nathan. She was curious to see if this was actually helping him. It surprised her to find that he seemed a little more relaxed. His shoulders slumped so his blond hair didn't brush against the top of his cage. He sat cross-legged with the blanket covering his genitalia, and his hands resting on the material, subconsciously picking at it.

"Yeah, I've got straight A's. Even taking college prep classes… I'm always studying…" His voice turned shaky. "I was at the bus stop… studying from the streetlight. I didn't see them walk up."

"No," Lizzy insisted as tears rolled down his cheeks. "Tell me about your hobbies."

"I do yoga and I used to do ballet, but I just don't have the time anymore with my schoolwork."

The door at the end of the hall flung open, scaring the crap out of all three of them. Chance and Nathan stared at each other for a few moments. Both took slow breaths to keep each other calm. A loud squeal echoed in the room, then stopped, then echoed again. Chance's eyebrows furrowed in confusion as she turned to see what was going on. The squeak was so shrill in the quiet space that it hurt her ears. It was coming from a cart that resembled an old metal trolley, very much like the food tray carts at the hospital. The server stopped in front of each crate and slid the tray through a small gap under the doors.

As the man bent over to slip the tray into Lizzy's cage, Chance got a good look at his face. The man was in his late fifties. He had a gray five o'clock shadow with white patches. His visage was grizzled and weather-beaten, but he still had a youthful twinkle in his soft, gray eyes.

Chance's dark eyebrows furrowed in a moment of recognition as she matched his features to someone she'd met. The wheels on the cart squealed once more and the man bent over in front of her cage. He slid a food tray that had about one metric cup of brown stew-like stuff into her crate.

Flinging herself forward, Chance dropped her blanket as she reached out to grab the cage door. Her slim fingers slipped through the small bars as she nearly rammed her forehead into it while trying to get a better look at the man.

"It *is* you!" tears welled in her eyes as she whimpered.

The man chuckled gleefully as his gaze trailed from Chance's multi-colored eyes to her exposed breasts. Chance quickly flung herself away from the cage door, snatching up her blanket to cover herself. Why was he here? THAT was the homeless man she'd give change to outside the hospital. He was always so jovial and made her day just a little better just by being there. Tears rolled down her cheeks as she tried to piece together what that same man was doing here, but nothing came to mind.

He served the final captive his meal and dragged the cart from the room. As Chance eventually got her emotions under control, her eyes trailed to the tray. She hadn't eaten in what felt like forever. Upon closer inspection, though, Chance realized her dinner was not stew, but chunky canned dog food.

She made a gagging sound after leaning forward and sniffing at the substance. Yep, definitely dog food. This had to be some sort of joke-. She turned her head to find that every captive who had been here before her was scooping up the chunks and eating them.

Lizzy crushed one chunk with her fingertips, then used it to sop up some of the sauce before pinching some and bringing it to her mouth. Chance swiveled her gaze to Nathan, who seemed to be the only other sane person there. He was curled in a ball, pressing himself against the backside of the cage, as far away from the tray as he could get.

Chance returned to examining the food and feeling her appetite dwindle.

She whispered, "That's disgusting."

"It's not so bad when you get hungry enough." Lizzy murmured, looking disappointed as she sopped up the last of the sauce with her last piece.

Chance made a face like she was going to be sick and shoved the tray back out of the slot. There was no way she'd be famished enough to eat that. Would she? There were historical events of people facing a chance of starving to death, so instead they committed acts of cannibalism. She'd never really known hunger before this, but wasn't yet ravenous enough to devour dog food.

She laid down, preparing to sleep as she mumbled her thoughts, "Ironic that hellhounds would feed the humans dog food and keep us in dog cages."

06

Sold To The Man In The White Hat

Chance

A loud clattering woke Chance from the light slumber she had eventually found. She rubbed her eyes as she sat up and scowled, trying to get her bearings.

A group of four people entered and walked down the aisle between the two rows of cages. Some captives waited and stared at them as they moved past, others hid themselves beneath their decrepit blanket in fear. They stopped in front of Chance's cage and unlatched the metal lock that kept it shut.

"Remember me, pretty girly?" The man in the leather coat asked with a cocky grin.

Chance sneered, crossing her arms over her chest. She tried to look angry, but the only thing she felt was terror. That was the same bastard who led her abduction team.

"Get out," the leather-coated stranger snapped.

"No." Chance turned her scowl to a glare at the bars along the side of the cage.

The hellhound in the leather coat grabbed the door and flung it open so hard it banged off the front of the next crate. He reached in toward Chance and pulled back, just in time to keep Chance's bare foot from hitting his face.

"Don't touch me! Espèce de connard!" Chance screamed in a combination of French and English at the bastard.

The prisoners gasped in surprise and fear, as if they dreaded how the hellhound was bound to react. Chance didn't care. She wasn't about to do anything they commanded. No way in hell!

"No!" she yelled as two of the monsters reached in, grabbed her flailing legs, and heaved her out of the crate as fast as possible.

The bottom of the cage scraped Chance's back, but it went ignored. Her hands clawed at the bars on the sides, attempting to get a good grip, as her fingertips dragged from one metal rung to the next. When they had her all the way out, all modesty disappeared as Chance tried to swing at the men with her fists, but the three of them quickly pinned her to the ground. The female hellhound stuck a needle into Chance's thigh with a painful pinch.

The drug's effects instantly attacked her senses and thoughts. Everything was spinning around Chance as her body became weak. She wanted to be touched; she longed to caress someone, anyone. She moaned softly, half closing her eyes as a wave of dizziness overcame her.

Chance no longer struggled against the grip of the men holding her. They yanked their prisoner to her feet, and instead of fighting against them, she clutched onto them, fearing that if they let go, she would fall.

"Help me," Chance whimpered, shaking her head as tears of frustration rolled down her cheeks.

The hellhounds partially dragged, half-carried Chance toward the door they had entered through. As they approached, she noticed more hellhounds coming into the room and opening the other cages, drugging the people locked in them before pulling them out.

Chance lost all sense of direction as they moved up and down long hallways and stairwells. At one point, Chance lost consciousness and had to be hauled the rest of the way.

"Hey, wake up," someone hissed, as the hellhounds who had her arms gave Chance a shake.

Gasping for air, she struggled to raise her head. As she barely raised her head, the men lifted her slightly to place her feet under her. Chance's neck surrendered to her weakness and her head flopped backward. Her knees buckled, forcing the hellhounds to hold her up.

"What's wrong with me?" she whispered over the buzz of muttering voices.

The hum of voices rang into the open space. She stared around with her hazy vision, trying to assess the room. It was a large space with a door on three of the four walls and a huge, red curtain dividing the space. She appeared to be backstage.

Voices echoed across the space, the sounds carrying within the room's acoustics. Her head tipped to the side and her eyes lingeringly closed while she struggled to stay alert. They marched her to a table. Her brows furrowed as she spotted a large metal pail resting on the table. Soapy water sloshed on the table as a feminine hand with red painted nails reached into the bucket.

Chance closed her eyes as her head slowly tilted backward. She couldn't force herself to stay upright. It was as though her muscles slowly became weaker with each moment that passed.

The cool fingertips began at her throat, moved down her collarbone, then across her shoulders. It smelled like bathroom soap from a mall. It had to be some generic brand, but the texture was greasy, as though someone was trying to oil her down like a wrestler. The wash was likely to hide the smell of the musty mix of urine and mold from the room they kept the abducted in.

The contact felt so good as the smooth hand massaged the oily soap into her skin. A moan escaped her lips before she could help it.

'No! I shouldn't be enjoying this!' Chance suddenly struggled against the grip that held her up.

The stranger that she couldn't see tweaked her nipple as they rubbed oil into her skin. Tears leaked from the corners of her eyes. She felt as though her mind and body were betraying not only her dignity, but her sense of self. The hand moved down between her thighs and massaged lightly, causing her clit to harden with arousal. She gasped softly, finally forcing her eyes to open so she could glare at the redheaded woman who had kidnapped her.

"Why?" Chance whimpered, with a voice that didn't want to work. "I don't understand…"

"You will soon enough, sweet little human," the hellhound responded in a musical tone, as though she enjoyed her job a little too much.

Chance couldn't help the whimper that escaped her as the woman reached around and massaged her back and ass with the oil. A group of three passed by with the man that had been in the cage beside her.

"Nathan?" Chance whimpered, struggling against the hands that held her.

Chance squinted as they dragged Nathan to take the first spot in line. Someone started rubbing him down with the soapy oil.

When the curtain fluttered open, light flashed into her eyes, blinding her for a moment. She blinked back tears as a vampire's pale face popped behind the curtain.

"Where the fuck is Elizabeth?" The pale-faced man snarled with his fangs glittering in the dim backstage lighting.

Lizzy appeared from somewhere behind Chance. She clearly wasn't drugged like the rest of them, as she easily moved smoothly and unassisted. Her hands hung loosely at her sides. Lizzy wore a pink dog collar around her throat. She bowed her head so low that her chin rested on the brim of the collar. Their gazes met for an instant, but Lizzy's eyes carried no recognition as she glanced at Chance from the corner of her eye.

"I'm here, master," Lizzy's voice was soft and submissive.

"Let's go, you dumb bitch."

"Yes, master," she responded, and quickly followed him onto the stage beyond the curtain.

Chance couldn't even process what she had just seen. Lizzy was wearing a dog collar, and she called a vampire 'master'. What had that woman faced for her to behave in such a way? Chance cocked an eyebrow, struggling to form cohesive thoughts. Lizzy… that poor girl must have spent every day in those cages.

As soon as they finished drenching Nathan with the soapy oil-and-water mix, they dragged the limp young man past Chance and onto the stage.

"Ladies and gentlemen, fangers and beasts of all ages, allow me to present to you our first piece of the evening." Chance heard an announcer's voice echo clearly through speakers and the commotion in the nearby room died down. It was the voice of the vampire who had summoned Lizzy. "This wonderful piece is in his early twenties and seems to be of mixed Latino ancestry. From what our informants tell us, he is not a virgin, in front or in back. But with a bulging weapon and muscle tone like that, why would it matter?! For those in the back without sensitive vision, his eyes are completely black, contrasting nicely with pale blond hair… Just look at those dark pretty things sparkling with fear! He has no acne and well-maintained teeth. Finally, what you've been waiting for… because as you all know, tonight is a special night… Tonight is our flavor pieces, and this delectable toy tastes like… strawberries! We will start the bidding at $15,000!"

Chance stood there with her mouth hanging open in absolute horror. She couldn't believe what she was listening to. They were being sold?! The price for the young man was slowly increasing. It had already reached $45, 000.

"No... Please, don't let them do this to us," she whimpered softly and struggled against the grip that held her.

"I think you like the thought of being sold..." the woman who oiled up her body responded with a mischievous smirk.

Chance's voice came out in a muted whisper, "Never."

"Really? Your perky little nips are still hard, and you're so wet, I'm sure you'd cum in seconds if I kept playing with you."

"No..." Chance whimpered, tears rolling down her cheeks. "You drugged me."

"With so much vamp venom you should be practically unconscious right now... Makes me curious how much a specimen like you will go for," one guard holding Chance murmured.

The second man responded. "With a physique like yours and those eyes. You're definitely quite the merchandise for any collector."

Before Chance could argue again, the announcer's voice reverberated backstage, "Let's see if we can't increase that bid!"

Following the presenter's suggestion, a scream from the slave who was being auctioned echoed throughout the area.

Chance flinched hard in fear, trying to move herself away from the stage area. The man who held her left arm laughed quietly as she helplessly struggled to break free.

The monsters sold Nathan for $270, 000. With every person they dragged past Chance onto the stage, her nerves increased. She watched them go, being sold off, one by one, to the highest bidder.

Eventually, Chance had to lean on one of her guards to remain on her feet. The drugs were wearing off, but it didn't mean she was in a better state. In fact, she was ready to drop and pass right out.

Chance suddenly felt someone giving her a light shake to wake up. The two guards had to keep holding her up, because she had indeed fallen asleep.

"Ready, little human? Cause it's your turn." One of them whispered to her, but she was so out of it, she couldn't tell which had spoken.

She could hear the announcer's voice, which sounded made for television commercials. "For our final offering, we have a unique treat for you. We believe this one is a Japanese and French mix."

Chance's head slowly lifted as they pulled her bare-naked through the curtain. The stage light struck and blinded her, creating white specks that danced in her vision. She blinked back tears as her captors dragged her onto the center of the stage. Once there, they brought her to her knees, facing an audience. The floor was cold and wet, triggering goosebumps to rise on her skin.

"This little toy is clever. Not just street smart, but studying to be a doctor! Pre-med!" The announcer's voice echoed in Chance's mind, sending her whirling through a torrent of horrific thoughts.

'THEY KNOW ME!' she panicked, floundering against the ironlike grip of the beasts who held her to her knees.

She tilted her head so she could glare at the announcer. Beside him stood Lizzy, whispering the answers to him. She was a setup! That traitor! Chance groaned loudly as she struggled again, wanting to run across the stage and punch Lizzy right between the eyes.

"Look at how this toy overcomes venom!" The presenting voice used the opportunity to upsell the product.

She trembled in their arms, her mind reeling. How was she going to beat them? She wasn't going to scream! Like all the others before her, she wasn't about to give them the satisfaction of shrieking and increasing the price.

"For those of you nearsighted, this special guest has one black eye and one blue-green. Unfortunately, it's from modern medical advances, not genetic blessing. Her dark hair is silky, likely from the hint of Asian ancestry…"

The announcer paused for theatrical flair as he grinned, marching to the other side of the stage to keep the spectators engaged with him.

"Our final flavor is one of the rarest. I've only seen two in my entire afterlife! VANILLA!!!!"

The audience erupted in a murmur of voices, some people even standing up and yelling out prices.

"Ten thousand!"

"Fuck the werewolf, $50, 000!"

"Eighty!"

In his glory, the announcer excitedly remarked, "We've got eighty thou- do I hear eighty-five?"

Someone called out from the back of the room, "Ninety!"

Chance couldn't help the tears that welled in the corners of her eyes as she stared around, trying to make out the features of the bidders in the auditorium. She couldn't see any of the faces beyond the blinding light. A part of her prayed the police would break down the door like in the movies… and another part of her wished Tyne would show up and rescue her like some sort of Prince Charming. But fairy tales were for children.

The bidding reached $145, 000 before it slowed, and the announcer's thrill dimmed.

"Maybe you all need to hear her scream to encourage you," he scowled over his shoulder at her as he spoke.

This was what she was waiting for. Chance sneered at the announcer until she noticed a man step in front of her with a large bucket in his hands. He threw the contents of the bucket at her. Freezing water with chunks of ice flung at Chance, splashing across her front, soaking her entirely.

Chance didn't even let herself gasp, though she desperately wanted to. As the urge to cry or scream out lifted, she turned a dark glare onto the presenter and snarled audibly.

Her reaction had the opposite effect than what she'd expected or hoped for. After a few moments of surprised silence, the crowd erupted once again with prices. Her mouth hung open as she slowly shook her head in disgust.

"Two-thirty? Did I hear-." The announcer was trying to catch the highest cost over the shout-outs of his patrons.

"Two eighty to the dark fairy."

Her eyes widened. Dark fairy?! What the fuck was that?!

One patron stood. He was easy to spot amongst the crowd because his clothing was entirely white, from his hat to his shoes. The dark-skinned man walked smoothly to the edge of the stage, making eye contact with her. Slowly, a smile emerged on his dark lips. The twinkle in his dead gaze made her skin crawl. He leaned forward, resting his forearm on the stage as his unblinking eyes appeared to delve into her soul. He was definitely a vampire.

"Five hundred," the man in the white hat announced in a quiet tone, though his voice seemed to carry above the call outs from the audience.

Chance wasn't trembling from only the cold. His stare terrified her. He didn't even flick his gaze from hers as he reported the ridiculously high price. The way Tyne looked when he was sleeping… like a corpse…that was how this monster appeared as he stood there smirking at her.

Automatically Chance shook her head, but her silent plea when ignored.

"Five hundred!" The announcer didn't hesitate to jump on the price, "Going once!"

"Six!" someone called out, followed by another bid. "Seven!"

The corners of the white-clad vampire's mouth curled up into a smile that sent chills down Chance's spine. She slowly shook her head, unable to break eye contact with the beast before her.

"One million."

The auditorium met the vamp's response with utter silence. Even the announcer hadn't expected that jump in price. Apparently, the creep wasn't fucking around.

"No." Chance whispered dejectedly.

"Sold! For 1 million dollars!"

It shouldn't have been possible for the vampire's smirk to turn darker… but as the guards dragged Chance behind the curtain, the creature's lifeless eyes followed, and his grin screamed of the pain she was going to endure before she begged for death to claim her.

07

Meeting Master

Chance

Chance couldn't help struggling against the hellhounds' grip as they returned her to the backstage area behind the grand red curtain. Their fingers dug into her skin as they fought to keep a firm grasp on her. Their fingertips gouged painfully into the flesh of her underarms.

There was no way she was sticking around to face that creature!

Her heart was thrumming so hard she could hear it in her ears. Her instincts put her into a blind panic. Chance attempted to throw herself back and forth to rip her arms from their grip. Her bare feet kicked at their legs, trying to add a little more umph to her side of the battle.

"Jeeze! I can't keep a hold of her. She's too oily!" one hound snarled as they pulled her to the backstage table.

The pair bent her over the table, pinning her while they fought to regain control of their prisoner. Chance almost got her right wrist loose, but as soon as his hand slipped, he caught it again immediately. She dragged the outer edge of her foot down the other man's shin, trying to distract him from holding her.

Chance knew she needed to break free! She was desperate to escape before it was too late. She had the feeling that if the monster got his cold, dead hands on her, she certainly wouldn't live long after.

"Give her more venom!" one hellhound noisily hissed, and the other responded, "Can't! Her heart could give out. She's had too much of the synthetic stuff."

Chance's teeth clicked loudly as she tried to bite an arm that accidentally got too close to her face. When she heard the announcer's unmistakable voice drawing closer, she suspected she was out of time. Nausea took her alongside a wave of terror. A cold sweat immediately spread across her body, leaving her trembling with the chill. Her hands became frigid and clammy.

Chance closed her eyes tightly, still refusing to give up her fight as the presenter's chattering went from an indistinct hum to a coherent, albeit one-sided, conversation.

"I can't believe you killed your last one already. Not that I'm complaining. The quicker you eat them, the more money I make! Oh, shit!"

He must have spotted the struggle between Chance and her jailers. She didn't dare look back to see how far away the announcer was, or who was with him. *Please don't be that vampire!* She'd been seeing a vampire for a little over a year and he never once scared her, but this monster was different. She was so scared that her bones ached with sheer terror.

"Do not presume to touch what belongs to me!"

A horrifyingly chilling voice rang out from directly behind Chance. The three halted their timeless struggle and became stark still while realizing who the owner of the drawling tones was. It seemed quite possible the men were just as anxious as she was.

Both of the hellhounds whipped their hands clear from Chance. The pair quickly stepped away from her. In her moment of blind panic, she attempted to grab onto them. As the duo bolted away from her, she gripped the edge of the table.

Chance bowed her head and closed her eyes tightly, unable to force herself to turn around to meet the vampire who had purchased her.

Her entire body trembled uncontrollably. If she had eaten the dog food, it was likely she'd have puked it up from the strain of her nerves.

Chance slowly shook her head as tears wanted to well up in her eyes. She stubbornly refused to allow them to leak out. It felt like an eternity that she stood there, frozen in terror. The drugs they'd given her had worn off, leaving her tired but alert. Being sober did nothing to improve the sensation through her extremities, which were still numb.

After a moment, Chance felt the material pressing against her bare back. The chill of his flesh radiated through his clothing, sending a shiver down her spine. Before she could process what was happening, he bent forward, encompassing her frame with his own. An icy breath crept across her throat as the vampire hissed against her ear.

"I could take your body here and now with all these eyes upon you, or… I can bring you home first. Choose quickly. A millennium or two has done nothing to instill me with an overabundance of patience."

"I.." her voice cracked and broke.

No other sound could be forced from Chance's lungs. All she did was vehemently shake her head again. Tears erupted from her eyes and silently leaked down her cheeks.

The vampire pulled away slightly, but not enough to free her from his clutches. He grabbed her wrist in a painfully tight, vice-like grip. Then he turned her around, compelling her to look up at him by pinching her chin and tilting her head back.

Chance closed her eyes when he brought his face forward. Her breath caught in her lungs, expecting him to press his lips to hers. He lightly dabbed the tip of his tongue against the tear that had streaked her cheek.

As he pulled away, Chance fluttered her long, dark eyelashes as she opened her eyes.

"Vanilla," he whispered.

That malevolent smile returned, causing Chance to tremble in fear.

"Feed me," he commanded her.

With a shaky hand, Chance lifted her hair from the sweat dampened skin of her neck and tilted her head to the side.

The vampire sneered, "Not from there."

He grasped her hips and easily placed her on the table. Her hands grabbed the table's edge as she watched him come to a kneel before her. The ancient vampire slipped his icy fingers between her thighs, slowly prying her legs apart. Her toes curled as she struggled to keep her knees together.

"No! Please! Take me to your home. Don't do that to me here in front of everyone," Chance begged, finally finding her voice.

The vampire smirked as he exposed her core. He licked his lips, eyeing her pussy. One of Chance's hands had moved to cover her most sensitive area to protect it from the vampire, while the other used her forearm to block her breasts from view.

As he opened his mouth, she gasped. His teeth were so long she worried they'd cut right down to her bone, but her fear was so great, she couldn't force herself to fend him off. Instead of bringing his face to her pussy, he turned his head and sank his fangs into her thigh.

As his fangs pierced into her skin, Chance drifted forward, closing her eyes tight as the entire world spun around her. She helplessly panted and bit back a moan that nearly escaped her lips. He withdrew his fangs and moved them further up her leg, penetrating her flesh once again.

He buried his fangs so deep into her, a wave of arousal broke through the spine-crushing terror.

Chance gasped, leaning forward and removed her arm from her breast to place atop his head. The soft felt of his hat was soothing against her fingertips.

Her head spun. Never in her entire time with Tyne had she wanted him to touch her in the way she desperately desired this stranger to.

Chance panted hard, finding it gradually more difficult to breathe as waves of dizziness made functioning a painful endeavor. She could hardly feel her fingers as a numbness spread across her body.

The room spun, making it a struggle for her eyes to focus on anything around her. She barely noticed the young man standing directly beside the vampire. Her brows furrowed as she blinked, taking in the attractive gentleman's features. When the boy caught her staring at him, he sneered in disgust.

08

THE MASTER

EADRICH

He slipped his fingers inside his new toy's beckoning center. The warmth that engulfed them was like the fires of humanity's hell, embracing him and welcoming him home. He desperately wanted to feel that searing heat with his entire being.

"Stop," the mortal whispered pathetically, but didn't use the hand atop his head to push him away.

He could feel her slim fingers curl around the brim of his hat, holding his face poised at its location. He dropped his hand to his side, then withdrew his fangs and progressed further up her thigh. Immediately, the girl moved to shield her femininity from him as he clearly intended to make his way there.

His cheek brushed the back of the hand that protected her

dignity, halting his advance. He could feel the penetrating heat radiated from between her dainty fingers. It caressed his face longingly. He opened his jaw wide and plunged his fangs so deep into her skin that his human teeth also bore into her flesh. The fiery feast of her life essence flooded into his mouth, quenching both his need for warmth and satiating the desperate hunger that had engraved itself into his soul.

A flavor he hadn't experienced in over a millennium drowned and embraced him. It took every ounce of self-control to break away from the delectable possession. As he withdrew, the ancient vampire wiped away a trickle of blood from the corners of his lips using his thumb and forefinger. He licked the remaining crimson from his thumb while allowing his gray eyes to observe his new toy as she wavered at the edge of the table.

"More..." Chance whimpered, drawing her bottom lip into her mouth as both her hands both grabbed the table's edge. She leaned back slightly, offering herself to him. "Please."

The girl would die if he drank too much more from her, and he planned to enjoy her thoroughly before he allowed her time to end. Yet she spread her legs wider, inviting him to devour her further. Blood seeped from one of the fang marks closest to her fiery center. He watched as the crimson trail taunted him in its delectable dance toward the ground. It dripped to the floor, mesmerizing him in a way that nothing else ever could.

He reached up and removed his hat, tossing it to the table next to the girl. His dark silver hair glittered in the incandescent lights that shimmered through the cracks of the stage curtain.

"I can't..." the girl whimpered, her entire body clearly trembling from the strain of withdrawal. "Please, more..."

So, he took her invitation. The vampire gladly returned his lips to her thigh, licking the remaining wound to encourage it to heal. As his tongue caressed her flesh, his victim moaned and rolled her hips. Her small hand moved to press against the top of his head. Those delicate fingers twined with his hair as she attempted to pull his face against her succulent entrance.

He withdrew his fangs to stare up at his new toy.

"Please. Feed on me," the delectable human whimpered hoarsely as she moved her gaze to meet the vampire's.

She rolled her hips toward him again, as if begging for him to enjoy her in more intimate ways than a simple meal. He sank his fangs into the girl's thigh again, feeling her body react as her hips pushed forward and a delirious sounding moan rushed out. The venom would not only extend her high, but it would give the toy a much-needed surge of energy to keep up with his stamina.

He retracted his fangs as he grew bored of feeding from a willing victim. He licked the wounds closed before standing. His dead eyes examined the small creature as she writhed helplessly on the table.

"Cadmael," he looked over his shoulder, "make a phone call."

Then his eyes settled upon the delicious girl. "Tell me what you want?"

Tears streamed steadily down Chance's cheeks as she floated in and out of a sense of alertness. The vampire's arms wrapped around her to keep her from collapsing backward. Against the bare flesh of her back and through the thick material of his shirt, Chance could feel a chill radiating from him.

"I want…" she mumbled, panting lightly as her head fell forward so her forehead rested against his lapel.

"Tell me," he purred with a smile.

Before she could respond, he turned his hips to press his rock-hard cock against her leg. The girl moaned loudly, lifting her head from his shoulder. As she stared at the vampire, she didn't seem to notice his companion holding a phone up, the black screen facing the master, while he plugged a headphone into the vampire's ear.

09

TORMENT BEGINS

CHANCE

"I want you inside me," Chance cried out in a desperate plea for some relief. "Please, I'll do anything."

The words rushed out before she could stop herself. She had never been this aroused in her entire life. The young woman truly thought that she might die of heart failure if she didn't get some respite soon.

Smirking, the vampire unzipped his pants and jostled himself about to free his throbbing cock. It lightly tapped against her clit as he readjusted his stance so his forearm could keep her leg up from behind her calf. His other arm remained wrapped across her back, holding her body in an upright position.

Chance gasped and moaned into his chest as she wiggled her hips, trying to force him to penetrate her. She was no longer focused on protecting her dignity that was long gone. When Tyne would bite her, there was always arousal and a burst of passion, but it was nothing compared to the potency of this creature's fangs.

"PLEASE!" she yelled up at him, tilting her head back to glare at the beast who was torturing her with sexual denial.

The horrible monster wasn't even looking at her. He was smirking at his sour friend with the phone. The men were making eye contact, as though having a silent conversation.

Suddenly, and without warning, the vampire rammed his entire length deep into Chance.

She screamed as an aching wave of spiraling pain and bliss slammed through her body. Her hands left the table to wrap around the vampire's neck, pressing her breasts against the material of his suit.

The vampire instantly became vastly more aggressive in his maneuvers. His grip on Chance tightened as he lifted her from the table, plunging himself as far into her core as his size would permit. He easily bounced her up and down, rocketing his cock into her depths as she helplessly screamed, clutching at him so firmly that her nails gouged the skin on the back of his neck.

"Hello? Chance?! Is that you? Are you okay?" a tinny voice echoed from the phone.

The jarring motions had unplugged the headphone from its port, allowing everyone in the room to hear the person on the other end of the phone call. As the familiar tone spurred her back to reality, a panic built up in her chest as her heart broke.

"Chance?" She could hear Tyne yelling for her, as he recognized her gasps and screams.

She couldn't even process that he was calling out to her as she finally started to lose consciousness. The only thing keeping her awake was the rage of the vampire's cock pounding deep inside. It was as if he was forcing it in so hard that she'd shriek in pain for the audience on the phone.

"Chance! Answer me! NOW!"

"Tyne..." she whimpered, but the vampire interrupted her.

"I own her now, Tyne." The vampire said as he pushed himself deep inside the girl, forcing another gasping moan out of her.

"Eadrich? I'll fucking kill you! I own her, you piece of-."

Click. The vampire's sidekick hung up the phone. He placed it into the breast pocket of his black pinstripe dress suit.

"I didn't tell you to do that," Eadrich murmured, sounding disappointed as his hips slowed their movements.

"My apologies master, I simply wished to protect you from his crass language."

The vampire stepped forward, setting the girl down on the table, without allowing himself to slip from within her. His hips continued to thrust into Chance as she allowed herself to lie down. She couldn't hold herself up without his assistance. Every part of her was so exhausted, it was surprising her that she remained conscious. Chance couldn't help the moans that erupted from the back of her throat as she streamed in and out of wakefulness.

The high she'd experienced had gradually lessened. She opened her eyes to see the two men kissing while the vampire pounded himself deep into her. Chance gasped, as she became slicker with arousal. She'd never seen two men kissing aside from tv. It was so much hotter in person! Her mouth hung open, and she felt her insides clutch the bloodsucker's cock.

When the vampire glanced down at her from the corner of his eye, clearly noticing the change. She felt her cheeks heat, but she couldn't force herself to look away. He pushed his tongue out and the younger man engulfed it with his mouth, slurping hard. No fangs. The young man who came with the vampire had no fangs.

She didn't belong here. This wasn't supposed to be happening to her! Tears rolled from the corners of her eyes as she struggled to find the strength to wiggle against his grip.

The harder she persisted, the more his massive cock ripped at her insides.

She whimpered, "It hurts."

The vampire broke off the kiss and loomed over her for a moment as his gaze scanned her features. She pushed her hands out against his chest with all her strength, but he was an immovable object…aside from his hips, which continued to pound into her.

"Stop," she hissed through grit teeth, feeling a pain build up inside her stomach.

He smiled.

The vampire bared his fangs at Chance, making her quiver with fear and regret. His deadened gray eyes seemed to examine her closely, staring at every curve in her flesh. She shifted her hands to cover her breasts, but he grabbed both her wrists. Placing them in one of his hands, he raised them and pinned them to the table above her head. He brought his face forward to her breast, just above her soft nipple. As the vampire drew his head downward with his lips drawn back, exposing his fangs, Chance panicked. She miraculously wiggled an arm free and swung her hand out, slapping the creature across the face.

Within an instant, the snarling vampire had both of her arms pinned to the table above her head again. The sound he made was so guttural that it sent chills across her body. Goosebumps rose across her skin as her nipples instantly became hard. Every muscle tightened and strained as she panicked. Even her insides tensed painfully around his cock.

"Is that what you like? You animalistic, little beasty," he growled… "But now is not the time to please you. You need to be punished."

"No. no… please. I'm sorry…" Chance whimpered, instantly regretting the fact that she had been defending herself. "Please, I'll do anything. Please…"

Fear was an excellent motivator for increasing energy. She was no longer on the verge of passing out, but wished she had. As she begged the vampire, she closed her eyes while shaking her head rapidly. She couldn't help the loud gasping sound that she emitted with every terrified breath.

"Open your eyes."

Chance let out a wail as she opened her eyes. She was sure the monster was going to kill her. She continued to mouth her pleas, but no sound escaped her.

"As your punishment, I will hurt you," he murmured, and she froze.

The monster chuckled softly, seeming to bask in her outright terror. Chance even stopped breathing as she stared at him with wide eyes. Her face quickly became red, as if she intended to lose consciousness from lack of airflow. Those beautiful multicolored eyes were full of emotional turmoil and were so easy to read. The more terrified she became, the tighter she squeezed his pulsating weapon, which he still hadn't withdrawn.

Eadrich continued taunting her after taking a moment to stare at her terrified face. "But only a little this time."

Tears welled in Chance's eyes as Eadrich raised a single finger. That finger elongated and hardened into a clawed weapon. Her face went from terrified to horrified. Yes, there's a difference. Any and all color vanished from her face. She was so scared, she couldn't even tremble.

"No. No, please." She begged as she felt the vampire's cock swell inside her while she clenched around him in terror.

He pressed his claw against the flesh just beneath her collarbone. Chance barely felt the skin tear.

The very point was so razor sharp that after being cut, it took time to realize what had happened because her body hadn't processed the pain. He seemed to take his time to ensure maximum sensation.

Suddenly, Chance pulled against the hand restraining her arms. He kept the finger poised, though her struggling made it slice her flesh in a jagged pattern instead of one smooth line. The more she struggled, the more his claw destroyed her.

"It stings!" she whimpered. "It burns!"

The wound felt very much the same as when she cut her leg shaving. First, there was no pain, but when air or water touched the wound, it seared. His lips pulled tight over a cruel smile as he slowly dragged that finger downward. He sliced over the sensitive skin of her nipple, watching as it took a moment for her flesh to realize it had been cut, before crimson spilled forth from the wound.

"It hurts! It hurts! Let me go!" Chance cried out, struggling hard against him, tears streaming from her eyes.

"Do you want the pain to stop?" He whispered in her ear. "I can be a merciful master…"

She quivered as he brought his face down toward her chest. His cold tongue licked her collarbone and dragged half down the cut. As he pulled away, she felt the skin weave itself together, easing a small amount of her suffering.

"I could heal the rest of it, but you wanted me to stop enjoying you…" He told her, his voice mocking sincerity.

"Please! Do it! It hurts! Please!"

10

Timing Is Everything

Eadrich

Eadrich sighed, feeling slightly annoyed with how slowly she learned. Apparently, the girl wasn't as intelligent as advertised. He lifted his hand from the table, but before he could do anything, the human started screaming.

"Please! NO MORE!!! I'M SORRY!" she broke into open-mouthed sobs with more incomprehensible babble.

He snapped his fingers.

The man standing next to him, who'd been quietly observing the situation without the slightest reaction, finally spoke. "Repeat after me. *Master, please enjoy me.*"

"Master! Please enjoy me. Please!" the girl desperately cried out, hoping to make the pain stop.

Her invitation was more than enough to satisfy him. He opened his jaw wide and pulled her nipple into his mouth, feeling it stiffen against his icy tongue. His fangs slashed at the skin, but received no visceral reaction from the human. Eadrich withdrew his fangs and plunged them into her breast again. This time, his tongue swirled around her nipple, enjoying every slight bump and ripple on the hardened pink flesh.

As his fangs delved deep into her skin, Chance moaned quietly, closing her eyes. Eadrich retracted his fangs and rammed them in anew, encouraging more venom to enter her body. He did nothing to move his hips, waiting for his bites to take effect. The desperate woman lifted her legs from where they hung and wrapped them around his waist, attempting to pull him further into her as she ground herself hard into his middle.

Instead of allowing Eadrich to resume his assault on her body, his companion interrupted him, "It's time, Master. Would you like me to bring the car around?"

Eadrich pulled his face from the girl's flesh to click his tongue and glared at Cadmael, "Malix Peek, you have terrible timing." He sighed and added, "Go ahead."

Cadmael's mouth tightened into an irritated knot, but the display of emotion was a minor flicker before it vanished once more. He said nothing, simply yanked a large purple dog collar from his pocket and placed it on the table before walking swiftly away.

A soft sound emitted from the back of Eadrich's throat as he chuckled. He gave the girl a few more deep pumps, knowing Cadmael would wait as long as Eadrich told him to. Finally, he let himself explode deep inside the woman, filling her with his toxic seed.

CHANCE

Chance gasped, screamed, and covered her mouth with

both hands as she tried to process what had just happened.

'Did he? Did he just cum?'

She felt like someone rammed a slushy up inside her, filling her to the brim. As he wrapped his hand around the back of her neck to sit her up, the icy liquid gushed, leaking off the side of the table. He then pulled her onto her feet, and it began dribbling down the inside of her thighs.

EADRICH

Without giving her an option, Eadrich picked the collar up from the table and smirked as he tapped one of the little electrical nubs on the inside of the collar. He slipped the leash handle around his wrist. He ignored her as she flinched away from him while he reached around her neck to attach the collar to her.

"Why-AH!" She started to say and screamed as the collar shocked her throat, then the silly human screamed again from the pain, causing her to scream a third time before practically ramming her own fist into her mouth to halt any further noises that she could make.

Tears streamed down her cheeks as she sat on the dirty carpeted floor, glaring up at him. Eadrich snorted, having enjoyed that far more than he should have.

"You can thank Cadmael for that. Apparently, he thinks you're too noisy." He smirked down at the girl. "Come now, little toy."

Chance didn't move toward him, her hands reaching toward the collar. Eadrich couldn't help the glee he felt as he gave the leash a light tug and the mechanism in the collar shocked the girl.

She screamed from the zap, only to have it shock her one more time. Chance sat on the floor, silently weeping as she trembled from fear and exhaustion. The electrocution was definitely enough to wake the girl right up.

Eadrich's head whipped around as Cadmael entered the

building from a side door.

"Master?"

"Yes?"

"He entered the front door."

"I see. Bring her." Eadrich dropped the leash and turned, marching toward the side door that the younger man had come in through.

11

LOYAL SERVANT, THE PET

CADMAEL

Cadmael's bright blue eyes observed the display before him. He licked his lips as he watched his master's cum trickle from the woman's hole, then down her ass, forming a puddle beneath her. She looked exhausted, high as a kite, and in pain, but her night was far from over if his master had his way.

Kneeling beside the weeping girl, Cadmael examined her damages, making a mental note on the medical care he would have to provide later. He slipped one arm across her back and another behind her knees. Her bare skin was so cold, he could feel the chill through the material of his suit. He groaned as he lifted his master's new toy. There wasn't much time, so he hurried out the door, following in his master's wake.

The dim emergency light of the building was barely

enough to chase away the evening's shadow. He blinked, trying to accustom his eyes to the dark as he trekked closer to the black car he had parked a mere ten paces from the door. Eadrich had left the door open, so Cadmael shoved the girl into the back seat of the car and closed the door behind her.

Cadmael swiftly marched around the vehicle, his blue eyes scanning his surroundings for danger. He adjusted his tie as he continued to make his way around the back end of the car. He reached into his pocket and withdrew the keys, then proceeded to open the driver's door before slipping into his seat.

He pushed down on the clutch, starting the vehicle with that ever-familiar roar of the engine as it came to life. Glancing in the rearview mirror, unable to fend off his curiosity, he spotted the new toy, Chance, glaring at the vampire in the seat next to her.

"Do you want to see Tyne again?" Eadrich asked, directing his question towards Chance, as Cadmael put the car into first gear. Eadrich then added in a more commanding tone, "Take your time driving, Cadmael."

Cadmael adjusted the rearview mirror so he could not only spy on the pair, but watch out the back window as well. Tears were welling in the girl's eyes again as she nodded. All her crying was getting on his nerves. He raised his foot from the clutch and tapped the gas, encouraging the car into a slow roll forward.

Chance nodded her head emphatically, her eyebrows drawn down in confusion. Her fingers lightly touched at the collar, as if reminding herself that if she spoke, she'd suffer.

Cadmael couldn't help the smirk that tugged at the corners of his lips when the girl silently responded. He hated the emotions he developed every time his beloved master got a new toy. A tiny part of him felt like someday soon one of them might replace him. His jaw tightened as he heard his master's reply to the girl.

"Encourage me to fuck you…" then Eadrich continued when he noticed the girl hesitating, "Quick, or your opportunity will expire."

Chance leaned forward and fumbled with his zipper. Her hands were trembling so hard that she could barely manipulate the material covering his cock. Instead, she simply rubbed over his clothing at the bulge. Cadmael licked his lips as he watched his master's shaft triple in length as it expanded. She kept mouthing the word 'please'. If she spoke, she'd suffer for it.

"Fine," Eadrich growled, giving an exasperated sigh as though he felt fucking her was only for her sake. "Close your eyes."

Eadrich devilishly smirked as he adjusted their positions. He placed an icy hand over her eyes as he maneuvered them, so Chance's naked body pressed against the backrest of the seat. He slipped in behind her, while using his free hand to guide his cock into the woman's hole. As he entered, Chance gasped.

"Are you ready to see your beloved?"

As his master spoke, Cadmael clicked a button on the door and all four windows in the car rolled down. The wind exploded into the vehicle, sending Cadmael's curly hair bouncing around on his head. He took a slow deep breath, but could only smell the stink of the city as it filled his perfectly maintained car. One other thing of importance floated in upon the breeze. A man's voice screaming a single name.

"Chance!"

Glancing in his rearview, he could see a tall dirty blond vampire with muscles for days chasing after the vehicle. The man's long hair fluttered in the wind as he picked up speed, attempting to catch up to the car. Cadmael pressed on the gas and sent the gear into third without even touching the clutch.

12

Wishes Are For Fools

Chance

Chance's fingers clawed at the vampire's hand, desperate to see the man attached to that ever-familiar voice. Her own nails gouged at her forehead as she flailed to free herself. It took everything for her to remember NOT to scream in frustration.

Eadrich removed his hand from her eyes and wrapped his fingers around her throat, keeping her pinned beneath him. His other hand slipped to her front and cupped her vagina, applying pressure to the area.

As soon as the vampire uncovered her eyes, Chance struggled to get her vision under control. Then... she saw him. Her hair flailed in the breeze, fluttering across her vision, but she could see him! Tyne was behind the car, chasing them as the driver moved the vehicle just fast enough that the vampire couldn't quite catch up. She raised both her hands and slammed them into the back window.

"TYNE!" Chance yelled for him, but broke off in a scream as the collar zapped her in return for her stupidity.

The way her core tightened as the collar shocked her made her body clench around the vampire's rock-hard cock, pushing deep inside her. He groaned and moaned into her shoulder as they observed Tyne chase after the car, gaining on it, only to have the vehicle's speed increase, but not enough to discourage Tyne from continuing to try. Cadmael seemed to enjoy taunting the running vampire.

Eadrich licked along Chance's shoulder as he moved his hips faster, thrusting into her. She didn't let that stop her from banging on the window. Every time her fists struck, it sent shooting pains up her wrists.

"I want you to cum while he helplessly watches…" Eadrich murmured softly before sliding a hand around to her front and claiming her clit with icy fingers.

Chance gasped loudly… too loud. The collar shocked her, and as she screeched, the electricity increased, making her scream again until no exygen remained in her lungs. Her mouth hung wide in a silent shriek with all the air dispelled from her body. She struggled to force a breath in as she gagged, fighting not to cough.

Tyne had finally stopped yelling as though he was conserving his strength to continue running. From the flush in Chance's cheek, she looked not only exhausted, but on the verge of an orgasm.

"Eadrich!" Tyne screamed as he slowed his pace, unable to keep up.

She shook her head, becoming uncertain about exactly *who* he was chasing after.

As the icy fingers worked her most vulnerable area, Chance gasped for air. She wiggled beneath the vampire as her core tightened around his rock-hard cock, which hadn't hampered its aggressive assault. As he massaged, she became gradually more sensitive, jerking her hips away from his icy fingers to stall the rising orgasm.

Suddenly, Chance halted all struggles, as her body grew tense. She stopped breathing and tilted her head back. It started in a slow trickle, but when he increased the speed of his cock ramming into her and slowed the fingers that toyed with her clit, she let out a desperate moan.

"Plea-uughh." She tried to beg, but halted with another zap that made her hips jerk forward.

"Say 'master'…" He encouraged, slowing his fingers, and pressed hard against the clit, barely moving them against the pulsating nub.

"Ma—ah… Master-aaagghhh…" She wept silently from the pain that seared at her throat.

"Good girl…" He whispered and sank his fangs into her shoulder, allowing his venom to intensify her every sensation, as his fingers strummed her clit with the speed of an ungodly reckoning.

As the vampire fucked her wildly, Chance couldn't help her body's betrayal. A sweeping orgasm spread across every part of her, as her limbs trembled through a tingling numbness that caressed her entire body. Everything tingled.

"Whoa," she whispered before she could stop herself.

It took a moment, during the waves of pleasure, to realize she hadn't been zapped. For a split second, Chance thought the batteries may have died and allowed herself to gasp a little too loud as liquid trickled down the inside of her thigh. The regret was instant. She screamed again, and the collar shocked her harder. The shock caused her cum to rush forth in a gush of overwhelming pressure.

Eadrich growled softly into the girl's flesh as he withdrew his fangs and sank them in once more. With a scream, she clenched around his cock, making it nearly painfully tight. As she came over that orgasmic edge, he erupted deep inside her.

Sighing, Eadrich released his grip on the girl, leaving her where she was as she continued banging on the rear window while he turned around and slipped his cock back into his pants.

"Say goodbye," Eadrich chortled, which Cadmael took it as a hint and pressed down on the gas, slamming the car into fourth and speeding away while rolling up the windows.

The scream that left Chance felt like it was being torn from her soul.

She could feel the monster watching her from the corner of his eye as she wept, staring hopelessly through the rear window. Her trembling hands still pressed hard against the glass. Eventually, the city seemed to slip away. She whipped around, grabbed at the door handle, and struggled to find a lock button. Chance felt rage bubble up inside her and punched the window with every bit of might that she could.

"Ow! Ugh." She yelped in pain, then groaned as an electric shock pulsated through the prongs on the collar.

Chance settled in her seat, shooting a dark glare at the monster that had violated her several times within hours of their meeting. Her jaw quivered as she sneered at him. Her arms automatically moved to cover herself while she watched those cold gray eyes trail up her tanned body. She could feel his cold semen, warmed by her body, continue to leak out of her, streaking the seat.

Slowly, she shook her head. Chance's multi-colored eyes glanced out the window, trying to memorize the streets and turns the driver took. The car flew over a speed bump, jarring everyone inside.

"Malix Peek!" the vampire snapped in irritation.

"My apologies, Master."

Chance quickly returned her focus to her surroundings, intent on formulating a plan of action. When she made her escape, she'd have to remember how to get back to the city. The further they drove, the more scared she got. As the city turned into a commercial area full of factories and warehouses, she had a gut-wrenching feeling that they weren't going to stop driving any time soon. Her eyelids were getting heavy and wave after wave of exhaustion tried to pull her into the depths of darkness. Chance wrapped her arms around herself tighter and pulled her knees up to her chest as goosebumps rose on her flesh from the chill of the car's air-conditioning being turned up so high. She blinked and realized that they had left the city behind. When? When did that happen? She had simply blinked her eyes and was suddenly staring out at the fucking farmland!

Why were they going so far away? Why had he come to that auction? How did Tyne know Eadrich? That was what Tyne called him. What a stupid name. It wasn't British like Tyne's name. She looked at the vampire from the corner of her eye, squinting in her attempt at not making her assessment obvious.

He was far more handsome than she had previously thought, with high cheekbones, a pointed nose and arching eyebrows. His skin appeared faded and ashen, though it may have had a dark tan when he was alive. His dark lips made her think of a drowning victim because they were nearly blue. The vampire was tall and slim. He stared out the front window with mild disinterest in his dead gray eyes. They looked like they could have been dark brown at one point, but decay had set in, dimming the colors.

Chance sniffed lightly, drawing his attention. Those blue lips of his curled into a malevolent smirk, making his fangs shimmer in the dark. With a faint squeak, she pivoted her face toward the window in hopes he'd leave her alone. She sniffled again, mostly out of habit.

Eventually, fields transformed into forest, then field, and then forest again. Over time, the lull of silence and the purring motor made the exhausted girl lose consciousness.

Chance woke up to the sensation of the vehicle turning around. The ding of the four ways clicking sounded extra loud as the car slowly backtracked. Chance hadn't realized she had slumped down in her seat. She sat up straight, snatching her seat belt and buckling it.

After a few moments of driving in what was clearly the wrong direction, the master muttered, "What is wrong, Cadmael?"

"I-I hit a little birdy…" Cadmael's tone was dripping with

concern.

"It's probably dead. Just go home and forget about it, like any normal person would."

"Yes, Master" his tone of voice was matter of fact, and he shut off the four-way blinkers, signaled and made a U-turn without another word.

Chance stared at the driver's reflection in the rearview mirror… She could see the worried set to his eyebrows as he cruised away from the scene of his crime. *What was his name again? Malix Peek?* If he really was as sweet as he appeared, she may be able to use that to her advantage.

Shortly after that, Chance lost her fight to stay awake and keep watch on her surroundings.

13

A New Home

Chance

Chance woke to find herself in a large, pale blue bedroom. There was no way to tell how long she'd been asleep, or what time of day it was because of the light canceling curtains that hung in the window. The room was brightly lit from a single sconce on the wall by the door. Someone had lavishly decorated the room with suspending drapes on the walls, a canopy bed, a fake fireplace, and two more candle-shaped lights mounted to the wall on both sides of the bed. A rather large antique armchair sat in the corner of the room as well.

Chance blinked several times, trying to process the world around her. She was far drowsier than she should be for the amount of sleep she'd gotten. That was, until something wet and warm seemed to glide up the inside of her leg, from her foot to her knee.

The girl gasped, trying to yank her leg away from the physical intrusion. Nothing moved. Chance lifted her head. There sat the driver from the car, holding a moistened, soapy sponge in his hand. Her legs and arms were spread to the four corners, bound with leather bands and cords, strapping her to the bedposts. She lay there, helpless, looking like a damned starfish with a strange man washing her naked body. There was a needle stuck in her left forearm, taped in place. The cord led up to a nearly empty bag of blood that was hanging on the wall from the mounted light. They were giving her a transfusion. She couldn't help worrying about the possibility of contamination. If he didn't drink her to death, she was going to die of any number of things from that blood.

Silently, Chance cried while the sponge slid back down her leg, leaving a bubbly trail in its wake. The vampire's underling leaned off the edge of the bed and she could hear the rattle of a bucket as he squeezed out the water and allowed it to refill the sponge several times. Then he held it up, giving one last squeeze, watching the soap bubble between his fingers and dribble down his forearm.

The vampire's servant inched further up the bed and twisted so he could reach between her thighs. He scrubbed up and down her thigh at each angle before rinsing the cloth again.

Chance wanted to recoil at his touch. She longed to scream, yell and try to attack him, but none of it would do her any good. Instead, she had to learn as much about him as she could. If she could win his trust, then maybe she'd have an ally.

He seemed almost shy in his mannerisms. It made her wonder if someone had abducted the servant as well. If that was some common ground between them, then maybe he'd want to help her escape. He brought the sponge to her middle. She gasped, turning her face away and closing her eyes. Chance tried to pull her knees together, but the restraints didn't give her that much freedom. He was thorough in his cleaning and definitely not as shy as he appeared.

Chance's toes curled. She couldn't believe that simply having this stranger wash her was turning her on. There was certainly something wrong with her now. Maybe, if she pretended to want him… he'd be easier to manipulate. It wasn't that too far of a leap for her to fake to be aroused. The slow rhythmic circles and smoothness of the soap combined with the perfect amount of pressure made her insides tighten. Her breaths came in sharp inhales as she pushed herself toward his sponge. Just as she was about to climax, he stopped.

"Wait," she whispered and immediately realized that she wasn't shocked by making noise.

No, he hadn't removed the collar. It was still on her with the prongs gouging into the skin at her throat. She realized she had told him to wait with no repercussions. The man sat there with the sponge held in the air, soapy water dripping onto her abdomen and also rolling down his muscular forearm as he waited for her to continue speaking.

"Sorry," Chance whispered, feeling a fire rise in her cheeks.

The man rolled his eyes and turned away, beginning the routine of thoroughly rinsing out the cloth.

"Malix?" she murmured and instantly regretted it.

The sponge dropped into the bucket, and the man whipped around to face her with a snarling growl.

"I'm sorry!" She cried out too loud and immediately suffered for it.

The shock sent a ripple of chills across her body, causing goosebumps to rise on her damp skin while her nipples hardened and became sensitive. Chance squeezed her eyes closed tightly and turned her face away as tears leaked from the corners of them. She shook so hard she was sure the bed rattled faintly beneath her.

"My name is Cadmael…" the man murmured after taking a deep breath to calm himself. "Malix Peek… is…"

He sneered slightly. After his reaction to the name, Chance suspected that the word was an insult that the boy's master used when he became displeased with Cadmael.

"I'm sorry…" she attempted to smooth things over. "I just thought it was a really pretty name."

Cadmael's eyebrows furrowed as he peered at her in a way that screamed. She was full of shit, and he knew it.

Trying to rectify the situation, Chance added, "Cadmael is a nice name, too."

He chuckled softly and shook his head, causing his ringlets to bounce playfully. Observing him now, staring down at her with that playful twinkle in his startling blue eyes, she could see that the man was truly exceptionally beautiful. His roots were brown, though he had previously bleached his hair and dyed the tips blue, and currently they appeared to have mostly washed out. He seemed to be somewhere in his early twenties, but his eyes held a sense of maturity to them that most young adults didn't have. Or maybe that was just the trauma of his life shining through.

After staring at each other for a short while, the boy let out a soft sigh before seating himself on the edge of the bed. He leaned forward and lifted the sponge from the bucket again. Cadmael squeezed out the soapy water and turned to face the girl. He started with her hand, then worked his way up her arm.

She whispered from beneath him, "Cadmael?"

He made an irritated noise in the back of his throat.

"Am I going to die?"

"Probably."

That one word was like freezing water being poured over her entire being. Her whole body went limp as she gazed straight ahead, seeing nothing at all. The numbness she felt across her extremities was no sensation like the high she'd been experiencing from the drugs they gave her or the venom of vampire fangs. This was stone cold terror.

Chance lay there, staring at the ceiling, feeling like nothing she had ever done in her brief life had actually mattered. The boy washing her body didn't matter, the vampires, her studies. Nothing in life mattered… nothing mattered, because she was going to die soon.

14

The New Toy

Cadmael

The change in her demeanor caused Cadmael to pause. Maybe he shouldn't have spoken at all to the girl. His newfound discomfort was why he chose the shock collar for his master's toys. If they couldn't talk, then it wouldn't hurt him so much when they died. He would be the one cleaning up the mess left behind from their brief presence.

The girl's loss of energy irked Cadmael more than it should have, considering she was just a toy. He grit his teeth as he turned his back on her and plunged the sponge into the warm water. Should he say something to soothe her? Could he repair the damage he'd done? No, there was nothing he could utter that would make her situation any easier for her. She probably had been better off not knowing her end was coming. Some lasted days, others potentially survived for weeks.

Once he finished rinsing the sponge, he shifted his position to kneel on the bed, placing a hand on the opposite side of her for stability so he could reach her other arm.

The girl flinched and whimpered quietly as he hovered over her, balancing. The sponge was wet and soapy. It left a filmy feeling on her hand after he scrubbed it. Cadmael washed down her arm, from her fingertips to her shoulder, paying extra attention to her underarms. Chance squirmed slightly when he touched her here, being as she was extremely ticklish.

Cadmael paused, raising an eyebrow at the girl, before realizing that he was practically face-to-face with her. Clearing his throat, he quickly pulled away and returned to the edge of the bed to rinse the cloth out again.

"Did he buy you, too?" Chance asked in a shaky voice.

"Yes," Cadmael responded, feeling that he owed her that much after bluntly telling her she was going to die.

"Does he hurt you?"

He paused, staring at the sponge as it dribbled water into the bucket. He tried to swallow, but there was nothing to swallow. His mouth had gone dry. Cadmael glanced toward the door automatically as a precaution.

"Sometimes… When I deserve it."

"Is that why you listen to him?"

Cadmael squeezed the sponge out and turned to face the girl once more. He shifted to his knees and used his free hand to adjust his tie before leaning over Chance once more. He swallowed as a nervous reflex before drawing his bottom lip into his mouth. Carefully, he used the back of his hand to brush aside some stray strands of hair from his brow. Water dribbled from the sponge down his wrist, dripping onto the pillow beside Chance's ear. Cadmael pressed the sponge gently to her forehead and dragged across her skin.

"My master loves me," he whispered under his breath as he tenderly washed her face. "He purchased me when I was very young and has always taken excellent care of me."

Chance's eyes widened in horror. She opened her mouth to speak, but could only gasp quietly as tears filled the corners of her eyes. She closed her mouth, struggling to stop her bottom lip from quivering as she stared at Cadmael. From her perspective, this gentle boy who took care of that loathsome creature got beat if he erred at all, but she was a stupid toy who didn't understand the complexities of his relationship with his master.

When Cadmael realized the girl was actually crying, he froze. The sponge fell from his hand, sliding off her cheek and landing on the pillow.

"What's wrong with you?" he growled in her face, feeling extremely uncomfortable by her reaction.

"I'm sorry," Chance whispered, shaking her head. "You must have been very young."

Cadmael grunted as he snatched up the sponge and swiveled away from the girl. He rammed it into the bucket with more force than necessary. This conversation was making him very self-conscious.

"If I'm a good girl… like you… like you are a good boy…do you think he will let me live too?" Chance questioned.

That was the moment Cadmael remembered toys would say anything to ensure their own survival. She didn't care about him. The selfish human was crying for herself.

"I am a pet. You are a toy." He clarified in a matter-of-fact tone, making sure she understood that there was definitely a distinction between the two.

He turned with the freshly rinsed cloth and scrubbed down her torso with more vigor than before. No matter where he cleaned, navel, clavicle or nipple, there was no difference in his motions. He kept his movements swift intending to end his time alone with the annoying girl who asked far too many questions.

"But, if I become a pet, too," she said, wincing as he washed across her hardened, sensitive nipple. "Then you won't be so lonely anymore."

It was a shot in the dark, but she was going to try whatever she could to gain any leeway with him. There was no way this sweet boy didn't feel isolated with a vampire lurking in the shadows all the time. How dare she assume he wasn't happy? That his mission in life wasn't to see to his Master's every whim! His reaction certainly wouldn't be whatever she had hoped it would be.

Cadmael pulled away, glaring down at the stupid girl. His face became red and blotchy as his eyes threatened to water. His hands trembled with untamed rage.

"You- don't- know- a-damn- thing!" the boy hissed at the girl as a deep, thunderous growl built in his chest.

A throat cleared nearby, and all eyes flashed to the door. There stood Eadrich, wearing a black and red silk dressing gown that draped lavishly off his body. He was far more muscular than his suit initially illustrated. His hair was dark silver, and his eyes looked gray and dim, though it seemed to glitter in this light. Undressed as he was, his many tattoos showed, contrasting with the ashen gray color of his flesh.

It was possible that vampires aged in their own peculiar way when they reached a certain point in their afterlife.

The devious vampire leaned on the doorframe, resting a hand on his hip as he observed the pair in the room.

"I'm not interrupting, am I?"

"Yes," Chance hissed in a whisper at the same time as Cadmael said, "Of course not, Master."

Cadmael's blue eyes flashed in irritation at the girl. His hand actually trembled as he stood and whipped around to snarl at the annoying little toy. His hands clenched, causing water to dribble out from the sponge as he squeezed it.

"Don't speak to my Master like that. You don't know anything ab--" A banging reverberated through the house, echoing down halls. "You awful-." He started again, but halted as the doorbell rang, interrupting him again.

"Malix Peek," the vampire snarled in irritation.

Cadmael's head turned to stare at his master, his mouth snapping shut so hard that his teeth clicked.

"Yes, Master," the younger man murmured and spun on his heels.

He marched toward the door, but as he drew closer to his master, his gaze dropped to the floor. He looked like a dog that was kicked around as he tried to slink past Eadrich unscathed. The doorbell rang, and Cadmael flinched before bolting out the doorway past his master.

15

MASTER OF THE MANOR

EADRICH

As soon as Cadmael walked out the door, slipping past him, Eadrich smirked at his new little toy, helpless on the bed. She was so adorable with those big almond-shaped eyes surrounded by long, dark eyelashes. One eye was such a dark brown that it was nearly black and the other a glittering sea green with a ring of blue around the outer edge. With every sharp inhale, her chest rose and fell hard. On either side of the collar, he could see her blood rushing through the vein. Cadmael hadn't found the time to brush her hair, leaving it a knotted mess on the pillow beneath her head.

The only reason he could spot each tiny detail was because he had the gift of vampire sight. The easiest way to describe it was like something akin to a camera lens, where he could zoom in and out, refocusing to remove blur and perceive the most minuscule details.

"We are going to have a guest in a moment. Please ensure to be on your best behavior…Or I will have to punish you."

Her brows drew down, and she twitched her leg as if testing her restraints. He was going to kill Chance no matter what she did. Her jaw clenched as he stepped to the side, leaning on the wall beside the door. He just wanted to watch her as the blood slowly dripped into her vein from the bag suspended over the bed.

CHANCE

WHAT THE HELL WAS HE WAITING FOR?!

Chance couldn't help the sneer that tugged at her lip as she glared at the handsome beast leaning against the wall beside the door. Her hands balled into fists as she tried to pull against her restraints.

"Why?" Chance whispered. "Why are you doing this to me?"

Eadrich slipped a hand into the pocket and cocked his head to the side before responding in a purr, "Because I *can*."

There was a rustling sound in the hallway, followed by the thudding of boots as someone ran toward the room.

Tyne charged in through the doorway. He made it two steps before he processed that Chance was laying nude on the bed before him. As soon as his eyes fell upon her, the corner of his lips tugged into the slightest of smiles. The words that spilled forth from his mouth were nothing close to what she had expected.

"Where's Eadrich?"

Eadrich's ashen colored hands slid up over Tyne's shoulders and fondled his chest as the ancient vampire stepped up behind him.

Tyne closed his eyes while Eadrich's familiar touch caressed his muscular chest. One of the older vampire's hands plunged down toward Tyne's crotch, and he did nothing to stop Eadrich's advances.

"I have missed your touch," Tyne whimpered as one of those familiar icy hands slid downward.

Eadrich smiled over Tyne's shoulder at Chance, who was staring wide-eyed at the pair. Her mouth hung open in shock. He grabbed Tyne's massive cock through his fitted jeans, feeling it harden instantly.

"What are you?" Eadrich muttered to the taller man, who immediately seemed to give over control to the dominant vampire.

"Property," Tyne sighed in a shaky tone, barely audible.

His gaze dropped to the floor as if he could not bear to look at Chance tied to the bed…the woman who thought he came to rescue her.

"Whose property?" Eadrich's hand clenched around the other man's shaft, almost threateningly.

Tyne breathed out the answer in a voiceless whisper. "Yours, father. Forever."

Father??? This monster was Tyne's father?! But they looked nothing alike.

"Good boy…"

A smile tugged at Eadrich's mouth upon hearing those words in that sultry voice.

"It has been well over fifty years since you sent me away…" Tyne whimpered, glancing hopefully behind his shoulder at Eadrich.

"Who does the toy belong to?" Eadrich interrupted, not acknowledging Tyne's whining.

Tyne's dark blue eyes shifted to stare directly into Chance's. His lips parted as if he was trying to respond, but couldn't. His eyebrows drew downward in an apologetic expression as his eyes narrowed.

"Whoever…" Tyne started and had to stop to clear his throat.

Chance slowly shook her head in disbelief. How could he say that? Whoever?!

"Pardon, my son?" Eadrich licked his lips as he watched

the light of hope leave Chance's stunning eyes. "Who does the toy belong to?"

Her chin quivered as she shook her head again, silently pleading for Tyne to lay claim to her. Tears burned in her eyes as his next words struck the very core of her being.

"Whomever my father wishes."

Eadrich chuckled in the back of his throat as he applied pressure to Tyne's shoulders, encouraging him to bend over.

"You want to be fucked, don't you? Like the dirty little bastard you are."

"Yes, father." Tyne closed his eyes as the tears that filled Chance's then rolled silently down her cheeks.

"Repeat after me," Eadrich murmured as his eyes developed an umbral ring of crimson circling the gray. "Daddy, if I'm fucked right now, I'll leave you alone. So, Daddy, please make sure I'm fucked good and hard."

"Leave?" Tyne whispered, with brows drawn inward, looking disappointed.

"I thought you took my toy to welcome me home…to lure me back. Maybe you believed I'd been punished for long enough."

Eadrich snorted, but his hand didn't slow its encouraging motions over Tyne's pulsating cock.

"No, my child, I was in the market for a new toy, and when my pet recognized her as yours… I laid claim to her."

"But father-" Tyne started, but Eadrich interrupted him.

"If you don't want to be fucked, then just leave." The older vampire dropped his hand to his side and stepped away from Tyne.

"No. Father." He turned his head so he could plead with the ancient vampire, but at the monstrous expression on Eadrich's face, Tyne froze.

He must have realized there was only one way to appease Eadrich. The younger vampire swallowed his saliva before repeating word for word the mantra he had learned moments ago, "Daddy, if I'm fucked right now, I'll leave you alone. So, Daddy, please make sure I'm fucked good and hard."

Chance would have screamed if she could. *He* was supposed to be her savior and the bastard just gave her up to this monster without a second thought! Tears were in endless supply as she could do nothing but silently beg for this humiliation to end. She knew he did stuff with guys as a stripper, but did not know he would be comfortable sleeping with other men… never mind asking for it like that.

"Brace yourself," Eadrich murmured as he cocked his head to the side with a deviant smirk that made his dead eyes twinkle.

Tyne's expression changed, but he seemed almost enthusiastic in the way he leaned forward, grabbing the railing across the base of the bed. He spaced his feet apart about shoulder-width and waited for Eadrich's touch.

"Please… fuck me daddy."

"Oh, stupid child… that wasn't part of our agreement." He flicked his fingers at Cadmael as he spoke. "I said you would get fucked. Never said who by."

Chance gasped so loudly that she surprised herself. She was glad that the collar didn't process her near scream as a sound.

No one noticed as Cadmael slipped into the room while his master toyed with the other vampire. The young man had been standing in the doorway with his hands clasped in front of him when his master commanded him. His jaw clenched, but he moved forward to place himself behind Tyne.

This was an unexpected turn of events. Cadmael seemed uncertain in the way he moved. He reached around the vampire's waist and undid his pants, pulling down both Tyne's pants and boxers. Tyne's throbbing cock bounced free of the material that held it down.

TYNE

Tyne snarled loudly, glaring at his father. How could he allow himself to be tricked in such a way? He didn't struggle or refuse the situation. He knew better than to refuse any form of kindness from the ancient vampire.

Eadrich kept his word, no matter how violent he needed to be to make it happen. If Tyne refused the offer, he'd suffer for it.

Suddenly, there was a hot, moist gush as something slipped between his ass cheeks, causing Tyne to gasp loudly, though he refused to take his eyes off Eadrich.

Cadmael had to push his face hard between Tyne's cold, muscular cheeks as Tyne tensed. The young man rammed his tongue out with the force of a torpedo, burrowing it directly into his hole. A warm hand slid around his hip, aiming for his pulsating shaft.

Tyne's purring moan seemed to encourage the hungry creature to work harder at eating out his ass. The warmth of the young man's hand enveloped Tyne's icy rod, making it pulse with energy as if coming alive with desire. Every stroke sent shivers of desire across Tyne's body, causing his hands to clench hard on the iron bed frame, bending it slightly with his inhuman strength. Still, he couldn't stop staring at his father with a look of utter adulation.

"Father, please," Tyne begged and moaned again, struggling not to cum as the boy so masterfully pleasured him.

Eadrich walked toward Tyne and encircled his fingers around the tip of Tyne's cock. "Now."

With a single word from Eadrich, Tyne's dick exploded with icy cum that shot into the vampire's cool hand. Then he helplessly watched as his master made a lingering stroll toward the head of the bed.

Eadrich spoke softly to Chance. "I doubt you ever saw my little boy blow his load. He hates it, cause it's painful for us vampires to finish…He's such a big baby…" Eadrich chuckled as leaned over the girl, "I'll give you something he never gave you before… something you can remember him by. Now, open your mouth."

Chance absolutely quivered as the vampire commanded

her. She had to know what was coming. The girl visibly forced herself not to cry as she opened her mouth.

"Stick out your tongue."

Just the tip pushed out the opening as her lips seemed like they tried to close against her will.

"Farther, or I'll rip it out."

As Eadrich threatened the girl, Tyne moaned loudly from the base of the bed. He seemed to enjoy it far more than he was letting on. Eadrich would give him something to remember her by, too. The ancient vampire raised his hand up over the girl's face and squeezed his hand into a tight fist. Slush-like semen oozed from between his fingers and the base of his fist. Some trailed down his wrist while most of it dribbled into the girl's mouth, making her gag loudly. Just as she seemed about to spit it out, he covered her mouth with the slimy hand, ensuring she had no choice but to hold it there or swallow. Watching his juices fill her mouth and spill out nearly sent Tyne over that edge once again. He hadn't been this aroused since the last time he'd been in his father's clutches.

Eadrich kept his hand over the girl's mouth as she choked and gagged, while struggling not to swallow Tyne's load. He leaned forward more, bringing his face to her breast, and pulled her nipple into his mouth. His fangs sank deep into the supple flesh as his tongue swirled around her puffy nipple. Tyne licked his lips, desperately wanting her blood to spill forth into his mouth as well.

Tyne saw the retraction in the girl's throat as she swallowed his juices. Immediately after, she began coughing against Eadrich's hand. The air came out her nose as there was nowhere else for it to exit.

"Good girl," Eadrich purred and leaned forward, pressing his kiss to her forehead, leaving a bloody imprint of his lips on her skin.

The ancient vampire stood and strolled to where Cadmael was still pleasuring Tyne, who was barely capable of staying on his feet.

"I'm going to give you something to remember her by. One last taste."

When he finally arrived in front of Tyne, he tapped Cadmael's arm to tell the boy that it was time. They all knew his intention was for Cadmael to ram himself inside Tyne while the two vampires kissed, sharing in the flavor of Chance's delicious vanilla blood. Unfortunately, as he pressed his lips against Tyne's and their tongues shared the same space between them, they realized Cadmael hadn't entered Tyne.

Eadrich broke off the kiss and both vampires glared at Cadmael as the boy's hands cupped over his own cock. The young man looked absolutely horrified.

"I'm… I'm sorry master…" he whimpered before adding in a whisper so quiet that without superhuman hearing, it was silent. "It won't work."

Tears filled the young man's eyes as he shook his head in delicious humiliation. If the boy could shrink in on himself, he absolutely would have, as his master's glare turned dangerous.

"Are you trying to make a liar out of me, Malix Peek?"

The sound that came out of the more was a strange mix of a gasp and a scream as he collapsed to his knees. "No Master! I would never!" He threw himself forward, prostrating himself, "Please forgive my weakness!"

"Punish yourself… I don't even want to touch you." Eadrich spat his words down at the trembling boy, then screamed, "GET OUT!"

Tyne couldn't help the tugging of a smile at the corners of his lips.

16

The Truth of Things

Chance

Before Chance could even flinch, the young man bolted from the room. She realized at that instant; she might be better off dead than living a life as that guy's pet, just like Cadmael.

"I guess I'll *have* to fuck you," Eadrich groaned, rolling his eyes and looking bored.

Within moments, Tyne was bent over the bottom of the bed, his blue eyes staring up at her naked form as Eadrich yanked on a fistful of his hair, forcing the younger vampire to look at the woman he gave up.

Suddenly, from the depths of the building, a scream of agony exploded, echoing through the halls. Chance gasped, becoming very concerned for the pet's welfare.

"Music to my ears," Eadrich hissed before ramming his

throbbing mass into Tyne's ass as hard as he could. Tyne groaned loudly in pain as his hands clenched harder at the metal bar.

Another scream erupted from the dungeon in the basement, and Eadrich smiled the cruelest of smiles. He gasped in pleasure as he pressed his v-line against Tyne's muscular ass cheeks, plowing himself all the way into his partner.

Tyne moaned louder than Chance had ever heard him. Her jaw quivered as the man she had been with for almost a year was being fucked right in front of her by the monster who bought her. Tears filled her eyes, but she blinked them away, glaring at him.

EADRICH

"Look at her naked pussy," Eadrich growled. "So wanting and needy… Is that what you like now? Was it a suitable replacement for *THIS*."

With that said, he went to town on the younger vampire, ramming himself without mercy into Tyne. His hands turned into claws, and he slid them down Tyne's back, watching as they shredded his skin. Blood spilled forth and splashed about the floor at their feet. Eadrich's foot slipped in the crimson liquid and both men toppled hard against the bottom half of the bed. The rail across the end of the bed rammed into Tyne's stomach.

Eadrich lost himself in the surreal passion with the smell of blood all around. He sank his fangs into Tyne's flesh and allowed himself to drink from that poisonous cup. His head spun instantly, and a burning sensation seared his throat, but it was worth it. His thundering hard-on grew to new unreached proportions as he drove it deep into the other vampire.

When they fell, Tyne's hand landed on Chance's calf. She whimpered quietly, trying to pull away.

Eadrich's fingers suddenly wrapped around Tyne's throat and reefed him back, so he stood straight and the contact between the pair would be broken.

"Do not touch what belongs to me!" Eadrich snarled, before moving out of the way and shoving the younger vampire toward the entrance.

Tyne slammed into the solid oak door, leaving a bloody imprint as the ribbons of his shredded skin was compressed between his body and the wood. The pressure reopened the deep lacerations, causing blood to trickle down the door and his backside, making a puddle at his feet. Tyne groaned in pain while glaring at his father.

The pair stared at one another for several moments. The only sound breaking the silence was Cadmael's agonized screams radiating through the building from somewhere in the depths.

"You've been fucked. Now, get out of my house."

Tyne took one last look at Chance, who shook her head, mouthing his name in a desperate final hope that he would save her. His eyes dropped to the floor briefly, as if putting off his departure.

"Father, please."

Eadrich walked over to where Chance struggled against her restraints as she helplessly watched the entire display of power. He climbed onto the bed and grinned at the human. How could he be so lucky as to have been there the one night that they had abducted the human Tyne had taken as his toy? She really was a delicious treat.

"Why?" Chance mouthed, tears rolling down her cheeks. The next bit was a barely audible whisper. "Why are you so mean?"

"I'm mean to you because you're special." The first portion of his response was tender, almost loving. The second part sent chills down her spine. "I like to watch you squirm."

Chance looked like she was going to puke. There really was no hope for her. Eadrich was planning to torment and torture her until he got bored. Then he would drink her until she stroked and died.

He undid the clasps around her ankles. He then shifted her legs so that they were bent and wedged himself between her thighs. As he rearranged her, she whimpered, likely from her muscles aching due to hours of immobility. His icy lips touched the side of her knee in a tender kiss.

Eadrich kissed further up on her thigh, sensing the girl tense with each brush of his lips, coming to his favorite place. He could feel the heat of her cunt on the side of his face as his cheek grazed those lips. Eadrich's mouth opened wide, and he sank his fangs deep into the delicate flesh of her inner thigh.

CHANCE

Chance gasped loudly as the vampire's teeth tore through her skin like razors. Within seconds, her head was spinning, and she was becoming aroused. She moaned resoundingly than she normally would have. This was the closest thing she could claim to revenge against Tyne for giving her up, for abandoning her to this fate. It wasn't that hard of an act with how the vampire bit again and again, each time making her higher than the last, while sending fresh waves of passion coursing across her body.

"Master," she whimpered as quietly as she could so she wouldn't get shocked.

Pushing her hips forward, she raised them slightly while glaring into Tyne's dark blue eyes.

As Tyne scowled at her, Chance felt the corners of her mouth tug into her own twisted smile. "Master, fuck me."

The words came out before she could stop herself. Chance wanted to say anything she could to hurt Tyne, and in her moment of rage, she really hadn't thought about the consequences of that decision. Her jaw clenched as her head did another spin when the vampire between her legs pounded his fangs into her flesh with so much force that it actually hurt beyond the numbing venom of his fangs.

Chance screamed out. The collar shocked her, and she welcomed the pain. She was glad to have anything to distract from the fact that she'd invited the vampire to take her body and use her willingly.

He twisted his head, adjusted his position and planted his face against the lips of her pussy, plowing forth with his tongue as though he planned to devour her soul from between her legs. Chance's ensuing cry of pleasure and surprise encouraged him to ram two fingers deep into her.

"Don't you dare." She groaned as the electric shock caused her body to tighten around the vampire's fingers. "Don't you leave."

That shock made Chance clench hard. Her toes curled, and she writhed in her oncoming orgasm.

"MASTER!" Chance yelled, then screamed again as the collar did its job perfectly and shocked the hell out of the girl.

The pain and tension pushed her over that delectable edge. She spilled out into the vampire's waiting mouth as he drank from her cup. His fangs cut and scratched her, but they healed instantly, leaving only tingling in the wound's wake.

Finally, Tyne could handle it no more. He turned his back and took a single step. That was what she'd been waiting for.

"She told you to stay." Eadrich wiped her juices from his chin as he hissed over his shoulder at Tyne. "You will stand there and watch me take her as many times as she wants."

Tyne slowly veered to face the pair. Chance was already so high she barely noticed the blood-curdling screams as that loyal pet beat himself somewhere in the distance, sight unseen. The sounds had become so repetitive and familiar that they were drowned out by the sounds in the room.

Tyne stood there and observed, his mouth pulling into a tight knot as his father undid the straps that held Chance's arms.

Eadrich chuckled as he traded places with Chance. He folded his arms on the pillow and rested his head on his arms so he could perfectly see Tyne at the door near the foot of the bed.

"Go ahead, toy. Fuck me."

She placed her hands on his chest. Every movement in her arms was pure agony after having them strapped up. The rest of her body was sore, but she was too high to care.

"Will you bite me, Master?" She asked in a whisper, wanting the pain in her extremities to stop.

"Face the other way. I mean for you to look him in the eyes while you fuck me."

Slowly Chance turned, placed her hands on her master's thighs and slipped a leg onto each side of him. She didn't have much experience being the one on top. The thought made her nervous.

The universe spun so hard around her, she had no choice but to use both hands on his legs to hold herself upright. She wiggled her hips but was failing miserably as she tried to push him into her. The smirk that formed on Tyne's face made her want to throw herself off the bed and attack him. The thought vanished as Eadrich's icy cock penetrated her dripping pussy.

Chance gasped softly, allowing it to slide slowly into her body as she eased herself down onto him. She whimpered quietly from the unimaginable length of his cock. As soon as he was all the way inside her, she straightened, arching her back and panted noiselessly as she struggled to grind her hips. Now that she'd devoured his entire member, she felt like she just skewered herself with his massive rod.

"Move your hips," he murmured softly and added, sounding threatening, "or I'll move them for you."

Attempting to roll her hips, Chance barely swayed them forward and back again. She gasped and moaned, trying her hardest to give the vampire beneath her as much pleasure as possible.

"I'm going to cum," she whispered a lie mutedly to antagonize Tyne.

Eadrich reached up. Using a single clawed finger, he sliced

the leather of the electric collar. Chance watched the damn thing fall. Catching it, she chucked it to the floor at her left, glad to be rid of it. The excitement of having the collar removed made her slick, which allowed her hips to move far easier than they had moments before.

"Oh, Master!" Chance exclaimed loudly, and then screamed as he grabbed her hips and yanked her down harder. "Master! Master, cum for me! Fill me!"

Eadrich and Chance smirked as they watched Tyne becoming more and more tense. The bastard looked ready to throw himself out the window. That was enough to help push Eadrich over the edge. She felt his icy fluid gush into her in an exhilarating rush of pleasure.

"Thank you…" Chance gasped out as she stopped moving to bask in the sensation of being filled to the brim.

"ENOUGH of this, father!" Tyne snapped. "You've made your point. I am nothing to you."

"Are you jealous?" Eadrich licked his lips hungrily as he watched Tyne's rage bubble over. "Join us then."

Tyne cocked an eyebrow at Eadrich's 'kind' offer. Chance glared over her shoulder at the ancient vampire. Judging from the skeptical expression on Tyne's face, she realized he suspected that there was a catch. It had already become clear to her that Eadrich was a master manipulator with a tendency to find the cruelest and most unexpected way to torture those beneath him.

"How may I serve?" Tyne murmured, as though he'd said those words a thousand times before.

"You wanted my load… come recover it from her."

Chance twisted to stare at her master in confusion. Retrieve it from her? *How*?

Eadrich spread his legs, moving Chance's with them. She moaned loudly, feeling his icy load leaking out around his cock as he shifted them to make room for Tyne. Chance panted softly, feeling a wave of dizziness overtake her. Her head tilted to the side as though it were too heavy for her to hold upright. Her entire body felt clammy, and her stomach turned, though there was nothing in it for her to lose.

Cadmael's distant screaming had finally stopped. It was possible that he had decided his punishment was over, but more likely that he passed out from pain and exhaustion.

The ancient vampire sat up and slid his hands beneath Chance's thighs, just under her knees. He sank his fangs into her shoulder and drank from her, basking in that amazing vanilla flavored delight. Chance watched as Tyne climbed onto the bed and lay down on his stomach. Her brows furrowed for a moment, until he pressed his lips against her pussy, his tongue lapping where Eadrich's cock penetrated her.

Chance screamed out, her hips jerking to Tyne's mouth. She was becoming so dizzy, but this time, she was sure it wasn't just the venom in the vampire's fangs. Blood loss was weakening her. Her eyes closed and her head tilted back to rest on Eadrich's shoulder. This was it. She'd be free of them both… This was how she'd escape.

"Master. Kill me. Drink it all," she murmured softly, thinking he would follow through.

Eadrich's fangs tore out of her flesh as he burst out laughing. Chance's fiery blood spilled from his lips, dribbling down her back. His chuckle made her loath herself for opening her big mouth. The ancient vampire lifted her slowly. She could feel bubbles of liquid ooze from around his cock, which Tyne suckled and licked up.

"Whoa!" Chance yelled as Eadrich's cock slipped free of her pussy.

Tyne immediately covered her hole with his mouth, sucking to slurp up everything he could of his master's seed from within the girl. The heat of her humanity had warmed it, making it almost taste good. Or maybe the sweetness he was enjoying was simply the flavor of Chance. That sweet vanilla that he would never have again.

Chance moaned and gasped loudly as Eadrich lowered her once more. The tip of his cock pressed its way between her ass cheeks. Her toes curled as she struggled not to tighten against the pressure that seemed to build pushing into her asshole.

"No, no! Please, don't! It hurts!" She yelled in pain.

Chance's hands moved to Tyne's head before her fingers tangled in his hair. He would do nothing to help her, and she knew it. As he suckled and licked at her pussy, his fangs cut and scratched at her. The wounds healed almost instantly, but it didn't mean there was no sensation involved. Once he removed all the juices and she was empty, he pushed his mouth to her clit, ensuring to give her maximum pleasure, as his master would want. The best part about it was that the closer she came to orgasm, the tighter she'd become and the more his father's cock penetrating her ass would hurt. As he ate her out, he stared up, watching for the moment it would happen so he could catch it as her gaze met his. He smiled into that delicious pussy.

As if her asshole couldn't take the building pressure, Eadrich's massive cock broke past the barrier and slipped about two inches inside the opening. Chance screamed, and everything tensed. Never had she felt such a stabbing pain in her life. Tears rolled down her cheeks as she struggled to force herself to remember how to inhale.

"Good girl… Breathe through the pain. Relax and let it subside."

Tyne worked all that much intensively against her clit, trying his hardest to push her over that edge to orgasm, where every orifice on her body would tighten. He slipped two fingers inside her, moving them slowly. Gradually, he increased his speed until she came. Liquid gushed around his hand.

Chance's breathing slowed as a tension built up in her abdomen. She felt the heat escalate and before she could help it, a trickle began.

"Ohh-nooo!" she cried out.

The more she tried to stop the flow, the tighter she clenched around the tip of Eadrich's massive cock.

"Oh! It feels… OH!!" The more constricted her hole

became, the better it felt.

As she orgasmed, Eadrich lowered her onto his cock, feeling himself filling the tight hole as it strained around him. He moved her slowly as though gently encouraging her to engulf him wholly. Her breathing hampered and her hands traveled to her breasts to massage the tender flesh.

"OH!!!" Chance screamed.

Her entire core tightened. Everything seemed to clench. Her toes curled as her back arched. Chance's nimble fingers fumbled to her nipples, pinching and lightly twisting them as hot liquid gushed from deep within her, spilling out into Tyne's waiting mouth.

Tyne hungrily lapped up every drop he could. When finished, he reached forward, slipping three fingers with force inside her entrance. As he wiggled them around, he found himself aroused by the simple thought that, through her vaginal wall, he was rubbing his father's massive cock. He spread his fingers out, stretching her so that he could massage her G-spot while pressing against the rod buried deep in her ass.

"Do you want to punish him, toy?" Eadrich murmured in Chance's ear before drawing it into his mouth, suckling lightly on her earlobe.

The vampire's icy breath sent chills across Chance's neck, and she moaned as he toyed with her ear. Her hips ground harder, following his lead. Eadrich's freezing hands clasped around her waist as he helped her body sway.

"Do you want…" Eadrich started, before rephrasing the question as he released her hips to allow her to continue moving her own. "He's deserting you… He will leave you behind. He said I can have you."

Chance felt her entire frame grow more tense with each word that the cruel vampire hissed in her ear. Her hands moved to Tyne's shoulders as the vampire didn't slow in his attempt to make her orgasm again.

"Your lover has abandoned you here to die."

With that, her nails gouged into Tyne's flesh, cutting into

his shoulders with so much force that blood trickled from the wounds. She felt tears filling her eyes, threatening to roll down her cheeks and drip onto his back.

Icy fingers wrapped around one of Chance's wrists, drawing it away from Tyne's shoulder. She whimpered, but cooperated. Her hips consistently rocked back and forth, unable to help herself.

Eadrich pulled open the drawer of the nightstand next to the bed and shoved his hand in. After a few moments of shuffling about, he found the tool he'd been looking for. He took out a short-handled cat-o'-nine-tails whip.

"Take it," Eadrich hissed as he slid the weapon into Chance's hand.

Chance froze. She stared at the leather tool. As her hand trembled, the slender pieces of leather hanging down from the handle seemed to dance, tickling her thigh.

"I- I don't…" she started

"Hurt him how he hurt you." Eadrich sank his fangs into her shoulder again.

He permitted some to roll down her body in slow, deliberate streams, simply allowing a small amount to bubble out from the corners of his mouth. He watched over her shoulder as crimson trickled down between her breasts, eventually between her thighs.

Her hand clenched in anger as Eadrich's taunting words appeared to wind their way into the depths of her soul. As his fangs pierced her skin yet again, a dizzying climax erupted. Chance couldn't even fathom why he suddenly changed pace, devouring her clit with a whole new level of desire. Her gaze moved down. Blood from somewhere seemed to trail down her stomach, welling against his lips, some seeping in, mixing with her juices as she orgasmed into his mouth.

He was loving this far too much. Tyne was drinking from her, enjoying the taste of her. BUT THE FUCKER WAS GOING TO LEAVE HER HERE!

Swish.

The tendrils of the small whip made contact across Tyne's

shoulders, spilling down his back in a tender caress.

"Harder," Eadrich commanded and smiled as Chance's body tightened around his cock as she tensed while raising her weapon, preparing to strike the vampire between her thighs.

"Ow!" she yelled out and glared down at the bastard eating her pussy.

Tyne's mouth remained firmly pressed to her clit like he'd been compelled to. He smirked into her pussy as he readjusted his hand to slip four fingers forcefully into her, tearing her tight little hole.

"BASTARD!" Chance screamed and brought down the whip with as much force as she could.

It took every ounce of power she had in her tiny body, and the only result was the slightest of pink lines on his back and a deep moan erupting from his mouth into her pussy. Chance yelled, trying to rise to her feet and escape the agony of Tyne driving his entire hand inside her. Luckily, as she tore, his saliva healed the wound.

Tyne was careful not to allow his fangs to cut her because he knew it would displease his father.

Chance had raised the whip to strike again, but in the onslaught of pain, her hands came down. She dropped the whip as her fingers tangled in Tyne's sandy blond locks.

"No more!" She screamed, "ENOUGH!"

Neither vampire stopped their advances. It felt as though Tyne was trying to rip her guts out of her crotch while her sadistic master pounded away at her ass, continually yanking her back down onto him every time she attempted to stand.

"I'm done!" Chance yelled as she pulled on Tyne's hair to force his face away from her hypersensitive clit.

"Then why are you about to cum?" Eadrich whispered to her before planting his fangs into her shoulder.

TYNE

Eadrich must have suspected the girl needed something to help dull the pain and bring about waves of pleasure. It was possible that he had already mentally fractured the tasty little woman. Centuries ago, humans would last months before their minds shut down. Their species were growing weak faster and faster every generation.

He pierced the mortal's flesh with his fangs repeatedly. He didn't allow his saliva to heal the wound. Each time he broke her skin, she'd tighten for a split second around Tyne's hand before Eadrich's venom numbed the area.

He suspected that with each bite, Chance felt her ability to resist the vampires wither and die. Gradually, she relaxed, settling onto her master's massive cock, while Tyne's fingers found it easier to move in and out of her. A lusty moan escaped Chance's lips as her hips twitched toward Tyne's mouth.

"More," Chance whispered. "Bite me."

Chance begging for someone to bite her made Tyne lose himself in his animalistic desires. His eyes glazed over black as his fangs carved up the succulent flesh around the woman's clit. His saliva healed it as quick as he cut it. Blood poured into his mouth. The most delicious blood in the world.

"NO!" Eadrich screeched in a rage.

The ancient vampire shoved Chance sideways off of them so hard that she flung off the bed, hitting the wall beneath the window. The human curled into a ball, both her hands covering where her pussy tore as she wailed and whimpered in pain.

Eadrich snatched up the whip from where Chance had dropped it onto the sheet. He lashed it so hard across Tyne's back that it drew blood. The amount of force behind his attack sent several of the leather tongues dancing about the air as they tore off from the weapon.

"How dare you presume to drink from my toy!" Eadrich yelled, kicking his foot out and hitting Tyne on the shoulder with more power than humanly possible.

Tyne knew he had made a mistake the second his fangs broke through her skin, but it was too late. Eadrich had been waiting for him to fuck up. The ancient vampire's kick sent him flying off the bed, shattering his collarbone. He landed hard on his ass, one hand cradling the arm belonging to the broken collarbone.

"Father! Please!" He begged as quickly as he could, ready to grovel if necessary.

"Leave or I'll slaughter you like the bitch you are!" Eadrich snarled, coming to his feet on the bed as he brandished his weapon while glaring down at the pathetic piece of property that had displeased him.

"It's almost daybreak-."

"Have I ever been the type to *care*?" Eadrich began a slow walk down the length of the bed, coming ever closer to where Tyne climbed to his feet.

Tyne could sense danger radiating from the ancient vampire. Eadrich's eyes hadn't changed from the dull carcass-gray they always had, but he could feel it in the air. If Tyne stayed, Eadrich would definitely kill him this time.

"Goodbye, Father." He whispered as he left the room with a painful bow to his body, his collarbone aching from the movement.

He didn't dare glance at Chance before bolting from the chamber. This would be the last time he laid eyes on the pet that he'd worked so hard to collect. He quickly turned and ran from the room, even leaving his clothing behind. There was no point in risking his life for a pair of pants.

CHANCE

Chance sat against the wall crying silently, unable to force herself to move. She didn't care that Tyne was gone. Judging from how he reacted to Eadrich, he would never have stood a chance at saving her. She was on her own. She needed to do this; she needed to make it believable. But most of all, she needed the pain to stop!

"Thank you, Master," she whispered between her tears.

Chance hadn't even heard him approach before he was kneeling by her side. She sniffled quietly as he slipped his arms around her, easily lifting her from the floor.

"There, there, my little toy…" the monster purred as he laid her down on the bed.

Eadrich took one of her wrists and pulled her hand away from her torn pussy. She tilted her head back to stare at her master in confusion. He enjoyed that delicious expression far more than he had expected.

"Wait, Master. Why?" Chance whispered, her voice cracking from the strain. "I did what you wanted…"

He wrapped the strap around her wrist, tying her down. Then Eadrich grabbed one of her ankles, forcing her leg to straighten, ignoring her cries of pain from the movement. He fastened down that leg, then repeated the same thing with the other. He came to the head of the bed and smirked at Chance's free hand, which was gingerly trying to rest on her pussy.

The girl's bottom lip quivered as he grasped that wrist. Her brows rose. Instead of placing it on the bed, where he could strap it down, he moved her hand so it would circle his still hardened cock.

"Give me a hand job," he commanded in a hiss.

Hoping he would leave that hand free after, Chance crept her hand up and down the incredible length of his cock.

"Do it with more enthusiasm or I'll fuck you instead." Her eyes widened in horror.

If he touched her pussy, she feared she would die from the pain. Chance couldn't help crying now. Hot tears poured from the corners of her eyes and across her temples, moistening her pillow. She was so mentally and physically exhausted. Every movement hurt, each muscle strained from exertion. She panted, gasping for air as more tears forced their way from behind her eyes.

"Not good enough." He adjusted to place a knee on the

bed.

"NO!" Chance wailed.

The prisoner moved her hand with a newfound force. On any human man, the amount of squeeze combined with motion would have bordered on being extremely painful. Vampires were different. Eadrich moaned a soft encouragement as he placed his hands on his hips and tilted his head back with his eyes closed.

"Open your mouth," he commanded without looking down. "I want you to get as much in there as you can."

Chance already felt like she was going to puke. She opened her mouth wide, sticking her tongue out, exactly as he had shown her before. If she did well, maybe he would leave her untied. The young woman moved her hand faster, encouraging his juices to explode onto her face and in her mouth. The flavor! Vampire jizz tasted like blood and ash. She retched instantly, turning her face away. The icy liquid began to dry into a crust on her skin. She gagged loudly, his cum poured out of her mouth onto her pillow as she dry heaved.

He grabbed her wrist as she drew her hand away from his cock to wipe her face.

"I like it like that," he told her as he strapped down her only remaining free limb. "Sleep well, my little toy. I'll be seeing you soon.

They left Chance laying in a moist, blood-covered bed, with vampire cum on her face while she cried into the night until she fell unconscious from pure exhaustion.

17

NEVER ALONE

CHANCE

At the sound of an explosion, Chance woke up screaming in terror as she struggled to sit up. She fought more intensely against her restraints than she ever had before.

Another eruption from overhead sent a chill through her body as a horrified shriek escaped her mouth before she could stop it. Now that she was conscious enough to process the situation, Chance could hear the shhh sound of the rain hitting the building. Though the blackout curtains blocked any of the lightning strikes, she knew it was a thunderstorm.

She knew that her fear was illogical. The probability of being struck by lightning were supremely low. But as another clash exploded, the girl screamed again as if life itself were being ripped from her lungs. She didn't care if she woke up the entire household. She didn't give a damn if he beat her senseless for disturbing his slumber.

Across the bottom half of the doorway, a black shape stopped and peered into the room.

After blinking away her tears, she realized it was a dog. A big fluffy husky. The dog turned back the way it had come, having investigated the disruption and found no danger.

"No puppy!" she whimpered. "Please!! Here doggy…"

She began making kissy noises, trying to encourage the animal to come to her. The dog froze and swiveled to face her, its head cocking to the side. Another flash of lightning and Chance screamed, closing her eyes tightly. When the clatter ended, she opened her eyes, squinting as she looked for the dog. It was gone.

"Please! Please don't leave me alone," she pleaded, helplessly tied to the bed, and no longer able to stop herself from going into heart breaking sobs harder than she had cried since the day she'd been taken.

Pressure changes on the bed caused her eyes to open wide. She instantly regretted all of her screaming, expecting to find Eadrich threatening her. Instead, big blue eyes surrounded by black and white fur were staring at her.

"Puppy," she whispered, but shrieked as an eruption of thunder exploded with a deafening sound.

The dog whimpered as he climbed the remainder of the way onto the bed. The animal looked around and then laid down, one leg stretched across her lower abdomen, his muzzle resting across her ribs. He closed his eyes.

Another rolling blast made the girl flinch, but this time she didn't scream. She winced hard, startling the dog. He grumbled and crawled further up her body, so his torso laid across her chest and one paw rested on each side of her head. He nuzzled his cold, wet nose into the side of her neck.

"Good puppy, good baby," Chance whispered, then whimpered as a deep continuous thunder noise echoed in the distance.

The dog lightly flicked his tongue out to lick her cheek and earlobe, attempting to unburden the girl. It took hours, but eventually Chance fell back asleep, soothed by the body heat the massive dog provided. The dog made a weird sound after he licked flakes of dried vampire cum from her face.

"It's okay puppy," Chance whispered mutedly as she fell unconscious. "Please don't leave me."

As she slept, she could feel the heat of the large dog keeping her warm and making her feel safe. It felt like it had only been a few hours, but there was the possibility that it had been days. With the blackout curtains, even the flashes from the lightning from that horrible storm didn't penetrate the windows.

Something warm and wet tickled her fingers, making Chance smile slightly as it woke her.

"Good puppy," she moaned softly, with her eyes closed.

"There's no dogs here." Cadmael's voice startled her awake.

"But- last nigh-"

Cadmael interrupted her. "You had severe blood loss yesterday. If you talk to the master about hallucinations, he will see how far he can push your mind. I'd suggest keeping those details to yourself."

Chance's jaw quivered. She was positive it hadn't been a dream. It had felt so real. She knew she wasn't alone in the bed when she fell back to sleep.

"But the storm…"

Cadmael swiped the cloth up her forearm, only to pause at her elbow. He looked at her with his brows drawn down and his lips parted. The young man shook his head slowly while cocking an eyebrow.

"There was no storm," he whispered softly, before returning the cloth to her hand and scrubbing between her fingers.

That was when she realized Cadmael was shirtless. Even when he had been sexually active the previous day, he wore that dress suit. He had on his pants and a belt, but there was definitely no shirt. His skin was so badly scarred that she couldn't spot a patch of flesh without an old or recent wound. Cadmael had both his nipples pierced, though she wondered if it was something his master wanted, or if he did it.

Chance blushed, realizing that he had caught her examining his six-pack, which flexed every time he leaned forward and back as he scrubbed her.

CADMAEL

Cadmael turned away from the girl, feeling a heat rise in his cheeks. Maybe it had been a bad idea to go shirtless. No one had ever looked at him the way she did. He leaned forward and rinsed out his sponge and heard her gasp at the same moment that he felt a wound on his back tear open from the exertion of bending over. That was his punishment for failing to follow his master's orders the previous night. Cadmael did it to himself to prevent his master from taking the whip into his own hands.

If Eadrich decided Cadmael hadn't disciplined himself at the level his master expected, he would have suffered far worse.

Blood dribbled from the reopened slash as he sat up and twisted to wash the girl. He began scrubbing dried blood and cum from her face.

"Are you okay?" Chance whispered with tears bubbling in her multi-colored eyes.

"Why wouldn't I be?" Cadmael murmured, trying to sound nonchalant as he kept his features blank.

"Your wounds. I'm not blind! I can clearly see them."

"I deserved punishment," he hissed defensively through grit teeth.

The girl needed to drop this line of conversation before the master woke. He didn't wish to be disciplined for not appreciating that his only punishment for failure was a lashing, which he got to do to himself!

Her face was finally clean, so he turned his back and rinsed the cloth out again.

"I'll change your sheets later."

Cadmael returned his attention to the girl, washing her throat, neck, and armpits. He wet the sponge again before scrubbing more of the woman's flesh. After he rinsed the sponge, he paused before he brushed it against the girl's most sensitive area.

She screamed in pain. The sudden loud noise scared the shit out of him, so he flinched away from her. He stood and backed away two paces, nearly kicking over the bucket as he traveled.

"It hurts!" she cried out and immediately burst into tears while struggling against her restraints.

His brows furrowed as he leaned over to get a better look at her wounds. He moved back to the side of the bed, kneeling on the edge as he examined her vagina. Using his fangs, Tyne sliced the area all around her clitoris with razor blade cuts. That resulted from unhealed fang slashes. Eadrich had perfected leaving vampire bite marks without allowing his saliva to touch the wound and heal it. The entire area, including around her hole was swollen, nearly beyond recognition. He shifted positions to see further up her taint in search of her anus. The area around that hole appeared torn and bruised, but clearly hadn't faced the same trauma as her front side. He cleared his throat before quietly speaking.

"I'll be gentle, but I *must* wash you."

He rinsed the sponge one more time and squeezed out as much liquid as he could. It was barely moist as he saddled her shin to get a better angle for trying to gingerly cleanse the girl. Against her will, he lightly dabbed the area around her clit. The screams that came out of the girl were horrific. She flailed around endlessly when he attempted to move the sponge closer to her entrance.

"Alright. Alright! Stop." He climbed off the bed to rinse the sponge. "I'll wash it last, okay?"

"Please, don't touch me there. It hurts… It hurts so bad."

As the girl complained, whimpered and whined, he scrubbed the rest of her body, being careful not to miss any area. She begged and pleaded for him to pass up on washing her private areas. She didn't understand that he really had no choice. Maintaining her was a part of his chores, and he didn't skimp on anything.

Cadmael pursed his lips as he returned the freshly rinsed sponge to her intimate area. He squeezed, letting the water runoff and splash her area, dribbling down. He hoped that the soapy liquid would disinfect the area without him having to touch the sponge to her flesh. Maybe it would be less painful for her. She cried out anyway, even though he didn't touch the sponge to her wound. He knew from personal experience that anything touching those wounds, even lightly blowing on them, would feel like agony.

The last time he told her anything, she panicked. This time, he didn't tell her she had tears in both holes and her privates looked virtually unrecognizable. It was possible telling her would make it feel more painful.

"I see you've gotten an early start today, my pet." The voice of the sinister vampire came from the doorway. "You've completed nearly all your chores around the house."

Cadmael stood quickly, dropping the sponge into the bucket as he faced his master. He smiled warmly, placing a hand over his heart, before bowing.

"Your praise honors me, Master."

CHANCE

The way Cadmael stared at his master with open adoration made Chance want to puke. There was no reason this idiot boy should feel so loyal to that scumbag master of his. Her mismatched eyes shifted to gaze at the vampire, who stood completely naked in the doorway. Was he already planning to fuck her again? She barely had the opportunity to rest! Was that creature really so insatiable?! AND SHE HURT SO

BAD!

"Cadmael, where are your clothes?" Eadrich questioned, though he really shouldn't be the one talking, considering his own state of nudity. "You know, I like you in suits."

"Of course, Master. I will adjust to your preferences before continuing my chores." Cadmael bowed again, then picked up his bucket and made his way out of the room, not even flinching as he passed by his abusive master.

Chance's eyes were as wide as they could go as she watched the master stroll up to the bottom of the bed. He rested icy fingers on her foot, toying with her toes for a moment before slowly making his way around to the side of the bed. He gradually made his way toward the head, dragging his icy fingers across her skin as he moved. His touch gave her chills, making goosebumps rise as she shivered. A very large part of her wished her reaction was purely from revulsion, but there was something in his caress that made her lust for more. The thought made her sick.

"Hmmm, which hole to choose…" he murmured, sounding as though he were teasing her.

Chance's eyes widened in horror. It was likely he remembered the night before, and simply didn't care about the amount of pain fucking her would cause. The fucking monster was looking right at her pussy as he said it! He knew she was suffering. She had seen Cadmael's expression when he saw what her privates looked like. She could only guess how horrific it looked down there.

"My mouth!" she suddenly blurted out in a desperate plea.

"Pardon?"

"Please, Master, fuck my face." She began begging, trembling for fear that he would choose a more painful path.

Hopefully, phrasing it like that would make him happy and he would accept just to encourage her to continue the submissive act.

"Well, aren't you the perfect little toy today?" Eadrich's smirk turned devious. "Tell me why, and I may comply."

"Because you-…" if she blamed him, would he torture her

further? He was like Tyne, a narcissist, where nothing was ever his fault. "I tore myself last night."

Chance's jaw quivered uncontrollably as she lightly struggled against her restraints. Her eyes desperately pleaded with him as she squinted up at his face, fighting not to let them fill with tears.

"Please, Master," she begged before opening her mouth wide and sticking out her tongue the way he had wanted her to the previous night.

Cadmael entered wearing a white dress shirt tucked into his pants. He was carrying clean sheets under his arm, while in his hands he had a broom, mop, and a bright orange bucket of fresh soapy water that sloshed around with every step he took. He froze in the doorway, clearly wondering if he should come back later to clean. Too late. His master's eyes narrowed in on him and a malicious smile formed on the ancient vampire's dark lips.

"How may I serve you, Master?" Cadmael insisted, bowing politely, though he was careful not to drop a single thing.

If Cadmael had dropped anything, anything at all, his master likely would have castigated him for his failure. He moved to the corner of the room and leaned the mop and broom against the large, floral-patterned, high-backed armchair. He meticulously set the bucket down beside his other tools and placed the bedding on the chair.

Following his master's gaze, Cadmael made his way around the bed, undoing the cuffs on Chance's limbs. When finished, he bowed his head to his master, glancing up at the vampire from the corner of his eye. She followed Cadmael's gaze to stare curiously at the vampire.

EADRICH

Eadrich flicked his fingers at the girl, shooing her off the bed. This was going to be fun. He enjoyed tormenting Cadmael. No matter how hard the boy tried, he'd always be an easy target for Eadrich to play with. As a tiny beasty, the boy was far too innocent and taking away the pure stare the little thing had, was one of the few pleasures Eadrich had left in this life. In fact, as a boy, Cadmael had a sweet disposition and no matter how hard he tried, Eadrich had yet to manage to turn the boy truly dark. If Cadmael ever became completely jaded, he knew the boy would become boring to him.

Chance whimpered as she slowly dragged her arms down from over her head. Relaxing the muscles between her shoulders seemed agonizing for the girl. The sweet expression she wore made his smile widen.

Following Eadrich's command, the human gingerly peeled herself from the bed. She struggled to come to her feet, cradling her arms as her fingers lightly massaged at the sore muscles in her upper arms. Chance's multi-colored eyes moved her stare from one man to the other as she wrapped her arms protectively around her body. That would do nothing to protect her.

When Eadrich waved his hand a second time at the bed, Cadmael clearly prayed it was to change the bedding. He bent down and grabbed the corner of the fitted sheet.

"No. I want you to lie down. Diagonally, so your head is here." Eadrich pointed at the spot right beneath his crotch.

It irked him that he had to explain to the stupid pet what he wanted. Cadmael should have known, but he was playing coy. Cadmael released the edge of the sheet. The elastic made it snap loudly onto the plastic under-sheet.

"Of course, Master."

But Cadmael didn't move. He was staring in disdain at the mix of red, yellow, and brownish stains on the sheets. It smelled as bad as it looked. At some point, the girl had pissed the bed in the night. Eadrich had expected that, considering she'd been there for days. Her bladder had likely released while she was asleep. The best part was Cadmael's loathing for dirty and unsanitary things. It made this part so much more enjoyable for Eadrich. The boy should be glad he was allowed to don a shirt to cover the open gashes across his back before he was forced to lie down.

Eadrich grew impatient and cleared his throat loudly, making Cadmael flinch self-consciously. He placed a knee on the edge of the bed and froze. Eadrich loved watching the young man's mind work. He hadn't instructed Cadmael on HOW he wanted the young man to lie. Face up or down?

Cadmael hesitantly relocated to the center of the bed, chewing his bottom lip as he seemed to consider his two options. Being face up meant he would protect his injured back from whatever Eadrich had planned. However, it would mean he could end up receiving wounds on his front side as well.

Cadmael lay on his stomach. Eadrich watched closely as several of the slashes in Cadmael's back opened from the excessive movements of simply crawling. The blood seeped through the white cotton dress shirt, creating distinct lines on the pristine material. Cadmael tilted his head back as far as he could to stare up at his master with his brows drawn down with a deliciously worrisome expression.

"That will work," Eadrich murmured as his eyes flashed to the girl, "Now you- lie on top of him, face up."

Chance crawled across the bed and rolled herself onto Cadmael's back as carefully as she could. Eadrich smirked as Cadmael tensed from the pain, making the girl physically wince. He was bleeding, but there was nothing she could do. If she didn't obey, Eadrich would torment them worse. The girl laid shoulder to shoulder, her body weight pressing her back against his, the back of her head rested on his.

Eadrich smirked as he placed his icy hands on either side of her head. The girl automatically opened her mouth and stuck out her tongue to prepare for him. Carefully, he positioned the tip of his cock on her tongue, rubbing it about so her saliva moistened his skin. The heat… that miraculous human warmth radiated down his shaft in waves. He nearly sighed in relief.

"Perfect height. Thank you, my pet." He purposely

emphasized that he was using Cadmael like a stool to raise her up so he wouldn't have to crouch while fucking her face.

"My pleasure, Master." Cadmael gritted his teeth, struggling not to groan as Eadrich chose that exact moment to ram his cock deep into the girl's mouth and down her throat.

Chance's entire body flailed as she gagged loudly on his icy cock. As soon as she got herself under control, he pulled it back out slowly. She began attempting to suck on it. It seemed the girl was going to make a genuine effort at pleasuring him, but a simple blow job was just so boring.

Without warning, Eadrich slammed his throbbing weapon as far into her throat as he could make it go. He held it there, feeling her constrict tightly around his bulging weapon as it stretched her throat. He refused to pull away, no matter how hard her arms flailed through the air or pushed at his hips. Her legs even kicked out at the mattress, occasionally striking Cadmael's calves. The poor boy lay there beneath her, bearing all her movements through those nasty wounds on his back. He must have been in agony, because Eadrich could even hear him quietly panting as he struggled not to show his pain.

Eadrich placed a hand on the girl's throat, using it to compress the space even tighter around himself. The human's face was turning purple from lack of air, and her eyes were bulging as she realized her death could come from choking on a dick. Her expression was something he could barely describe. It only made him so much harder to watch that horror paint her pretty features.

She bit down, but her teeth did no damage. He wasn't a young vampire. Thousands and thousands of years had changed him in ways that he would never have imagined when he first transformed.

"Open wide, or you'll die like this."

Chance unclenched her jaw as a large vein pulsed in her forehead. He pulled his cock out and the guttural sound that erupted from the back of her throat echoed loudly in the small room. She rolled off of Cadmael's back and began hacking and coughing. Strings of drool and stomach acid dangled from her mouth and nose as she struggled to get herself under control. There was nothing in her system to puke, as she hadn't eaten in forever.

"I guess we'll have to do something else." Eadrich purred, far more excited than he should have been.

"Nooo…" Chance cried out between coughing and gagging from her failed attempt at throat training.

"Oh yes. I don't give second chances." He snorted at his own pun. "Cadmael, you can do your chores. You're boring me now."

Cadmael rapidly rocketed from the bed and started lifting the fitted corners of the sheet. He tugged lightly on the sheet as if to tell the girl that she needed to move. Cadmael wasn't an idiot. If he touched her without permission, he could undoubtedly face his master's wrath, and a tiny part of Eadrich hoped the boy would fuck up.

Chance carefully climbed off the bed, watching as the servant quickly attached clean sheets overtop of the plastic, not bothering to wash the staining that had leaked through to the clear underlay. He moved as fast as possible because if he took too long, he knew Eadrich's focus would turn on him. He snatched up the pillow and switched its casing before placing it back at the head of the bed.

Eadrich observed as the young man carried the soiled bedding into the hallway. He listened as Cadmael's footsteps stopped, just out of sight. The wounds across his back had completely torn open and stuck to the shirt, making them pull further with every one of his motions. The agony the boy must have been in that entire time had to be excruciating, but he said nothing. Chuckling in the back of his throat at the thought, his gray eyes drifted to the young woman.

Chance was staring at him with wide, terrified eyes. She'd finally got herself under control, though her hand rested on her throat as she took slow, deep breaths.

"Please Master, forgive me." She murmured softly. "Teach me to do better. I'll do anything to please you."

Eadrich ignored her pleas as he watched Cadmael enter the room again. He kept his back on the pair and his focus on his task. He quickly picked up the broom and began sweeping in the corner, purposefully facing away from the center of the room. Eadrich smirked, knowing Cadmael was doing everything he could to remain invisible while tending to his chores.

"You want to please me?" Eadrich questioned her with a devious smirk that widened as a thought crossed his mind. "Bend over so I can fuck your ass."

"Wait. I'm still hurt… NO!" Chance staggered as he grabbed her arm and forced her to bend over so far that her face buried into the mattress with his hand pressing on the back of her head.

She struggled against Eadrich, but he was so insanely strong with his vampire power it was utterly useless. He pushed the tip of his cock against her asshole, preparing for the explosive heat that would rush over his flesh. Unfortunately, the weak little human screamed in agony, with her legs giving out, narrowly avoiding penetration. Eadrich growled as she tried to crumple to the ground, thinking it would save her ass.

"Please, Master!" She screeched as his fingers tangled in her hair, pulling her further up onto the bed so it would hold her up. "PLEASE! AAAHHHHH!"

Eadrich forced his pulsating cock deep into the human, feeling her tear around him. Her tension as she screamed and struggled only tightened her hole's grip on his cock. No lubrication and no toying. Blood and tears were her lubricant today. He was obviously hurting her on purpose.

"I paid a million dollars for you, toy," he growled, wrapping his hands around her throat and squeezing. "I *will* get my money's worth."

Eadrich exhaled an icy breath onto the back of her neck as he buried his face into her hair. As the girl yelled, he squeezed to see if he could force her vocal cords to stop working. He counted to five and released her throat, then did it again. Her cries broke into sobs as he toyed with her. Eventually, he grew bored with choking and rested a hand on the back of her head so his fingers could tangle in her hair. That was the moment he decided to finally move his hips, swaying to glide his cock in and out of that glorious little hole.

Chance screamed endlessly into the mattress, barely able to force air in through the material pushed against her face. He was sure she thought this was the worst pain she'd ever experienced or would. She was wrong. As long as she was alive, there was so much more he could do to her. One of her hands reached down and pushed behind her, trying to stop or even slow the ruthless vampire. It did nothing. He felt her warm fingers on his hip when he'd rush into her, but ignored it.

Her other hand stretched out over her head, as if subconsciously reaching for Cadmael.

CADMAEL

As the broom dragged across the hardwood, his eyes flashed to the screaming girl while his master rode her hard. She did not know what she was doing, and all her struggling was only making it worse. It was more painful if you fought or resisted. He pulled his bottom lip into his mouth, lightly chewing on it as he watched their pair.

Without slowing, Eadrich spoke. "Are you jealous? Do you wish you were the one beneath me?"

It unnerved Cadmael how his master sounded like he was talking about the weather or some other mundane thing.

"Yes, Master," Cadmael responded, dropping his gaze to the floor shamefully.

"Do you wish to spare the toy from her pain and take her place?"

Cadmael's eyebrows drew down, knotting tightly to the middle of his face as his mouth hung agape. His master was a tricky one who loved to play games. There was no saying how

Eadrich would react to whatever answer was given.

Chance lifted her face from the mattress enough to stare at Cadmael. Her eyes pleaded silently for him to save her as she screamed soundlessly, no longer having a voice. Their master continued to pound himself into her, even as he carried on a conversation.

It was time for Cadmael to take a gamble. "If I say yes, would you fuck me, Master?"

"Come here, then."

Quickly, Cadmael leaned the broom on the wall and skirted around the base of the bed. He stopped at his master's side, careful not to even glance at the toy, still pinned beneath the cruel vampire. Eadrich finally pulled out of the girl and stood, raising an eyebrow at Cadmael before speaking to Chance.

"Roll over, toy."

Chance whimpered softly as she turned herself over. The girl had actually thought that their master had been done with her. Foolish human. She left her legs dangling off the side of the bed, while using her arms to cover her breasts, while one hand moved down to protect her pussy.

"How may I please you, Master?" Cadmael questioned with raised eyebrows.

"Open your mouth."

Cadmael obeyed instantly. The words had barely left his master's lips and Cadmael was following through. He didn't even flinch as Eadrich spat in his mouth. Flecks of spit missed, hitting his cheek and chin. The girl gasped loudly in surprise as Cadmael continued to stand with his mouth wide open, tongue hanging out in the expression his master preferred.

"Lick her."

Cadmael nodded and slid to his knees. She didn't move her hands from her pussy, so Cadmael was forced to take her wrist and make it move. His master's spit dripped from the tip of his tongue as he wasted time struggling with the girl. He reached up and parted the girl's lips. He could see where the small tears in her flesh from the previous night were, so he leaned forward to lick at the wounds.

Still, with his tongue out of his mouth, he looked back at his master as his hands slid beneath her knees. He lifted her legs to expose her ass, holding them wide apart to improve his access. Eadrich nodded and bowed, spitting in Cadmael's mouth again, smirking as the boy's own drool dribbled down his chin.

Cadmael leaned in, burying his face between her ass cheeks as he plunged his tongue into the detrimentally damaged cavity.

Chance had prepared to scream out in pain as she felt his soft cheeks press between hers, but when his tongue pounded into her asshole, she gasped in surprise. It didn't hurt. Her holes no longer hurt. It took her far too long to realize that the saliva had healed her.

"Good enough. Toy, sit at the head of the bed. I want you to watch this and learn quickly. Tomorrow, I will test you and if you cannot do what Cadmael does, I will severely punish you."

Chance quickly flung herself to the pillow, sitting on it and pulling her knees to her chest and wrapping her arms around her legs. She observed as Cadmael took her spot from before, barely making a face as he laid down on his back. He kept his tongue out of his mouth, with his jaw held as wide as he could. In that position, he couldn't stop the gasp from the pain across his back when his wounds pressed into the mattress.

Cadmael tilted his head back, letting it hang off the edge, mentally preparing for his master's grand entrance.

Eadrich didn't take his time. He rubbed the tip on the flat of Cadmael's tongue, likely enjoying the overwhelming heat that rushed across his flesh. Within a heartbeat, he rammed his cock so far into Cadmael's throat that tears of pain formed in the corners of his eyes. His master's giant cock suffocated him, but he did nothing to resist.

Without hesitation, Cadmael brought his hands up to his

head. One moved to pamper his master's cold testicles, which rested on his forehead. The other hand massaged his own throat with as much strength as he could to constrict the area and give his master maximum pleasure. His toes curled from the tension as he felt his face heat. His head throbbed agonizingly from the lack of airflow, though the smooth flesh of his master's balls oddly seemed to ease some of the pain.

As one of his knees bent, the pressure in his throat eased, and Cadmael took a deep, gasping breath of air around the massive cock that filled his mouth. He kept his tongue pushed out but moved it back and forth as if trying to add a massage to the exposed shaft.

Again, his master thrust it so deep that Cadmael could no longer find air. He made a soft gurgling noise around the bulge in his throat as his legs moved, pushing his feet into the bed while he focused on pleasuring his master. He could feel his own cock twitching as it pushed against the front of his pants.

Eadrich pulled his cock most of the way out of Cadmael to allow him to breathe. He gulped three deep gasps before the impatient vampire slowly slid the entire length into Cadmael's waiting mouth.

"Time for a proper face-fucking," his master was kind enough to warn him.

He mentally prepared himself as Eadrich placed his hands on Cadmael's chest, knowing how painful it was going to be. There was no way his master didn't know that his slash marks would be pushed harder than ever into the mattress beneath him.

Cadmael tried not to, but a soft groan escaped him from around the cold, meaty flesh that took up residence in his mouth. He took one final deep breath, knowing he would not have the luxury of breathing again for a while. Then it happened, as though all hell broke loose. His master began pounding hard, thrusting the entire length of his cock into Cadmael's throat.

Each time it reached its maximum depth, Cadmael gagged

and choked loudly as it was ripped back out along with whatever air had been trapped beyond it. His master's hands pushed so hard into the young man's chest that the creature's claws drew blood. Cadmael laid there, his arms flinging to his sides to prevent himself from trying to stop his master. His hands balled into fists, gripping the sheet as if it might give him some form of support.

Chance looked absolutely terrified. Her arms shook and tears rolled down her cheeks. She slowly shook her head in horrified denial.

Every few minutes, Eadrich would pull himself far enough out of Cadmael's mouth that he could catch a deep breath before another round would befall him. After about twenty minutes, Eadrich pulled most of the way out of Cadmael's mouth. He left just enough cock in that when he finally blew his load, it filled the Cadmael's mouth instead of his throat.

"Open."

Cadmael opened his mouth, sticking out his tongue properly as his master would want. He simply allowed the cum to drizzle out, running up his cheeks and into his nose and eyes.

"Keep some in." Eadrich smirked. "Swish it around."

Cadmael, ever obedient in his undertaking, struggled not to gag on the blood and ash flavor that he swirled around in his mouth.

"Now swallow."

Cadmael swallowed and opened his mouth to show his master that he followed the instructions perfectly.

"Good boy," Eadrich praised, patting Cadmael's fresh claw marks on his chest. "You can strap the girl down and go get me dinner."

Cadmael sat up and used the edge of his shirt to wash his face. He turned to stare at his master as he attempted to wash the cum out of his curls.

Eadrich walked toward the door. "Oh, and make sure it's young. The last one was disappointing. Don't dissatisfy me again. I'm going to take a nap."

"Of course, Master." Cadmael held a bow until his master had completely left the room.

"Lie down, please," he told Chance, walking toward the head of the bed.

"Wait. We can leave while he's sleeping. We can run away together to somewhere he will never hurt us again."

Cadmael shook his head slowly. "You're so naïve, it's almost adorable," he murmured before grabbing her wrist.

As he strapped her down, he told her. "There is nowhere to go that he won't find you. He would never stop hunting for you as long as you belong to him." As he finished with the last strap, he added, "He owns us until we die."

Cadmael finished with the last strap before speaking, "It's best for you to sleep while you can. He was in a good mood today. He won't be so gentle every day." With that warning, Cadmael left, leaving his cleaning supplies behind as he left to follow his most recent orders.

He paused outside the door to catch his breath, listening to the girl snarling loudly. Her bed creaked as she struggled hard against her restraints like she had every opportunity she got.

The movements stopped, and he knew what had happened. One hand. One restraint. That was all it took. Her hand slipped free of the cuff. He nodded slowly to himself before walking down the stairs, knowing what was to come.

18

ONLY CHANCE

CHANCE

As Chance's wrist and hand slipped free of the cuff, she stared at it in surprise. It took her far longer than she'd like to admit for her to get over the shock of sudden freedom. Using her available limb, she quickly undid all the other restraints that held her captive to that awful bed.

It was now or never. She had to at least try!

Carefully, she pulled the fitted sheet off the plastic covered mattress. Chance enveloped it around herself like she would with a bath towel, tucking the corner between her breasts. She wrapped it extra tight, hoping it wouldn't slip off as she ran.

She rested her hand lightly on the door frame as a bout of dizziness nearly sent her toppling to the ground. Panting weakly, she had to close her eyes for a moment as her free hand moved to her stomach. The pain was becoming rather unbearable. There was no way to tell how many days had passed by after her abduction, but she knew she hadn't eaten a single scrap of food since.

This was going to be her only opportunity to escape. She wasn't going to waste it cowering in her cage. Chance took a final deep breath while mentally preparing herself for one of the most life altering events of her life. If she made it to safety, she could simply move forward and forget about this hell.

An idea occurred to her, and she slipped back into the room. Chance marched to the window and ripped open the decorative curtains to expose the blackout material taped to the window. She quickly tore the tape that held it sealed tight to the window and grabbed the edge of the frame, and pulled up with every bit of strength she had. Chance checked to make sure there were no locks… she had been in such a rush that she wasn't thinking clearly.

There, across the bottom and side edges. They screwed the fucking window shut! She was on the second story. There was another window outside, to the left, and under the windows was a slanted roof. That might be Eadrich's room. So close to hers that he could hear everything.

Chance pulled her lower lip into her mouth. The skin felt painfully cracked and dry from dehydration. Her flesh was no longer plump and healthy, like before they took her. The dim bedroom lights glittered on the glass, so her reflection could gaze back at her. Her cheeks had become gaunt and dark patches had developed beneath her eyes and in random spots on her body. She looked like a drug addict. Her own appearance terrified her. As tears welled in her eyes and her chin shook, her fingers touched her bruised cheek as if checking to make sure that the stranger staring at her through the reflection was her own face. Her foster parents wouldn't even recognize the emaciated creature she'd become in only a few days.

She needed to see them again! She needed to go home!

With a newfound fire, Chance ripped some of the tape off the edge of the blackout material and made a square with an x in the middle. The tape would keep the glass from being too loud as it cracked. It would also prevent too many pieces from clattering to the hardwood floor.

If she made it out, would her rustling around while trying to find a way down draw too much attention? Maybe this wasn't the best plan. There had to be other ways. Obviously, there were going to be entrances to the building that she could leave through. Morning was coming. She could almost feel the sunlight wanting to greet her beyond the horizon.

The vampire wouldn't be able to follow once the sun was up.

Chance quickly and silently made her way to the door once more, peeking around the edge. She could feel anxiety bubbling in the pit of her stomach. Her instincts drew her in two different directions. She could climb back into the bed and wait for someone to come. Maybe she'd even receive praise for not running away. The other option… the thought of returning to the life she'd worked so hard to mold and build was far too tempting. If she stayed, she'd die. If she ran and got caught, she'd die. Her only way of surviving was to get out and make it to safety.

She cautiously moved toward the top of a grand staircase, beside which was a balcony overlooking the main entrance. Chance rested her hand on the railing as she leaned forward to ensure that no one was waiting for her in the region below.

The grand feature of the area was an enormous door. A big, hard oak-looking portal. The rest of the overly decorated space seemed to simply be an entry room with several doors spread throughout. Only one door mattered to Chance!

As she practically flung herself down the endless stairs, her eyes didn't stop flickering around the entrance room, terrified that the vampire would make an appearance.

Once at the door, she turned the handle to find the door wouldn't budge. Of course, there was a big bolt lock that needed a key stopping her from opening it.

Carefully, she snuck into the room to her left. An elaborately decorated fireplace sat on one side of the room. Opposite it was a wall of paintings and murals of famous places all over the world. Leaning against the corner closest to the door was a stack of what appeared to be portraits. In front of them was an easel with a half-finished portrait.

It was her! Would her portrait end up with the pile of other paintings of whom she could only assume were Eadrich's previous toys? There were at least fifty canvases in that pile! Chance rested her palm in the center of her chest and rubbed the ache that seemed to build from her terror.

Above the scenic paintings that lined the wall were windows, each with a blackout curtain taped tightly to it. Why were all the windows so high up?! Further into the room were rows of bookcases filled with literature, some looking to be hundreds of years old. The room seemed both beautiful and sickening at the same time. She could picture them enjoying this room after toying with her. Cadmael would be in the corner painting the toys, so there'd be some evidence that they existed, while Eadrich sat in the large armchair before the fireplace. The bastard vampire had placed the chair with its back toward the books, where he could observe Cadmael painting while he read.

She felt goosebumps spread across her skin. This room would offer no way out, unless she wanted to try climbing up the chimney. No, not a way out now. That was an option she might risk in the future, if no other presented itself to her. Shaking her head, Chance left the library behind.

Once again, she stood in the large entranceway. Beside the base of the stairs, there was a door across the space from her, which was closed. She turned to her right and followed the hallway. Maybe under the stairs she'd find a door leading to the basement. Basements had windows and she could get out there! But the wall was flat. There was no door to a set of stairs.

Chance surveyed the rest of the entry hall. There were four sets of doors, three of which were grand looking double doors with inlaid gold designs. The space held stairs to the second level, then at the end of the hall was an enormous set of double doors. Between those doors and the library was another set, which was also closed.

She marched to the flat wall alongside the stairs, glancing up to the balcony overlooking the entrance to make sure the vampire hadn't come. Chance approached the door of the room directly beside the library. If he was in there, her escape attempt would end prematurely. When she rested her fingers on the gilded handle, Chance took a calming breath and lightly applied pressure.

Click. It was locked. All that stress and anxiety and the fucking door wouldn't open. Chance wanted to scream out her frustration.

If the door had opened and that beast was in there, her life would be over. Trembling, she stumbled her way to the next door at the very end of the hall.

As her fingers brushed against the cool metal of the handle, Chance swallowed the bile that rose in her throat. She had never been one for horror movies. This feeling was exactly why!

The door creaked open. The sound reverberated in her bones with a shrill sensation, almost making her legs give out. The sound made her wish she'd just broken the window upstairs and thrown herself head first off the roof.

Exposed beyond the oak door were two sets of stone spiral staircases. One leading up, and the other down. Two choices. Which was the better option? Basement. Definitely down.

Chance's fingers dragged along the dark stone, feeling it become damp with moisture as she moved deeper underground. This had to be the remnants of a castle. Someone fashioned a Victorian-style manor around the ruins of a distant past as if encasing history in a protective barrier. At the bottom of the stairs, there was another door. Solid planks clasped together with iron rods, certainly from the same era as the stone walls and stairs.

She used her shoulder to push the heavy door open, surprised by how quiet the hinges were. Her feeling of regret was instant.

Eyes wide with horror, she stared around the dank dungeon. Those monsters had filled the walls with portraits of young men and women, with no space to spare. Her hands clasped over her mouth to muffle the scream that wanted to erupt from the back of her throat. She slowly turned, taking it all in.

A part of her had expected all his victims to be of Asian descent. Serial killers had a type, didn't they? No nationality, no appearance, no physical size was spared. It was as if Eadrich had no specific taste in what he enjoyed. He'd torture and make anyone his pet or toy. From beautiful golden frames, there were countless faces staring at her with matching expressions of fear and uncertainty.

The room smelled deceptively like a hospital, sterilized with bleach. The items decorating the open space were like something from the worst horror movies about ancient torture devices. Equipment hung from the ceiling or appeared sorted on tables which lined the outer edges of the room. Their tools were innumerable. There were wooden objects and furniture that she had never seen and couldn't even imagine a use for them. This room would not lead to freedom. There wasn't a single window, or any other door.

"No," she whispered and turned, running up the stairs to the first floor.

A hopelessness built up in her mind, creeping its way into her heart. Her hands shook uncontrollably, and her legs were so numb that as she climbed the steps, she had to use the wall for support.

Once on the main level, she walked toward the base of the grand staircase. There was one more door that she hadn't checked. If there was no escape from that room, then she'd sneak back upstairs and decide from there if she should go out the window or wait for them to come back, then build their trust so she could try another escape at a later date.

Chance rushed into the last room, glaring around at… a kitchen? Of course, it was a kitchen. A part of her had expected another torture chamber. She pushed the door shut behind her and examined the space. There was a counter on the far wall with cupboards overhead. The wall directly to her left had one window, which was far too high for her to reach, even if she found a chair to climb on. There were also three skylights on the ceiling, each with a blackout curtain taped over it.

She pulled open a drawer, hoping to find a knife. But there was none. The next drawer, followed by another cupboard. NOTHING! Everything was empty. How the hell did Cadmael eat? What did he eat?! There were two fridges in the space. She approached the one beside the entrance and pulled it open. Then closed it faster than she'd opened it. Blood. Bags of blood and saline. They really had quite the set up.

She walked over to the other fridge, which was at the counter beside the sink, beneath the skylights. It was full of protein drinks and meal replacements. The top shelf of the fridge looked like a pharmacy of nutrients and vitamins. Why? How could a man survive like this?!

A banging sound in the hallway sent Chance into a panic. She could hear keys jingling as someone relocked the entrance door from the inside.

There was a door to her right, next to a pantry style closet. She grabbed the handle and found it locked. Chance whipped around and pressed her back against the exit door as she stared the way she had come.

No way was she giving up! She moved to the pantry, ripping the doors open, and entered the empty space. She pulled the doors closed and stared through the slats in horror as Cadmael marched into the kitchen carrying several large takeout boxes. He set the boxes down and walked to the first drawer she had opened. He dropped the large key ring with several house and car keys on it into the drawer.

Chance smiled… until he used a key on his necklace to lock the fucking drawer! She had to get that necklace! The young man walked back around the counter to the takeout boxes. Her stomach ached, desperately wanting the food. The smell filled the space, making her mouth water. Cadmael froze in the middle of the room with his eyebrows climbing up his face. His eyes widened and his head slowly swiveled to stare in her direction. His brows drew down and his mouth hung open. Chance felt the color drain from her face. She could swear that he was looking directly at her through the slats in the cupboard.

"What the fuck is that awful smell?!" Eadrich's voice yelled from upstairs. "Malix Peek! What are you up to?"

Cadmael whipped around, picking up the takeout from the counter. He balanced them on one arm as he opened the door.

"You gave me permission to feed your toy, master," he started speaking before he was even fully out of the room. "I didn't know what she liked, so I got her a bunch of different things."

The kitchen door clicked shut, making the voices sound distant and faded out. Her stomach clenched with nerves and she suddenly felt as if she had to void her bladder. They were about to discover that she had tried to escape, and she would not survive the punishment.

"Leave it there. You can feed her after you bathe me."

Chance couldn't help the sigh of relief that came out in a breathy gasp. She pulled open the cupboard door and stared around the kitchen in a panic. She needed to find a way out! Chance opened the fridge and pulled out a protein drink, chugging it. She had never been one to enjoy those, but this was survival! Holding the empty bottle in her hand, she put the lid back on and placed it on the shelf she'd gotten it from.

Her stomach hurt from the sudden and speedy consumption. The transfusion was the only reason she'd made it that long without food and water, without her body shutting down. Her eyes scanned the room in terror.

What could she do now?! Maybe she could sneak back upstairs and hope no one noticed that she had slipped out of her room. No. Cadmael definitely saw her. But… if he saw her, why didn't he say anything? Maybe because he knew there was no way out! That stupid locked door.

She marched over to the door, grabbed the handle and twisted while pushing her bodyweight against the door. It did nothing. Then she saw her path out of here. The skylights were the only other way.

Chance carefully climbed onto the counter, then onto the fridge, where she could reach the skylight directly over it. The opening between the top of the fridge was only two feet, but being small, she easily maneuvered herself around in the space.

She peeled back the tape holding the blackout material to the window, careful not to drop it. She took the tape off the curtain and placed it onto the window in the shape of an X. Upon closer examination, she realized the window was single pane and would be easier to break with less noise.

As someone turned on the faucet, she heard water running inside the walls. The extra sound was welcome, as it would help hide the ruckus she was about to make. Chance glanced at her hand. She wanted to be a surgeon, but if she fucked up her hand now, that would not be an option for her in the future.

Ah-hah!

Cleverly, Chance wrapped the curtain around her hand to protect it. She'd done nothing like this before, but it seemed like a logical plan that just might work.

Chance took one final soothing deep breath before closing her eyes, turning her face away, and swinging her fist up through the skylight. There was a crack sound, but it wasn't as loud as she'd expected it to be. She opened her hands and barely caught the taped-up glass before it could fall onto her. Several small shards scattered onto her, but most of the glass had been held together by the tape.

Carefully, she set the shards on the fridge behind her. Using the material to protect herself from cuts, she picked out any jagged pieces still stuck in the frame around the hole.

The skylight would be a tight fit, but she could wiggle out. Chance grabbed the glass window, picking up a piece that made a perfect pizza slice shape. Carefully, she set her makeshift weapon on the roof, then grabbed the edges and pulled herself most of the way out. She hadn't even made it all the way through the hole, and she was gasping at the fresh scent of the forest.

It was entirely a miracle that she didn't cut herself at all throughout the risky endeavor. She stared around, feeling the unforgiving grooves of the roofing material beneath her feet. If that hurt, the forest floor was going to be awful.

Planning ahead, she tore the old material into three slices. Two, she wrapped around her feet, much like a tensor bandage. The final, smaller piece, she wrapped around the shard of glass, making a handle to help prevent her from cutting herself. This was it. She was not going back without a fight!

Chance wiggled out through the skylight, careful not to let her sheet catch on any of the shards of glass still sticking from the frame. She didn't let herself hesitate. Now was her time for action!

Carefully, Chance moved to the edge of the building. Peering over the side, she felt her stomach drop. That would be quite a fall. She made her way around the perimeter. She realized that the window in her bedroom overlooked the roof she was standing on. There was no way down. So, she carefully went back around the edge of the roof until she reached the skylight. This was ridiculous! She was so close to freedom, and yet she was stuck!

Any minute now, they could discover her absence. As she approached the front of the house, she spotted a lower roof, which likely belonged to a porch. She wasn't too afraid of being spotted by either of them at the second-story windows because of the blackout curtains. Chance laid on her stomach and inched her way to the edge. She carefully dropped her material wrapped shard of glass onto the grass nearby, relieved not to hear it crack and break.

Grabbing the side of the roof, she slipped her leg over the edge, letting it dangle before doing the same with the other leg. The rough roof scraped at the delicate flesh that rubbed against it. The sheet provided very little protection.

Holding on for dear life, she inched her way down until she hung in the air. Panting, Chance pointed her toes, feeling them touch the railing for the porch below. She let go of the roof's edge and grabbed onto the support beam as she carefully climbed down. EVERYTHING HURT. She did not know how she held onto the roof's edge as long as she had.

Her eyes flashed to the door for a split second before she whipped around and bolted down the steps. She rounded the railing and ran across the grass to where she had dropped her makeshift weapon. In the dark, she fumbled for far too long to find it, but as soon as her fingers claimed her weapon, she ran as if the devil was on her heels.

Chance almost allowed herself to laugh at the exhilaration of her newfound freedom, but the pang of terror that sent shivers across her skin was enough to remind her of the danger she was still in. She tripped over logs, slipped on rocks and took several tumbles, scraping the crap out of her knees, shins, feet, elbows and forearms. At one point, she fell so hard, her hand squeezed her glass shard tight enough that it cut her hand. Tears streamed down her cheeks in a flow that she thought would never end.

As a child, she had lived on a farm. Hiking and camping were part of that upbringing, but that was long before her parents died. The skills Chance had learned were too far back in her memory to be of any use.

Eventually, she ran out of energy and her wild running slowed right down. Chance used a tree for support as she gasped for air. Every inhale burned her lungs, and each exhale felt like it would be her last, or that she'd puke from the strain. Nope. She gagged loudly, but swallowed the protein drink back down. After this, she really needed to take up track and field or something. She should have never quit running after high school. Her face burned from exertion and sweat dribbled from every pore. Her legs trembled, but she suspected that if she hadn't already been so worn, tired and tortured, she'd have been able to run a lot farther, much faster.

A twig snapping in the forest behind her ripped Chance from her thoughts. Within a heartbeat, it annihilated her feelings of relief. No! It couldn't be them! She had come so far! Her eyes scanned the trees behind her. Her gaze was flashing this way, then that, as she covered her mouth to silence her panting. It didn't matter how much she tried to stay focused on being calm, panic set in. Her instincts screamed at her, and she turned back around to keep running.

Chance ran until her lungs were on fire, and her body was coated with sweat, mud, and grime.

THERE! The sky had incrementally turned rouge as the sun climbed into the horizon. Daybreak. The most glorious thing Chance had seen in what felt like an eternity. Tears streamed in a steady flow as she desperately ran toward the rising sun. That was the evidence she needed for hope to spring up anew. That was her sign of freedom!

CRACK!

Chance tripped over a branch as it snapped loudly. She slammed down onto the ground with a hard thump. The wind knocked completely from her lungs, Chance lay there unable to force air back in. Her arms and legs went numb, as if she was on the verge of losing consciousness.

Forcing herself to breathe, she started coughing. As she finally began drawing a breath again, feeling returned to her extremities. She pressed her face into the forest floor, letting the cold ground cool her overheated body. She lay still in the dirt, feeling the soil beneath her fingers.

Something was building in her. This was a sensation she never thought that she'd experience again. It was the feeling of freedom. Chance rolled onto her back, panting hard but unable to force herself to climb to her feet.

The morning sun glittered through the trees, warming Chance's exposed skin. She came to her knees and closed her eyes, taking a deep breath of fresh morning air. She could literally smell the mildew. It was such a glorious morning.

Barely audible, a soft rustling drew her attention. Chance twisted to stare at the trees behind her. Her skin prickled across her arms and a chill ran down her spine. She was frozen in terror. The sun wasn't high enough in the sky for her to feel completely secure. The canopy barely let light trickle down to the ground. She wrung her hands to stop them from trembling, but it did no good. Chance grabbed at her sheet to make sure it was securely wrapped around her.

Another light rustling sound to her left drew her focus. Her head whipped to stare with flared nostrils and tight mouth toward what she hoped would be some small animal. Nothing. There was nothing there. Nothing she could see. What if…?

In a flash, Chance was on her feet, running hard. Between the exertion and the protein drink, Chance's stomach lost its battle. She bent over and puked every bit of what she'd taken in. Bracing herself on a tree, she was sick until there was nothing left in her system. She wiped her mouth with her forearm, then stood straight and pressed her back to the tree, accidentally stepping in her own throw up. She ignored it, unable to force herself to look down as her multi-colored eyes darted at her surroundings. Chance could swear it felt like something was watching her.

When she could, Chance was on the move again. With the sun being out, her only problem would be Cadmael. Her hand clenched around the shard of material-wrapped glass, as if reminding herself that there was one last thing she could do to ensure her freedom.

Her mismatched eyes shifted to stare the way she had come. She felt bad for having the thought. Cadmael was just as much Eadrich's prisoner as she was. The sweet boy with sad blue eyes was just too far gone to realize it. She would kill him if she had to. The thought made her feel guilty, but her life mattered too and if he was going to bring her back to the monster who would kill her, then he would die trying.

When she could no longer run, she started walking. Once her breathing was under control, she forced herself to increase pace. Her legs burned, but it was nothing compared to the feeling across the bottom of her feet. She didn't dare stop moving again, for fear the pain would stop her from walking again. Eventually, she'd hit a road and from there, she could follow it to civilization. Surely, she'd either be able to hitch-hike to the city or find it on her own.

What would she tell her parents?! A mental breakdown. That's what. They would be horrified, but not as much as they would be if she tried to tell them about vampires and hellhounds.

CRACK!

Chance whipped around, knowing that time it wasn't in her head. She heard something from somewhere nearby. In the distance, the sound of wood breaking, but deeper than any noise before. It was definitely a tree falling. She could hear the wood splitting and cracking as it fell, then the boom was loud enough to rumble the ground. A random tree falling in the forest not even 15 feet behind her? No!

There was no way! THE FUCKING SUN WAS UP! There was no way the vampire could be hunting her down!

Chance whipped around, ready to break into a dead run, when she bolted face first into something hard and sturdy, sending her tumbling backward. She was so scared and surprised she couldn't even scream.

No sound came out of her as she stared into Eadrich's soulless gray eyes, glittering in the morning sun. He took a step forward, his expression horrifying as blistering wounds gradually appeared on his face. They festered as the sunlight hit them.

"I'm going to devour you…" he hissed, reaching out toward Chance's face.

"NO!" Chance yelled and rammed the shard of glass into his chest with every bit of strength she had.

Her hands slipped along the glass edge as it sliced through the material that she had twined around it. Then it shattered.

Shards poked through the cloth, shredding her hand. Impossible! That should have at least cut him, but it did nothing to his bare, tattooed chest.

"No…" a muted whisper escaped her as she stared at the undamaged location on his skin.

"I'm not as weak as the young vampires you're used to dealing with."

Chance shook her head, whipping around to run away, but Eadrich caught her hair in an iron grip.

As Chance struggled against the grip he had on her, she screamed, "Why don't you just kill me?!"

Eadrich pulled her in close, turning her face so they could stare into each other's eyes before speaking.

"When will you learn?" he purred in a dangerous tone. He lifted her from the ground and pulled her in close, wrapping his icy arms around her small body. He embraced her so tight, she could barely breathe. With his lips tickling her earlobe, the monstrous vampire growled, "I own you. Your life and death are mine to decide."

"Please… no more…" she whimpered before feeling his fangs sink into her shoulder.

She gasped and moaned. Eventually, her eyes closed, and all went dark. Her last thought was a question of how he planned to punish her for running. Secretly, Chance wished she'd never wake up again.

19

Ancient History

Chance

The vampires abducted Chance and then sold her to this monster. Without so much as a word, Eadrich took her to this mansion against her will. She'd been physically and mentally tormented while being starved. It was clear she was going to die here, and yet he was somehow surprised that she tried to escape. How could he even be mad?!

Chance startled awake. She was lying on something cold. She wasn't even strapped down this time. Her eyes cracked open, and she could see Cadmael standing guard by the door with his hands clasped in front of him. His clothing appeared ruffled. He looked tired and sore. The way he stood spoke volumes.

"Leave it," Cadmael snapped, his eyes narrowing.

She realized her hand had been moving to scratch an itchy

spot on her forearm. There were two injection sites. One on the back of her hand was pumping saline, and the other on her forearm pushing blood. Both bags were nearly done. They really wished to make sure she survived as long as possible.

Hoping for death would do nothing, and she didn't really want to die. Chance wanted to survive, to make it through this and get out. No matter what they did to her, she would try again and again! Chance would never give up her freedom and would continue to fight for it.

She slowly sat up as she frowned at Cadmael, before asking, "You okay?"

The young man's face was pale. His hands were clasped in front of him as if attempting to seem professional, but his laced fingers tightened when she questioned him about his well-being. Maybe he didn't like that she noticed how 'off' he seemed. His eyes narrowed as he glared at her. His mouth tightened into a knot as his jaw locked.

Chance pulled her knees to her chest and realized they were no longer scraped from her numerous falls in the forest. The thick cut down her shin was also gone. The material wrapping her feet was removed, and they were also healed. Apparently, vampire saliva could heal bruises as much as it healed cuts. She suddenly had a distinct mental image of Eadrich spitting into a bowl repeatedly for Cadmael to apply to her skin. Maybe they had vampire saliva repositories or something where vampires got paid for their spit. That way, overlords like Eadrich wouldn't be subjected to doing something so below their station.

"You guys healed my wounds, but why?" she asked curiously.

"He wants you in peak physical condition while he tortures you." Cadmael's response was in a flat, emotionless voice.

Chance felt panic bubble up inside her. Her stomach turned and her head spun. She felt like she was going to faint or puke. Though she didn't think she had much of anything left to puke up. In her panic, she blurted her wishful-thinking out loud.

"We should run away together," Chance whispered to him, knowing she stood a better chance of escaping if he helped her.

His dark expression turned into a straight up glare as he responded, "What makes you think something like that is even remotely possible? Do you think it was an accident that one of your cuffs was left just loose enough for you to slip yourself free?"

Her face paled. "Why?"

"I followed my orders," he said through grit teeth, as his face turned a peculiar shade of green.

"Why would he want me left loose? Why would he want me to escape?!"

"He wants to punish us."

"So, he's not actually mad?"

Cadmael snorted softly, then responded, "He's pissed. You got farther than any other toy before you."

"I don't understand what the point of all this is."

"It helps to keep things interesting."

"What happens when he stops finding us interesting?"

"We die."

Her stomach dropped, and a wave of dizziness struck her. Chance shook her head, glaring at the boy as she whispered in a muted voice.

"I don't want to die."

CADMAEL

"We all die. Everyone who enters this house dies young." His eyes moved to the portraits on the walls, scanning the countless faces of Eadrich's victims.

Cadmael had come to terms with dying young when he was still a child. Eadrich had made sure that Cadmael would welcome the day when this all stopped. He even painted his own portrait, though he knew no one would see it. Cadmael's replacement would help Eadrich burn the portraits belonging to his last pet, just as Cadmael had done to the works of the pet before him. Once Cadmael was gone, no one would bother to remember the faces of the many toys that died here throughout his time of service. He was simply waiting in line for his turn to die.

Chance's brows furrowed. "I'm so sorry," she whispered.

Cadmael gave her a flat stare, emotionally distancing himself from the girl. "For what?" he growled through gritted teeth.

"I'm sorry for thinking that you were just like him," her jaw quivered as she shook her head. "I'm sorry for hating you."

Cadmael's jaw locked so hard that he felt like his teeth could shatter from the strain. His eyes burned and his nostrils flared. The way she looked at him was freaking him out.

"Stop it," Cadmael snapped, his hands balling into fists at his sides. "You don't know anything about me."

Cadmael's voice cracked as he spoke. Stupid girl! Stupid toy!

His fantastic hearing picked up the soft scuffling of feet coming down the stairs, long before his master came close. Cadmael stepped aside so his master could grace them with his illustrious presence.

Eadrich cocked an eyebrow at Cadmael, who submissively dropped his gaze to the floor. If Eadrich knew anything of the conversation from moments ago, he'd never let Cadmael live it down.

EADRICH

"Hello, my naughty little toy," Eadrich purred in his slow, drawling voice as he walked to the center of the room. "It's time for your punishment."

Chance snarled up at him as her arms moved to cover

herself. It amused Eadrich that after so much time had already passed, she still wanted to cover herself. He found it peculiar that she seemed so disgusted at him seeing her naked body, when she'd been fine with Cadmael. It was probably because the younger man never looked at her sexually or with cruel eyes. The pathetic human didn't see Cadmael as a threat, but she didn't know what he knew. That sweet looking boy had snuffed out countless lives. Maybe even hers if he seemed like he got too attached.

"What's the point?" the silly little human hissed up at him, her entire body trembling.

"To teach you a lesson, my sweet thing." He crouched beside her, his forearms on his knees as a wintry smile appeared on his lips.

His toys were no fun when they broke too easily. If he occasionally gave them a little taste of freedom and took it away, sometimes it destroyed the toy, other times it reinvigorated their urge to fight. There were some who didn't even try to escape, and those were the ones who bored him.

This one had a fire in her. She pissed him off for real, only because, for the first time, a plaything got away. Normally, they caught them after they got out onto the roof from the bedroom window. But she hadn't broken the window, so he assumed she was slinking around the house in a desperate search for any other way out. Never would he have expected a toy would climb out of a skylight. None of them had ever thought of doing that.

"Why?" she smirked, but her voice cracked, betraying the strain she was under. "Did I exceed expectations?"

His hand flung forward using vampiric speed, so she wouldn't see it coming. He wrapped his hand around her throat as he sneered down at her. The heat of her skin felt like an insatiable fire he wanted to wrap around his entire being. Her thrumming of her pulse beneath his fingers quickened, but her expression didn't change, aside from initially flinching from surprise.

"Do I look to be in the mood to deal with your attitude?"

He brought his face threateningly close to hers. He left his lips parted to ensure his fangs would glitter in the dim candlelight of his torture room. The dancing shadows emphasized the unhealed burn wounds on his cheeks and forehead. Luckily, they were no longer painful, but he looked absolutely hideous.

"No…" she responded, his fingers tightening on her throat seemed to piss her off. "You *look* like a crater face."

Snarling, Eadrich shoved the girl so hard she was flung backwards until the back of her head smashed off the stone floor. He grabbed the tubes that connected to her arm and reefed on them, tearing the needles from her flesh. Enough of giving her sustenance to help her regain her health. She seemed to have certainly gotten back plenty of strength.

"Tabernac!" Chance cursed in what he knew was French as she screamed in pain.

She hugged her arm, squeezing her fingers across the wounds, applying pressure to slow the bleeding.

Eadrich maliciously smirked. "You will concede to my might," he told her as he stood to glare down at her. He added in a threatening hiss, "Or you will suffer my wrath."

"Why are you like this?" she screamed at him, glaring.

She was being far too dramatic for the small amount of damage he'd inflicted. Eadrich's face changed for only a split second. At first, he was surprised, but that quickly changed to amusement. Maybe this could be entertaining.

"What do you expect me to say?" He gave an overly enthusiastic laugh that sounded far too cold as he walked away from her. "You want me to go off like in the movies, tell you how I'm not really evil, just misunderstood?" He chuckled at the back of his throat. "Maybe it will help me see the light and I'll change my ways…" He walked to a counter and picked up a reed. "… fall in love with you… and then we can live happily ever after."

He loved watching her expression change as he taunted her. She was such an easy mark and those delicious expressions she made. The girl had no poker face. Her bottom lip quivered as she hugged herself tighter. He held each end of his new weapon in his hands and bent it in the middle to check how supple it was.

"How about we play a fun little game?"

"Go fucking play with yourself."

"Or I could just beat you." Eadrich felt the smirk on his lips widen as he made his offer. "Guess why I'm like this and I'll set you free."

"Yes!" the silly girl agreed without hearing the rest of the terms for his game.

"But if you're wrong, you accept five lashes."

"Yeah, right!" she snarled defensively. "You're not actually going to tell me the truth. You'll lie just to torture me anyway!"

"Cadmael?" Eadrich didn't even look toward his servant, but the boy responded as required.

"My Master is many things, but a liar is not one of them." Cadmael murmured the truth from his position by the door.

On that note, if Eadrich wanted Cadmael to lie, he would have without a second's hesitation. The boy's features didn't change in the slightest, but for some idiotic reason, his words were enough to sway the girl.

"Fine," she grumbled, likely realizing that she didn't have much of a choice.

"Tell me your theories. You have three tries before I get bored and move on to something else. Proceed."

The girl's hands moved to her stomach as though it were upset. She would have eaten if she hadn't pissed him off. The thought occurred to him that her upset stomach could be from nerves. She likely thought she stood a chance at guessing why he did all this.

This little game was nothing to him. The dim sparkle in his dead eyes should be more than enough to tell her that. She swallowed, the muscles in her neck flexing, and Eadrich caught a whiff of bile. It was possible she had more in her system than he thought.

"Maybe you had such a horrible human life that you're a

psychopath now."

He chuckled, enjoying her explanation. That was a good one. She must have taken some psychology classes, among the other things she studied.

"You'll have to be clearer. That's quite a catch-all hypothesis."

With narrowed eyes, the girl made an irritated noise in the back of her throat. That look of concentration and deliberation on her face was far too enjoyable. He could practically hear her thinking *'either she was close, and he didn't want to give in, or she was way off, and he wanted her to think she was close to keep her from guessing the correct answer.'*

She was a smart, scientifically inclined woman. It was possible that she'd consider nature versus nurture after trying to figure out why he would push for a more exact answer. Of course, there was no way for him to really know what she was thinking, but he'd studied human behavior long enough that his educated guess was often spot on.

"I want to change my answer."

"Oh?"

"You were born that way."

Catch-all answers. The toy had found a clever one. It would cover the entire portion of nature, leaving only nurture. This girl never ceased to impress him. He read and studied this stuff out of boredom, she had a thirst for knowledge.

"What if I told you, I wasn't sure what you meant?" he questioned, "How could we possibly know if I was born like that?"

He watched her jaw clench in frustration. She had to know he was toying with her.

"As a child, you'd torment other, younger and weaker children. You'd hurt small animals. You might even have known you were different because you enjoyed the pain of those around you, even all the way back then."

"Is that your final answer?"

"Seriously?" Chance snapped, her hands balling into fists.

Eadrich smirked as he said, "Turn over."

"Are you fucking serious?" The girl looked panic stricken as she struggled to maintain her glare through her fear.

He flicked the stick through the air in a circular motion, cocking an eyebrow at the silly little human. The dark expression on her face was absolutely delectable. Eadrich knew it wouldn't take him long to get bored with her resistance. In fact, he was sure she'd try to escape again. The girl was slowly becoming too predictable.

"It's time to hear you sing," he purred, stroking the long thin reed, readying himself to strike her with it.

Chance took her sweet time rolling over. The young woman hissed between her teeth as her breasts pressed against the stone. She kept her head tilted back so her face wouldn't touch it. She took a slow, deep breath and closed her eyes. He smirked, watching every muscle in her tiny body tense as she mentally prepared for him to thwack her across her back and ass.

Eadrich took a lingering stroll in her direction. He examined the flexible stick, picking the end he planned to hit the girl with.

"Would you hurry up already?" she snapped, turning her face to glare up at him.

His eyes narrowed. This attitude of hers was getting annoying. Eadrich stopped beside the girl and raised his weapon above his head. When she closed her eyes, he brought it down… across the bottoms of her feet.

Let's see how you run now, you little bitch.

Chance's eyes snapped open in surprise. She screamed before she even seemed to realize she was the one making the noise. The girl rolled onto her side, pulling her knees to her chest as she wrapped her arms around her legs.

"What the fuck?!"

Eadrich grinned, brandishing his stick as he chuckled, watching her get more pissed off. Even though her attitude problem pissed him off, it also amused him.

"That should count as two!" Chance childishly demanded.

"But I only hit you once."

Four more hits and Chance would get to try again to be set free. She couldn't even think clear enough to come up with an answer. Her feet stung across their soles. Even though it was a single line, she felt the pain radiating across them. She almost wished he had hit her ass!

"I'm waaaiting," Eadrich hummed, to antagonize her.

Grumbling, she turned back onto her stomach. As her body pressed against the cold floor, the chill gave her goosebumps that rose up her arms, across her back and then down her legs. This time, she didn't point her feet. She pulled her toes up, flexing her calves so the bottoms of her feet wouldn't be so accessible.

She seemed to prepare for him to hit her bottom or back. He moved down, trying to make her think he planned to strike her across the back of her thighs. Eadrich chuckled before leaning over and whipped her hard at the bottoms of her feet, hitting across her arches.

Chance screamed a string of cuss words that were a Frankenstein combination of French and English. She curled in the fetal position again, glaring through her tears at Eadrich.

"What the fuuuck!" She finally finished her swearing rant. "You bastard! Why?!"

"You tell me. That's the point of this, isn't it?"

"UGHHH!" she growled at him angrily. "I don't fucking know! Were you-."

"No!" he snapped. "I have three more strikes."

Chance took a deep breath, ready to yell at the monster that she was sick of this game. Then the thought occurred to her. As long as he was toying with this game… he was being gentle compared to what he could do to her.

Three more hits. She could handle three more… couldn't she?

He wanted to laugh out loud as the girl laid back down and spread her legs. She thought he was going to have to pick a foot to hit. She was so tense, and this was taking too long for his lack of attention span. He placed a barefoot on her calf, pressing down hard so she couldn't pull away. In a flash, he slapped his stick across the bottom of that foot three times while she screamed and struggled to get away.

When he moved his foot from her calf, she came to a sitting position and twisted her foot so she could see the lines across her foot.

"You damn psycho!" She hissed at him before blowing on the bottom of her foot.

Chance

"Yeah. We know. I'm a psychopath… but *why*?"

"Were you abused and tortured?"

"Nope… now submit."

That fucking psycho wanted her to approach and lie at his feet to willingly ready to accept his punishment.

"I can't," Chance whispered, her jaw quivering as she shook her head. "I'm done playing your stupid game."

Tears rolled down her cheeks.

"I can't understand why anyone would be the way you are." Chance could barely speak as she shivered. "I still don't believe you. How can it be neither nurture nor nature?"

"Do you want me to tell you? I'll tell you and forgo striking you with the reed."

"Please," she whispered hoarsely, knowing that it didn't mean he wasn't still planning some other form of torment.

"Nature was a 'no'. I was not born with these desires. As a human, I was so utterly perfect that they specially selected me to become…" Chance sneered. Of course, the fucking narcissist would think he was perfect. "I guess it would be equivalent to what you would call a priest, only better. I was in service to the gods."

That was hard to believe. This bastard would never put someone else's needs before his own. She couldn't picture him being even remotely kind, never mind attaining a state of priesthood. Why would he lie about something like that?

Eadrich walked away, picking up some rope from a table at the side of the room.

"What about trauma?"

He snorted as he walked over to her. He grabbed her arm in a grip that made her gasp out in pain. As she yelped, he pulled her to her feet.

"Nope. We had a severe drought, and I became a virgin sacrifice." He paused, cocking an eyebrow at her as her mouth hung open in utter disbelief. "I accepted it as part of our way of life. It was an honor."

As Eadrich spoke, he began tying the rope around her upper arms, drawing her elbows tight behind her back before tying them together. She tried to resist, but he was so strong that it was entirely pointless.

"You were murdered. Could that have been the trauma? - Ow!! It's too tight." Chance whined as he finished tying the rope down her arms, trapping them behind her back.

"Dumb ass. I said Sacrifice."

"If you became a vampire, how exactly did that work? Whoa!"

Chance gasped as he bent her over and picked her up under his arm. The fucking freak with unbelievable strength held her like a football! He carried her across the large room.

About 8 feet up the wall, they attached a metal bar so it protruding outward. At the end of the bar was a wheel. Eadrich set her down beneath the arm, then took the end of the rope, stepped on a stool, and slipped the rope through the hole over the wheel. He kicked the wooden stool away with the bottom of his foot before turning around, looking ready to hand the rope off.

That was the moment Cadmael marched quickly across the room like he was on a mission. He accepted the rope, stepped back, holding it so tight in his hands that his knuckles turned white.

Chance glanced over at Cadmael with a frown. He always looked so cold, even though he was warm. His face reflected no emotions, though he stood stiff as if he were in pain. She felt her eyebrows draw down, but hadn't really realized how obvious her expression was until Eadrich spoke.

"Are you concerned for my little pet?" The vampire murmured, "He left your cuff too loose and wasted all that money on human food for you… So naturally, I made him eat every- last- bite."

Chance gasped, staring from Eadrich to Cadmael. The young man was right, Eadrich really just wanted any excuse to torture them. Any reason would do. When she considered Cadmael's diet of protein drinks, vitamins and water, his stomach had to be in agony. Yet, the man was so stoic, showing no pain at all aside from holding himself extra stiff.

"I think he's still hungry," Eadrich mussed. "Would you like him to eat your ass, too?"

Chance cringed with her brows drawing down in a dark glare as her gaze swiveled to Cadmael's face. He didn't move. Not even a little. His expression remained the same cool vacant mask. Yet, she felt so much pity for him. There was no way he didn't feel like everything was going to come up… or that his guts were going to burst.

"Fine, let's ask him. Malix Peek? Are you still hungry?"

"If my master wishes it, I am a starving man at a banquet."

"No." Chance interrupted breathlessly as she struggled against her restraints. "Urm, no, thank you."

She stared at the boy with so much pity in her eyes that he turned his gaze away from her. She knew he hated being called Malix Peek, but there was nothing he could do about it. Everything about him was at his master's discretion. As his master signaled to him, Cadmael pulled the cord. Chance screamed as he forced her tied arms to pull up behind her, which made her bend over.

"Are you sure you don't want him to moisten you?" Eadrich confirmed, pushing his thumb up against her asshole, which she clenched in fear.

Chance gasped from the pressure on her rear, before snapping, "Fuck you, asshole."

"That's the plan."

Before Chance could react, he grabbed her waist, pulled open his robe, and rammed himself into her ass. Her scream echoed loudly, echoing off the dungeon walls. She screamed until no air was left in her lungs, but that didn't stop the monster who penetrated her. He slid his entire length into her, using her blood from the tears as lubrication.

Once in, he paused, giving Chance an opportunity to get her bearings, but it did her little good. She shrieked and cried, wailing loudly as she struggled while he stood there with his cock pushed all the way inside her.

When Chance finally caught her breath, the maniacal bastard grabbed a handful of her hair, pulling her head back. She screamed, feeling herself painfully clench around his massive cock. Pulling her hair made her arms twist upward, nearly dislocating her shoulders.

"A large enough jerk, and your arms would be done for." She could practically hear the smile in Eadrich's voice as he taunted her.

The only sound Chance could muster in response was a soft, desperate whimper. Tears filled her eyes and cascaded down her cheeks as he began wildly fucking her. His hips swayed, starting off slowly and increasing in speed. She wished he would bite her. It would give her some form of mental reprieve from the agony shooting across her midsection.

He was going to kill her. She knew she had a zero percent chance of survival, but she'd make damn sure they'd never forget the one that didn't break. They would damn well remember her!

Suddenly, there was an icy gush that filled her, making her toes curl and insides squirm.

"Finished already?" Chance snarled, wishing she could glare over her shoulder at the monster as he pulled his cock from her ass. "That was fast."

In the corner of her eye, she could see Cadmael's face drain of color. He really didn't like her baiting his master. She was done trying to be a good little toy.

Goosebumps rose across her skin as some of his icy cum dribbled from her puckering asshole. Eadrich suddenly spat on her asshole. That wasn't a good sign. He seemed to only provide her with any form of healing or medical care when he planned to increase the level of torture. She felt the tears around her anus healing and the skin tightening to what it was before his cock stretched her out.

"I think I've upgraded you. A promotion." Eadrich chuckled as he walked to the nearby table. "You, my annoying little bitch, are now a slave."

"Like there's much of a difference." Chance watched the vampire return with his hands, hiding something behind his back.

"Someday, I'm going to kill you." She snarled, but broke off into a gasp as he inserted something that felt like a bubble into her butt. "What the fuck was–!" she gasped again as the next bubble slipped in. His cum luckily provided some lubrication. "Oh, my Geh!" Another bubble, one that was definitely larger than the last. "Oh!" Another.

That was why the fucker healed her ass. It was back to the same tightness before he stretched it out so that every bubble on those beads would stretch her all over again. Chance squirmed, feeling her stomach become tight with discomfort.

"Being a slave means I will torture you, not just toy and play with you…" He spoke while he shoved the last three large balls of the anal beads into her tiny asshole.

"Still not seeing much of a difference," she hissed through grit teeth

He walked around to stand in front of her, smirking down at Chance's scowling face. "You will."

20

You Knew It Was Coming

Chance

That fucking asshole rammed a ball gag into her mouth just as she opened it with another glorious, smart response. She screamed into the gag, flecks of drool already trickling through the small holes, when she snarled at him like the little beast she was. Chance screamed in pain when he had to use force to push it past her teeth.

Her jaw ached in its refusal to allow the damn thing to fit, but he forced it in anyway. She screamed and struggled against him. When Chance pushed her tongue forward against the ball, she choked, nearly puking.

"Go ahead, give me attitude now." Eadrich snarled at her, obviously enjoying her misery, as he put himself nose to nose with her.

Instead of trying to scream at him, she took the deepest

breath she could and blew hard. She forced the air out through the holes in the ball, sending flecks of drool and saliva spraying out at the suddenly very pissed off vampire.

Chance wanted to close her eyes in an attempt at cowering, but she needed to stand firm, more in that moment than ever before. His movements were so fast that she barely saw as he snatched the cord that trapped her arms. He reefed it down, yanking it from Cadmael's hands so it came loose from the wheel and fell to the floor. His hands circled her throat and squeezed. He squeezed so hard she was sure her neck was going to snap. She closed her eyes, preparing for her end. Without warning, he released her. Chance hacked and coughed into the ball as he snarled in her face, ignoring the flecks of saliva that had flung through the ball.

"Your death will not come so swiftly. I will make you suffer."

WHY WOULDN'T HE JUST END HER LIFE!?

Chance kept mentally bouncing between wanting to die and wanting to survive. Either way, she wanted this pain and fear to end. The human mind could only handle so much, and she felt like she was already going crazy.

Rage bubbled up as she snarled at him from beyond the ball gag, making drool dribble down onto her chest. She couldn't even understand why she did it. Chance's knee came up right between the vampire's thighs, nailing him in the nuts with all the strength she had.

He released her and as he bent over to grab his groin, she whipped around and ran toward the door. *THAT WAS SO STUPID!* She wasn't even running to escape; she was running out of sheer terror.

Eadrich practically roared behind her as she came closer to the door. The sound bounced off the walls as he slammed his foot down on the rope that trailed behind her.

Coming to a dead stop, Chance was clothes-lined by her own arms. They suddenly pulled backward, though her body was still going forward. There was an agonizing crunch followed by a grinding feeling deep inside both shoulders as she fell. The pain was so intense that she couldn't breathe. Her mind reeled with every fact about disarticulation that she learned during her studies. The pain was so great, she couldn't even scream. She laid on the cold stone floor with her arms twisted up behind her back until they rested above her head. She couldn't even breathe to force herself to scream or cry.

After several minutes, which felt like an eternity, strong, warm arms scooped Chance up from the floor. She couldn't even force herself to open her eyes as she screamed in pain when Cadmael jostled her about. He set her down on her feet, but had to keep his hands on her waist or she would have collapsed to the floor in a trembling mess. She just knew Eadrich was right in front of her and the thought made her shake harder. Chance felt like crying, but nothing was coming out. Her head flung forward to allow vomit to erupt through the ball gag. It was mostly stomach acid with trace amounts of protein drink. When she stopped puking, Eadrich's icy voice echoed in the recesses of the darkness surrounding her.

"Apologize to me and submit."

Chance's breathing was so hard and the pain shooting down her arms and across her back was so brutal that every exhale was nearly a groan-like moan. With the gag in her mouth, every sound seemed amplified. There was nothing she could do to prevent it.

There was nothing she could compare this to. It was akin to an out-of-body experience where nothing mattered. She wasn't in pain and seemed to have developed a numb feeling across her entire body, as if the physical and mental trauma disconnected it from her soul. She was barely aware of what was happening to her. Cadmael had to hold her up while following his master's instructions on how he wanted her immobilized. She could barely hear Eadrich's words as they maneuvered her.

Her consciousness teetered on the verge of slipping into total darkness, when a single thought drew her back.

Don't give up. You can't give up. You are a survivor! With each word surfacing in her mind, she began to *feel* again. She struggled against her restraints, feeling both rope and chain gouge into her flesh. Had she been asleep or awake? How did she end up in this new position?

Eadrich And Chance

Eadrich ripped the anal beads from his slave's asshole, sending bits of feces and old sperm flinging through the air. Flecks of the secretions from the young woman's ass splattered the wall behind the ancient vampire, who had moved out of the way as he reefed on the cord.

Chance wailed in agony against the ball gag tied snuggly with a leather cord which wrapped around the back of her neck. She coughed, gagged, and wailed in protest, while struggling to free herself from the monster who tortured her during her every waking moment. The hollow ball gag with holes did nothing to silence the young woman. It was far too large and had to be forced into her mouth, making her jaw ache more painfully the longer it was in there.

Eadrich could control every agony and each pleasure that his slave experienced. This was not the time for pleasure, and there was nothing the youngster could do to ease her suffering.

As the human cried, mucus trickled from her nose, dribbling down the ball gag, mixing with saliva as she drooled. At one point, in the evening, Chance had even puked, though there had been nothing in her system, so phlegm and bile filled the gag before trickling in strings toward the ground. The secretions formed a small puddle on the floor beneath the prisoner, suspended from the ceiling by ropes.

Chance's body, damaged from head to toe, with bruises and cuts marring her formerly nearly flawless skin. Naturally, the human's marks could be readily covered in public, ensuring that no one would learn of her deviant experience.

"Are you prepared to give up?" Eadrich enquired of the young toy, a nasty smile on his face as he hoped she would not succumb.

More tears spilled down from Chance's eyes as she furiously shook her head, desperately straining to scream her displeasure beyond the ball gag. The chains that held Chance in place seemed to tighten on their own as she trembled, cutting off more circulation to her extremities and causing her to swing uncomfortably in the air. The metal clanged loudly, sending vibrations along the bindings, increasing the intensity of every sensation.

"What? I can't hear you…" the deadly vampire mockingly interrupted his victim's desperate pleas.

The girl's body seemed to hover parallel to the ground. Ropes held her head back at an unnatural angle so that it forced her to stare straight ahead.

The ancient vampire walked around to Chance's face, the girl's mismatched eyes following the creature. At the sight of Eadrich's fangs, the human's eyes opened unnaturally wide with icy terror. She tried frantically to shake her head, but the movement caused vibrations to travel their way down the chains holding her in this awkward position. Chance cried out in pain, sputum dribbling from the gag, as the straps holding her seemed to shoot searing pain down her limbs.

Eadrich reached a hand forward, pressing on the ball gag, feeling spittle surge through the small holes against the palm of his hand. As Chance choked, more mucus rolled out from the girl's nose.

"Oh- no…" Eadrich whispered, putting on fake concern like a horrible mask. "You made a mess, my little toy."

Then, he rubbed his palm under Chance's nose and across her chin, before washing the human's face with the collected mucus.

He dropped the sincere mannerisms for a more homicidal tone as he aggressively moved his hand. "You can have it back!"

The chains rattled as Chance struggled to avoid the

vampire's icy hand, but in the end, all she could do was close her eyes tightly. The young woman desperately prayed for it all to be over. Her jaw would have quivered if the ball gag hadn't locked it as wide as her mouth could go. She gagged as the smell of vomit became stronger, mixed with the saliva and mucus that was rubbed all over her face.

With the last ounce of strength she had, Chance gave one last scream through the ball gag. Bits of spittle and vomit flung through the holes in the gag, spraying in front of the vampire's precious little victim. When the girl was finally out of air and strength, she lost consciousness.

Chance woke moments later, screaming in agony as a searing pain radiated from her abdomen. The only other sound in the room was the chains clanking soundly and Eadrich's sadistic laugh. It echoed through every crevice of the room.

EADRICH

While Chance was unconscious, they changed her position to meet Eadrich's desires better. By the time the girl came to, she was hung right-side-up with a new strap wrapped around her shoulders and two long chains hooked to each side, stretching out to the walls to keep her erect.

"You know..." Eadrich walked a slow circle around the girl as he spoke, his fingers trailing her warm, naked flesh. "They say when someone suffers a knife wound, you need to leave the blade in to slow the bleeding until help can arrive."

The stupid human wiggled, but they had tightly strapped her arms behind her back. There were shackles holding her legs together, and a chain leading from it to the floor, making sure she couldn't swing her feet about to use them as a weapon. Eadrich had learned that fucking lesson. The ball gag had also been removed.

He cocked an eyebrow as he waited for the idiotic girl to realize what had just happened. Chance's eyes slowly trailed downward, likely following the pain to find out what was wrong. He smirked as a look of understanding and terror dawned on that pretty little face. The hilt of a decent sized blade protruded from her stomach.

"Please!" Fresh tears streaked the mud on her face as they rolled down her cheeks. "I need a doctor. Please don't let me die."

"Why shouldn't I?" Eadrich snarled, coming around to her front again. "Look what you've cost me?"

He brought himself face to face so she could see the blistering wounds across his forehead and cheeks. The wounds stung and burned like nothing he'd experienced in centuries! This little bitch had the nerve to beg for her life.

"Exactly!" Chance announced, sounding far too excited. "A million dollars. Has my torture already been worth a million to you?"

It was a desperate idea. Even he had to admit that it was a desperate push for survival. She probably thought that if she could make him want to keep her around, she'd find another window of opportunity to escape. He sneered, wondering what benefits he had from keeping her alive. She had definitely been entertaining. She was far different from any toy or pet. Her resilience bordered on insanity.

Eadrich sneered as he placed a hand on the knife. "Bored now."

"I'll be the perfect toy!" she shrieked, sounding desperate.

He ripped it out of her stomach, basking in the ensuing scream that ruptured from the little plaything. It struck him odd that she was so out of it that she hadn't noticed the knife enter, but once she was aware of it… the pain was unbelievable for her.

The knife fell to the ground with a loud clatter that echoed off the stone walls of his torture chamber. Eadrich dragged his finger along the slit as blood dribbled from the wound. He felt mesmerized as the crimson ooze made its way down her v-line, then her thigh, dribbling down to make a puddle at her feet. Her sobbing was like music to him. The rhythmic sound alternated with the percussion of her wailing screams as he toyed with the wound.

"Should I lick it? Would you like that?"

Chance was crying too hard to answer, but she nodded so hard it shook her body.

"Would you be a good girl?"

He slipped his fingertip between the two flaps of skin, wiggling it to massage the tender meat beneath.

The prisoner screamed in agony but flailed her head up and down, nodding desperately. Eadrich knew now that the girl would do anything to earn the right to return to that room upstairs. Being slowly starved to death while having him violate her repeatedly was a far better option. That place was a haven compared to this cold, dank basement that smelled of a strange mixture of bleach, blood and shit.

As her screaming settled down, he murmured, "Maybe I should make a new hole to fuck… like this one."

Then, as if for emphasis, he forced his fingertip in until the first knuckle.

Chance screamed so hard that there was no air in her lungs, but she didn't seem capable of forcing herself to breathe in again. She dangled, her face turning red as she gasped hard, but barely received any oxygen.

He needed to keep her alert. He wouldn't let her go into shock. It would mean she was one step closer to death and the pain would be over.

Her skin turned clammy and pale. He touched her fingers and realized a cold spread across her extremities. When he prodded her knife wound, she gasped quietly, but didn't scream in agony, as if it were being numbed. He felt her hot blood seeping from it, trickling past his icy finger.

Yes. Shock. Ruining all his fun, shock. Her lips slowly curled into a smile as she took a lingering breath. Slowly, her head tilted forward so her chin could rest on her chest as if she were about to lose consciousness.

"Will you be a good girl if I let you live past tonight?"

CHANCE

Her eyes scanned the room, passing over Cadmael, who stood in the corner with his head bowed and hands folded in his lap. She wished she could see his face. His fingers gripped each other so tight that his knuckles were white.

Then her gaze fell on the twisted vampire. "Please."

Her whisper was almost inaudible. Chance's eyes closed, and she hoped it would be for the last time. Someone was screaming. Nope! Not someone. Her. She was screaming in agony as the vampire forced two fingers into the wound on her abdomen.

"No dying yet!" he yelled over her screeching.

Chance finally opened her eyes as his fingers stopped moving and glared at the monster tormenting her. He pulled his fingers from the wound, making her scream again. More tears would have rolled down her face, but she didn't have enough fluids left in her to cry.

He rubbed one finger against her mouth, trailing her lips with her blood as they quivered beneath his touch.

"Hmmm," he moaned. "That's my good girl."

Then he put the finger in his mouth, sucking that sweet vanilla flavored crimson. Eadrich swallowed before coating them with his saliva. He chuckled before pressing his lips to hers in a fiery kiss, filled with so much untapped passion that she'd never experienced in a kiss before.

Chance returned the kiss with everything she had. She kissed him like her life depended on it. Her tongue slipped out, rushing into his mouth, trailing across his teeth, before withdrawing as his tongue advanced. She sucked hard on his tongue, massaging it with her own as her eyes closed tightly. He withdrew his tongue and sucked on her bottom lip lightly.

Without warning, he slammed his saliva-soaked fingers knuckle deep into the knife wound. Chance broke off the kiss and shrieked so hard that when she ran out of air, her head fell back, hanging behind her as she completely lost consciousness.

EADRICH

As he withdrew his fingers, Eadrich could feel the wound closing and healing shut. She had a very valid point. The girl had cost him far too much money to just throw her away. He needed a new plan of action. But first, he needed to rest and heal.

"Bring her upstairs, tie her to the bed, and monitor her," Eadrich ordered Cadmael as he marched from the cellar.

21

ALTERING THE PATH

CADMAEL

Cadmael sat by her bed for nearly two days while the girl slept. He had given her nutrients, saline, and another transfusion. Over those two days, his master would walk by the room, pretending like he wasn't peeking in.

Cadmael had placed himself in the corner armchair to rest when she finally woke. He heard her speak before he even realized she was awake.

"Am I dead?" her voice sounded dry and raspy.

"Sorry. No," he whispered as he opened his eyes.

He continued speaking as he approached the bed. "You weren't that lucky."

At the side of the bed, Cadmael picked up his protein drink from the nightstand. He opened it and stuck a straw in. Cadmael held it out for her to drink and moisten that sore throat. He hadn't really been able to even look at anything meal related in days.

"About time!" a sinister voice announced from the entrance.

Chance released the straw to stare over at the doorway, appearing to be making her best efforts to imitate Cadmael's vacant stare.

"I thought we were going to have to use smelling salts for you to wake you in time for the party." Eadrich waved his hand in front of his face as if wafting away an unpleasant smell. "But that horrible stench would be detectable for weeks."

Chance

That was when she took in everything she was seeing. He was wearing a freaking kimono. *Why?* There was no way to continue imitating Cadmael's vacant stare anymore. Her mouth hung partially open as she squinted to get a better look at the blue, pink, and purple floral outfit the vampire wore so confidently.

"You've got one too. I enjoy matching outfits with my toys…" he waved his fingers toward the large chair in the room's corner, where a black, green and blue, flowered kimono rested. "I upgraded you to a toy again." He plucked a piece of lint off his chest. "It's not entirely your fault that Cadmael was lax in security, so he received the rest of your punishment."

Chance's eyebrows furrowed in pity as she looked up to where Cadmael stiffly stood, expressing no emotions on his face. How much punishment had he received because of her? Didn't he say her escape attempt was something the twisted vampire wanted, anyway?

Her gaze returned to the ridiculously dressed vampire. Talk about cultural appropriation. She wouldn't even feel comfortable wearing something like that, and she at least had *some* Japanese blood. She gritted her teeth and balled her fists, but there was nothing she could do.

"Cadmael will get you ready for the party…" Eadrich smirked as he turned to leave. "Oh, and Cadmael, you can pick her symbol."

As she turned her face up to look at the servant, she saw his eyebrows flicker in surprise. It was rare for him to be so expressive. Eadrich walked away before she even looked back at the doorway.

"Seriously?" Chance whispered, aghast.

Cadmael quickly began undoing the cuffs that held her to the bed. Once finished, he helped her sit up and lightly massaged her arms to improve the blood flow. Chance hissed between her teeth as the searing pain in her arms subsided and her hands tingled less.

Chance groaned quietly as Cadmael attempted to help her to her feet.

"I'm so hungry…" she whimpered and then gasped as Cadmael suddenly grabbed her upper arms and forced her to face him.

"Don't eat or drink anything unless the master gives it to you." His blue eyes had a sternness to them she never would have imagined.

He often could come across as cold and distant. But commanding… no. Cadmael was soft-spoken, bordering on sweet. He appeared as though he could be stoic, but not someone with leadership qualities.

"I-uh," Chance stuttered as she clutched his dress coat to keep herself on her feet.

She was so tired and so hungry. Everything on her body, including her eyelashes, hurt.

"You're going to get a proper bath tonight," Cadmael informed Chance as lifted her up into his arms.

She couldn't help feeling relieved as her feet left the ground. The muscles all the way down the length of her legs were aching from disuse. Her jaw trembled as she buried her face into Cadmael's chest so he couldn't see that she was on the verge of crying, yet again. He probably thought she was such a baby because she was always crying. He'd suffered this life for years and in the time she'd been there, she had never seen him cry.

The strong young man carried Chance out into the hallway. He turned left and entered the room next to hers. He set her down and reached out, flicking the fight on. The fluorescent light was blaring, making Chance blink several times.

The room was a white marble bathroom without a mirror. To Chance, it looked like the tackiest, most overdone room she'd ever seen. The bathtub, floor, walls and counter were marble. When she looked up, it surprised Chance that the ceiling had drop-in tiles and pod lights. She had almost expected the ceiling to match everything else.

Cadmael bent over the tub and turned on the water. As he reached into the water flow, testing the temperature with his fingers, Chance glanced at the doorway. For only a split second, she considered running out the door and making another escape attempt. Her mismatched eyes stared at Cadmael's backside for a moment as she convinced herself not to try. She slowly shook her head, settling on waiting. She would pace herself, maybe find a better opportunity to get out, which would be more of a sure thing.

As the tub filled with water at the temperature he had set, Cadmael turned to face Chance, holding a hand out for her. Shakily, she slipped her fingers into his, which were unexpectedly callused. She carefully stepped into the tub and allowed him to help her sit down in the lukewarm water.

A part of Chance wanted to lie down and let the warm water wrap around her like a soothing blanket. Another part of her feared that if she let her guard down, Eadrich would appear from nowhere and drown her.

She whipped around to stare at the open doorway as classical music began playing downstairs. Chance's hands flung to her chest to cover her breasts as strange voices rang out over the music. Cadmael turned to the door and slid it closed. He clicked the small lock into place, making Chance relax instantly.

It was strange how relaxed she had become with being naked in front of the young man. He had never seemed to look at her with lust or sexual desire. He'd probably be beaten by Eadrich if he did. Chance watched as he moved to the sink, opened the cupboard and took out a small basket that had everything he could need for her bath.

Oh, my God! Why did I just look at his butt?! What the hell is wrong with me?

Cadmael had only ever been interested in Eadrich. She couldn't explain why she kept snatching glances at the pretty man. Cadmael picked up the white plastic cup from the basket and tucked his tie into his dress shirt to make sure it didn't dangle into the water.

His warm hand slipped beneath Chance's silky black hair to cup the back of her neck. As he leaned her back, her hands suddenly flung out to grab the edge of the tub, halting her descent. Chance's eyes were wide, and her jaw trembled. She gasped lightly in her panic, unable to stop the fear that she was going to drown.

"It's alright. It's just us in here. My order was to only care for your needs."

His voice was so soft and comforting that it barely echoed over the sound of water gushing from the faucet. Chance stared into those sweet blue eyes and let her fingers peel themselves from the edges of the tub. Though, as the servant lowered her into the water, her hands dragged along the sides as if slowing the movement to a speed she could feel more comfortable with.

When the back of her head touched the bottom, she felt like an idiot. The water barely reached her ears. The vampire and his servant had wound her up so tight, making her so mentally ready to be tortured, ready to die, that she expected it to come at any moment.

Tears leaked from the corners of her eyes and she angrily blinked them back. No! No more crying. Thankfully,

Cadmael seemed to ignore them, as he scooped up water and poured it along her hairline. His fingers delicately slid through her locks, massaging her scalp lightly. It felt so good, so soothing. Chance closed her eyes and took a slow breath, trying not to moan her approval.

The water's warm embrace had become strangely comforting. She sensed him move away and squinted up at Cadmael as he turned to pick up a small bottle of shampoo from the white wicker basket.

"Hmm," Chance moaned as the smell filled the room. "Strawberry. It smells so good."

Cadmael gave her an extremely brief, warm smile as he squeezed out some shampoo into the palm of his hand. That smile gave her butterflies. The water level slowly rose until it was just about to block her ears. Cadmael set the bottle down and used that hand to turn off the water before turning back to her. He rubbed his hands together, making the shampoo bubble and froth between his palms and along his fingers.

Chance couldn't help returning his serene smile as Cadmael leaned over the edge of the tub. His fingertips gently slid along her scalp. He massaged as though his fingers were conducting the symphony playing from the ground floor beneath them. She slowly closed her eyes, enjoying the soapy fingers rubbing her.

His hand slipped to the back of her neck, massaging the tense muscles from beneath the water. He used the hand on the back of Chance's neck to sit her up. She had been feeling so good in the water with his massage. She sighed softly and bowed her head forward, feeling a trickle of soapy water roll down her forehead. She closed her eyes to make sure it didn't go into them. He rubbed the shampoo thoroughly into her hair.

"Tilt your head back," Cadmael whispered softly, but Chance stubbornly didn't obey.

Sitting in a nice warm bath, with the smell of real shampoo wafting through the air. Cadmael's tender touch was so comforting that it almost made her feel safe. Tears made their ways from the slits in her tightly closed eyes, dripping into the water alongside the soap.

Cadmael didn't seem interested in trying to force her to follow his request. He simply scooped up water into the cup and drizzled it into the top of her head. He did this several times, while using his free hand to glide along her hair, helping rinse the bubbles out. Soapy water trickled down her face as she kept her head bowed.

"I'm sorry…" Chance whimpered, not even knowing why those were the words that slipped from her lips.

Cadmael started massaging her scalp again. Judging from the smoothness of his finger movements along her hair, he must have applied conditioner. He collected her hair and pulled it over her shoulder so he could have access to her back.

"For my punishment?" the young man asked, sounding confused.

"I- I dunno…" Chance whimpered and flinched as she felt a soapy cloth rub against her back. "How can you live like this? How do you survive?"

The cloth stopped moving in the middle of her back. Slowly, Chance turned her head to stare up at him as she fought the tears that wanted to roll down her face. The young man had a 'far away' expression. His blue eyes suddenly flashed to meet Chance's mismatched eyes for a split second, before his brows furrowed and he glanced away.

"I won't survive," he whispered and dragged the cloth across her skin again. "This has been my life nearly as far back as I can remember." She watched him closely, and he fixated on his task, moving on to washing her arm. "I'm going to die."

The way he said it was so matter-of-fact that it freaked Chance out. How could he seem like he didn't even care? How could he be so calm about it?

"When?"

"When my master wishes." He maneuvered her hand to wash between her fingers and then the palm.

"What? So, you don't even know when? He could just decide tomorrow?!"

"Master will find the next pet before then. I will teach that pet, like the one before, taught me." Chance felt her cheeks heat as he washed across the tops of her breasts. "Once my replacement is ready, my legacy will end." He rinsed the cloth and brought it up to add more soap. He washed the rest of her chest as he continued speaking. "I have the honor of choosing how, though."

He took a slow, deep breath as he rinsed the cloth again.

"You have the honor!? That's it?" The pitch in her voice surprised herself.

"That's not all. I will be cremated, along with all my paintings. Every trace of my existence will be removed from this world."

Her expression must have been one of pure horror as she stared at the man who she was sure was only a few years younger than herself. He was so ready to die at such a young age that he'd completely come to terms with it. The damned fool seemed ready, almost like he was waiting for it to happen!

"This is all your life is? That monster tortures you and then kills you. A pet is the same thing as a toy."

"Vampires will be our end," he murmured and slipped the cloth between her thighs, pushing his material covered fingers between the lips and wiggling them.

Chance gasped loudly, her hands flung to his forearm to hold on tight. He didn't linger in that area a moment longer than he needed to. Cadmael lifted the girl's leg and washed its length before scrubbing her foot. He nonchalantly switched feet, then worked his way back up her leg.

CADMAEL

They did the rest of the bath in silence. It seemed she was basking in her sorrow or plotting her next escape attempt.

There was no way for him to be sure. A tiny, insignificant part of him wished she would have escaped. There was something different about this toy. Ever since he was a child, countless toys had come and gone.

It took Cadmael nearly fifteen minutes to thoroughly scrub the rest of her body. He constantly glanced at her face to read her features, but she did a decent job at hiding her thoughts for once. He hooked a hand towel over his forearm before lifting her from the tub, soaking his suit. He quickly carried the girl, naked and wet, to her room.

Chance's arms snaked around the back of his neck, her cool fingers toying with the short curls at his nape. As her fingertips tickled him, goosebumps prickled their way across his skin. He set the toy down on her feet and allowed his eyes to examine her briefly. She had not a single mark remaining from her punishment. His master had given him a chore to ensure that there would not be a single blemish on her skin.

The girl suddenly gasped as she stared down at her body.

"My scars," she whispered.

"I cut them open and applied vampire saliva to heal them. Master didn't want any defects in his toy for this evening."

The girl looked far more upset by the removal of her old scars than she should have been. Her hands traced her pristine skin as though in search of a mark that she would never find. Her jaw trembled before she blinked back tears that threatened to roll down her cheeks.

For nearly a split second, he felt tempted to question what her problem was this time. Did she like having flaws?

Her eyes met his before she answered his unspoken question, "The scars were from a car accident." Her hand stopped tracing where her scar had been on her stomach and moved to her thigh, where he had also removed an extremely grotesque looking piece of tissue damage. "My parents died… and these scars were all I have left of them."

Cadmael cocked an eyebrow at the girl. He never would have thought that scars could hold a sentimental value for someone. He had countless scars. She looked so pathetically heartbroken as her unique eyes searched her perfect skin for any remaining flaws.

"Some scars are only skin deep." Cadmael murmured softly to Chance as he lightly patted her skin dry, never rubbing for fear of scraping the cloth against her flesh. "Healing the outside will never remove or undo the damage within. Those wounds you will carry until you die."

Chance lifted a hand and placed it in the center of her chest as if feeling for a heartbeat. Apparently, his words of empty comfort were enough to soothe her. *Until she died… however soon that might be.* Even if he knew the meaning behind those wounds, he still would have removed them as per his master's wishes.

It took Cadmael nearly forty-five minutes to dress the toy in her outfit. He had studied how to put the kimono on the girl properly. He placed each fold in the fabric meticulously. Everything had to be perfect for his master. He also applied makeup and three different perfumes to different areas of her body to ensure a uniqueness to her smell, no matter where their master breathed in her scent. One could say that Cadmael was a man of many talents, though he had no choice but to be a jack of all trades. He simply never knew what his master would require of him.

Neither of them had said a single word for the rest of the time it took him to perfect her appearance.

Finally, Cadmael stopped fussing over the lingering details of her outfit and gave a satisfied nod while crossing his arms over his chest. He allowed his eye to trace every detail of her outfit, looking for the slightest wrinkle or imperfection.

His hand slipped into his pocket, feeling the permanent marker that still waited to be used. Cadmael took a slow, even breath as he contemplated what to do with the marker. His master had clarified that the decision was Cadmael's… But he knew that if he made the wrong choice, his master would take it out on him. When given any opportunity to do anything or exercise his freedom of choice, he needed to ask, 'what would please Eadrich the most?'

Cadmael tentatively retrieved the marker with his eyebrows drawn down in deep thought as he contemplated his options. He toyed with the cap before pulling it off and raising the marker. As he stepped toward the girl, Chance lifted her hands defensively and waved them through the air while stepping away.

"What are you doing?" she demanded.

"All owned persons must be marked tonight."

Her eyes narrowed for a second. Owned persons meant toys and slaves. She nodded hesitantly and pulled her arms in to wrap around her torso. As Chance hugged herself, Cadmael pressed the cold felt tip of the marker to the center of the girl's forehead. Before he really thought about it, his hand moved of its own accord, drawing a small, bold circle on her otherwise unmarked skin.

He sighed as he withdrew his hand, hoping his selfish decision would also please his master.

"What did you do?" Chance questioned, raising a hand to her forehead.

"Don't touch it." Cadmael warned, catching her hand in his. "With that mark, you are protected and should survive the night."

She nodded, wrapping her fingers around his in a brief display of appreciation or possibly affection.

"Thank you," Chance whispered softly, giving Cadmael a shaky smile.

It was likely that she had just realized that it was his decision to ensure her safety with that mark. He pulled his hand from hers and stepped away. There was no point in getting attached. He needed to remember to keep himself distanced from her.

"Don't move from that spot. Master will be in shortly."

Cadmael backed away, giving her an encouraging half-smile before turning around and leaving Chance standing in the center of her room, by the base of her bed.

22

To The Party

Chance

Chance stood there for what felt like forever, though it was probably only about 20 minutes. She had closed her eyes while listening to the music from the main floor as it echoed up the stairs and into her room. Her room? It revolted her that she actually accepted that this space was hers.

"Now that is a sight to send a man into oblivion." A familiar, drawling voice resounded from the entrance. "You look like you were almost worth every penny of the million dollars I wasted on you."

Chance's brows drew down as she opened her eyes to stare at the vampire in the doorway. Her breath caught in her throat when she took in his appearance.

"Wha-? I thought…" she started, but cocked an eyebrow as she examined his clothing.

Eadrich rested his forearm on the frame of the doorway as he leaned his weight on it. His graying skin, that had once been brown, was covered with odd tattoos that resembled cave paintings. He wore a long white skirt with lime green trim and a green sash around his waist, holding the skirt on. Over his shoulders, Eadrich wore a see-through cape that did nothing to hide his many tattoos. If she didn't loathe him, she likely would have found him mesmerizingly attractive, especially in such peculiar traditional-looking garb.

"The theme of tonight's party is nationalities and origin stories," Eadrich divulged as a mischievous grin pranced its way across his dark gray lips. "I was going to show my respects to your heritage, but Cadmael told me the outfit I wore was the female version. Turns out he bought two for you in case I'd like for you to do a costume change midway through the party. I'd have worn it anyway, but I feel it would be disrespectful to your ancestors for me to cross-dress." He sighed, looking sadder than he should have.

"But… is that some sort of ancient Native American outfit?" Chance asked, feeling rather ridiculous for needing to.

"Have you forgotten already, silly toy? I'm Mayan." His hand waved through the air in a flourish, drawing her attention back down to his skirt that reached midway down his thighs. "This was every-day garb, which I had Cadmael weave for me several years ago. That boy is gifted with a loom."

As her eyes traced the intricate designs on the white and green skirt, her eyebrows rose. How was it possible for Cadmael to have yet another talent?

"Let us go! We are already fashionably late," Eadrich announced as he turned his back on Chance, placing his hand on his hip and nudging his elbow out toward her.

Chance stepped forward, nearly stumbling as she realized the tight wrap of her skirt severely constricted her legs' movements. It took far too much focus to make sure her steps were meticulously small. Shuffling herself forward gave her the appearance of gliding across the floor.

"So much focus on your face for such a simple task as walking," Eadrich taunted her, sounding more playful than cruel.

He seemed to be in an exceptionally good mood. Hopefully, it meant that she'd be safe from any torture for the evening. As they left the room, he thankfully walked at a pace that matched her abilities in that skirt. Reaching the top of the stairs, Chance hesitated, hearing a ruckus of voices, music, laughter, and screaming from the floor below. Her free hand reached out to the railing, adding extra support as the pair began a long descent down the stairs. She could already see people and creatures milling about, entering and exiting through the main door.

An Englishman with a long black tailcoat turned to face them with an enormous smile, slightly obscured by a large handlebar mustache that seemed to float aimlessly across his top lip.

"My lord!" the rotund man exclaimed as he bowed deeply to Eadrich. "It's a pleasure to see you again!"

Chance gasped, realizing that the man had no eyes. She froze, unable to take the next step, only to be dragged down the remaining stairs by Eadrich, who hadn't slowed in the slightest. Staring into those dark holes made her stomach turn as her hand removed itself from the railing to clasp tightly onto Eadrich's forearm.

"Calvetein, you grow younger with each millennium," Eadrich drawled, complimenting the stranger.

"Oh, dear man, it must be the virgin sacrifices. They do wonders for skincare," Calvetein responded as the two creepy old women with him nodded enthusiastically.

The term 'women' should be used lightly to describe them as they had wrinkle upon wrinkle, so intensely that their gender was nearly indistinguishable. One of them had a blue tinge to her skin, while the other had fluorescent green swirls that vanished between the folds of her skin. Chance's breath caught as the blue-skinned creature turned to her with red eyes far too big to be human.

Chance accidentally let out a soft whimper as she hugged Eadrich's arm while trying to put the ancient vampire between her and the monsters.

"What a delicious looking little human you've found, my old friend," the old, green, witchy looking creature hissed through jagged fanged teeth, resembling the mouth of a shark.

Chance's eyes widened in horror. She could barely breathe, because Cadmael had wrapped the material around her waist so tight. That wasn't the only reason that her breaths came in sharp, short panting gasps for air. Fear bubbled up inside her, making her head swim and her chest constrict in pain.

"Vanilla," Eadrich responded, sounding prideful while flicking his fingers toward Chance.

"So is mine!" Calvetein responded, waving his hand at a young man with an 'O' marked on his forehead in black marker.

The boy waited with the same expressionless features Cadmael had as he stood with his back to the corner by the kitchen door. Chance tilted her head to the side, eyeing him curiously. He seemed well-fed and cared for. She actually felt envious of the boy with haunting, sad eyes.

"Mighty young, isn't he?" Eadrich questioned with a raised eyebrow.

"In this day and age, it's the only way to ensure that they are untainted." The monster waved his hand impatiently at the boy, who quickly bolted to his master's side to hold up a hand for him. "Care for a taste?"

"He's too young for me to really enjoy." Eadrich shook his head slowly, giving a frown as he wiggled his arm free of Chance's grasp to wrap around her shoulders.

"Oh, but wasn't that pet you drag around only a wee thing when you bought him from his mother?"

Chance's hands came to her mouth as she gasped louder than she would have liked. She raised her eyebrows while turning her gaze to stare up at Eadrich. His own mother sold

Cadmael to the twisted vampire?! How old was 'wee thing'? He must have been really, really young, considering this creature's own slave looked to be no older than fourteen.

Calvetein dribbled saliva from his lips onto the boy's wrist. The mucus splashed the young man's skin, sizzling loudly as it seared his flesh. The burning flesh created a smoke-like vapor that rose in the air toward the monster's face. Calvetein breathed in the essence, basking in the aroma of burning flesh.

The boy silently gasped, attempting to pull away from the creature's iron tight grip. His face was full of resolve as he clearly had expected the pain, but when it came, instinct made him try to withdraw. The boy was left weakened, gasping for air as if the monster had sucked all his energy out. Calvetein released the young man's wrist, letting the boy drop to his knees. The boy simply sat on the floor with his eyes closed, looking like the creature had sucked the life-force from his body.

Chance fought the urge to yell at the monster as she stared down at the boy that she could do nothing to help. She couldn't even help herself. She turned her body toward Eadrich, pressing herself against him as though hoping he would simply bring her back upstairs. She closed her eyes tightly, praying for some way to leave this terrible party.

"I bid you adeiu, as I have other guests to greet." Eadrich nodded to the group before leading Chance past the library.

As she glanced in, the room seemed full of people and monsters socializing. At this rate, she was certain it was monsters and their slaves. There wouldn't be any free humans in this awful place.

They had locked the second door in the entranceway when she'd made her escape attempt. Now it stood wide open, welcoming guests to enter. The first thing she noticed about the room was that the many smells permeating the space were overwhelming. It smelled of perfume, incense, death, and blood. But the aroma that drew her attention and made her mouth water was the scent of food. Chance took a slow deep breath, having to swallow the saliva that built up from the intoxicating aroma. Her abdomen ached painfully with a hunger that it never knew before her abduction.

A Great Dane pranced out of the room and quickly stepped aside to make way for Eadrich and Chance to pass. It bowed its head and Chance knew it had to be a Hellhound. As they approached the gaping mouth of the double-door wide entrance, a creature that Chance was sure could only exist in some Hentai stumbled into the entrance. Tentacles. Just tentacles.

"Oh! I see you've come as entertainment tonight, Lucifer." Eadrich said to the monster.

LUCIFER?! There was no fucking way…

Lucifer's response was something completely unintelligible, while the tentacles hanging from what she assumed was its head waggled back and forth in excitement. Chance pressed her cheek against Eadrich's cold chest as her arm snaked its way across his lower back. If she could have melded with the vampire, she would have. The smell coming from the tentacled beast was likely the scent of death that had wafted through the air as they approached.

"Oh, you like her, do you?" Eadrich chuckled, tightening his grasp around Chance's shoulders to press her harder against himself. "If my toy isn't a good girl, I'll change her mark for you."

Chance's eyes bulged as she whipped her head back to stare up at the vampire.

"Master," she pleaded in a shaky whimper while her free hand snaked its way up his chest.

Before she could say anything more, Eadrich continued walking past Lucifer to enter the room. Chance gasped loudly as she stared around. The walls were two floors high, with innumerable chandeliers hanging from the ceiling. Another gasp escaped her when she realized half those chandeliers were people! The slaves were hanging from chains and ropes at different heights, each with candles placed across their flesh to create some macabre human light. To top off, further into the space, on both sides were several tables filled with foods that she could barely make out through the crowd. Beyond them, at the furthest end of the room, was an entire orchestra on a stage.

Directly to Chance's left hung an exceptionally pretty woman with bright red hair worn in ringlets, nearly touching the ground. She had a single line down the center of her forehead. The girl's green eyes met Chance's, and they stared into one another's gaze for far too long.

"Do you wish to be a light in the darkness?" Eadrich whispered in her ear and guided her closer to the chained woman.

"How?" Chance whispered, but realized nearly immediately how it was done.

"Hot wax." Eadrich murmured, before reaching out and yanking a candle from the girl's upper arm, which was twisted behind her back. "And glue." He added as she screamed mutedly into the solid ball gag tied into her mouth.

Chance's eyebrows drew down as she stared pityingly at the woman who was just as trapped as she felt.

"It's a macabre art exhibit from a rather famous dark forest sprite." As he smirked down at her, he held the candle close enough to Chance's cheek that she could feel the heat from it. "Want to know a secret?"

Chance hesitated. She didn't want to know anything. She wanted to lock herself away in her room and never come out again. However, the last thing she wanted to do was displease Eadrich. He seemed to be in an exceptionally cheerful mood, and she feared destroying that and facing his wrath. She was careful not to allow her eyes to stray from his gaze to the candle.

"If my Master wishes to share one with me." She gave an answer that was nearly as perfect as something Cadmael would say.

Eadrich chuckled softly before responding, "The artist tied each slave with both chains and ropes. Then placed some candles in such a way…" He moved the candle so the flame could lick at one rope holding the red-haired slave. "That at random, a slave risks falling to their death."

The rope, which was tied around the girl's shoulders, cracked loudly as it snapped and gave way. The upper half of her body suddenly swung down toward the floor in a rattle of chains and a gurgling scream.

Chance gasped, flinching away from the girl as she swung toward the ground. Her hands shook as she instinctually reached out to the slave. Before she could make contact, Eadrich dropped the candle to the ground and used his grip around her shoulders to guide her away from the other woman, who had clearly fallen unconscious after her head hit the ground. Chance couldn't help trembling as she constantly glanced back at the redhead.

She barely noticed when more monsters greeted her master, praising him for such a successful event. When he realized she hadn't been paying attention, his fingers painfully dug into her upper arm. She turned her gaze toward his face as she tried to pull away from his hand by pressing herself against him. She touched her cheek to his chest, listening to the silence from within. He clearly wanted her undivided attention, like she was some show piece. That much was clear from the jealous way he had reacted.

She kept one arm beneath his see-through cape, wrapped around his waist as he guided her around the room. Her free hand trailed his six-pack, tickling the icy flesh as he spoke to his guests.

She was so tired and so hungry. The smell of food made her stomach twist painfully. Among the monsters were other slaves. More than half had a large circle on their foreheads, others stood at the side with X's or wavy lines. Two or three slaves had squares marked on their foreheads. All the slaves hanging from the ceiling had a single line down the center of their foreheads.

She enviously watched as people approached the buffet tables, taking heaping helpings of food. Even some slaves approached the food table. No one stopped them. No one cared. Chance licked her lips, desperately considering trying to sneak some food.

Chance glanced up at Eadrich, who was speaking a foreign language to another vampire who wore an orange and blue skirt in a very similar style to Eadrich's. She couldn't help the surprised gasp as the vampire's hand flung forward, grabbing Eadrich's throat. He didn't even flinch, though she did, before staring in surprise at the scene that unfolded just above her head.

Eadrich smiled at the other vampire. Chance could feel him grow stiff against her beneath his skirt. He had a hard-on! She thought Eadrich was all domination and would never be aroused from being in a submissive position.

"Papa…" Eadrich purred, and Chance gasped again, staring from her master, then at the stranger.

Was this ancient creature Eadrich's sire?

"You can wander around down here, toy. Stay in the house," Eadrich murmured and finally dropped his arm from its resting place across her shoulders.

"Yes, Master," Chance whispered, trying her best to sound obedient, but he clearly didn't care.

Eadrich immediately began ignoring Chance as he slipped his arm through his Papa's and the pair began a gliding march toward the door while murmuring in the foreign language.

It took only a moment for Chance to realize how truly alone she was. As she stared around, no one even appeared to notice her, and when they did, their eyes landed on the 'O' on her forehead before they walked away.

This was what she had been praying for! Chance made a beeline toward the buffet table. The aroma rising from the food was inexplicable. Her nostrils were filled with the smell of spices she had only ever dared to imagine, but upon closer inspection, a sinking feeling erupted in her gut.

She didn't recognize anything at first glance. Maybe a glass of punch from the large crystal bowl would satisfy her. She carefully slinked along the table, toward the punch. Chance's eyes scanned the delicacies, looking for anything that would remotely resemble edible human food. There were gizzards and platters with crackers that had jelly and bugs on them. She spotted some other things that she recognized, but wouldn't dare eat them, like the crushed fingers and a dip that seemed to be congealed blood. Why did it smell so good?!

Finally, she got to the punch bowl, beside a bear sized.... Bear? The bear stood on its hind legs, using a ladle to scrape the bottom of the crystal bowl, trying to get to whatever was resting on the bottom. Chance picked up one of the clear wine glasses from the table, cradling it in her fingers as she waited for her turn.

The bear spotted her and scooped up a ladle full of liquid before turning to her. She held the glass out and he filled it, pouring the liquid into the cup. A soft plop sound came from the cup as something chunky fell into her drink. Chance sighed softly, hoping beyond hope that it was ice or some kind of exotic fruit. As Chance stared into the side of the crystal glass and gasped, a brown eye stared back at her. It had the pupil of a cat that freakishly dilated as if the thing could actually see her.

Chance quickly set the glass on the table while the bear guffawed down at her in a deep rumble which sounded intensely like a growl. Her hand flinched away from the cup as her eyebrows drew down and together. Why? Why was nothing here edible?

"Why?" she whimpered out loud by accident.

A voice rang out beside her that resembled a thundering purr, "Warlock eyes. Nearly extinct, they are." He tilted his head back and poured his glass of punch into his gullet, spilling much of it from the corners of his mouth, dampening his thick brown coat. "There's berries over here."

The bear moved down the length of the table as he chomped on a squishy eyeball that fell into his mouth from the bottom of his glass. He set his cup down before scooping up a handful of berries to hold out for Chance.

"See, berries," the bear-like creature encouraged, as he used his free hand to scoop a second handful for himself.

"They are delicious."

He shoved his pawful against his snout. The bear's lips peeled back, exposing his sharp teeth as his tongue snaked out to help scoop up the berries.

"Thank you," Chance whispered politely, as she tentatively reached out to the food that the bear offered her.

As her fingers scraped the pad on the bear's paw, it surprised her that the texture was rougher and less leathery than she'd expected. It reminded her of an older dog's paw.

Chance hesitantly brought one berry to her mouth, dabbing it with her tongue and sniffing it before actually inserting it. It's not that she didn't trust the bear, but she was in a room full of monsters. Reminding herself of that, made Chance stared around suspiciously. A few of the monsters seemed to glance in her direction, some openly staring. It was hard to read their faces, because some creatures didn't even have faces.

Chance drifted her hand that had the berries in it behind her back to hide her misdeed. Maybe she shouldn't have accepted them. With a pout, she glanced up at the bear. It was like he could read her mind. He nodded and lifted the edge of the tablecloth while slipping himself behind her to use his massive size to block her from the view of the nearby party guests.

"Thank you."

Following his lead, Chance slipped beneath the table. As soon as she was out of view, she gobbled down the few remaining berries. A part of her desperately wished the bear had given her more.

From beneath the table, Chance could see both foot and hoof shuffling about the room as creatures milled around in an unrecognizable pattern of socialization. Her breathing quickened and her heart raced when the thought occurred to her that any of those creatures could find her and suspect she was up to something. She could almost hear her pulse strumming inside her ears.

Her multi-colored eyes scanned the feet, watching for a

face to appear beneath the tablecloth's edge. It was only a matter of time before a monster found her. The last thing she'd want would be for someone to change the mark on her forehead. She could end up being tortured or fucked by a lineup of endless creatures. Her face felt hot, and she panted, finding the material wrapping around her chest and stomach to be more constricting than before.

The ever-familiar sound of a rope snapping echoed across the large hall. The slave screamed in terror as their chains rattled loudly. Monsters clapped and cheered, some collecting bets on which slave was going to be next and if they'd fall all the way to the ground or not.

If she got caught hiding, maybe she could end up being one of those chandelier people! Slowly, Chance's gaze moved toward the red-headed girl her master had tormented earlier in the evening. How could she forget about her?! This was her opportunity to help the girl, and she wasted it selfishly thinking of her own needs. She had to get to that girl. Maybe she could relieve her pain and suffering.

Chance forced herself to crawl out from beneath the table, on the opposite side than she had entered. There was about two feet of space between the table and the wall, so she teetered toward the wall, catching herself, while on the verge of collapsing. The room was spinning and not in the vampire venom kind of delirium.

She turned her back to the wall and leaned against it for support as her multi-colored eyes scanned the room to see if any of the creatures noticed her reappearance. The cold marble wall radiated a chill into the air that felt so good against her feverish skin. There were some glances in her direction, but the only one who openly stared at her was the bear, and she could swear the lips of his muzzle had curved into a dark smile while he watched her.

Chance's eyes closed and her legs nearly gave out as she swallowed the saliva that built up in her mouth. The nausea was almost too much to handle. Her head swam and darkness ascended before lifting. It was as though there was a veil over her eyes, making everything around her disorientating.

The one thing Chance knew was that she needed to stay focused and get to the redheaded slave. Chance used the wall as support while she groggily stumbled her way toward the door, slipping past innumerable monsters along the way. When she reached the girl, she slipped on something slimy covering the floor. The small flat slipper that squished her toes wasn't made for slick surfaces.

"Ugh!" Chance gasped as she landed hard on her hip.

Her hand slapped the floor next to catch herself, though it did no good. The hand slipped in the slime, landing Chance on her side. She squinted down through the haze at her crimson-soaked hand and arm. Blood covered the entire side of her outfit as she wound up sitting in it.

Chance's gaze shifted to the redheaded girl hanging upside down from chains strapped to her legs and waist. The chandelier girl's head pressed hard enough against the ground that her neck tilted uncomfortably to the side. There was a severe gash on the girl's forehead, which was likely where the blood came from. A head wound like that, along with her being hung upside down, would have created a greater flow of blood. This was too much blood.

Whatever Chance could see of the girl's face was far too pale. She reached forward, pressing her fingers to the slave's neck, smudging the blood from Chance's hand onto the girl's freckled skin. There was a pulse, and it was stronger than she'd expected!

Chance carefully stood, slipping and falling back down, twice. Her bloody hands fumbled with the Velcro straps, holding the girl in the air as Chance struggled to free her. Velcro, rope, and chains. They had used everything imaginable to hang the girl up.

If she could help just one person, maybe someone could help her in return someday. She glanced around and realized all the monsters in the room were staring at her. No. That wasn't possible. There was no way they'd all be looking at her. Chance's hands trembled as she froze, making eye-contact with many of the creatures watching her.

The noise in the room hadn't stopped. If everyone was really staring at her, then the sound of them conversing and listening to music would have halted. She was hallucinating?! The berries! That fucking bear!

So… she could trust nothing.

Chance took a deep breath, finally undoing the Velcro on the girl's waist, then her ankles. Both the slave and Chance crumbled to the floor in the redhead's puddle of blood. She did everything she could to ignore the surrounding creatures and keep her focus solely on the other girl. She wrapped a forearm around the girl's torso and dragged her toward the nearby wall by pushing out with her heel while heaving with her free hand. Her outfit made maneuvering nearly impossible. Once there, Chance sat the girl up against the wall, hoping to slow the blood flow.

Chance turned her back on the girl as she looked around, hoping to find something to press against the wound.

Before she could scream out, a hand covered her mouth from behind and dragged her into utter darkness.

WHAT THE FUCK WAS HAPPENING?

She struggled, trying to scream out as her attacker pulled her into the depths of hell.

NO! It had to be another hallucination!

The monster dragged her part of the way down a passage that was so narrow her flailing arms scraped the stone as she fought. The hand covering her mouth was icy, and the breath that beat down against her throat was strangely cool. The smell wasn't the strange cinnamon that hung on Eadrich's skin. Her mind was reeling, and her terror, combined with toxic berries, wouldn't let her think straight.

Chance bit down hard on the hand that covered her mouth, breaking the skin. Ashen flavored sludge filled her mouth, making her gag loudly as she turned her face away. She choked on the ooze while she struggled to spit it all out. Chance was positive that she actually swallowed some, which made her dry heave loudly. To silence her, the hand moved to her throat and squeezed until barely any air could pass her lips.

"Cadmael!" she whimpered out the only name that came to mind.

Fangs sank into the side of her neck as claws scraped along her skin, easily shredding the many layers of the thick materials of the kimono. From her chest, down past her groin. She barely managed to keep the material wrapped over her shoulders.

They moved down the long stone corridor while it fed on her. Chance's feet were forced to attempt walking, but with the kimono skirts still wrapped so tightly around her ankles, she had to be dragged. At least, until her legs gave out, and she collapsed, the monster followed her to the ground, landing so hard on top of her, it knocked the air from her lungs. Her head pounded as a pressure built behind her eyes. There was no way this was a hallucination caused by eating the berries. She was dying! Face down in a dingy passageway where no one would ever find her body.

The icy hand on her throat released its grip to slide down between her skin and the stone under her to grope her breast. Chance coughed and gagged with her throat burning painfully from the toxic sludge she'd ingested. She raised her hands up, clawing at what felt like cobblestone as she tried to wiggle her way out from beneath her attacker. His icy skin and fangs made her realize the monster was, in fact, a vampire.

Chance gasped as she felt something slick penetrate her core, pushing deep inside her as his fangs plunged into her flesh. Of course, the vampire wanted to fuck her as he drank her dry. They were horrible creatures. She tried to kick her heels behind her, but her legs were so tangled in material she couldn't move them.

"No," she whimpered in a throaty gasp.

From further down the hallway where they had come from, she heard a thunderous, snarling growl. Was it the bear? Why would he care about a vampire touching her when he was the one who encouraged her to eat toxic berries?

There was a scuffle overtop her, and the vampire's cock slipped out of her as he struggled with the beast. She could hear the monster snarling and its teeth snapping as it attacked the vampire. Chance cried out, wiggling forward by just a little bit as she tried to free herself from beneath the vampire.

There was a whimper as the vampire hurt the animal and it collapsed to the ground next to them.

"Damn mongrel." An English accent echoed in the dark, making Chance's heart skip a beat.

"Tyne?" she whispered before icy hands coiled around her throat and his throbbing cock rammed its way back into her.

23

FLAVOR WORTH DYING FOR

TYNE

Tyne had to throw that damn beast into the wall with enough force that he likely broke many of its ribs. The creature whimpered on impact and fell unconscious immediately, which allowed him to turn his attention back to the girl, who had nearly wiggled herself free from beneath him.

As she whispered his name, the horror in her voice sent him into a rage. He had never wanted to hear his toy call out to him in such a way, but the damage could not be undone. She knew what vampires were now, and no matter what, she'd see him as one of them. That pissed him off more than anything else about this whole damn thing. He had her trained to do whatever he wanted, and she believed it was her own choice!

He grabbed her arm and rolled her over so she was facing him. His hands wrapped so easily around that slim throat like it was made just for him. He felt her weak, warm little fingers digging into his hand as they clawed desperately at him, attempting to free herself from his grip.

Her mouth gaped open when she tried to scream. The only reason he could see the look of horror on her face was because of his vampire abilities. His original intent was to kidnap her and bring her home, never letting the girl out of his sight again, but the blood that coated her body sent him into a feeding frenzy. As he breathed in the blood, and her vanilla scent combined with the faint aroma of Eadrich's cinnamon essence, he lost all self-control.

As he sank his fangs into her breast, he could practically taste Eadrich's lips on her skin. It was like kissing his beloved sire once more. Tyne mentally cascaded into oblivion as he rammed his throbbing cock deep inside his prey.

Drinking from her had him so caught up that he didn't notice when she stopped struggling. He released her throat and licked the wound his fangs caused. He could hear her pulse slowing.

If he couldn't have her, then neither would Eadrich. He pressed his lips to hers, desperately wanting Chance to wake and return his kiss. He could taste something unexpected and familiar on her lips. Vampire blood. His blood.

Tyne turned his gaze to the smudged black blood on his palms from where she had bitten him. It was very possible that Chance had ingested some of the toxic blood from when she bit him. It dawned on him that if she died, he'd have sired her. If this human passed on with his blood in her body, she could turn into a vampire. It could take one drop or a thousand. There was no actual science to who could be sired and how much it took or how much time needed to pass.

If she turned, he'd be stuck with her stalking and following him for eternity. She would be drawn to him in the same way he was with Eadrich, and his father toward his own sire.

At that moment, Chance's heartbeat stopped.

The sound of silence in the corridor was deafening.

"No!" Tyne hissed in panic.

He quickly shifted his position and pressed his hands in the center of her chest like he'd seen on the television. One. Two. Three. Four. Five. He pumped hard against the area below her chest and above her abdomen. It looked like the right spot.

The longer her heart remained at rest, the more frenzied his movements became. CRUNCH! Something broke beneath her skin. Probably a rib.

Tyne didn't dare stop. He needed to bring life back into the helpless human body before it was too late. There was no huge gasp like in the movies and her heartbeat didn't spring to life with the excitement of a new lease on life. He hadn't even noticed her taking a breath. The only sound in the corridor was the slow rhythmic beat of Chance's heart as it eased awake once more. The thrumming was so soft, as though it struggled to find the desire to awaken fully.

For a few moments, Tyne wasn't sure if the beat would suddenly stop again. He waited. Tyne listened closely as it gradually picked up the pace. When he was sure the girl's heart wouldn't give out once more, he finally relaxed.

He carefully eased Chance up into his arms, having to turn sideways or her legs and head would scrape the narrow sides of the corridor. Tyne marched away, making his escape with his toy nestled in his arms.

When she awoke at home, things would be different. Tyne no longer had the patience to keep treating her like an equal. He was a vampire, and she was his dinner. She needed to start acting like it.

At the end of the corridor, Tyne unbolted a large oak door before slipping outside. The cool night air hit him with a fresh breeze that smelled of forest with the barest hint of decay. There was such a variety of creatures present in the house that the entire area smelled more of a graveyard than normal.

As long as the smell of cinnamon was nowhere near, he might succeed in his plan. If anyone else bought Chance, he would have either purchased her back or killed them and taken her. Tyne snarled loudly, glaring over his shoulder at the house as he marched away through the forest. He jostled Chance about slightly as he stepped over a large fallen tree.

"I saw you take that tasty treat," a deep, grumbling voice snarled from the trees to his left.

"Damn it." Tyne quickened his pace.

"I reported it to Master Eadrich immediately," the same voice hissed, but from somewhere in front of him.

He felt the skin prickle across his body as his rage built up. This damn forest beast was toying with him.

"Show yourself, you damned coward!" Tyne snarled, his accent growing thicker with his rage.

There, directly in front of Tyne, appeared a deer with massive antlers. The creature stared straight at the vampire and he could swear it was smirking. The deer's shadow appeared darker, denser and elongated, stretching farther than the dim moon overhead should allow.

"Don't make me say it," the monster taunted him mischievously, cocking its colossal head to the side which shifted the shadow beneath into the shape of a bear.

Tyne needed to attack quickly, before the forest dwelling spirit in front of him spoke again. He carelessly dropped Chance's unconscious form to the ground with a loud thump. It was possible something crunched beneath her as she hit the forest floor.

With an audible snarl, Tyne threw himself forward, stepping over Chance as he flew toward the spirit. In the moments that it took for him to cross the distance between them, the beast melted into shadow.

"Get back here, yeh little bastard!" he snarled, whipping around, trying to follow the creature with his gaze as the shadow snaked across the forest floor.

A giant bear suddenly appeared next to where Tyne had dropped Chance.

"Your sire commands you to return to him immediately," the bear blurted out in a growl before Tyne could charge in its direction.

Every word felt like a stamp on his soul, binding him to follow the command. He barely took two more steps upon the last word the spirit spoke. As the monster finished, his body robotically turned and began a solid but speedy march toward the house, where he could feel his master's presence.

The summons felt like a heavy burden on his chest. A weight crushed him from all sides, shooting pain down his limbs, growing more and more agonizing the harder he tried to resist. Tyne breathlessly panted for air while turning his head to look back in search of his prey. She was gone, as was the monster who'd caught him.

Eadrich was going to be so pissed. The ancient vampire had a temper and had warned Tyne that he shouldn't let Eadrich see him there again. He followed that command. Eadrich never even knew Tyne was there, and wouldn't have if that stupid spirit hadn't been watching Chance so closely.

He arrived at the house far quicker than he would have liked. His hand squeezed the handle too tight as he unwillingly twisted it. The door swung open, seemingly of its own accord, welcoming him to his doom.

One step. Two. A third. Each one sent an echoing reverberation of terror across his flesh. He didn't need to be told where his sire was. He could feel the pull as if it ripped at his insides.

He pushed past the milling people and creatures who were still enjoying the party. The sound of music rushed at him as the flickering candlelight blinded him. Even without sight, his feet kept moving him forward. His boot thumped into the front-side of a step before lifting higher to set down upon it. The stairs felt endlessly long and yet far too short.

At the top of the staircase, he stiffly turned to the right, took four steps, then turned left, finding himself at a closed door. Above the music, muffled screams of pain barely echoed from the other side of the door.

Tyne opened the door, exposing the decently sized bedroom that was once his, some 80 years prior. It was almost the same as the last time he was there, practically identical to the barren wasteland it was when he lived there. The chair in the corner had clearly been refurbished and the rest of the furniture had been restained. He had hated this room for decades, until he'd pissed Eadrich off and was sent away. Before then, they kept slaves and toys in the basement. Eadrich was telling him how easily he was replaced. He had slaves living in Tyne's room, as if announcing that all he ever had been to his sire was just another toy.

His eyes immediately turned to locate the source of the screaming. It was Cadmael, Eadrich's manservant. The young man lay naked on the floor next to the door, tied and gagged. Shadows blocked his ears so he couldn't hear, his eyes so he couldn't see, and his mouth so he couldn't scream. The shadows slithered and moved like snakes, searing his skin where they touched. Tyne could see through the shadows to where the boy's skin blistered across his face, arms, and torso. The torture made him scream against the magical shadow gag, which burned the inside of his mouth as he opened and closed it without noise.

The key feature of the room was a canopied single bed in the center of the space. Chance was sound asleep on the bed with a thick blanket covering her, hiding her nude body from his sight. The forest spirit who had returned with her was standing by the bed, speaking with Eadrich.

"As I said," Eadrich purred at the creature, his back to the door as he compelled Tyne to enter. "Having powerful allies means creating bonds. I cannot simply accept your charity. Please, tell me how I can repay the favor."

"The girl," the creature responded, shifting from the shadow creature to a bear as its paw reached out toward her face. "When you become bored with the creature… I wish to receive her."

Eadrich glanced over his shoulder and smirked as his eyes met Tyne's. Of course, the bastard would be tempted to agree to those terms, just to spite Tyne's attempt at stealing her back. He slowly shook his head, silently pleading with his father not to release the girl to that creature.

"May I inquire why you wish to have the girl, what you want with a human?"

"I have found this creature interesting. I will make her my bride."

Tyne gasped at the same time as Eadrich snorted loudly. Naturally, the sadistic vampire would find this to be a hilarious twist of events. He turned to the side, so he was facing the bed and could easily glance from the creature to Tyne. His smile was so enormous that his fangs glittered in the room's candescent lights.

"As her owner, I declare that when I no longer have a need for the girl, she will be your bride." Eadrich purred in satisfaction with a deviant smile pulling at his lips.

"NO!" Tyne yelled in a snarl. "That fucking human belongs to me, you goddamned thief!"

He took three steps before his sire hissed a single word, "Stop."

The amount of desire behind the command compelled Tyne to halt every motion. He could barely even think, never mind speak. He gagged on his desire to yell at the pair who made plans for HIS human. Tyne's entire body trembled fiercely as he opened his mouth, attempting to roar at the pair.

"My son…" Eadrich whispered, suddenly looking mournful.

The ancient vampire moved toward him at a lingering pace. His hand took up a corner of the blanket and peeled it back as he approached.

"Take a good, long, last look." The ancient vampire hissed as Chance's naked body came into view.

Tyne's gaze forcibly shifted to stare at the unconscious woman, memorizing every detail of her form. Her forehead had a nasty bruise, and there were scrapes on her cheeks, elbows, forearms and knees. The most disturbing of her wounds were the long slash-like claw marks down the center of her body, from her collarbone down to her navel. Tyne hadn't realized the damage he'd caused her in his bloodlust.

Eadrich released the blanket, letting it fall to the floor at his feet as he circled Tyne. Sometimes, his sire reminded him of a shark circling his prey before the kill.

Eadrich's arms wrapped affectionately around Tyne. His hands lightly traced Tyne's muscular shape as the sire embraced him from behind. Tyne could feel his father's icy cheek resting on his shoulder blade near the nape of his neck. He closed his eyes tightly, enjoying every second of having this much sought-after affection from his father. Eadrich turned his face so his chin rested on Tyne's shoulder. His icy breath cascaded across the younger vampire's neck. It was odd how an older vampire felt cold to a younger one.

"Now…" Eadrich hissed, finally releasing his grip on Tyne while walking around the face off with the vampire he sired over two hundred years ago. With the most sorrowful voice he had ever heard from his sire, Eadrich whispered one last command, "kill yourself."

The order that he thought would never come rang out in his father's voice.

"Pleas-!" He started to beg, but it was already too late.

His fingertips formed dagger-like claws, and with lightning speed, he plunged his weaponized hand into the center of his chest, piercing his heart.

There was no other agony like it. Every part of him burned like he had descended into the flames of hell. He stood there trembling, his eyes still unable to leave Chance's body to stare at his father. Slowly, Tyne shook his head as a tear rolled down his cheek.

How could his father kill him over a human? His claws sank deeper, shredding his heart, inevitably killing him.

Tyne couldn't even look down to examine his body as it turned dark and ashen. Eventually, his legs gave way, breaking in half, like a log in a fire that had been burned too long. The younger vampire fell to his back, feeling the burn spread across his extremities, searing his hair away to ash. He could feel pieces of his face flaking as it took over his eyes and nose. The flutter of movement sent warm ash from his body dancing toward the ground as he blindly waited for nothingness to come.

In moments, he would be this blackened, burned corpse, completely unrecognizable. Vampires turning to dust was a myth. It was as if the flames of hell had finally come to collect his demented soul while searing his body. His thoughts dimmed as all sounds vanished. The last of his senses were gone. Tyne was no more.

24

The Breeding

Cadmael

It had been nearly a week since the party and Eadrich had ordered for Cadmael to keep the girl heavily medicated while she recovered. He had maintained her medical health to the best of his abilities as he healed from his punishment for failing to ensure everything at the party went smoothly. Cadmael wasn't sure what had happened to Tyne for his disobedience, but there was a burned-up body at the base of the bed when he finally came to. The smell of burning flesh was still rancid in the room, even though Cadmael had cleaned, scrubbed and sanitized the area. His eyes flickered to the burn mark on the floor at the base of the bed. That was one hell of a way to die.

Cadmael sat in the corner armchair of the human's bedroom waiting for her to wake. His fingers subconsciously traced one of the long, thin burn marks on his cheek, which was already scarring. Normally, his master would have provided him with vampire saliva to heal his wounds and ensure his precious pet wouldn't have any visible permanent scarring. Not this time.

Chance moaned softly, drawing the Cadmael's attention from his deep thoughts. He heaved a sigh as he stood to approach her bedside. Those peculiar eyes of hers fluttered open, and she quickly glanced around her room.

"Wha…?" Chance coughed softly.

"You needed much rest to recover. I told you not to eat the food." Cadmael murmured as he limped carefully across the small room.

"Are you okay?"

"Always," Cadmael responded, and turned to face the door as his master's voice rang out.

"I know what I want." Eadrich smirked as he stalked his way into the room, glaring playfully from one of his victims to the other.

"How may I serve you, Master?" Cadmael made the mistake of asking.

He bowed smoothly to Eadrich. He was careful not to show how much pain he truly was in. His Master would punish him for it if he did.

"You're going to fuck her… and Malix Peek, do not disappoint me like last time."

"Yes, master." He quickly peeled off his pants and boxer briefs.

He left his shirt on, hoping to hide the horrible burn marks twining and snaking their way across his body. It didn't stop the ones on his legs from behind visible. Her eyes stared at them in horror and surprise. His eyes narrowed, daring the silly girl to point them out as he carefully climbed onto the bed.

Cadmael's eyes kept flashing nervously at his master when he leaned over her. His left hand trembled as he desperately massaged himself, attempting to stimulate a response. His brows drew downward, showing more expression than normal, but he couldn't focus on keeping his emotions hidden when under this sort of pressure. For some strange reason, this humiliation was far more unbearable than anything he'd yet faced.

"I'm waiting, Cadmael."

"Forgive me, master. I will do it now."

CHANCE

Cadmael rammed his hips into hers, but she felt no penetration. She couldn't help the look of pity that appeared on her face. There was also a feeling of dread. If he failed to do it, the violent vampire could become cross with them both.

He kept moving, smooshing himself against her in a desperate effort to fulfill that twisted monster's desires. Cadmael panted as he laid forward on his elbows, trying to bury his limpness into Chance.

"I'm sorry, Master." With those words uttered, he rested his forehead on Chance's breast and wept. "I can do it with you in me. I can make it hard like that… but, I'm so sorry, Master!" He blubbered as he cried hysterically.

His hot tears rained down onto her skin as he wept with such hopeless agony. The vampire growled, uncrossing his legs as he seemed about to stand. Chance needed to do something! ANYTHING!

"Wait, Master!" Chance begged. "We will do as you wish."

She watched as their master sat back in his chair, crossing his legs and waiting impatiently for them to fuck. Cadmael reached up and undid the cuffs on her arms.

"Get off me." She growled at Cadmael and pushed him, so he'd roll over.

Chance quickly undid the cuffs on her ankles and they switched positions, so he was the one laying with his head on the pillow. Chance glanced at their master and then examined

Cadmael's limp dick as the young man wiped tears from the corners of his eyes with the back of his hand.

She put his full extension into her mouth and began sucking gently, massaging the malleable flesh with her tongue. He had to get hard, or she would definitely receive his punishment, too. No matter how much her mouth worked, nothing happened. She reached out a hand and massaged his balls, desperate to get any reaction…except the one she got. Cadmael started whimpering again, hiding his tears by placing a forearm across his eyes.

Eadrich cleared his throat, obviously becoming very bored.

Cadmael had said he could get hard for Eadrich! But why not for her, or Tyne? What if she…

Cadmael moaned loudly. His heels dug into the mattress and his cock sprung to life in the back of her throat, nearly choking her as she slipped her fingertip into his asshole. She slid her finger in and out as her head bobbed up and down. The young man in her clutches had no choice but to lay there twitching helplessly in her grasp.

EADRICH

"Hurry up." Eadrich hissed, probably feeling irritated that they actually succeeded.

He had been looking forward to punishing them for failing. His mouth tightened in a knot as she went to climb on top of the boy. Maybe mixing it up, he would lose the hard on.

"No, I want him fucking you, not you fucking him." Eadrich's snarl rang through the room loudly.

CADMAEL

Cadmael nodded and quickly switched positions with the girl, scared that he would lose the strength in his throbbing cock. It tingled, almost like it was desperate for touch. He'd never experienced such a desire before. His master had always used him, but he received little to no gratification.

It was already becoming soft as he fumbled with himself, trying to put it inside her waiting hole.

"It's okay. Come closer," she whispered encouragingly.

As Cadmael pressed the tip of his cock against her core, Chance reached down and grabbed his ass cheeks in both hands. She pulled him hard against herself. Gasping as he filled her center.

Chance

The pair laid there gasping and panting in surprise and pleasure as the heat they shared was nothing like either had experienced with vampires. She moved her hands, encouraging him to sway his hips. He pulled out and pushed back inside, gasping again as he trembled from the strain. Each time he moved in, he did it with more enthusiasm and power until his movements were swift and vigorous, no longer in need of her encouragement.

"Kiss me," she instructed him and as their lips met, she felt a hot gush deep inside her.

Cadmael

He moaned into her mouth and pressed himself hard against her, unable to move as he filled her. Suddenly, Cadmael broke off the kiss and buried his face into the crook of her neck. He seemed unable to move or think. It was as though he suddenly realized that another person was in the room.

His head whipped up to stare in surprise at his master. As he examined the smile on Eadrich's lips, he seemed to become hard all over again.

"Do you wish us to be done, master?"

"No."

Eadrich stood and pulled off his robe. He was covered with tattoos that looked like a mix of cave drawings and Celtic designs. He straddled Cadmael and pushed himself into the boy with no preparation.

Cadmael screamed in agony into Chance's throat as his arms clenched tightly around her shoulders. His master pounded harder and harder into his asshole, uncaring if it ripped. All Cadmael could do was focus on ensuring his muscles remained relaxed, so he didn't tear. Luckily, he had years and years of practice.

Eventually, the pain gave way to pleasure, and Cadmael was panting alongside Eadrich. His cock still hadn't pulled out from deep inside Chance. It seemed unlikely, but as their master thrust deeper and deeper into the younger man, he became harder and even larger than before.

"I'm going to cum again," Cadmael warned, feeling his ass tighten around his master's throbbing cock and the tip of his member pulsated deep inside Chance's core as she writhed in pleasure beneath him.

EADRICH

"Good. Breed for me, my pet," Eadrich hissed loud enough that both the young ones froze in horrific realization.

It was too late though, Cadmael had already erupted a second time, even further inside Chance than the last time.

"Breed?" Cadmael whispered as Chance croaked the same word.

In that moment, with both those naïve creatures staring at him in fear, he couldn't help but cum. His icy juices filled

Cadmael's asshole.

"Get it out!" Chance cried out desperately as she pushed her hands against Cadmael's chest, but there was nothing he could do as long as Eadrich was rammed hilt deep in the young man's ass.

After a few minutes, Eadrich climbed off the pair, allowing Cadmael to get away from the girl. Chance pulled her legs up to her chest and moved to lean against the headboard, where she pressed her eyes into her knees and cried.

"Why?" she whispered, then lifted her head to glare at the vampire. "Why do this?"

"For the pups." Eadrich responded in cruel honesty, "Your offspring will follow in its parents' footsteps. It will live to serve me. Maybe you'll even have two and I can play with them and breed them, too."

CHANCE

Chance's face looked horrified. Pups? What the fuck did he mean by pups? Slowly, she turned her face to stare at Cadmael as if seeing him for the first time.

"You're a hellhound," she whispered, horrified by the thought. "Like those monsters who kidnapped me."

She couldn't even process everything the vampire had said. He wanted them to breed the children…with each other? She felt like she was going to be sick.

"Strap her to the bed. I don't want to risk another escape attempt…" Eadrich smirked as he leaned against the doorframe to enjoy the oncoming struggle.

Cadmael moved forward and reached for her arm.

"DON'T TOUCH ME!" she screamed at him.

He had no expression on his face as he grabbed her leg and yanked, dragging it to slide her down to the center of the bed. He was stronger than he looked. It didn't matter. She kicked at him with her other foot, smashing it into his fingers.

"Don't fucking touch me, you monster!"

He jumped on the bed. Spinning himself around, he saddled her thighs to hold them in place. As he struggled to wrap the straps around her legs, she sat up, and began scratching, slapping, and punching his back to force him to release her.

"I hate you!" She screamed as he shackled her other leg.

He stood on the bed over Chance and turned to face her. She nearly punched his groin, though his reflexes were thankfully fast.

"Do you even care? They'd be your children, too!" She hissed in his face as he grabbed both her wrists and pinned them to the bed over her head.

CADMAEL

Cadmael was careful to mask any emotions he had as he attached the straps to her wrists. He climbed off the girl and stood next to the bed, facing his master.

"Oh, one more thing I forgot to tell you… I won't need you after they are born. So that's when I'll finally eat you." Eadrich chuckled and walked out of the room, making his way toward his own lavish room.

The young hellhound took a moment to glance at the girl he'd just strapped to the bed. The girl who might very well be carrying his offspring.

"Get away from me!" she snarled. "Don't even fucking look at me!"

Chance twitched hard against her restraints.

"As you wish," Cadmael whispered, bowed to her, and marched to the door.

He grabbed the handle and closed it with far more force than necessary. Once outside the room, knowing his master was not around, Cadmael panted lightly, grabbing at his chest where an agonizing ache had erupted. Through the unimaginable tortured he'd grown up enduring, he never once experienced a pain like this. It only intensified as Chance's heart retching sobs penetrated the door and shot like an arrow straight into his soul.

25

THE ONE CHOICE

CADMAEL

Every day for three days, Cadmael returned to Chance's side to care for the girl. She screamed and yelled, whipping around and struggling every time he entered the room. He had no choice. He set up her IV's, brushed her hair, teeth, and washed her body. The entire time, she'd fight him, trying to bite him and snapping insults at him. Other toys that belonged to his master usually acted like this in the beginning, right until they died. Few even realized that Cadmael's shackles were invisible and eternal. She knew what his situation was like, and now she treated him horribly. She was only treating him like the monster he was.

Cadmael stood in the doorway, watching her sleep. He hadn't been able to force himself to rest since *it* had happened. He slipped his hands into his pockets and leaned on the doorframe. There were so many chores to do, but he didn't want to leave that room in case anything happened to her.

His master continuously taunted him. It was nearly impossible to keep his true feelings masked. If Eadrich had even the slightest suspicion on how much this whole breeding thing bothered Cadmael, he'd set up a breeding farm.

Maybe, if he was careful, he wouldn't wake her and could fluff her pillow. She had to be sore after laying there for so long, but his Master said she wasn't to be unshackled for any reason.

If she wasn't with child, would Eadrich force him to do it again, to try a second time? Or even a third? Cadmael closed his eyes, placing his hand on his abdomen, feeling bile rise in his throat. His mouth tightened as Chance groaned in her sleep.

Cadmael fanned his hand in front of his face, attempting to cool himself down. Two days ago, he noticed her hands and feet were freezing, so he did the only thing he could. He turned up the heat. His master didn't want a blanket placed on her, because he wanted the girl naked at all times. He wasn't concerned about getting into trouble for playing with the thermostat. Eadrich couldn't feel the temperature from the air and wouldn't notice the bill because Cadmael dealt with the finances.

"The older you get, the harder it is to tell what you are thinking." A drawling voice hummed from behind him.

Cadmael closed his eyes and felt the smallest of smiles tug at the corners of his lips. He took a slow, deep breath and allowed the rosewood and cinnamon scents that wafted from the ancient to caress his senses. He tilted his head to the side, basking in the ambiance of his master's presence. His heightened canine abilities were the only reason the hint of rosewood was detectable.

"Is that why you wish to replace me so soon?"

"*Soon*?" Eadrich slowly slid his hands up Cadmael's back,

toward his shoulders.

The vampire stepped forward, pressing his slender body against Cadmael's backside. His fingers trailed their way down Cadmael's front, sliding across the muscular curvature of the shorter man's chest and abs. His fingers strummed the rippling architecture that the hellhound worked so hard to sculpt. He had done his best to be so exceptional at everything that Eadrich wanted, hoping he would become completely indispensable.

"The one before me… he was older than I am now, but you've already decided to replace me with my offspring."

"You remember when I purchased you?" Eadrich whispered, dragging his cool tongue up the length of Cadmael's ear. "You just stared at me with those beautiful blues."

"I always wondered why you chose me. I wasn't even the most attractive pup in the litter."

"You were different." Eadrich began kissing his way down Cadmael's neck.

Eadrich's fingers unclasped the buttons on the dress shirt, making his pulse quicken. Having his master undress him made it difficult to remember his train of thought.

"How so?"

"You weren't afraid." Cadmael could feel his master's lips twist into a smile as Eadrich pressed them against his shoulder.

"I've lived with you most of my life, and yet, you shared more about you with this toy than you ever have with me in all that time."

"Are you envious, my loyal hound?"

"Always, Master"

"What do you wish to know?"

Cadmael paused. He hadn't expected this turn of events. Maybe it really was over. He would accept whatever his master decided his fate would be.

"I want to know how old you are and how old you were when…" His voice trailed off, unsure of what to say.

"I don't know how old I am." Now that Cadmael's shirt was open, Eadrich's hands slid along his skin, tracing the scars and lines of a tortured past. "A couple thousand years, at least."

Cadmael gasped out as Eadrich's icy fingers slid under the waistband of his pants. It dragged slowly across his sensitive skin, making his stomach muscles twitch and tense up.

"Fifteen."

"You don't look fifteen."

"Vampires age and decay simultaneously at an extremely slow rate, which decreases over time."

"Why are you willing to share this with me now? Is it because my time of service is coming to an end?"

"You've lasted longer than any who've come before you, my sweet boy."

Cadmael moaned softly as Eadrich tweaked his nipple. The feel of his master's icy hands wandering over his body gave him goosebumps, making him instantly aroused. He felt a tingle in his lower extremities as he hardened from the mere thought of Eadrich entering him.

"How will I die?" Cadmael whispered, feeling uneasy.

He had accepted that this was the way things were, but he also felt fear that he couldn't push down.

"It is your choice, as promised," Eadrich murmured before gliding his cold, wet tongue along the back of Cadmael's ear.

"When will she die?"

Eadrich snorted softly before answering, "I forgot you were a little busy when I made that decision." He chuckled softly. "You'll just have to wait and see."

He stuck his tongue in Cadmael's ear. It took a lot of focus not to instinctively flinch away from the uncomfortable sensation.

"What about the pups? Having her like this will weaken her during the pregnancy. She needs mobility."

"Do as you wish, then. It's your responsibility to care for the toy and my future pets."

"Why me? You've never done something like this before, have you?"

"You have been exemplary, and your time is ending. No others have been as perfect. I wish to see if I can replicate that."

Goosebumps rose on Cadmael's flesh. It was all just an experiment. He should have known that. He knew Eadrich well enough.

"I- were the other ones before me… were they scared?" His voice cracked as the vampire suckled on his earlobe.

"Does it matter?"

"No," Cadmael whispered, tilting his head to the side to offer his throat to his Master.

"Are *you* scared?"

"Sometimes."

"What do you fear?"

As Cadmael opened his mouth to answer, Eadrich's fangs sank into his flesh and the only thing to escape him was a deep, lusty moan. Eadrich's icy hands pulled Cadmael back against him, pressing his hardening cock between Cadmael's ass cheeks. He wished he wasn't wearing pants, but made no effort to remove them. He wouldn't. Not without an order or a sign that it was what his master wished.

"That I'll be alone," Cadmael answered as the vampire's venom made him rock hard while the blood-loss made his head throb and his mind spin.

Cadmael moaned softly, swaying his hips as he gradually became more and more high. His hands reached out, grasping the doorframe to keep himself on his feet. His master's fangs pulled out of his flesh, then rammed back in. Cadmael sucked air into his lungs with a twist of pain and pleasure that made him exhale in another desperate moan.

"Master," Cadmael purred softly, feeling his cock press painfully against the front of his pants.

Eadrich's nimble fingers undid Cadmael's pants. Cadmael gasped as his master freed his cock from his pants and boxers. The vampire's cool fingers massaged the entire length. Cadmael's head spun so hard that his knees grew weak. It took all his strength to remain on his feet. His legs trembled with the strain. With every gulp of blood that Eadrich took, Cadmael felt himself come closer to dropping to the floor.

Eadrich's forearm wrapped around his abdomen. He felt it holding him up like an icy iron bar across his gut, trapping him against his master.

"Do you want me to fuck you?" Eadrich hissed, but before Cadmael could respond, he added, "Or do you want to fuck her again?"

"I want to make my master happy." Cadmael answered Eadrich, feeling himself nearing orgasm.

"I think you should cum right now." Eadrich commanded and sank his fangs back into Cadmael's shoulder.

Cadmael moaned, letting himself explode hot semen into Eadrich's hand. His knees were giving way and his grip gradually slipped down the doorframe as his hands weakened. His eyelids grew heavier and his head bowed forward.

Eadrich touched his cum soaked fingers to Cadmael's lips. "Taste yourself, my sweet little pet."

Cadmael opened his mouth, sticking out his tongue. Eadrich's cum drenched fingers pressed gradually further into his mouth until he slipped them into the back of Cadmael's throat. Cadmael felt his throat constrict around his master's fingers as he struggled not to gag.

As he faced extreme blood loss, a thought crossed his mind, '*was master going to drink every drop?*'

Suddenly, Eadrich released him, dropping Cadmael to the ground, though it felt more like the floor came up to meet him. Cadmael lay there, with his face pressing into the hardwood as he struggled to hear his master's words.

"Drinking from you is disgusting. Like eating a wet dog."

"I'm sorry, Master," Cadmael spoke softly with tears rolling down his cheeks.

He wanted so badly to please Eadrich. He would never be good enough, but it didn't stop him from trying.

"Oh, and Cadmael. Find me a new toy to torment. This one is going to be boring for the next nine to ten months. So, make sure it's something that will entertain me."

"Anything for you, Master," Cadmael barely had time to voice before losing consciousness.

26

GENTLE MASTER

CHANCE

The hum of voices stirred her from the depths of darkness she traversed in her sleep. Chance didn't even think she had dreamed anything and could barely remember what happened the past several days. She would have groaned in pain from her throbbing limbs and sore back, but she didn't want them to know she was awake.

If he knew she was awake, he could end up torturing her more. The words he hissed at Cadmael, the conversation that was meant to be private. How could Cadmael sound so devout to that monster?! She swallowed, remembering that he'd practically grown up with Eadrich's twisted nature.

She wanted to hate both of them. Cadmael could set her free if he really wanted to. But the results for him would be catastrophic. SO WHAT?! Why should she worry about the results for him? If she told him she was going to try again, he'd probably try to talk her out of it. Or worse, he'd report it to his *beloved* master.

Hearing this private moment between the pair made her pity Cadmael, knowing that if given half a chance, she'd try to escape again. It was clear where his loyalty was.

There was a soft thump near the base of the bed. Did his request of Cadmael mean he would no longer torment her? The floor creaked right beside her bed and she knew Eadrich must have been there, watching her. She hadn't even heard him approach!

"You are so delicious," he told her, lightly stroking her bangs from her forehead with the back of his fingers.

His cool touch nearly made her flinch. If she could stay still enough, maybe he'd leave her alone, thinking she was sleeping.

"Normally, my toys die in the dungeon… but you've already survived longer than most… This room has been *your* dungeon. I think it's only fitting that this be your deathbed."

She wanted to flail and fight against her restraints, but she didn't dare move a muscle. Chance focused mostly on her breathing. She felt the mattress shift beneath her as he sat on the edge of her bed. He was probably watching her face for even the smallest of reactions, so she gave him none. She didn't even let her eyes move beneath their lids for fear he'd see her eyelashes flicker.

Eadrich's icy fingers trailed down her temple, cheek and then throat. His touches were featherlight, tender caresses like nothing she'd ever experienced. It took all her focus to keep her breathing level as his fingers slid down her breast. He circled her nipple, not quite touching. Chance heard him take a deep breath… an icy breeze cascaded across her breasts, erecting her nipples. Goosebumps rose, prickling her skin, but she stayed perfectly still. Why was his touch so arousing?!

"I cannot kill you… I can't even feed from you for nearly a year."

Chance could hear him ruffling around in the drawer

beside the bed.

"Don't worry, my precious little whore… I'll be back."

Nope. She wasn't falling for it. She did not open her eyes and didn't dare move. Even if he left the room, he was going to come back.

There was no actual way to know when he was coming back, or if he had already returned.

Without warning, something hot splattered onto one of Chance's nipples and trickled down the side of her breast. An obnoxiously loud gasp erupted from her, but thankfully, she squeezed her eyes shut tighter.

"Oh, clever girl…" Eadrich purred, and more hot liquid splashed onto that breast.

Chance didn't gasp. She barely kept it in. Her jaw quivered from the strain, but she clenched her teeth to stop the movement. He seemed to enjoy her being asleep and if she ruined that now, he'd definitely find a horrible way to torture her.

Whatever he poured on her seemed to have solidified as it cooled on her skin.

"Prepare for the other nipple," he warned her.

Thankful for the warning, Chance mentally readied herself for the hot wax to be poured on her other nipple. Hot wax suddenly splashed against her skin, but not where she expected. Her toes pointed and knees tried to draw inward to protect her center as Eadrich trickled hot wax onto her pussy's lips.

Chance groaned loudly as tears leaked from her eyes.

"Oh, does that mean you give up? Are you awake now?"

His taunting voice made her want to lash out at him. Instead, Chance forced herself to relax her entire body. She almost opened her eyes, but squeezed them tightly shut.

"Let me help you with that."

She felt panic rise as she waited for whatever that horrible monster had planned. She felt a droplet on her eyebrow and clenched her teeth to stop herself from gasping as it rolled down onto her eyelid. Then another droplet. Two more…

Slowly, the wax bled down from her brows to her eyelids as he slowly created covers to seal her eyes shut.

Once her eyes were firmly sealed shut, he trickled some wax across her throat, nearly making her gasp in surprise. It trickled to the sides of her neck, disappearing into the bed beneath her as it cooled, leaving wax paths across her flesh. Chance considered telling Eadrich that she was awake, but quickly decided against it. If wax play was the worst part of her experience for the day, then she would lay there and take whatever he offered.

After she was thoroughly covered in trails and splat marks of wax, Eadrich peeled the wax from her eyes. Chance refused to open them. As he pulled the wax, she had to hold her eyes closed tighter, feeling like he was trying to rip her eyelashes out. There were a few spots where she was sure the wax had burned her, but she still barely reacted.

Without warning, his fingers swirled, pressing the edges of her clit as they moved. She felt it growing like a beacon, demanding his touch. It took all her focus to keep her breathing level as her abdomen tightened. His fingers slowed, and she relaxed.

Chance's clit tingled as it grew desperate for more stimulation, and Eadrich complied, increasing the speed that his fingers moved. Her pulse quickened, but she forced herself not to gasp as her stomach tightened, preparing for the edge of oblivion.

His fingers slowed once more. A tear leaked from the corner of her eye in frustration. She couldn't believe that she wanted him to make her have an orgasm. It was the closest thing to a kind touch he'd given her since she'd been there. Her own thoughts and body were betraying her!

His speed increased again. Chance's toes curled before she could stop them. Her stomach muscles tightened as she felt her insides clench. She struggled not to tilt her head, though her lips parted as a tingling sensation spread across her body. Chance held her breath so she wouldn't pant during her orgasm.

"Don't want to breathe?" Eadrich murmured, sounding almost tender.

An icy hand, feeling like glass, covered her mouth and nose while she met with a whole-new level of pleasure. His fingers maliciously stroked her hardened clit, trying to push her beyond her limits. As the finishing waves of her release lessened, Chance panicked. Her hand balled into a fist. She tried to turn her face as her body desperately struggled for air. His fingers still hadn't slowed, and the tender sensitivity of her post-orgasm softness made her twitch uncontrollably as he continued his assault.

It started in a trickle which turned into a gush. Liquid escaped her body. Eadrich released his grip on her face. Chance's eyelids snapped open as she gasped for air. She coughed lightly as she stared up at his cruel, red eyes.

"No manners," he murmured as she got herself under control. "I'll have to 'talk' to Cadmael about that."

Did he mean to punish Cadmael yet again? Manners, for what?! The orgasm! That bastard was holding her prisoner and wanted her to *thank* him for making her orgasm.

Chance took a deep breath. "I'm sorry." She whispered out the apology, then added. "Thank you, Master."

Tears leaked out. She couldn't stop them. Just saying those words made her feel repulsive. After listening to him torment the young man, she couldn't just encourage him to beat the boy. These head games he played, he probably had Cadmael thinking he'd never survive without his master. It made her sick.

The room was quiet.

After what felt like an eternity, she finally opened her eyes again, hoping not to find Eadrich standing there. He was gone. There were no words to explain the amount of relief she felt at finding the room empty.

27

ONE MORE TRY

CHANCE

Chance was sure she must have laid there, dozing in and out of consciousness for hours. She really had to pee, but was so tired of pissing in her bed. Achingly, she lifted her hip, shifting her position as much as possible while still tied. The sheet was still damp because of Eadrich toying with her and making her cum. If Cadmael woke up, he might let her pee in the washroom.

Her stomach hurt so badly that Chance felt like she was going to puke. She knew it was actually very unhealthy for her to hold her bladder like that, but she was so tired of being treated like a feral animal.

A soft groan from the bottom of the bed made her eyebrows raise. Stiffly, Chance lifted her head to see more. Cadmael was still out of sight on the floor.

"Cadmael? Are you alright?" Chance whispered.

"Yes, toy, I am fine," He grumbled softly.

It annoyed the shit out of her that Cadmael had never called her by name. She suddenly spotted the top of his head rising above the edge of the bed as she slowly clambered to his feet. Cadmael teetered, grabbed the wall and stood with his eyes closed for a few moments.

A trail of blood trickled from his neck, down his muscular chest and stomach, staining the partially undone dress shirt.

"If he drank until you died, would you turn into a vampire?" Chance blurted out without thinking.

"No," Cadmael responded, and walked to the foot of the bed.

For a moment, she had forgotten how mad she was at him for the whole impregnation thing. It really wasn't his fault! She kept trying to remind herself, but every time she looked at his face, she wanted to scratch it right off. Her brows furrowed, and she turned her face away. Chance closed her eyes as she struggled with her desire to scream profanities at him again.

"You only turn if you ingest vampire blood and then die," he told her. "Urm… while it's still in your system."

His voice sounded tender, yet sad. Chance felt warm fingers lightly touch her ankle. She opened her eyes enough to squint at the man, who was undoing the straps.

"Oh good. I really have to pee."

"I'll set you up to have a bath and I'll change your bedding for you."

Chance's stared at the hellhound in a combination of elation and surprise. He was actually going to let her bathe herself?! Her enthusiasm faltered when she looked closely at Cadmael's features. His lips had a blue tinge to them and were pulled tight together. His brows seemed set as they drew downward over his beautiful, pale blue eyes. He squinted when he undid the strap on her arm. As he leaned over her to reach for Chance's other arm, she instinctively took a deep breath.

His scent was so deliciously sweet. She closed her eyes and took another breath. When she opened them, their eyes met. Chance swallowed, her lips parted as she struggled with herself on what to say.

Cadmael cleared his throat and stood. Chance stared curiously up at him as he seemed to fidget with adjusting his dress shirt, doing up the buttons. He looked… uncomfortable.

Slowly, Chance sat up. She groaned softly as she wrapped her arms around herself, trying to rub her upper arms. Everything was so stiff from being stuck in one position for so long. Her arms and shoulders throbbed agonizingly from constantly being over her head. Chance took a slow breath as she paced herself. She slowly turned her body and slipped her legs off the edge of the bed.

She wasn't sure if he was being sweet and trying to help, or if Cadmael had suddenly lost his patience, but he slipped his arms around her and easily lifted her from the bed. She wanted to wrap her arms around his neck, but as she went to do so, she couldn't make them move. Instead, she simply leaned against his chest, resting her forehead against the bloody collar of his shirt. It still felt moist, and around the stain the material had turned crusty.

He carried her swiftly to the bathroom and set her down on the toilet. Stepping back, he made eye contact, watching her with crossed arms. Slowly, Chance shook her head.

"I promise I won't try to run away right now. I just cannot pee with you watching me."

Cadmael cocked an eyebrow, as he seemed to consider his options. He suddenly nodded, then moved to the cupboard under the sink and pulled out the basket that had all the bathing materials. Her brows furrowed in irritation. That wasn't what she meant. She wanted him to at least go into the hall and face away from the bathroom.

"Master has made it clear that he will punish me in your place if you displease him," he explained clearly to her. "Knowing this, I will trust you to act accordingly."

He moved to the faucet and carefully set the temperature. As the water loudly filled the tub, Cadmael turned and bowed to Chance.

"I will return shortly."

She watched as the hellhound left the room. This newfound freedom gave her a pang of anxiety at the bottom of her stomach. She promised Cadmael she wouldn't try to escape, but the temptation was so much that she felt sick to her stomach. She needed to be logical about this.

One point would be that if she ran, she could escape. Trying to escape would destroy the small amount of trust Cadmael had for her. Did she have enough time to wait for another opportunity?

Chance stood, realizing that she hadn't had a bowel movement since arriving… Nothing in, nothing out. Cadmael was likely glad for that. The poor man washed her bedding nearly every time she soiled it. Her hands moved to her stomach, which no longer felt hunger. It simply felt like an empty hole, reminiscent of her soul. Broken.

Chance climbed carefully into the tub. Every movement caused her some form of pain. It took far too long for her to even sit down in the water. She pulled her knees to her chest and wept quietly. Everything hurt so badly, from her body to her heart. She pressed her eyes against her knee caps as she cried. Her arms hung at her sides so her hands rested in the water.

Time felt endless. She did not know how long she had cried for, but stopped when the water suddenly turned off. Her head whipped up, and she stared at Cadmael, who was leaning over the tub to turn the faucet. Her brows furrowed for a moment, before realizing that the tub had filled to the brim and was actually splashing out across the floor.

"Sorry," she whispered, knowing he was going to have to clean it.

"I watched it happen. I could have stopped it sooner, but you seem to have needed the cry." Cadmael's gaze dropped to the floor. "I will wait if you wish to continue."

He spoke as he leaned back on the counter. His shirt was still stained, and he had clearly not washed the bloody imprints from his skin.

"No, I'm sure I'll have plenty of time to cry later."

Cadmael nodded before approaching the tub. He kneeled at her side and took up the cup. His hand firmly cupped the back of her neck, so Chance tilted her head back.

She closed her eyes, feeling unshed tears leak from their corners. Warm water trickled across her forehead and cascaded down her hair. He applied the water three more times before sitting her upright.

Chance opened her eyes to watch as he lathered the shampoo between his hands. His warm fingers grazed her temples lightly before gliding into her locks of dark hair. Cadmael massaged her scalp for longer than what was necessary, but she wasn't complaining. His eyes would flash to hers for a moment, then to his task, as if noticing she was watching him, too. Her pulse quickened as he slipped one hand to rest against the back of her neck.

Slowly, she tilted her head back to rest on his strong hand. Chance could feel his warm breath caress her cheek and down her neck as he reached for the cup floating next to her in the water. Cadmael poured the warm liquid down her scalp again, careful not to trickle any into her face.

He dropped the plastic cup into the water and turned his gaze away as he reached to his left for the bottle of conditioner. His collarbone seemed emphasized by his movements, as did the blood stains. Why did he clean her before bothering to care for himself?

He maintained that supportive hand across the back of her neck as he poured some conditioner on her hair. He set the bottle down before using that hand to massage it into her scalp. Chance lifted her hand from the water and slowly reached out to him. Her fingers tenderly touched his neck, rubbing it to remove the bloodstain.

Cadmael's blue eyes stared into hers for a moment, as though captivated by her. Chance slowly traced her fingers down to his collarbone, following the blood trail. His face was so close to hers that his feverish breath delicately washed over her supple lips as her own breath aligned with his. Chance noticed her breathing quickened in time with her heartbeat.

Her butterfly finger touches changed to her palm as she massaged up the side of his neck, then down his collarbone. Chance's hand slowly made its way along his smooth skin. He twitched as if being awoken from a dream.

Finally, breaking their connection, he turned his gaze from hers and cleared his throat lightly. Cadmael's breath came in rapid gasps for air as he reached for the cup. He quickly rinsed Chance's hair. Too fast. She sighed in disappointment as he sat her up, releasing the back of her neck. Cadmael moved away, taking a deep breath as if trying to soothe himself. He cleared his throat again as he picked up the cloth.

Cadmael stared at the material in his hand with his eyebrows drawn, as if he were hesitating. He dipped the cloth into the water and held it up to apply liquid soap.

Chance felt butterflies floating around her stomach. There was no need for them. It was only Cadmael. Since her abduction, he had washed her countless times. He held the cloth up but paused. He drew his bottom lip into his mouth, chewing on it lightly as he seemed to contemplate what to do next.

The warm, soapy cloth touched Chance's neck, moving to her throat. She tilted her head back to help him, closing her eyes. As he moved closer to her breast, a soft gasp escaped her parted lips. She could feel the heat of his hand on the other side of the material, as if the fire in the man could penetrate anything.

He washed her breasts without lingering, though a part of her wished he would. When the cloth left her skin, she opened her eyes to look at him. Cadmael refused to meet her gaze as he rinsed the cloth and applied more soap. His hand trembled slightly as he broke the water's surface to reach for her hand.

His fingers felt callused and rough, but his touch was unimaginably tender. He washed her arms and hands as quickly as he could. Maybe he was less aroused than she thought or less responsive than she was. If she didn't get some relief from him, she'd end up masturbating. She certainly couldn't blame vampire venom for her random arousal.

The cloth moved downward. She closed her eyes, but to her disappointment, he washed her abdomen. He suddenly leaned in close to her. Chance gasped as his arm wrapped around her, his clothing getting soaked. She wrapped her arms around him and pressed her lips against the side of his neck.

His loud gasp erupted in her ear as her lips brushed his feverish skin. She could feel his pulse racing in his neck against her forearm. The cloth slipped into the water and slid across her plump little butt. As it rubbed her anus, Chance moaned softly, trying not to clench. Once he finished washing her ass, he hurriedly set her back down. She wanted him to linger there, with his arm wrapped around her, but he drew away.

Cadmael rinsed the cloth and quickly added more soap. He rubbed her abdomen again. The cloth passed over her pussy as he moved to wash her leg. She gasped when her stomach muscles tightened. Chance's hips even bucked toward him. She was so aroused by his touch, her pussy was pulsing with desire. He finished washing her leg and foot before moving onto the other. As he washed her inner thigh, her hips swayed her center toward him.

He rinsed the cloth and turned away from her to pull the plug. He didn't wash her pussy! He didn't! The cloth was still in his hand, beneath the water. She could feel the material tickling her thigh.

Chance reached out with both hands, grabbing his wrist and thumb firmly. She dragged his hand with the cloth up her inner thigh, slowly coming closer to her pussy. As their entwined hands moved to her aching, desperate center, their breathing turned into panting as they gasped for air. Chance drew her knees apart, inviting him to touch her.

His fiery gaze met hers in a moment of unbridled passion as he rubbed the cloth against her sensitive area. She released his hand, moaning lightly as her hands trailed up his arms. He washed her for a moment before the cloth slipped and she felt his fingers massaging her. Her climax happened instantly. Chance wrapped a hand around the back of his neck as she came.

"Cadmael," Chance sighed in a throaty moan as she staring longingly into his beautiful eyes.

Chance couldn't help herself. She pulled him down to her. She had barely brushed her lips against his before he gasped, pulling away and dropping to his ass in the middle of the bathroom floor. She stared at him with furrowed brows, but he was staring at the hand that had been touching her. He looked terrified.

Cadmael's other hand moved to the center of his chest, rubbing at it as if he were in extreme pain.

"Are you okay?" Chance queried, cocking an eyebrow.

"Fine," he responded, before standing.

The tub's drain made that annoying sucking sound as the last of the water disappeared. Chance wrapped her arms around herself and shivered lightly. Cadmael seemed to shake himself back to reality before standing and grabbing a towel from under the sink. As he approached, Chance stood. He wrapped the towel around her and lifted her up into his arms.

Cadmael carried her back into the bedroom and set her down in the center. He didn't meet her gaze. He bowed to her, muttering something about having errands to run for his master. He claimed that when he returned, he would brush her hair. It was as if he couldn't leave the room fast enough. Cadmael bolted from the room, leaving Chance standing in the middle of it, soaking wet with a towel wrapped around her.

She heard the door handle click locked. It sounded louder than it should have, as if announcing she'd never get out through that door.

That's okay. She was going out the fucking window!

Chance ripped off the towel and tossed it soaking wet onto the armchair. She ran to the window, threw the curtain out of the way, and tore off the blackout material taped to the glass. She stared at her own reflection in the glass with her mouth hanging open in surprise. On the outside of the building, someone had secured iron bars to the external frame of the window.

"What the fuck?"

She couldn't believe it. There was no way of knowing when in the past week that Cadmael had installed this. It had to have been him that had installed the bars. Eadrich didn't really 'give commands' so much as he expected Cadmael to read his mind, then guess and do what was expected.

Slowly, she shook her head. What could she do?!

Chance pressed her cheek against the cold glass, trying to see through the dark to figure out how the bars were installed. A large bolt would be a great axis point, and using something extended, she could create leverage to turn the bolt. Chance had always loved the sciences. What if she broke the window, then they caught her because of it? There really weren't many options left for her.

Chance's hands subconsciously moved to her stomach. If she got pregnant, it would weaken her more than she already had been. That was a huge IF. Chance wasn't about to disclose to them that since dating Tyne, her menstruation had stopped. Blood loss from feeding the vampire had done some serious damage to her body that she simply refused to acknowledge. That didn't mean she COULDN'T conceive… it just lowered the chances. There was no way to know how virile hellhounds were.

Tears welled in her eyes. It didn't matter. Chance was not about to allow her child to be raised by that monster. She would die first.

Copying her previous plan of escape, she peeled the duct tape from the blackout curtain and taped it onto the window in an X shape. This was it. She took a deep breath and then whapped her elbow into the center of the X. Chance's eyebrows rose as the strike made a deeper than expected thud.

Nothing… Not even a crack in the glass. Did they replace the fucking window itself? Using her palm, she hit the window hard. The deep thud resounded, deafening in her ears.

"No way," she remarked, rubbing her upper arm.

That strike hurt her far more than she'd admit. Not just her palm, the pain shot up every muscle in her arm and across her back. For a second, chance considered trying to kick the window. Could her leg lift that high with how stiff her body felt? She'd probably hurt herself.

She would give it one last try. She took a step back. After taking a deep breath in, Chance exhaled as she stepped forward, ramming both palms into the glass as hard as she could.

"Ughhh." She groaned, trying not to collapse to the floor in pain.

It hurt so horribly. Tears welled in her eyes, which she blinked back as she rubbed her arms.

Nope. That was absolutely not going to work. She didn't have the physical strength to break that window. What they replaced the glass with was far too hard. Maybe it was some sort of shatterproof glass.

Chance took a step back from the window and examined her surroundings. What if there was something long and sharp that she could use to stab a hole in the glass? It could weaken the entire thing and she could … wow… this was not some hero fantasy book. This was real life, and if she failed, she would die. There was no 'redo' in life.

She couldn't let panic and hopelessness set in. Chance ran to the nightstand and pulled open the drawers. They hid nothing there. After moving around to the other side of the bed, she ripped open the drawer of that nightstand. It held hand cuffs and three candles! That's why he seemed to never run out of wax. Fucking bastard.

Candle wax likely wouldn't do her any good. The cuffs, no, they didn't present any opportunity, either. Maybe she could rip a piece of the baseboards and try to use that. She would need tools to remove them. Chance put her hand through her hair, ignoring the moistness. The only other objects in the room were the bed, armchair, and curtains.

She didn't have the strength or skill to rip apart the armchair for some wood or metal that she could use. The curtains… her multi-colored eyes scanned the length of them as they hung from floor to ceiling. THE RODS!

Chance ran over to the curtain and grabbed the material, hugging it to her body. She reefed on it as hard as she could, but the brackets holding the awnings did not give way. Nothing. Chance ran along the wall, grabbed the curtain and swung on it like she would have as a child. There was a soft grinding sound, but the rod did not shift down. AGAIN! Chance jumped, grabbed hold, and attempted to yank it down. There was another grinding sound, louder than the last time.

Grabbing the bottom edge of the curtain, Chance marched away from the wall. Maybe leverage from an entirely different direction would work. Once she had a fair distance from the wall, she pulled with all her might. The hinges released, making Chance stumbled back in a flurry of material. Her calves slammed the side of the bed, sending her toppling backward.

The curtain rod clattered loudly to the ground. Far louder than she had expected. She felt a pang of fear twinned with a rush of exhilaration.

The thrill she felt from her accomplishment went far beyond anything logical. Exhilaration flooded through her as she rolled around on the bed, kicking the heavy curtain off herself. Chance thumped to the floor and crawled across the weighty material as she searched for the bar. Chance felt it hidden between the folds in the curtain. She lifted it, gasping in surprise. It was far heavier than she'd expected. She freed it from the material and held it up to examine her new tool. It was a two-and-a-half-foot long cast iron rod she struggled to even carry.

Everything in this ridiculous building was so over the top. She honestly hadn't expected it to be this sturdy. Chance dropped the rod onto her bed. She began moving the curtain to the side of the room to make sure she wouldn't slip on it, then picked up the iron rod. Chance smirked as she hoisted the rod to rest on her shoulder. She squared off with the window and mentally prepared herself.

Ready… CHARGE!

She ran straight toward the window, using the rod as a lance. DING. The rebound juddered through her entire body. Chance fell back, landing hard. The wind was knocked out of her lungs, leaving her gasping for air on the ground. The rod rolled away from her, ending up beneath the bed.

It surprised Chance that with all the racket she had made, Eadrich never bothered to check on her. No. He wouldn't, would he? It was Cadmael's job.

Chance sat up, staring around the room. What else? She doubted she could throw herself through the wall, or the door, for that matter. Chance walked over to the door and knocked lightly. It was solid oak. There was no kicking her way through the damn thing.

She wiggled the door handle just in case. If it was like one of those bathroom door handles, she would just need a pin to poke inside, and it would release the lock. There wasn't even a keyhole. Chance turned around, leaned against the door and let herself slide to the floor as she stared around the room. She looked from one corner to the next, considering how anything in the room could be used.

Chance adjusted her position, feeling stiff and sore already. She stretched her hands above her head, keeping her arms straight as she brought them down to her sides. She could feel every muscle from her forearms, upper arms and shoulders pulling and stretching as she moved. Her left arm bumped into something, startling the crap out of her. Chance stared in surprise at the large hinges. Of course, the hinges would be huge for such a heavy door. Regular ones would twist from the strain of so much weight. She rested her hand on top of the pin as her fingers toyed with it while she assessed the room.

Her fingers traced the hinge and the pin subconsciously. Suddenly, her jaw dropped. She slowly turned her face toward her hand. Gradually, her eyebrows climbed up her face as she considered the possibility of this new plan working. But what could she use?! The rod could create a focal point for impact. Chance crawled across the floor and reached under the bed for the rod. She wiggled harder, turning her face away as she stretched hard to reach it. As her fingers curled around the rod, her eyes spotted one bracket that the rod had hung from. It had fallen when she tore the curtains down. She pulled the rod out from under the bed. The tip dragged loudly against the hardwood floor. Chance lifted the rod and dropped it onto the bed with a soft groan.

Chance moved to the bracket and grabbed the long, thick screw. She twisted until it was finally free of the other piece of metal. Chance dropped the bracket to the ground with a clatter. If no one investigated all the noise yet, no one was bound to, no matter how much more racket she made. She heaved the rod up from the bed and made her way to the door.

Chance placed the screw beneath the bottom of the two door hinges, then balanced the pipe in the crevice below that. How was she supposed to have enough coordination and strength to do this?

She tried sliding the rod upward to hit the head of the screw. Her intention was to push it up hard enough to slide the screw into the underside of the hinge, pushing out the pin. It didn't work. Chance sighed, laying her tools down on the floor. She needed to either make the pin push up smoother or make maneuvering the rod easier. Chance's eyes scanned the room, seeing nothing that could help.

THE WAX! She leaped up and ran over to the nightstand.

She grabbed one candle and returned to the door. With all the force she could muster, Chance rubbed the candle against the large hinges. Slivers of wax crumbled off the large candle sticking in the cracks between the loops, while some fluttered to the floor. For extra measure, she rubbed the candle up and down the crack between the door and the frame.

This needed to work. Chance set herself back up with the nail and rod. With all her force, she slid the bar upward. The pipe moved so much easier than the last time. It thudded into the nail, which surprisingly moved up half a finger-width. Chance gasped loudly as she realized this fucking ridiculous plan was actually working! She didn't give up. She continued hammering away at the pin until it finally popped out of the hinges.

Chance pushed on the door, but nothing happened. She stood and stared at the upper hinge. This one was goin' down! And she was getting the fuck outta here!

It didn't take her as long to push out the second pin as it had with the first one. Eventually, it clattered to the ground. Chance pushed the door, but it didn't budge. WHAT THE FUCK!? Oh, yeah, doors have framing to stop them from hyper extending. She needed to find a way to pull the door inward. She needed something that could somehow hook under the door so she could pull it toward herself. If she used her fingers, she'd likely lose them from the extreme weight of the door.

Chance was so physically and mentally exhausted. This was the most exercise she'd had in weeks.

The curtain? She could try to slide it under the door and pull it up around the edges of the frame, gliding it upward. She frowned. It wouldn't work. The curtain was such a thick material it could never wedge around the door inside the frame. Something else… the bedding. The fitted sheet had an elastic which would help with making it hug the door as she pulled it upward.

Chance pulled the sheet off the bed and hurried back, dragging it behind her. She grabbed the top edge of the sheet and pushed it along the bottom of the door from corner to corner. At the corners of the door, she picked up the edges of the sheet, carefully lifting them so the sheet would slide upward between the frame and the door without simply being pulled back into the room. Once the elastic of the sheet rested just under the hinge, she heaved far harder than necessary. Too hard! The door came loose, and once the hinges were free of the doorframe, the locked handle did nothing to slow the door from collapsing inward.

Her heart raced as she stumbled backward. She fell onto her back and raised her arms to protect herself as the giant oak door fell toward her. She lay there for far too long, panting in fear with her eyes closed, before she realized nothing hit her. Chance cautiously opened her eyes, then stared around, trying to figure out why she hadn't been completely flattened. The door had landed across the bottom half of the bed, preventing it from hitting the floor and quieting the noise as it had fallen. Talk about luck!

Chance wasn't about to stick around. Her fucking sheet was stuck under the bottom edge of the door. That was supposed to end up covering her. She snatched her damp towel from the armchair and wrapped it around herself. This would have to do.

Stepping over the bottom corner of the door, Chance slipped into the hallway. She stared up and down the hallway cautiously before running for the stairs. At the bottom, Chance practically flung herself against the main door. It was LOCKED!

That was fine. Just another minor obstacle. She'd climb out of the skylight in the kitchen again. She didn't waste any time at all. Chance ran into the kitchen, climbed the counter and then on to the fridge. Without hesitation, Chance ripped the blackout curtain from the window. Her features froze, and a sense of horrifying dread filled her. Bars. They were making damn sure she wasn't going to get out of there again. The library likely had bars on the windows, even if she could get up that high. The only other room she remembered having seen with a window was the dance hall. She vaguely recalled ending up in a passageway inside the wall.

Chance ran from the kitchen headed to the party hall. Her hand hit that door handle, but nothing happened. Damn it. She was running out of time! Every second that she wasted on useless plans made her feel one moment closer to death.

Keys! Chance ran back into the kitchen. She moved to the counter and pulled open the drawer she had seen Cadmael store the car keys into. Her legs burned with exhaustion, but the only thing keeping her going was the smallest glimmer of hope.

There was nothing in the drawer. She groaned, reaching into the darkest area at the far back and sliding her hand around. It was dumb luck. There was a single key resting in the back of the drawer, as though forgotten. She picked it up. Staring at it, she felt that glimpse of freedom fading into the distance. She didn't know what she'd do if the key didn't fit any of the locks. She'd try the front door first. Then the party hall, and if neither worked, she'd come back and try the door beside the fridge.

Chance entered the hallway. She was so exhausted that she leaned against the door frame as she stuck the key into the lock and turned.

Click.

She stood there, staring at the key in the lock for entirely too long as it registered that the door had unlocked. Her hand slammed down onto the handle and she twisted, pulling the heavy door open and stumbling out into the chilly night air.

To her surprise, there stood Cadmael with his mouth hanging open in disbelief. He had a grocery store bag looped around one wrist and a leash handle around the other. The leash attached to a collar that was wrapped snugly around the throat of a red-haired woman whose eyebrows raised as she saw Chance.

"No." Chance whimpered and tried to run past Cadmael.

His hand flung out, catching her wrist in an iron tight grip. He walked in, dragging her with him. The new slave followed easily, without need for command. The door slammed shut behind him, closing out Chance's last hope of freedom.

28

His Punishment

Cadmael

Cadmael held her wrist and led the troublesome girl upstairs. At the top of the stairs, he stared at the entrance to her room in utter disbelief. How was this even possible?! His gaze slowly shifted to stare at the woman as if seeing her for the first time.

How could someone so small, so weak, do something so unbelievable?

That door would be hard for him to even *lift*! Somehow, this tiny woman pulled it down. He looked at the bedsheet wrapped around the bottom of the door on the ground and cocked his head to the side.

"Impossible," his voice cracked loudly as his gaze moved to stare at the toy one more time.

"Master," Cadmael whispered, spotting Eadrich coming

from the shadows further down the hall. "Forgive me for my incompetence."

Cadmael bowed, knowing he was to be punished for failing his master once again. He shook his head slowly as he rose, his eyes darting to the door once again.

"I cannot even imagine your disappointment in me." Cadmael's eyes flashed to Eadrich's face as his master still hadn't responded.

Eadrich's face was a mask as his red-rimmed eyes assessed the situation, looking from Chance, to Cadmael, to the slave and the door. Why couldn't Cadmael tell what he was thinking?! That was far more terrifying than facing his master's wrath.

"Please, Master, tell me how I can be punished to make this better," he pleaded, his hands trembling.

He released the slave's leash, the toy's hand and the small bag of groceries.

"What is *that*?"

"You told me to research breeding and what would need to be done to ensure its success. I purchased vitamins and some food for your toy." He paused for a moment, but when Eadrich said nothing, Cadmael continued. "You wanted me to bring you a special surprise for another toy… This is the candle whom your toy attempted to assist the night of the party. She is only alive by the will of your toy. I thought it would be fitting if this one fell into your possession."

Cadmael closed his eyes. He couldn't keep staring at his master, hoping beyond hope Eadrich would say or do something. His master would wait until the anxiety from silence was too much. So Cadmael did the only thing he could do; he bowed his head and waited.

After several minutes of silence, Eadrich murmured, "You never cease to impress me, my pet."

The knot between Cadmael's shoulders did not loosen. An offhand compliment did not bode well for Cadmael. He knew his master far too well to fall into a false sense of security over a few words. Eadrich loved instant gratification, and it pleased Eadrich to watch those around him suffer.

Cadmael glanced at the toy, who might be pregnant with his pups from the corner of his eye. She looked horrified, staring at the new toy. She shook her head as her hands moved subconsciously to her abdomen, tears rolling down her cheeks.

"I'm so sorry," Chance whimpered at the new toy.

His mind reeled as he struggled to comprehend what he was witnessing. There was no way this tiny, malnourished human had the physical strength to tear down that heavy door. The woman couldn't be an actual human! This shouldn't have been possible. He shook his head, frowning. Cadmael couldn't even imagine how she pulled this off. Countless toys had been locked away here and none had the stubborn, creative genius this woman had. This human was amazing!

The silence was unbearable. Cadmael did his best to ensure his master couldn't read his facial expression. It helped that Eadrich wouldn't be able to see Cadmael's face with how deeply he bowed.

"Clean this up and await your punishment," Eadrich murmured before turning away and marching down the hall.

The moment Eadrich vanished in the shadows, Cadmael rounded on Chance with an audible growl. His hands balled into trembling fists as his eyes narrowed.

"Get the fuck in that room," he hissed in a barely audible voice.

To his surprise, the girl bolted in, stepping on the door to get beyond it. She whipped around, glaring at him as she wrapped her arms around herself, over the towel. His blue eyes shifted to stare coldly at the new toy.

"Enter," he told her sternly, trying not to sound as aggressive.

The redhead bowed smoothly and walked into the room, with the leash dragging behind her. She stepped on the door and moved to stand next to the other slave. Cadmael snatched up his grocery bag and followed. Once inside the room, he tossed the bag onto the bed and turned to examine the door.

"Cadmael," Chance whimpered, "I'm sorr-."

"Shut up," Cadmael snapped, but when she had the nerve to look mad at him, he lost his temper. "You are a toy, and I am a pet. Don't talk to me like we have anything in common. I will not be so easily manipulated by you in the future. Shut the fuck up and do what the master says."

Cadmael turned his back on the toy and bent over, grabbing the edge of the door. It took far more strength than what he would have thought to heave it up in the air.

As he worked, Chance responded.

"Why are you being so mean?" she sounded so indignant.

With the door lifted, balancing against the doorframe, he glared over his shoulder at the woman who had brought him so much misery. "Because *you* are going to get *me* killed."

That shut her up. The girl stared at him with her brows drawn inward. He didn't care if his words hurt her feelings. This wasn't about mental wellbeing. It was about survival. She risked his life, and she fucking knew it. He told her that if she pulled something, he would receive her punishment.

Cadmael took a step back to examine the door, attempting to understand exactly how she dismantled it. How did she come up with the idea to remove the pins?! Cadmael used his foot to move Chance's tools out of the way. He was careful not to scuff his perfectly maintained dress shoes. He spent far too much time polishing them to allow them to come to harm. Cadmael adjusted his tie before grabbing the edges of the door and sliding it to fit within the frame.

"Tsk," he hissed as he caught the fingers of his right hand between the door and the frame.

Cadmael growled in the back of his throat, his eyes flashing at Chance. This was *her* fault. All of it!

This wasn't going to work. He needed to lift the door by almost half an inch before pushing it into the frame. Cadmael groaned as he hoisted the door to slide into place.

"Fuck!" he hissed under his breath as he, once again,

pinched his damn fingers.

He balanced the hinges on the door against the ones attached to the door frame. He slipped his hand carefully out of the gap and then slipped the door into place. Cadmael put a hand through his sandy blond curls as he examined the door. He sighed softly, picking up the large pins from the ground where the little escape artist had left them.

"Cadmael," Chance started, but at the dark glare from Cadmael, she stopped.

The fucking pin wouldn't go into the hinge properly! He picked up the cast iron bar and rammed it down onto the pin. One solid strike and it slid into place. Cadmael easily slid the next pin into place with just his fingers.

He took a deep breath and sighed softly, without turning to face the two women. It wasn't for him to discipline his master's toy. The failure was on Cadmael for trusting someone. How could he have been so foolish? Cadmael used the moment to reset his way of thinking. He had to remember to distance himself from the toys.

He had felt as though Chance differed from the previous toys because he had been stalking her for nearly a year. Not by choice, either. His entire life, he'd been compared to Tyne, while having to keep his master apprised of what the vampire was up to. As Cadmael aged, he got smart and often hired detectives to do most of the dirty work. It struck him as odd that his master suddenly stopped caring about what the younger vampire was doing. Eadrich stopped all the information gathering as soon as he got his claws on the girl. He must have known how out-of-his-mind desperate the younger vampire would become.

Chance's connection to Tyne was the only reason Eadrich bought the girl from the auction. If Cadmael hadn't recognized her from the reports, she likely would have been sacrificed by the dark fairy who tried to outbid Eadrich. If it weren't for him, she'd have died a long time ago.

Slowly, Cadmael turned toward the women. He wore a vacant expression, devoid of all emotion. He certainly would not lower his guard again.

"Give me the towel."

He foolishly let her have more freedom on the off-chance she could be pregnant with his pups. That was a foolish mistake that would cost him.

"No," the stubborn woman growled, gripping the towel tightly around herself.

Cadmael felt really annoyed, bordering on angry. He didn't show it at all, but he was at his wit's end from dealing with this creature. He really wanted to have everything perfect for when his master returned. Cadmael couldn't get physical with her, because he wasn't her master and didn't have the vampire's permission.

He would have smiled as the thought crossed his mind, but he didn't want her to catch on that this was a manipulation tactic.

"New toy, you may be seated in the chair."

"As you wish," she intoned and immediately placed herself on the chair.

The new toy's gaze would remain on the floor unless told otherwise, though he caught her glancing at Chance from the corner of her eye.

Cadmael picked up his grocery bag from the bed. His plan would be genius if he could be sure his master wouldn't become cross if he gave food to the new toy. His plan to say the new one could have it for being an obedient toy. If he did that, his master could become cross with him.

His blue eyes coldly met Chance's dark glare. He grunted softly, pointedly peering into the bag. The corners of his lips twisted into a devious smile.

"I guess you're not hungry," he muttered, attempting to sound thoughtful.

He heard a soft gasp and looked at Chance, just in time to see her raise her arms. The large white towel fluttered to the ground at her feet. The girl's arms moved to cover herself as if by instinct. When her cheeks flushed, he cocked an eyebrow. Being naked should really have become natural for her by now. There was a short period of time where she seemed completely comfortable naked in front of him, but now she protected her body from his gaze. It was ridiculous to him that she was taking so long to change her way of thinking. This girl really was going to be the death of him.

Cadmael pulled an apple from the bag and held it out for her. Chance's eyes widened, her lips parted, and she walked toward Cadmael with an outstretched hand. She delicately collected the apple from him and hurriedly took a bite.

Cadmael spun on his heels, planning what needed to be done next. He suddenly felt as though he were running out of time.

"Eat it quickly. Master will want to play with his toys very soon," he informed her while collecting the fitted sheet from the floor.

Cadmael hurriedly made the bed. His master wasn't the most patient creature. Just as Cadmael pulled the final elastic edge over the mattress's corner, Eadrich threw open the door.

At the ruckus of their master entering, Cadmael faced the door with his head bowed. The new toy followed his lead by standing and bowing her head.

Cadmael tried to glance at Chance from the corner of his eye. He prayed she had enough intelligence to do as everyone else did.

"My new toy," Eadrich purred, making Cadmael smile.

He really wanted to please his master, hoping it would extend his lifespan. He felt no shame in placing his life before the toys. They always died first. In fact, he'd dug hundreds of graves over the years. He was ten the first time he painted a toy's image and buried the body. It was a boy who was several years older than Cadmael was.

The previous pet had him do everything by himself to ensure that Cadmael could. He must have known his time was at an end. It took Cadmael three days to dig the hole. Someday soon, he'd be digging the graves for these two toys. Cadmael felt a pang of regret. If his master's plan came to fruition, Cadmael will soon dig the grave for the mother of his own pups.

His bright blue eyes followed his master, but he really wanted to be staring over his shoulder at Chance.

Eadrich's hand cupped one of the new toy's breasts. His icy touch made goosebumps rise on her pale, freckled flesh. Cadmael felt envious, watching the girl's lips part as their master pinched and toyed with her nipple.

"Your body's reaction is decent for a pre-trained toy."

"Thank you, Master." The girl whispered, sounding pleased.

"Do you have any special talents?" Eadrich's eyebrows rose as he questioned her.

"Yes, Master," the toy responded smoothly. "Would you care to learn them, or shall I tell you, Master?"

Eadrich chuckled in the back of his throat as his fingers lightly trailed their way down her body.

"What is your name?"

"Whatever you wish it to be."

Cadmael heard Chance gasp from somewhere behind him.

"Cumslut? Do you like the name?"

"Only if it pleases my master."

The girl's responses were immediate, and she seemed to truly believe what she was saying. That artist had his slaves meticulously trained to accept whatever would happen to them. Eadrich's slaves never lived long enough to have any real training. Though Cadmael was sure his master preferred his slaves a little wild and resistant. Having a completely obedient toy in the house was something new for Cadmael to witness.

As their master's fingers finally reached her center, her legs tensed. The toy wouldn't move unless she suspected he wanted her to.

"Would you like some time alone with your master?"

As the slave heard the question, her eyes lit up with excitement as she raised her chin to stare lovingly up at Eadrich.

"If it would please my master, I would love that."

Cadmael's mouth tightened for an instant as Eadrich's fingers slipped between the girl's lips in search of her clit. Cadmael's eyes narrowed, suspecting that his master was being so tender with the new toy to taunt the ones who displeased him. The envy was overwhelming. It made him miss the days when he was a pup and his master spoiled him with affection and tender touches.

Eadrich's fingers continued toying with the new toy's clit. Her legs trembled, though Cadmael wasn't sure if her reaction was sincere or simply a show for the sake of her new master.

"Stand on the chair," Eadrich told the new toy, dropping his hand to his side.

The new toy turned to climb onto the chair. Eadrich groped her ass as he turned his attention to Cadmael and Chance.

"Put that toy away where it belongs." Eadrich command Cadmael with his eyes narrowing at Chance.

There wasn't a moment of hesitation. Cadmael whipped around and plucked the half-eaten apple from her hand before the toy could stop him. He pointedly stared at the bed as he reached past her to set the half-eaten apple on the nightstand.

The glare Chance threw back at him made Cadmael want to shove her onto the bed. Instead, his brows furrowed, and he moved his hand, desperately showing the bed.

As Chance climbed onto the bed, Eadrich commanded, "Only cuff her legs. She will need her hands."

While they got set up, Cadmael couldn't stop staring at his master from the corner of his eye. Eadrich had maneuvered his new toy, so one foot rested on the arm of the chair. The one simple change exposed her most intimate area to the room.

Cadmael pulled Chance's leg, forcing them to spread so he could strap her down properly. His eyes flashed to where his master stood, trailing fingers up and down the new toy's inner thighs. His master's voice easily distracted him from his chore.

"What is your name?" Eadrich questioned, likely smirking because he knew she would repeat the name he chose for her.

"Cumslut, Master," his new toy stated in a matter-of-fact voice.

"Good girl," the ancient vampire purred before ramming three fingers inside the woman.

As Eadrich's fingers moved with the fury of a man possessed, his eyes flashed to Cadmael. "Malix Peek, strip." Eadrich's voice snarled as he gave his command.

Cadmael flinched, then hurriedly moved in front of the window where he removed his clothing. Cadmael quickly folded everything and left it on the windowsill before sliding off his shoes and socks.

Completely naked, he turned to his master and bowed to show Eadrich that he had completed his task. When he finally looked, his master was staring up at the new toy.

"You're not allowed to cum," the vampire instructed the girl in a tender tone. "Hold it in until I give you permission."

"Yes, Master!" the stupid toy sounded far too excited about the events that had transpired.

Cadmael sneered at the new toy, even though she wouldn't see it. The woman's eyes never strayed from their master's face as his fingers gave her pleasure beyond measure.

"I want your mouth on that one's pussy, Malix Peek." Eadrich signaled at Chance, using his free hand, without even glancing away from the toy on the chair. "Your tongue is not to leave her flesh."

"Yes, Master."

Cadmael quickly made his way to the bed. As he crawled onto it, Chance glared at him. She'd get over it. She had to know that he had just as much choice in any of this as she did. He wedged himself between Chance's legs. He pulled her toward the bottom of the bed to loosen the straps that held her legs so they could comfortably rest over his shoulders. He started with some gentle licking from her labia up to her clit.

"Here, toy." His master's voice announced from somewhere behind him. Within a second, something that felt like a coiling snake with nine tails landed on his back.

He couldn't help the gasp he made, vibrating her sensitive spot. His hands moved from where they wrapped around her thighs to rest his forearms on the bed.

"No," he heard Chance hiss.

"If you don't sufficiently punish him, he will face far worse."

Eadrich could feel her fingers lightly touch the top of his head, twining with his curls. His tongue swirled around her clit, attempting to encourage her, to tell the girl it was okay to strike him. Instead of cooperating, the foolish woman argued with their master.

"Punish!? For what?" she snapped at Eadrich.

Cadmael lightly grazed his teeth down her pussy lips as a warning to her. Chance gasped loudly, her hands suddenly slapping the top of his head.

"Good try, but use the whip," Eadrich taunted.

Cadmael snorted softly.

"Keep that tongue busy. I will not warn you again."

Cadmael buried his face between her thighs with far more enthusiasm than necessary. His tongue swirled and pounded her clit as if attempting to wreck her. His lips pursed around his teeth to protect her from the sharp edges while he rubbed his taut lips around the swollen nub that pulsed against his tongue.

"Pick. It. Up," Eadrich demanded, sounding so intimidating that Cadmael tensed.

His hands balled into fists, catching the sheet under him. He held tight to the material as he prepared for the lashing to begin.

"Please, Master," the new toy interrupted, "may I cum?"

Eadrich ignored the toy as he yelled at Chance, "Pick it up now, or Cadmael will beat you instead!"

Cadmael felt her hand on his back. Her fingers traced the old scars from previous beatings as they moved closer to the handle of the whip. Her fingers delicately dragged across his flesh as they wrapped around the wooden handle of what he knew would be the nine-tail whip. Chance raised the weapon from his back. He could feel the slender tendrils of leather tickling his flesh as they slid across his skin. The tails stopped, lingering, almost trembling. Cadmael's eyebrows furrowed in confusion as he anticipated a hit that didn't come.

"Strike him."

The tendrils of leather left his skin, only to return a moment later. The way the whip lightly dropped across his flesh reminded him of raindrops. He moaned encouragement into her delicious pussy.

"More power!" Eadrich snarled, sounding more annoyed than he should have.

The strumming sensation across his back improved in strength, but it would not be enough for his master.

"Cadmael! Do it yourself."

Cadmael's tongue pressed hard against Chance's clit to make sure it never ceased contact. He slipped one hand partially under her hip to brace himself for what was to come. His other hand raised, palm up, waiting for her to place the whip there. It took a moment, but after he opened and closed his hand, she placed the handle against his palm.

Cadmael took a deep breath, her aroma filling his nose. The amazing vanilla scent overwhelmed his senses. He straightened his arm, considering exactly how the strike needed to be placed to avoid hitting her legs. If he struck diagonally, he'd certainly hit her. Straight down it was then. He flexed his elbow, bringing the whip down toward his back with every ounce of strength he had. All the while, he ensured his tongue didn't leave her pussy.

He struck. The tendrils of the whip hit their mark, every one of them pounded his flesh in an attack that felt cutting. He grunted hard, gasping against Chance's clit. The woman screamed in surprise, her legs tensing against his back. Slowly, he lifted his arm, straightening it out. Cadmael counted four seconds, then struck again with the same amount of force. He growled in pain as the tails of leather met their mark. The length was enough that they hit him all the way down his back and halfway down his ass. He would have preferred a diagonal attack, but her leg was in the way. Cadmael straightened his arm, preparing to strike again. Both of Chance's hands clutched his arm, preventing him from completing his task.

"You want it to stop?" Eadrich questioned.

"Yes… please," Chance responded.

Something wet dripped onto Cadmael's forearm, but he couldn't look to see what it was.

"Please," Chance begged, then sniffled lightly.

She was crying. For him? His tongue slowed its assault on her as though trying to ease her pain by being gentler. The hand he had braced under her relaxed. He allowed his thumb to lightly rub the skin there by moving back and forth slowly. Cadmael realized in that moment he forgave her for attempting to escape and causing him so much trouble.

"You do it then," Eadrich ordered her.

Cadmael opened his hand and felt her take the whip from him. Her body tensed as she raised it over her head, and he prepared for her to land the tendrils across his back. Instead, she threw the whip away from them. Cadmael heard it hit the wall and clatter to the floor on the opposite side of the bed, from where Eadrich played with his new toy.

"You don't want to beat him? Then mate with the hellhound." Cadmael could practically hear Eadrich's smile as the vampire spoke. "Fuck him, and I won't make you strike him."

"Okay." Chance agreed without hesitation.

Cadmael finally lifted his face from between her thighs. He stared into her multi-colored eyes as tears streamed down her cheeks. Why would she agree to doing the very thing that had caused so much anguish for her? If the stupid human had just beat him, their punishment would be over, and this wouldn't have been happening.

The girl's hands trembled as they circled the back of his

head. She drew him toward her, encouraging Cadmael to crawl up her body. She pulled him until his lips met hers. This time, Cadmael did not need any assistance to have a bodily response. He had been hard from the moment his lips touched her flesh. Being a hellhound made him a simple creature. Their loyalties lie with their masters in every way imaginable. Cadmael had never really enjoyed anyone else's touch. His master was all he needed.

When their kiss broke off, his eyes scanned the room in search of that master. Eadrich was watching them, ensuring the pair followed through with his command. As his eyes met Eadrich's, Cadmael rammed himself as deep as he could inside Chance. The entire time he ate her out, he'd been on the verge of an explosion. Entering her now was all the poor man needed. Cadmael gasped, clutching her tightly as he felt his hot mess erupt inside the woman.

"I'm sorry," he whimpered quietly in her ear.

Cadmael really thought he'd be able to hold off longer. As he lifted himself onto his forearms to stare down at the girl, he knew he looked absolutely mortified.

"It's okay, Cadmael," Chance whispered.

Cadmael turned his attention back to his master. Eadrich looked far more disappointed than Chance had.

"I'm sorry, master." Cadmael still hadn't withdrawn his deflating cock from inside her.

He wouldn't without his master's command.

"Strap her down."

"Yes, master." Cadmael finally pulled himself from inside the girl.

He didn't even bother to wipe himself down without a command from Eadrich. Cadmael moved to the side of the bed as his fingers fumbled with the Velcro cuff for one of Chance's wrists. He made sure it was snug, but not so tight as to cut off circulation. He hurried around the bed and quickly strapped down her other arm. Once finished, he turned to his master and bowed.

"You still need punishment, Cadmael." Eadrich hissed as

he finger-fucked his toy so hard the woman struggled to stay standing. “You will use the whip on yourself. Do it till you drop.”

29

Hellhound's Devotion

Chance

Chance felt anger bubbling over in a white-hot rage as she processed Eadrich's words. That fucker made them breed again so she wouldn't have to beat Cadmael, and now he was beating himself!

"Yes, Master." Cadmael made it two steps before the new toy spoke.

"Master, please can I cum?!" At the same time, Chance screamed.

"You lying bastard! You said he wouldn't be whipped!" Anger

"No, I said you wouldn't have to do it. I never said he'd forgo punishment."

He finally withdrew his fingers from the woman standing on the chair. Her legs trembled so hard that she shook the entire chair. Eadrich threw her over his shoulder and marched out of the room, leaving Chance and Cadmael to their own devices.

"Cadmael, you don't have to do it," Chance told him in a desperate whisper.

The moonlight had disappeared, and sunlight had begun to trickle in through the window. After being in the darkness for so long. The trace amounts of light was blinding.

She squinted through her tears as she watched the hellhound kneel where the whip had landed. Chance shook her head silently as he turned his back toward her. Cadmael braced one hand on the wall, while the other lifted the whip. In a flash of movement, his arm swung upward, then down behind him. The tendrils of leather slapped loudly against his flesh, making him grunt in pain.

Chance gasped loudly and struggled against her restraints. She wanted to stop him, save him from himself.

"Please, you can stop. I won't tell him you didn't do it!" she hissed at Cadmael but went ignored as the leather hit its mark again.

Over and over, he struck his flesh with the whip. His back had turned red and begun to purple from bruising. Chance cried, closing her eyes tightly, but it did nothing to block out the sound of the strikes and his grunting as it became louder as the pain increased. The strikes stopped, and Chance opened her eyes to look at him. A trickle of blood rolled down his back from where the skin had split open. He was switching hands to lash himself using the other hand.

"Wait, Cadmael, stop! You're bleeding," she begged desperately as the striking resumed. "Please!"

Hours went by and the only pause taken was when Cadmael switched hands. Chance would look over, hoping he had finally stopped, only to be disappointed as he began again. His grunting turned into screams of agony as his skin became so swollen and destroyed that the slightest strike caused it to split. The muscles across his back and arms flexed and twitched as he continued his vigorous attack. The time between strikes increased until they stopped coming completely.

A loud thump made Chance open her eyes. She lifted her head to find Cadmael laying on his side with his back to her. Tears rolled down her cheeks as she watched blood seep from rips in his skin. His back was an array of black, blue, purple and red with streaks of crimson trickling across the wounds as gravity drew them to the floor.

"Cadmael?" Chance whispered, but didn't receive a reply. "why didn't you stop? Why?" she panted as she cried her words to him.

Hours passed by when she finally heard him stir. Chance softly called out, "Are you okay?"

His throat cleared before he answered, "I will be fine."

Chance lifted her head from the pillow so she could check on him. Fresh tears made their way down her cheeks. There was a puddle of blood beneath him. Slowly, Cadmael peeled himself from the floor while Chance laid there sobbing quietly. He limped to the side of the bed. Chance blinked back tears as he fitted a finger under the edge of her cuff. She realized he was checking to make sure she couldn't try to escape again. He probably couldn't take another punishment without his back turning into hamburger meat.

More tears flooded down her face. They simply came out on their own. At one point, Chance was sure there were no tears left in her body. Now she realized how very wrong she had been.

Chance's voice cracked as she whispered, "Kill me…"

After a moment's pause, Cadmael responded, "Is the thought of bearing my seed so unbearable to you?"

"The thought of my children suffering at his hands horrifies me." Chance responded immediately and began crying once again. "I don't want my babies to feel this pain."

Her heart was breaking. The pain in her chest was unlike any agony she'd ever experienced. If she had to choose, she'd take physical beatings every day, but this psychological torture was simply too much.

There was a strange tugging at her wrist that she'd come to recognize as her cuff being undone. She opened her eyes, but no amount of blinking could slow the tears that blinded her. The moment he freed her hand, she used it to cover her face.

The hellhound climbed on top of her as he reached for her other arm. Blood from his back trickled down his ribs in a steady stream, dripping onto her and the bedding.

Cadmael undid her other arm and then her legs. Chance drew everything in as she curled herself into the tiniest protective ball she could. She must have sobbed for a really long time, because when she stopped, the sun was on the verge of setting. The orange light dimly glowed through the window, making shadows from the forest dance across her room.

Chance sniffled and looked around. Cadmael was standing in front of her. His eyes were closed and red, as though he too had been crying. As a tear squeezed out to moisten his eyelashes, his hand came up and rubbed it away.

"Cadmael?" Chance tried again. "Please? Please kill me."

She knew it wasn't in his nature to end her life, but she was too scared to do it herself. Slowly, her head shook. She didn't want to die, but sometimes, there was no other way out. Chance shakily reached out a hand towards the hellhound, whose eyes finally opened. His brows drew down as he moved forward. His calloused hand felt rough against her soft fingers.

He took a deep breath and exhaled before kneeling at her bedside. "I have something to tell you."

"Hmm?"

"I can smell it. I can smell it if it worked." He looked away from her. "You're not pregnant, yet."

Her hand squeezed his so tight that her knuckles turned white. What could she do now? If Eadrich had his way, she would eventually end up pregnant.

"Last night?"

"I don't know yet, but from mating a few days ago, you aren't with child."

Cadmael's voice was soft, and his eyes didn't meet hers. There was no way to tell what he was thinking. She reached her free hand toward his face, lightly caressing his cheek with her thumb as she cupped his jaw. Chance's chin quivered as more tears rolled down her cheeks. His bright blue eyes flashed to the door before he leaned in close. He smelled like a mix of mint and cologne, combined with the iron scent from his bloody wounds.

"I'm going to help you leave," he suddenly whispered, catching Chance completely off guard.

Her mouth hung open as a numbness spread across her entire body. She had to be dreaming. The hand that had been touching his cheek dropped to the mattress as she stared at him like she was seeing him for the first time.

"Why?" she blurted out before she could stop it.

Her voice cracked over that single word. Her eyes couldn't open any wider. Was that really what she wanted to be asking him? He'd seen so much, done so much. He prevented her from escaping, and suddenly, he planned to assist her?

"Because eventually," Cadmael's eyes darkened, "you will be..."

It was like he couldn't say the last word. Maybe he didn't want to admit she was going to end up having his baby if something wasn't done. She wasn't sure why she had to ask this, but she needed to be certain.

"You're stopping any potential for your children to exist... why?"

Cadmael moved his face forward and pressed his lips against hers. She returned his kiss with equal fervor, terrified that this was some sort of plan from Eadrich to torment her further, but Cadmael's touch was so sincere, like it was a goodbye kiss.

Their kiss ended, and he pulled away, smiling lightly at her. The first smile she'd ever seen on his lips. It changed his features entirely, softening his cool eyes and warming the set of his brows.

As her hand relaxed, Cadmael pulled his fingers from their

entwined embrace with hers. Her hand suddenly clamped down on his and when their eyes met, she gave him a wavering smile. There was a bubble in the pit of her stomach that screamed this was a trick, but she had to believe in Cadmael.

"Stay with me," she whispered to him. "Run away with me."

With that, his smile disappeared as though it had never been.

"I am nothing without a master," he whispered as his calloused fingers trailed along her hairline.

"What do you have planned for yourself?"

"Don't worry about it. Everything will turn out just fine." He pulled his hand from hers.

He was nothing without a master? What if he was planning to die after setting her free? Chance felt sick, like the apple she had eaten was about to come back up.

"You're coming with me." She pulled on him, daring the hellhound to respond. "I'll save the money and bring you with me overseas, and he will never find us."

"Do you mean that?" his brows furrowed as he glanced at her.

"I won't leave you behind."

Cadmael slowly shook his head, a tear leaking from the corner of his eye. She knew he planned to drop her off somewhere and then he was going to come crawling back. This was his goodbye. The hellhound planned to die for betraying his master.

30

BROKEN TOY

CADMAEL

Cadmael wrapped his arms around the girl and easily picked her up from the bed. She weighed a fraction of what she did the first time he carried her up. As he stood, many of the wounds that had clotted trickled fresh streams of blood down his back, splattering the floor. He had decided. It was likely the first actual choice he had ever made with no thoughts of what anyone else wanted.

He needed to get her out of here. If she ended up pregnant, he'd have to watch his own offspring suffer the life that was his! They would share in his own personal hell.

"What-? Right now?"

"Shh." He hissed, silencing her as he carried her from the room.

Once he reached the top of the stairs. Something struck

him dead center on his back. As he flung forward, down the stairs, his arms clenched protectively around Chance. By the time they hit the bottom, he had lost his grasp on her.

There were a few moments of darkness before he came to. He could still feel Eadrich's foot between his shoulder blades. The bloody mess from his back had smeared, leaving a puddle beneath him.

"You traitorous mutt!" Eadrich hissed down at Cadmael from where he stood at the top of the stairs. "You were running away?!"

"I was going to come back, Master." Cadmael whispered, his voice echoing in the large, empty entrance hall. "I am nothing without a master."

"Liar!"

"I swear! I was only getting rid of the girl. I'm sorry, Master, but what you're demanding of me is a torment I cannot abide!"

"You…" Eadrich whispered in surprise. "Cannot abide?"

"Please, Master, just let me release her." Cadmael felt tears roll down his cheeks as he crawled toward the unconscious girl. "Let me set her free. I'll come right back to you. I belong to you and will face whatever consequences you deem fit."

His shin was pretty badly torn up, and he was sure his right shoulder had dislocated when he fell. Eadrich was halfway down the stairs, leaving a bloody print on every second step from the foot that had struck Cadmael's wounded back. His hand dragged along the dark wood railing as he approached at a menacingly slow pace.

"Hey, wake up," Cadmael whispered as he grabbed Chance's shoulder and rolled the girl onto her back.

Cadmael gasped in surprise as he stared into her wide, lifeless eyes. His skin prickled across his arms and neck as he shook his head. He'd watched countless toys die. He killed some with his own hands because it was his master's order… and the one he tried to save died because of him.

"No," his voice cracked as he whimpered. "Wake up, Chance!"

He suddenly sprang into action. Cadmael began chest compressions, though they would do nothing to undo the damage to her body or repair her clearly broken neck. Her head rested at the most peculiar angle, but he didn't see it through blinding panic. Cadmael simply did compressions, desperate to bring the girl back. He pressed hard enough in the center of her chest that he was sure the crunching was her ribs breaking. Tears streamed steadily down his cheeks as he mentally pleaded for her to wake.

"YOU KILLED MY TOY!!!" Eadrich's scream was so deafening that the words reverberated through Cadmael's soul.

The compressions stopped when Eadrich's leg brutally made contact with Cadmael's ribs. His vampiric strength sent Cadmael flailing helplessly through the air. He rammed into the door, knocking the antique corner table next to it over. With tears streaming down his hopeless face, he couldn't even get up. He rolled onto his side, coughing and grabbing at his chest.

Eadrich was on him in a heartbeat. The vampire grabbed Cadmael's throat in one hand and his hair in the other to heave him easily to his feet. He kept both hands dangling to his side as he accepted his master's rage. His tears had already stopped as Eadrich screamed in his face.

"I'll kill you," Eadrich slammed Cadmael into the hard oak door so hard that the wood made a loud cracking sound. "Worthless Malix Peek!"

Cadmael felt the wounds across his back split, causing blood to lead down his backside and trail down the door.

The vampire's icy hands both wrapped around Cadmael's throat. He had never felt such fear before as he did the moment his feet lifted from the ground. His hands grabbed at Eadrich's arm for support, but it did nothing to relieve the pain. Why was he so scared when he'd been ready to die all this time?

"I'd snap your neck, but you don't deserve the same death as her." Eadrich snarled, squeezing a little tighter. "I'll just have to settle for squeezing the life out of you."

Cadmael's head throbbed as his arms went numb. A tingling rippled across his entire body. There was a moment of clarity where he accepted his end. Cadmael let his hands fall to his sides as he closed his eyes. He didn't want the last thing he saw to be his beloved Master's enraged face. His vision had already blurred, so it was only a matter of time until death took him.

Cadmael lost consciousness for only an instant. When his eyes opened again, he was sitting on the floor with his back resting against the door while he choked and gagged on air as it forced its way back into his body.

There, in front of him, with her eyebrows furrowed, kneeled the woman he was sure he'd gotten killed.

"You?" he mouthed before breaking into an awful coughing fit.

31

TURNING FATE

CHANCE

"Chance!" she heard a familiar voice screaming her name into the void of never-ending darkness.

It was Cadmael! No. It couldn't have been him. Cadmael had never once said her name. She stared around blindly and fumbled her way toward the voice who called out to her.

"NO!" a less familiar voice rang out.

"Maman?" she stared around, desperate to hear that sound once more. "Maman! Ou est tu?"

There was no answer. Only darkness. A light appeared in the dark, like a glimmering flame on a candle… but it seemed to shrink farther and farther away from her. Chance ran toward it. She could sense her mother's presence, smell her perfume.

"Mammaaaaaan!" Chance screamed as loud as she could, desperately trying to close the distance between her and the light.

Like a tidal wave, another voice perforated the dark, "YOU KILLED MY TOY!!!"

Chance halted, flinching in terror as she searched for the owner of that horrifying scream.

"Eadrich?" she whispered into the dark with a shaky voice, then cried out, "Maman! I'm scared!"

The single light flickered as though it were a star, too far for her to reach. Like a whisper in the wind, she heard her mother telling her to hurry. Chance broke into a dead run toward the light.

"Maman! Jai—"

Eadrich's voice interrupted once again, "Worthless Malix Peek!"

She froze, staring around once again. Cadmael? He risked everything to save her. A loud crashing noise exploded nearby, drawing her attention to the waking world around her body.

"I'm sorry…" Chance whispered to her mother…

And then she awoke. Her neck throbbed in agonizing waves as she tried to move it. There was a hollow feeling in her chest, as if the world owed her something. It felt as if she didn't belong there anymore. Chance reached around her head, tangling her fingers in her hair as they dragged across her scalp. She pulled hard, forcing her head to straighten. That seemed to repair the discomfort that radiated across her throat and down her shoulders.

Chance slowly sat up, struggling to fend off the wave of dizziness that assaulted her. She felt high without the nauseating and heart palpitating traits of some toxic chemical. She tilted her head from side-to-side feeling something pop and grind painfully in her neck until the issue seemed to resolve itself. Chance closed her eyes, trying to drown out the visual overstimulation. The floor beneath her, the surrounding walls… she could see every single detail to the smallest hair or speck of dirt. That was too much to handle all at once. Add the sound behind her… it all drove her crazy!

With her eyes shut, Chance could 'feel' the surrounding room and everything in it. The entire universe felt as though it were closing in on her like an icy vortex. The cold gradually devoured her as it spread from her extremities.

There was a scuffle nearby, drawing her attention from the sickening agony of hunger that erupted in her stomach and burned her throat. With her icy hands pressed to her abdomen, Chance twisted to see where all the ruckus was coming from.

There was a tall, dark man with graying skin who had a shorter blonde man pinned by his throat. There was only one heartbeat in the room, and it was slowing. The soft thrumming echoed loudly in her ears.

She blinked in confusion as her dark eyebrows furrowed. It took a moment, but as she glimpsed the shorter man's face, everything came flooding back in a hurricane of horror.

"Cadmael," she mouthed the word before charging to her feet.

She could hear Eadrich's obnoxious, slurring voice hissing obscenities at *her* Cadmael. Chance ran towards the monster, who had spent a hundred lifetimes torturing others. Those few months of Tae kwon Do training she received as a child likely were no match for the vampire. When she closed the distance between them, Chance raised her right leg and swung it across in front of her body. Her shin connected with Eadrich's ribs just under his right arm. The shock of the impossibly powerful strike made him release his hold on Cadmael. The hellhound crumpled to the floor, unconscious.

For a moment, she had trouble forcing herself to look away from Cadmael. Chance desperately wanted to make sure he was alive. He lay on his side with his eyes closed. He had dark bruising already apparent around his throat. There was a thick streak of blood down the door. As Chance focused her overactive senses on listening for his heartbeat, Eadrich's voice echoed in a shriek across the empty entry hall, making her flinch. It was far too loud.

"What the fuck?!"

Eadrich held the wall as he dragged himself to his feet. Chance's eyes widened as she fully took in the ancient vampire's appearance. He had his silken robe hanging askew off his shoulder. His cheek was torn just below his eye from where his face struck the wall. His dark blood slowly trickled from the wound down the side of his face.

The blood dripped from Eadrich's chin, splattering the floor. Chance couldn't take her eyes from the bubbling wound that strangely made his natural cinnamon scent stronger, but now there was some sort of woody scent mixed with it. Her gaze followed the stream of crimson, as though mesmerized by the flow. Chance licked her lips when a large droplet left his chin, then fell as if in slow motion. It struck the ground with an explosion of noise as it scattered, becoming several smaller droplets.

Eadrich's yelling drew Chance's attention back up to his face. She cocked her head to the side, trying to process the words as he roared.

"This is impossible!"

Chance swallowed hard. The sweet, yet acidic scent of Eadrich's blood kept pulling her focus back to his wound.

"I never once allowed you to consume my blood." Eadrich hissed, shaking his head.

Chance tilted her head to the other side as she licked her lips. She simply shrugged her shoulders in response to his question.

"I'm so hungry…" Chance whimpered with a pout.

"Tell me how this happened, you stupid whore!"

Chance opened her mouth to answer and instead she smiled, feeling her razor-sharp eye teeth shred her bottom lip. Her own blood trickled down her chin and filled her mouth. The lukewarm liquid was awash with flavor. Chance moaned, suddenly more aroused than she'd ever been in her life. She knew her blood was cold, though it felt warm against her icy flesh as it dribbled down her body.

Chance moaned again loudly, over Eadrich speaking, "Respond, I command you!"

She moaned harder, just to bug him as she raised her hand to her chest. Chance massaged her breasts, smearing the dark blood across her skin.

"I'm so horny!" she whined, sliding that bloody hand

down, leaving a crimson trail leading to her pussy.

Her fingers slipped between the lips in search of more pleasure. Chance's other hand moved to her breast, pinching her nipple and tugging lightly.

Chance drew her bottom lip into her mouth, then purposefully bit down. Blood dribbled once more. She desperately swallowed what spilled into her mouth, attempting to satiate her hunger. The blood-soaked fingers of the hand fondling her breast rose to her mouth. The tips traced her lips with crimson.

Eadrich shook his head, snarling audibly. His lips peeled back as he shoved himself away from the wall. He stumbled two steps toward Chance. His eyes narrowed in rage, but he seemed distracted, as if slightly interested by Chance's actions. She watched closely as the muscles in his throat flexed while he swallowed. The sound was so loud it made her smile.

"I'm your sire! You must obey me!" Eadrich growled through gritted teeth.

"Sure, what do you want?" Chance purred her response.

She was so aroused that she couldn't stop staring at his cock peeking out from the opening in his robes.

Before he could respond, she asked, "Do you want me?"

She licked her lips when his dick bobbed up and down enthusiastically. Chance felt her lips draw into a smile when it hardened as a direct result of her actions. The little thing had already doubled in length and seemed to anticipate some action.

"I never wanted another offspring." Eadrich snarled, his hands balling into fists.

He took a careful step toward Chance. She sensed he was trying to get closer so he could attack her. Chance squinted quizzically before her face broke into a mischievous grin.

"Oh! I get it! That's why Tyne called you his father… Do you like that?" Chance slid one foot outward, making access to her pussy easier as she began massaging her clit more vigorously.

Chance put on her sweetest, most seductive voice, "I'm so horny, daddy. Please fuck me so hard…"

Eadrich took another step forward.

"Please daddy," Chance begged, "I need you inside me."

One more step and he closed half the distance between them. The wound on his cheek was already nearly healed.

"Daddy, tear me open with your giant cock."

Chance felt her orgasm looming ever closer. It was unlike any sensation she'd felt before. Her core vibrated with both pain and pleasure, but her climax was just outside her reach.

"I'm going to cum for you, daddy." Chance growled, coming ever closer to finishing, but still unable to climax.

Chance's body teetered painfully on the cusp of oblivion. Her mismatched eyes pleaded with the ancient vampire for him to assist her.

A devious smile pranced its way across Eadrich's lips. He seemed to have other plans than simply pleasuring her. Even with that grin on his lips, he looked to be one very pissed off creature. His hands stayed clenched at his sides.

Chance realized that she wasn't afraid. Normally, she'd instinctually feel absolute terror when looking into those red-rimmed eyes.

Without warning, Eadrich lunged at her, closing the distance between them before Chance could even gasp in surprise. Her eyes widened, though she still felt no fear. There was a hollow feeling where she knew that feeling should be.

His hand closed around her throat. To her surprise, it caused no pain. The force behind his attack caused Chance to step backward in a feeble attempt at keeping her balance. Something caught the back of her leg.

The way his body pressed against hers, along with the shimmer in his eye… she knew he had tripped her. As Eadrich threw himself forward, his robe came loose, fluttering behind him when he moved.

Chance fell backward with Eadrich on top of her. Her hands flung outward in search of anything to slow her fall.

Her back landed hard on the small antique table that had been on its side in the middle of the entryway. The wood gave way to their combined weight, cracking loudly as it collapsed beneath them. Chance could feel an uncomfortable pressure against her back, knowing she should feel outright agony, but there was no pain at all.

Eadrich squeezed her throat so tight it was impossible for her to force air through. She wasn't bothered by the lack of oxygen. It simply felt different to not breathe. Clearly, she didn't need to, and was only doing it out of habit.

Feeling Eadrich's hard cock rubbing against her thigh, Chance opened her legs to invite him to enter her. She rolled her hips, feeling his tip taunt her entrance.

The ancient vampire's free hand pinned Chance's wrist to her side, where it landed when she tried to stop herself from falling. He released her throat and dragged that hand across her collarbone, sliding it down her arm until it found her other wrist. His fingers wrapped so tight around her wrists, she felt the bones crunch. Chance knew without pain that he had broken both her wrists. The wound carried a severe discomfort, and the bones seemed to grind together irritatingly as he applied more pressure.

It made pulling her hands free from his grip impossible. It was almost like her body refused to force a movement that would risk causing more damage, even though there was no pain associated with the wound. If she were still human, she'd be able to struggle against him. It would hurt like a bitch, but the ability to try would be there.

Eadrich had literally paralyzed her arms. Even then, she felt no fear. The only actual sensation Chance seemed to experience was a dire need to both eat and fuck. She was hungry and horny.

"Tell me what you desire the most?" Eadrich tenderly purred against her throat.

"Fuck me!" Chance screamed, desperate for relief.

Eadrich shifted his hips, so the tip of his cock teased her clit, rubbing against it. Chance moaned, jerking her hips to force it inside. She whimpered when she raised her hips, and it tickled her entrance. The bastard moved his own hips away to stop his cock from entering her.

"What do I get in return?" Eadrich growled before licking up the side of her neck, sending fresh waves of arousal washing over her body.

"What do you want?" Chance cried out, ready to give him anything he desired.

"I want to devour you."

Eadrich opened his mouth to exhale an icy breath upon her flesh, making goosebumps rise on her skin.

"Why bother asking?" she couldn't help questioning.

"I am not your sire… or I'd have bitten you already."

"Will you satisfy me?" Chance questioned.

She could feel her wrists healing under the weight of his grasp. Chance smiled, hoping he hadn't noticed. As a distraction, she licked his cheek, enjoying the cinnamon flavor of the drying blood. She giggled when she realized her fangs had slashed her tongue.

"Just a taste," she told him, purposefully slicing her tongue more before sticking it out for him.

Eadrich's mouth tightened in irritation for a moment before he complied. His mouth wrapped around her tongue, and he sucked hard, sipping only a small amount of her blood before their saliva healed her wound.

When he broke off the kiss to smirk down at her while carefully pressing his cock to her entrance, she tried to bite his shoulder, but couldn't make herself penetrate his flesh with her fangs.

"Fuck me!" she screamed up at him. "Fuck me and you can bite me!"

In unison, Eadrich's fangs and cock penetrated Chance one last time.

32

SOLACE OR NOT

CHANCE

Eadrich's cock plowed into her with more force than ever before. She suspected it was to distract her from noticing how much blood he was drinking. The longer she laid there, the closer Chance came to dying. Her body weakened and the healing in her wrists slowed to where she was concerned that they wouldn't heal in time to attempt defending herself.

Eadrich must have been high from the overwhelming amount of blood he'd taken, because he released Chance's wrist to cup her cheek on the opposite side from where he drank. He probably assumed she was too weak from blood loss to do more than lightly struggle. Even as she grew weaker, her libido still screamed for sexual contact or anything to make her feel more alive.

Chance wiggled and dug her heels into the marble floor.

She raised her ass from the cold floor for a few moments while Eadrich pounded his cock deep inside her. As amazing as it felt to receive some pleasure, his icy cold cock didn't have the same cool flourish for her as it had before. She was still nowhere near that overwhelming climax feeling she had reached so easily with him in the past. Dying was not worth this fuck.

Her legs grew weak, to where holding her hips up became impossible. Chance expected to feel afraid as Eadrich drained her. Instead, her mind took a more logical approach. Without fear slowing her down, her mind seemed to work clearer. Her free hand moved across the floor in search of anything she could use to help her survive. She reached out toward the unconscious Cadmael. When her fingers wrapped around his shoe and pulled, feeling no resistance, it was clear he could not help her.

"I finally understand," she whispered, hoping to distract him. "I know why you hurt others."

She felt his movements slow, as if he were listening to her. His hips withdrew, then lingered a moment before pounding into her. He stopped moving his hips up and down to grind himself against her depths. His sucking on her neck slowed, but didn't stop entirely.

Chance stayed quiet, forcing herself to stop breathing as she let her body become limp. His mouth finally broke away from her flesh. Her skin healed nearly instantly from the remnants of his saliva on her neck.

"I know you're not unconscious, clever girl," he purred in her ear. "You didn't stop your heart from beating."

Chance felt his fangs pierce her throat once more. It didn't take long before her vision blurred, darkening.

"You can't remember…" Chance whispered, struggling just to speak, "What anything… feelsss… like…"

As she blacked out, a whimper from nearby yanked her back to consciousness. Cadmael! He belonged to her now and if she died, Eadrich would kill the boy.

Chance's eyes snapped open. Her hand that rested on the

hellhound's foot moved in search of a weapon. She took hold of a piece of the small wooden table. She raised her make-shift weapon into the air and brought it down toward the center of Eadrich's back with all the force she had. She used every ounce of strength her weakened body could muster. The instant the shard of wood entered his flesh, Eadrich screamed and attempted to get up. Chance slid her newly freed arm around the back of his neck while wrapping her legs around his waist. She locked her ankles to force Eadrich to remain plunged into her depths.

Chance had the merest inkling of a thought which should have disturbed and revolted her. Instead, she found herself aroused by the idea. If he died while so deep inside her, it might be enough to push her into that elusive orgasm she'd been struggling to reach. She could feel him fighting for freedom on top of her, snarling and growling reminiscent of a feral animal.

His struggling aroused her more while his cock miraculously maintained its hardened form. She could feel her insides tightening around it, almost pushing her over the peak into euphoria. She was so close, but it still wouldn't come!

Eadrich repositioned himself on his hands and knees, lifting Chance up from the ground. She hung beneath him, clutching tightly, feeling annoyed that he was being so stubborn. Chance pulled the wooden shard from his back. He struggled hard, grabbing her throat and using it as leverage to keep her back against the floor while trying to push himself upright. She knew she didn't have his strength, especially after he drank so much from her. Chance quickly rammed her weapon into his back once more, hoping to plunge it deeper.

Eadrich wailed, throwing himself around wildly. Blood rolled down his ribs, splattering the surrounding stone floor. She wanted to bite him so badly, but found herself unable to plunge her fangs into his flesh. In her anger, she twisted the wooden shard in his back. Eadrich's hands pushed down on her chest and throat as he tried to get free of her, arching his back. Her hands lost their grip on the aggressively flailing vampire. Chance barely kept her legs locked around his waist, preventing not only his escape, but forcing his cock to remain inside her. His struggling only caused his pubis to massage against her clit. She was so close to cumming, but it simply wouldn't happen! Eadrich snarled down at her while raising his right hand. His gaze turned to his fingers, the nails of which were shifting into sharp claws. Chance gasped loudly when she realized they were slowly blackening from the tops, moving toward his palm.

Chance couldn't help the amused giggle that escaped her. Eadrich's nostrils flared in outrage.

"You fucking bitch!" Eadrich hissed as he closed his fingers tightly together to make a spear from the tips as they turned into claws.

"Whoa!" Chance gasped loudly, watching as the darkening moved down to his wrist.

If fear were an issue, she'd have panicked, knowing death was imminent. Instead, she quickly considered her options. It didn't take long, as her options were so limited. Chance didn't have the strength or energy to throw the powerful vampire off herself.

Eadrich smirked down at her, likely enjoying the view as she floundered beneath him. As Chance reached toward her saving grace, the broken table, he snarled and attacked.

"I'm going to kill you!" Eadrich screamed and brought that weaponized hand down toward the spot between her breasts.

Her eyes widened, surprised by the speed his hand flew down at her. Chance grabbed the only thing she found, the small tabletop. She dragged it quickly on top of her, bracing it with her forearm, like a medieval shield. Eadrich's clawed hand smashed the wood into smithereens, sending slivers and chunks exploding outward. However, that wasn't what made Chance cry out.

Both vampires stared in surprise at Eadrich's hand. His blackening claws vanished into her forearm. All the luck in the world would not have made that happen twice!

The shooting pain was nearly on the same horrific level as she experienced when Eadrich dislocated her shoulders. The shocking pain quickly seemed to dim into an aching annoyance.

Blood trickled, pooling between her arm and her chest. Chance would have expected not only more pain, but far more blood. His clawed fingers appeared to vanish into her arm in the gap between the two bones of her forearm. His hand went so far that his claws sliced through the other side, cutting her chest. The darkening of his skin had moved up his arm, nearly at his elbow.

His icy smile made Chance reconsider her few options. Eadrich's fangs glistened as he wiggled his fingers. They sliced the skin at the center of her chest, and the damage to her nerves made her fingers twitch. Chance growled, refusing to give him another scream. The ancient vampire placed his free hand on her arm to brace it as he moved to pull his claws out. Chance had two options. One, let him pull his hand free so he could try again or…

Chance used her free hand to grab his wrist, stopping him from withdrawing. She grit her teeth as shockwaves of pain spread out from the wound. When there was no movement, the pain immediately numbed. Eadrich pulled back so hard her shoulders lifted from the cold stone floor.

He twisted his arm to loosen her grip, but she refused to give in. As his hand turned, Chance snarled loudly, trying to hold back her scream. The movement inside made her fingers tremble and twitch reflexively.

"Going limp already?" she hissed through gritted teeth.

Forcing a mischievous grin, Chance wiggled her hips, grinding herself against him. His cock instantly grew harder and more girthy than ever. Somehow, she'd turned this into the most fucked up battle of wills. Eadrich growled loudly, releasing his bracing hand to use it to strangle Chance. She knew this had to be an attempt to silence her.

"That's it? No wonder," Chance forced out in a breathy growl, "you died a virgin."

Eadrich roared as if damaging his ego was on par with a physical blow.

Their gaze met, and he raised his free hand as if to use his claws to stab through her throat. There were no more limbs left to use in her defense. He seemed frozen, staring down at her with loathing and outrage.

His raised arm shook as his features contorted with a grimace. The ashy dark color had reached his shoulder and ascended down to his chest. As Chance peered up at him, she noticed the darkness had become visible, slowly rising on his abdomen, blending with his tattoos.

As Eadrich's brows furrowed, bloody tears filled his eyes.

"I am," he whispered, dropping his hand to his side and slumping forward to stare down at her.

His charcoal fingers lightly grazed Chance's cheek as he hissed the last word, "Afraid." His voice cracked as it left his lips.

Chance smiled, feeling herself clench lustfully around his cock.

"Don't think about it," the new vampire responded. "Just lose yourself in me."

She was going to help him go out with a bang. A devious smile matching hers appeared on his darkening lips.

Using his fangs, Eadrich bit his bottom lip, easily piercing it. Blood dribbled down his chin, splattering Chance's stomach. As he leaned forward, hovering over her, his cinnamon scented blood splashed onto her breasts, throat, then chin. Finally, his lips pressed to hers in the most amazing kiss she'd ever received.

The moment of contact, an explosion of flavor enveloped Chance's mouth. His tongue twined with hers in an embrace the moment it entered her mouth. He easily threw her into oblivion through that timeless kiss of death. With the taste of Eadrich on her tongue and the feeling of him so deep inside, a wave of agonizing pleasure engulfed her entire body. His hips pressed hard against Chance as he stopped moving. Eadrich's last act in this world was to fill Chance with cum.

Chance lay there in the debris, panting hard. The whole breathing thing was a habit she didn't need to do, but found it comforting. Her orgasm had been the most intensely pleasurable and painful thing she'd ever experienced. Her entire body trembled in the aftermath.

Her shaking legs finally released their cage around the older vampire. Using her undamaged hand, she pushed him off her, so he stiffly rolled onto his back next to her. As his body moved, the clawed hand embedded in Chance's arm tore free, making her groan from discomfort. She lifted it in the air to examine the wound curiously. She opened her hand, watching the remaining exposed tenons flex and loosen from the friction of movement. She couldn't move three of her fingers, likely from the damage she'd incurred. The medical student in her wanted to experiment with the wound and learn from it.

Frowning thoughtfully, she brought her forearm to her lips. Her tongue slipped out and dabbed at the edge of the wound, wanting to watch how it healed from her saliva. As her blood touched her tongue she gasped loudly, feeling something far more desperate take over. It was a similar sensation to her desperation for sex she'd recently experienced, except this was much, much worse. Chance stuck her tongue into the wound, wiggling it around to taste as much of the blood as she could.

Eadrich's blood was spilled onto her wound, giving her the strangest combination of vanilla and cinnamon. It was a struggle not to allow herself to suck on the wound, drinking herself dry. Eadrich had drunk enough from her. She finally forced herself to lick the length of the gash, allowing it to heal. She watched closely as the skin cells duplicated, literally stitching the wound closed as if it had never happened. There was still a faint pink line where a scar should be.

She slowly sat up, staring at Eadrich's ashen body. He almost looked like a mummy from the way his skin had lost hydration. Miraculously, he still had a fantastic hard-on. His cock remained fully exposed. Some parts of him had turned ashen and crumble off his corpse as if it had been burned.

Too bad he was dead. She would have loved the opportunity to reap her revenge upon him in the most brutal ways imaginable. Chance remembered there was another survivor in the room. Her head slowly turned to stare at the young man.

Chance carefully crawled toward Cadmael. Once in front of him, she cocked her head to the side, examining his features. His closed eyes had dark eyelashes so long that she felt envious of them. His hair hung in messy ringlets that had gotten long enough the tips tickled his eyelids. The blue dye job he had on the tips of his hair when they met had faded into a sandy blond, and his dark roots had grown out. Had she really been there so long?

Chance's icy fingers tenderly brushed his forehead to move his bangs. Cadmael's eyes fluttered open. His brows rose in surprise as he took in what he was seeing.

33

FINALLY

CADMAEL

"Chance?" Cadmael whispered in a shaky voice.

"I heard you. You said my name for the first time," Chance told him and received a sweet smile in return, though tears filled his eyes. "So, I came back."

"Master!" Cadmael exclaimed in a panic. His skin turned ghostly white as he whispered, "He's going to--"

"He's dead." Chance told him in a flat voice, not expecting the despondent look on Cadmael's face.

He slowly shook his head as if he didn't believe her. Tears welled in his shimmering blue eyes.

Chance shifted herself to the left, exposing the ashen vampire behind her. Her robe was askew, hanging partially removed, so his rock-hard cock was fully exposed. She raised an eyebrow as Cadmael's face twisted into a strange expression combining panic and hopelessness. The way the beautiful boy's features strained sent a chill down Chance's spine. A part of her expected him to be relieved, but she enjoyed the strange feelings his face shared with her.

Chance realized her fingers had found her clit while she observed the hellhound. She instinctively breathed in and was caught completely off guard by Cadmael's scent. Chance could easily distinguish between his deodorant, cologne, aftershave, and two different body sprays. All of which made him smell wonderful when she was human… Now that she was a vampire, it barely masked the dog smell that rose from his flesh.

CADMAEL

Cadmael bowed his head. He couldn't even force himself to look at Chance. He was so ashamed of his own feelings.

His master was a monster. He knew that. But it didn't mean Cadmael didn't love him. Who was supposed to take care of Cadmael now? Who was supposed to love him?

Cadmael turned his face away, to hide the tears trailing down his cheeks. His hands squeezed into fists so hard that his fingers ached.

Who was he without a master!? He really was just some Malix Peek now.

"Malix Peek." He whispered softly, his voice cracking.

"What does that even mean?" She whispered, putting her free hand on his shoulder while the other continued toying with her clit.

"Stray dog. I'm nothing but a Malix Peek now." As he spoke, his head slowly turned to stare at the girl who he lost everything for.

"You're not. You're just Cadmael." She brushed her thumb against his cheek to dry his tears.

Her skin was so icy against his, it was almost reminiscent

of Eadrich. Cadmael closed his eyes, feeling his tears mesh across his long, dark eyelashes.

"Where do you want me to take you? Home?" he asked, but raised his eyebrows when she shook her head.

He couldn't imagine where else in the world she'd want to go after the nightmare she'd been through. She was a vampire now, so he couldn't guess what she could want from her old life.

"We are going to the police."

"We?" Cadmael responded.

"First, we need to show the police where all of *his* victims are. Those families need closure. Second, I'll be going overseas because I'm not giving up my life. I'm going to continue the path I was on before all this."

"I certainly can drop you off." Cadmael's jaw quivered.

His eyes closed tightly before he shook his head. He could smell her arousal and it was agony for him. How could she be in such a mood? She was a vampire now. That's how. They were in constant search of warmth, as if looking for the heat of life. Food and sex were what vampires craved.

He wouldn't tell her, but he would take her anywhere she wished and return to his master. He opened his eyes. He was never meant to outlive Eadrich.

"*We* are going to the police station." Chance repeated herself harshly.

"I'm scared," Cadmael whispered.

"Why?"

"Because of what I've done for my master."

"Don't worry, I'll make sure they know you were a prisoner, too."

"But I could leave any time. I had the keys."

Cadmael was certain that he was just as much of a monster as Eadrich was, if not worse, because Eadrich was honest about being a monster. Whereas he always played up being a victim, when he'd willingly done horrific things.

"And what would have happened if you left?" She finally stopped touching herself.

"I don't want to know."

"Exactly. You were a prisoner, too. Your chains were just different from mine."

"Can't I just drop you off there?"

"You don't want to stay with me?"

His breath caught as his gaze flashed to her face in surprise. His eyebrows rose and mouth hung open for a second as he considered how he should react. Before he could think logically about it, his words spilled out.

"I do. But why would you want a burden like me around?"

Chance growled, scaring the shit out of Cadmael. His gaze snapped to meet hers and his jaw locked. Every part of him tensed as he waited for her words.

"I am your master now," Chance snarled at him. "I refuse to allow harm to come to you. And you may never speak of yourself in such a way again. Do you understand me?"

Cadmael swore his heart skipped a beat as she said she was his master. His pulse suddenly raced. He couldn't help the glimmer of a smile that forced its way onto his face as he stared up at her. She touched her icy hand to his cheek before leaning in and pressing her lips to his. Chance's lips were cool and full, so tender and delicious. Her vanilla scent encompassed him like a passionate caress. As a vampire, that smell was far stronger than it had been than when she was human. He couldn't help the smile that pulled his lips tight mid-kiss. Cadmael took a deep breath, basking in her aroma.

CHANCE

"Something smells amazing, like pineapple." Chance whispered, standing and turning as if to walk upstairs.

"It's the toy from the party," Cadmael informed her, quickly coming to his feet and reaching out toward Chance as if to stop her. "She must be bleeding or a vampire wouldn't smell it."

Chance stood and walked toward the stairs, her eyes

searching for the origin of the scent. Her hands moved to her stomach, which was empty and aching with thirst. Her throat practically seared with desire and the thought of quenching that thirst sent rippling chills across her body, making her aroused once again.

"I'm so hungry."

Chance reached the bottom of the stairs. Her fingers lightly fingered the wooden banister as she lifted her foot to set it on the bottom step.

"If you go up there as you are now, you'll kill her!" he warned with wide eyes, taking two steps forward.

"Why would I care?" she asked without thinking as she glanced back at him over her shoulder.

Cadmael's features shifted, no longer tender and concerned. He swallowed loudly and took a slow, deep breath. He was suddenly expressionless, like a doll or a robot. Swiftly, Cadmael bowed, his eyes never leaving Chance's face.

"My apologies, Master."

She never wanted Cadmael to treat her the way he did Eadrich. He feared for his life, so he wore an emotionless mask as a shield. Chance's jaw locked in annoyance. Her hand recoiled from the railing as if it burned her.

"Cadmael?" Chance softly called as she slowly backed away from the stairs.

Every step away from food was pure agony. It took everything in her not to just bolt forward, throwing away the last shred of human decency she had left. She could not pull her eyes away from the second floor. The blood lust was serious and completely overwhelming.

"Don't fear me… please."

She shook her head as she struggled to hold on to her humanity. One of her hands moved to her stomach and the other to her throat, both of which yearned for the taste of blood.

"I know I'm revolting, but I can offer myself to you." Cadmael's soft whisper washed over her as he approached from behind.

His body was so close to hers, but not quite touching. His forearm appeared in front of Chance's mouth. She could feel heat radiating from him against her backside. Chance stepped back, leaning her body against his as her hands tenderly stroked his arm.

"I don't want to lose control," she murmured, unsure why she cared.

There was an internal struggle for control, as if the bits of remaining humanity inside Chance were fighting for Cadmael's survival. She could feel his hot breath cascade down the side of her neck when he exhaled before wrapping his other arm around her waist, holding her pressed against him.

"If it pleases you, stop when or before I lose consciousness. Hellhounds can survive far more blood loss than a human and we replenish quicker."

Cadmael bowed his head forward over her shoulder to press his lips against her neck. His ringlets tickled Chance's ear, making her nipples harden with desire. She couldn't believe that she was already this aroused. No wonder all the old vampire stories had them written as intensely sensual creatures. Chance could feel the sun blaring up in the sky outside, even without seeing it. They had time before she could leave anyway, and what better way to spend it than in his arms?

"Fuck me," she whimpered softly, lightly kissing his forearm.

Chance bent forward, making it easier for him to have access to enter her. She pulled his arm with her, so he had no choice but to cocoon her body with his own. The feel of his overwhelming body heat overtook her in waves. She hadn't realized how cold she was until his warmth enfolded her.

"So cold." She trembled from his touch as his free hand caressed her flesh, sliding up her hip, to her ribs and around to her breast.

"Touch me more!" Chance purred, desperate for more of his fiery caress.

"Drink, and I'll touch you everywhere."

Her teeth sank into his forearm, but the blood didn't spill forth until she pulled her fangs back out, biting again. She barely got a gulp of blood before her saliva healed the wound. WHAT THE FUCK! How was she supposed to feed?!

But that flavor! It wasn't as bad as Eadrich claimed. Yeah, his blood tasted a little how dogs smelled, but it really wasn't so bad. It temporarily quenched her thirst and was fulfilling enough that she could probably survive on it. She pulled her fangs out and licked the skin, watching it heal before biting once again. Chance moaned, sinking her fangs into his flesh again. She turned her head slightly, wiggling her teeth to shred his skin, allowing more blood to spill into her mouth. She chugged hard, swallowing gulps of blood, failing to keep it from dribbling down her chin and onto the stone floor.

She used one hand to keep Cadmael's wrist firmly planted against her mouth, while her other reached behind, grabbing his cock through his dress pants. It's girth tripled beneath her fingers as she massaged its length.

Cadmael cupped his hand over her breast for a moment before pinching her nipple, twisting gently until she gasped from pleasure and surprise. Chance moved her hips automatically as her arousal increased. His hot fingers made her skin burn. He twisted her nipple the other way, sending shockwaves of pleasure into the depths of her breast.

Why did that feel so good?! It should hurt or be uncomfortable. She wanted more, so much more.

"Cadmael, please. I need you."

CADMAEL

Cadmael gasped against the back of Chance's neck as she rubbed him into oblivion. There was no other sensation, like the icy caress of a vampire's touch. His blue eyes flashed at Eadrich's ashy corpse.

"It looks like he's staring at us," Cadmael whispered in a shaky voice.

Eadrich's eyes had blackened and partially caved in, but Cadmael still felt like they were watching him, judging him. His stomach turned, though there was nothing in it. Chance pulled her fangs from his arm and whipped around, glaring up at Cadmael, who stared down nervously.

"Let him watch us," she purred, pulling her bottom lip into her mouth.

Her eyebrows rose in shock as blood dribbled down her chin. Chance slid her tongue out, licking her lip to heal the wound. Her hands moved to his belt. The unbelievably sexy vampire hooked her fingers around the edge of his pants and belt.

Cadmael's breath caught in his lungs as her icy fingers tickled his skin under the edge of his briefs. His breath came in soft gasps, but as she used her grip on his cock to pull him to her, he tried to hold his breath. She might find him revolting if she smelled the dog scent from him. He turned his face away, trying not to exhale on the vampire.

Her beautiful face appeared full of focus. He frowned down at her with furrowed eyebrows. He wanted to reach out to her, but did not know how his new master would react. Vampires did not keep the same traits they had when they were human.

"Tell me what you want?" she whispered, her icy breath tickling his lips and chin as she tilted her head back and drew closer.

He licked his lips, practically tasting the vanilla on her breath. He wanted so badly to kiss her, to tell her he wanted her, but the paralyzing terror stopped him. Vampires were cruel creatures by nature, and he had no way of knowing if Chance would be any different from them now that she was one, too.

His eyes fluttered closed to stop the tears from welling. Normally, he would hide his emotions, but she forbade that and though she was trying to be different from Eadrich,

Cadmael had known vampires his entire life. Things don't change in an instant. At any moment, she could decide he was boring and end him.

It had always been easy for him to hide his thoughts and feelings from Eadrich, but Chance wasn't the cruel, ancient vampire. When Eadrich would ask Cadmael what he 'wanted' it was to gauge how well the hellhound could guess what Eadrich desired.

The girl in front of him may wear Chance's face, but she was a vampire, so she would have certainly changed.

"What do you want?" Chance repeated in the same tone of voice, conveying no emotion.

Her harsh voice echoed loudly in the entrance hall, making Cadmael flinch. The way she asked freaked him out more than anything because it sounded like she genuinely wanted to know what he desired. But what if she used it against him? No. She may have changed, but maybe what remained of Chance was the core of who she was.

"I want you to love me," Cadmael finally whispered, tears rolling down his cheeks, knowing that vampires can't feel love.

The silence that followed was deafeningly loud, but he refused to open his eyes for fear of seeing disgust on his beloved's face. His hands balled into fists at his sides to stop them from trembling as he waited for a reaction.

After what felt like an eternity, she still didn't respond, and Cadmael became more afraid of opening his eyes. His brows drew down and his eyes closed tighter, crinkling the bridge of his nose from the pressure.

Why wasn't she responding? Cadmael took a slow breath, taking in as much of her scent as he could. She was standing so close, he could feel the icy chill of her presence radiating through the air, caressing him. He cleared his features of all residual emotions. His mask was a defense mechanism, like a safety net for when he became afraid.

"Don't do that," Chance whispered, making him flinch again.

"My apologies, Master," he murmured, still unable to force his eyes to open.

"Say my name."

He cleared his throat. He didn't think he'd ever said Eadrich's name out loud. She was his master, so shouldn't he call her 'master'?

"I…" he lost his voice and had to clear his throat again, though he was only trying to buy time.

"I'm waaaaiiiting…" she hummed to Cadmael.

Her voice… the inflection was something he'd never heard from her. She sounded happy. His eyebrows rose slowly as he breathed in her scent before speaking.

"Chance," he whispered, unable to stop a silly grin from appearing on his face.

Cadmael couldn't take it anymore and opened his eyes to find Chance smiling up at him. Her fangs glistened in the chandelier's glow. He stared down at the beautiful woman in front of him. He opened his mouth, but no words would form.

"Cadmael? Do you love me?" she asked as she slid her hands up his chest.

"Since before I met you," he told her truthfully, but dropped his gaze, realizing she wasn't aware of the complete story of how she came to be at the manor.

Chance's hands clutched his shoulders, drawing his eyes back up to her face. She walked backward, leading him to the library.

"Tell me what burdens you?"

"Maste-uh, Eadrich knew about you because he had me investigating Tyne," he confided. "If it weren't for that, he would not have purchased you. We hadn't expected to find you at the auction, though."

They reached the doors by the time Cadmael finished speaking. He reached around her, without having to be told to do so, and opened the door, pushing it hard so it would swing wide. Instead of allowing his hand to fall back to his side, Chance slid her hand down his arm until it reached his wrist. She moved his hand so his palm rested on her hip.

"If you want to touch me, do it."

"I- I need permission."

"Do you wish to be my lover?" Chance asked, and his eyebrows rose.

Cadmael nodded, feeling his cheeks heat.

"Then behave as my lover, not my pet. I am not your master. Now, what do you want to do?"

CHANCE

"I want you." Cadmael exhaled his words in a quiet breath, a pained expression painting his face.

If he didn't behave as her equal now, he would forever be her slave. Chance didn't think she had the strength to be constantly reminding the hellhound that he was to be her lover, not her plaything. Her new found predatory instincts were screaming at her to dominate him and torture the boy.

"What are you going to do about it?" she sounded more forceful than she intended, but the point finally got across to him.

Cadmael timidly brought his face closer to hers, bending his neck. The hand on her hip slid to the small of her back, pulling her body against his. The fire of his warmth encompassed her, making her gasp with pleasure. She melted into his body, her hands sliding up to the back of his neck. Her fingers spread through his adorable curls as she rose to her tip-toes. His lips barely touched hers in a flutter of restrained desire. In a burst of electric passion, he firmly claimed her mouth with his, sending shuddering waves of frantic desire across her body. And as soon as the kiss began, he ended it, pulling away before she could deepen it with her tongue. Chance audibly whimpered in disappointment.

He moved his face forward again and her lips parted a fraction in anticipation, only to be disappointed as he laid a gentle kiss on her cheek. And another. And one on her earlobe, his chin brushing her neck.

"I love you, Chance."

In that moment, Chance realized all those natural vampiric instincts couldn't dampen the feelings she had for the hellhound.

"I love you," she responded, tilting her head to the side, offering her throat to him. "Now, show me your feelings!"

With a thunderous growl, the hellhound opened his mouth and bit the vampire's throat, laying claim to his mate.

THE END

Just kidding, I made a bonus chapter, cause I couldn't leave it like that.

EPILOGUE

SAY MY NAME AGAIN

CADMAEL

Circling his arms around his beloved, he moaned against her lips as their mouths collided in a wild entanglement of tongues and gnashing fangs. His hands felt frozen where she placed them, so afraid that he would displease her by giving into his waves of passion by caressing her flesh. Her glacial touch melted away all his worries and concerns. Her fingers traced every part of his frame, sending a rapture of chills across his body which caused goosebumps to rise. He slid his tongue along her fangs, allowing them to slice him so she could enjoy the blood that filled their mouths and rolled down their chins. Her moans encouraged him, making him want to find other ways to please her.

His right hand finally felt free to wander from its perch on her hip to slide down and groped her ass. His other hand eventually moved from where it dangled lifelessly at his side to cup her face. Her hair tangled around his fingers as his thumb slid along her cheekbone. He broke off their kiss to glide his lips along her other cheek, lightly kissing his way to her neck. He wanted so desperately to bite her throat again. It gave him such a feeling of overwhelming power and dominance, something he'd never known before her.

The hesitation lasted only moments before Chance's hand circled the back of his neck and her head tilted to make access easier for him. A deep growl erupted from his chest as he opened his mouth as wide as it could go. His hands trembled as his teeth dug into the vampire's throat. She tasted like a combination of three types of blood from the fighting. He could taste hers, his and even Eadrich's on her flesh.

As Cadmael showed his dominance, his lover moaned loudly, echoing her lustful sounds across the grand library. He had become so aroused that his cock pressed painfully hard against the front of his slacks. She was his everything.

His arms pulled her harder against him, so she could feel the might of his attraction to her. As she grabbed the front of his pants, Cadmael finally released his hold on her throat. He kissed a trail down her neck, stepping away so he could kiss along her collarbone, then down to her breast. Her nipples were already hard, urgently signaling their need for attention.

He suckled lightly on one nipple while massaging the other, as if trying to warm her skin with his touch. Both her hands were struggling with his buckle, desperate to release his cock from the material confining it. Cadmael suddenly gasped, but didn't allow himself to step back from the abrupt agony in his groin area. The sound of material tearing followed the searing pain. Hot blood trailed down his thighs as his pants fell to the floor.

His lover dropped to her knees when she realized what had happened. Her hand had shifted into claws from her frustration from fighting with the belt. As she hooked her fingers under the edge of his pants and briefs, they had morphed into weapons, scratching his lower abdomen and pubis.

"Cadmael! I hurt you!" She looked horrified as her eyes followed the trail of blood that streamed down his thighs.

With a thundering heart, he cocked his head to the side. Her concern for him nearly made him finish. Precum leaked from the tip of his cock, dribbling down the underside.

"Then maybe," he said with a mischievous smile he was sure she'd never seen him wear, "you should lick it better."

Her expression was absolutely adorable! Her eyebrows rose and a grin lit up her eyes as they suddenly glazed over black. It had triggered her peak arousal moment. He mentally prepared for a vampiric frenzy feeding that she wouldn't be able to stop. He smiled down at her as she excitedly stuck out her tongue.

He gasped enthusiastically as Chance's icy tongue touched his thigh. She slowly dragged it, licking her way up. He couldn't help the noises he made. This was the first time anyone had ever caressed him with so much genuine passion.

"Chance!" he yelped as she licked up his pubis to heal the wound.

"What?" she whispered, pulling away to stare up at him through long dark eyelashes.

He nervously stared down at her, unsure if she was cross that he didn't call her 'master'. Licking his lips, he trailed a hand up his chest.

"I - I said… you…" he cleared his throat nervously as his brows furrowed.

He felt panic rising as his pulse quickened. He knew she could hear it, but had promised not to mask his emotions.

"Say it again," she moaned, wrapping her hand around the base of his cock so tight that it bordered on being painful.

He blinked back the tears that wanted to trickle from his eyes. "Chance?" He whispered, then when she smiled up at him, he said it with more enthusiasm. "Chance!"

With no warning, she stuck her tongue out and slid it along the underside of his cock, collecting his juices. He nearly yelped in thrilled surprise from the icy sensations. His fingers tangled in her silky hair as he struggled with his frantic desire to touch her.

"Chance!" he growled her name as her tongue swirled the tip of his cock. "Wait, wait. I've never!"

He curled his body around the top of her head so his chest touched her hair as her cold mouth engulfed his cock. His hands trembled as they slid down her bare back, desperate to touch more of her flesh. As he bent over, the wounds across his back painfully tore, causing blood to trickle down his ribs and splatter onto the floor. Between her marvelous technique and the agony in his back, he exploded in her mouth.

He stood up, releasing her head to set her free. She continued to bob her head, sucking hard on his cock as it slowly became flaccid. She swallowed every ounce he shot out.

"I'm sorry," Cadmael whimpered softly, embarrassed that he's already finished.

She removed her mouth from his cock to smirk up at him as her tongue licked the blood from her lips. He chuckled faintly, knowing her fangs had sliced his dick. The venom made it entirely painless and even made his head spin. He stared down at his cock to find rings of blood from her lips.

Her chilly hands grabbed his hips as she leaned in and kissed a trail from his dick and up his abs. He gasped and whimpered, feeling worthless as he stood there, too nervous to do anything for her. Cadmael was so used to being ordered around that, without explicit instructions, he felt lost. His hands trembled as she kissed her way up his body. His stomach muscles tensing up with each brush of her cool lips. He moaned loudly and forced himself to move his hands, tangling his fingers in her hair, while the other hand slid down her back, enjoying the sensation of her glass-like skin.

When she reached his chest, Chance murmured, "I never even noticed your nipples were pierced."

She giggled and licked one of his nipples, making him moan as he wrapped his arms around her. He felt so desperate to be touching as much of her as possible.

"Say it again," she told him again with a warm smile.

"Chance, I love you."

He pressed his lips to her forehead, just above her left eyebrow as he cupped the side of her face with the hand that had been in her hair.

"Chance."

CHANCE

Every time he said her name, a fresh wave of arousal stirred deep within her core. Sadly, his ability to fuck was already spent. Chance's hunger and thirst wouldn't be quenched so easily. She still felt so cold.

"Cadmael," she whispered to him, taking a deep breath, focusing on the minty smell that seemed to radiate from beneath the scent of dog. "It's your turn."

"What?" he responded in a shaky voice.

"You are in charge."

The expression the boy made was so horrified that she nearly burst out laughing. His hands actually trembled against her skin as he shook his head.

"I–" he started, but Chance wasn't about to let him complain.

"You don't wish to reciprocate?" she feigned disappointment as she bowed her head to look up at him through her long dark eyelashes. "I thought I did such a good job. I'm sorry."

It worked like a charm. The boy went from too scared and nervous to really touch her, to wrapping his hot arms around her. He was so desperate to comfort her that his grip was tight enough that if she'd been human, it would make breathing difficult.

"Please!" he whispered, kissing the top of her head. "You're amazing. I don't know what to do. I do not know how to- to be in charge."

"Close your eyes," she encouraged, reaching up to press her palm over his beautiful blue eyes, shielding his ability to see. "Now my love. Is there anything you wish to do to me, whatever you wish to show me? Just know that I long to feel you. I want to see it all with your arms wrapped around me."

"My secret place," he suddenly whispered, and gave her the most adorable, boyish grin. "May I share it with you?" He paused for just a moment before adding, sounding panicked, "But you need to trust me. Trust that I will not let you come to harm."

Chance's eyebrows furrowed curiously. He seemed so thrilled that if she still had a heartbeat, it would be fluttering.

"Okay," she told him, tilting her head to the side. "I trust you, my sweet Cadmael."

"Look!" he exclaimed in surprise, staring down as his cock sprang to life. "You made it want you all over again."

He appeared almost frantic as he slammed his lips against hers. Before she could push her tongue into his mouth, he pulled away, leaving her standing in the middle of the library alone. He bolted to the door, closing it quickly. She suspected he was going to show her a secret passageway, like in the other room.

"Come!" he instructed as he slid his hand around hers, his warm fingers gliding between her own.

The sweetness was so strong she whimpered hungrily. She wanted that warmth all around her. The intention was to make him fuck her. Preferably on the floor in front of the old fireplace.

"I'm horny," she pouted as he led her to the bookcase closest to the external wall.

Staring at that wall filled with Eadrich's victim's portraits had horrified her before, but now she couldn't remember why it felt so disturbing. Above the portraits were eight insanely large windows, each covered by a blackout curtain. They were the only thing protecting Chance from frying to a crisp in the setting sunlight. Several feet from the wall were sets of double wide bookcases. There were three rows of them, and each row had three cases positioned back to back so that books would be on both sides of the viewer, who walked down the center aisles.

"We are going up." He picked her up as high as he could so she could climb on top of the case, which was easily nine feet high.

She found it far too simple to pull herself up. She looked

over the edge and watched as he slipped off his shoes and socks before following her up. He scaled it far easier than what should have been possible. As he came over the edge, Chance noticed a rope dangling nearby.

"Wait!" he yelped as she reached out for it. "Just give me a second."

He crawled toward her, still wearing that mischievous grin. Her eyes flashed to his cock, bouncing between his thighs as he moved. It was so big and warm. She wanted to put it in her mouth again, but had to remind herself that he was the one in charge.

He faced the wall with the windows and portraits and sat down, allowing his legs to hang over the side of the bookcase. He leaned back, glancing at his hard cock, before grinning at her.

"Chance, face the same direction as me and climb on."

She cocked an eyebrow at the mischievous-looking boy. She wanted to feel him, but she couldn't help the curiosity about the rope. It seemed to be attached to the ceiling, then it was connected to all the blackout curtains. Her brows furrowed as she saddled him.

Chance couldn't help the explosive moan that erupted from her lips. His cock slid into her at the same time as he sat up and wrapped his arms around her. His eternal fire enveloped her entire being. Her hands moved to his forearm to hold on tight as she moved her hips, riding him. His other hand moved so his fiery fingers could massage her clit.

"I'm so close that I might cum."

With her insides clutching his cock, she trembled, desperate for that push to send her into oblivion. Her fingers felt his arm flexing and tensing as he helped her maneuver, pulling her down hard and lifting her up.

"Yank the cord," he commanded her in a growl that made her nipples hard.

She looked at it for a moment, still moving her hips. The sun. She could feel it outside, still slowly setting on the horizon. The cord was connected to her only protection from it.

"If you love me," he told her, "pull that cord with all your might."

Chance snatched up the cord in her hand and reefed it down, blindly trusting the hellhound. His cock seemed to throb, becoming larger as she obeyed him.

Orange and red sunlight glittered into the library as every one of those protective blackout curtains fluttered to the ground. Chance screamed.

Both her hands moved to cover her face in terror as the light streamed in, reflecting dust particles in the large space. Cadmael didn't even slow in his fucking. In fact, he became harder than before, moving her body as she tried to protect herself.

He came, but miraculously, he remained hard.

"Look at it!" he snarled at her, moving his hand from her clit to grab her forehead and force her face to turn toward the light.

It was blinding and painful. Blood tears rolled down her cheeks as she forced herself to open her eyes and peer at the sun disappearing into the horizon. It was the most breathtaking thing she had ever witnessed. A chill swept across her body as the warmth of the light tickled her skin.

"As long as you drink from only me, you will be able to bear the light." Cadmael whispered softly. "You cannot partake in human feeding, or this blessing will be denied to you." He kissed down the side of her neck as his hand reclaimed her clit.

Her insides clenched around his cock as he hissed, "Walk with me in the light, Chance."

She thought she would never see sunlight again. There were no words to describe the way the light fractured across the sky like crystal shards of purity. Chance couldn't hold in the shriek of pure ecstasy when she orgasmed in the arms of her lover as the sunlight caressed her icy flesh.

Now, it's the end! I hope you enjoyed this

tragic tale.

Printed in Great Britain
by Amazon

44095962R00189